Emelyn Morley and the House of Galecliff

Saunmoor Book 2

For Mom, Dad, Laurie and Susan

Chapter 18
Travellers

Holborn district of London, Friday June 24ᵗʰ 1735

The night rain had turned to mist when little Penny Attridge hastened from her writing lesson in the high brick edifice of Furnival's Inn. Clutching her bonnet she moved briskly through the fog, making her way to a waiting coach on the street.

There was a woman there already, standing by the vehicle in an elegant powder blue dress under a grey cloak, just pushing the door closed with a white gloved hand.

"Excuse me ma'am," Penny said, holding her books in front of her. "Is it a *Hack & Humble*? Then it's my coach, if you please."

With a broad smile the woman turned to look at her, presenting a careworn wrinkled face, shiny with makeup. "Oh my dear child I must have got turned around," she said, bending to meet her eye level. "Is this your coach indeed? And how does a girl of ten have business at Furnival's Inn, never mind afford a night coach on her own?"

"I'm twelve ma'am," Penny said. "And I've a friend what helped me find lessons here. But I'm off home now."

The woman straightened up with a grin. "Lessons? Then you must be learning your letters. I don't suppose you're looking for a situation?"

"Yes ma'am. But nothing shabby."

With a tittering laugh the woman touched her hair. "Nothing shabby? Oh you are a little lady I can see that. What is your name darling?"

"Penny ma'am. Penny Attridge."

"Well met Penny; I am Mrs. Marybel Billings," the woman replied, presenting her hand for a shake. "Now do you suppose there's room inside for me? As it happens I know the Duchess of Kent herself seeks a lady's undermaid. We're dear friends she and I, and I've an idea she would be enchanted to meet you! Shall we talk it over?"

"Undermaid to a duchess?" Penny marvelled. "Well, Papa would be happy to hear of it, if you're pleased to come with me, to meet him."

"Of course," the woman replied. "But I'll not ride for free; I pay my way. Climb you aboard, and I'll pop in after a word with your driver."

Moments later the coach set out, and encouraged by her inquisitive companion, Penny talked excitedly of her private tutoring at the inn under a kindly professor and his wife, who made time for her in the evenings after regular classes, teaching all manner of subjects including arithmetic, writing and elocution. So engaging was Mrs. Billings that it was not until the fourth or fifth turn that Penny realized something was amiss.

"And which histories do you like in particular?" the lady asked. "You must spare no detail."

"I'm sorry ma'am, but this isn't the way," Penny said.

"Of course it is. I only want you to meet a friend first; and fear not, she is a lady."

Penny shifted in her seat, eyeing the window. "My father will be expecting me home."

"But aren't you a mite curious? I've told you the duchess requires a maid, and in fact, we are going to see her just now!"

"Are we? Truly? But first to my father ma'am, if it's no trouble."

"Oh my dear, you shall see him directly afterward, and with wonderful news to share!"

With a halting movement Penny reached for the door latch, but Mrs. Billings caught it first. "Now now—the duchess will be delighted with you. I'm sure you'd not wish to appear ungrateful."

Penney smiled weakly. "No ma'am."

Mrs. Billings slowly released the handle. "There we are."

The coach trundled down the darkening road, and Penny swallowed, hugging her books. "Does the duchess live in town ma'am?"

"Certainly not. Few persons of quality do my dear. Now, but I should find your father in neglect, letting a young girl out after dark. Have you no one else in the world?"

"No ma'am . . . it's been he and I since Mama went to her rest, when I was six."

"Well, perhaps it's time for you to find better society. A girl can't stay with her father forever."

There was something in her smile that made Penny reach for the latch again—but Mrs. Billings caught her wrist, and in that moment the door opened.

A beautiful woman, cloaked and hooded in black, slipped inside like a shadow, sitting beside the girl without a word.

"Mistress Vaela!" Penny gasped.

The vampiress shut the door, pulling it closed as she stared at the woman.

Mrs. Billings stared back, eyes wide as she panted for breath. "*I know you*," she rasped, her voice high and thin.

"Penny close your eyes," Vaela commanded.

The girl obeyed at once, covering her face, as with a long mewling sound Mrs. Billings shrank back.

"What is your business with her?" Vaela asked coldly.

"Dark mistress, I *know* you," Mrs. Billings repeated. "I know you, I swear it!"

Vaela bared her fangs. "I needn't touch you to feel your rotten heart—you mean to sell this child into the care of a brothel."

"Wait! You must remember me, please!"

Snatching her wrist Vaela yanked her closer, landing her on the floor between them, but with a gasp the vampiress recoiled, watching as the whimpering madam clambered back into her seat.

"I never forgot you," Mrs. Billings said desperately. "I knew your name, even before the girl spoke it aloud!"

Vaela scowled at her, scarcely believing. "Little Marybel Billings . . . has it been so long? What has become of you?"

"The world became of me!" Marybel cried, pulling out a kerchief to dry her eyes. "You cannot know my suffering . . ."

"Your heart was good," Vaela said quietly.

"Can you think I wanted this, to grow old into such indignity?"

"Did I not deliver you from just such a fate when you were a girl?"

Marybel nodded vigorously. "You did . . . of course you did," she sniffed, "but life conspired—not a month later I fell to another, my worth as a maid for ten guineas. You weren't there to deliver me, not then! From that night I swore to do what had to be done, to survive."

Vaela hissed, her nails stretching to claws. "Not children . . . You had a choice, as did those who took you."

Marybel's jaw trembled, but she sat up straighter. "Unaccompanied girls should know better. They come to the city with dreams no storybook could fulfil, and fall to their own ignorance, just as I did."

Unmoved Vaela stared at her, her vampire eyes darkening to black.

The lady smiled through smudged tears. "You pity me, dear creature," she said, reaching out. "You pity me don't you; you would not hurt me . . ."

"Your own suffering taught you nothing," Vaela said.

There was a scream, short with terror, and narrowly Penny peeked, finding Mrs. Billings pressed down on the bench with Vaela atop her, attached to her throat as the lady twitched. Penny covered her face again, and a swoon of dizziness carried her off.

"Open your eyes."

Penny did as she was bade, finding the coach had stopped. The vampiress sat across from her, and there was no sign of the ill-fated Mrs. Billings.

"Where is she?" Penny asked timidly.

"You need fear her no longer—she is gone."

"But where?"

"She is in the river, Penny." Vaela leaned forward. "She has only suffered the fate of the rotten; you must think no more of her."

Penny nodded, clutching her books tighter than ever. "Yes mistress."

"Now, your father's office as one of my spies is very important to me," Vaela said. "He could not carry it off if he thought you in danger. You must be more careful; you must not trust nor speak to anyone until the driver sees you home from your night lesson."

"But he didn't," Penny said in a small voice. "She spoke to the coachman, to pay her fare she said, but then he was driving us wrong."

"*He* was, but he's gone now," Vaela said, opening her arms. "Henceforth you shall have a different driver, loyal and watchful."

Penny moved across to embrace her, and when the door opened she found they were in a familiar courtyard.

"Up the stairs and home," Vaela said. "Tell your father the hackney coach was delayed, and tender my apologies."

"Yes mistress," Penny said, collecting her books to climb out of the carriage, and with both feet on the pavers she paused. Turning back she peered up at the coachman to find he'd been replaced by another, a still and silent figure who sat hunching over the reins, shrouded all in black, even his face invisible.

"Go on," Vaela said.

Penny twitched with hesitation. "I promise, mistress, I shan't grow up to be rotten as she was."

Vaela slipped out of the coach, and crouching before her she took Penny's hand. "Of course you won't," she said, smiling as the carriage rattled away. "But I must share the blame, for what became of little Marybel. I might have watched over her, as I have watched over you, but I was not so alive then . . . as I am now."

"I'm sorry," Penny said.

"Never doubt, you are stronger than she was. But you *are* late, and your father will be worried. Come . . ."

The familiar door at the top of the stairs was unlocked, and creaking it open Penny startled to find her father almost upon them, throwing on his cloak.

"Penny!" he cried, dropping to his knee to embrace her. "I was set to come after you—"

"I'm only late Papa, the coach was delayed," Penny recited. "Mistress Vaela tenders her apologies."

"Come in, if you please," Attridge said quickly, getting to his feet as Penny dashed into the other room with her books.

Vaela drifted over the threshold, shutting the door behind her. The living space was warm, the bedclothes clean and tidy, and there was a new table and chairs between stove and windows. "Good," she observed. "You present a proper home now."

Clearing his throat Mr. Attridge removed a pistol from his belt, laying it on the bed. "By your generosity," he said. "But did you not promise I should expect my girl not an hour after dusk."

"Yes," Vaela replied. "She'll not be delayed again, you have my word."

Mr. Attridge nodded, going to the table to unwrap a small parcel. "Penny! Get your supper lass."

The vampiress stood by the windows as father and daughter tucked into mugs of stew off the stove with bread and cheese, and looking up between bites Penny offered her some cider.

"No, thank you." Vaela smiled, peering down into the dimly twinkling courtyard.

"I suppose you'd have what lately I've heard, at the Devil's Inn," Mr. Attridge said thickly.

"Has there been any talk," Vaela asked softly, "of Lord Abbot's disappearance?"

"Oh yes ma'am, with much wrath and agitation. The Brotherhood fear him murdered, though they were quick enough to bring his son into the order. That cold spinster Miss Winter urges caution; she blames vampires, if you'll pardon . . . but no proof have they found. Chills my blood that woman does. I might wonder if she suspects me."

"Then you must effect ennui," Vaela said. "There is nothing less suspicious than a man bored to sagging at his post. As for Lord Abbot, they won't find a stitch; the brotherhood shall forget him soon enough."

Mr. Attridge swallowed hard, watching her. "Aye, I suspect he'll not be much missed, tyrant that he was. And if he made himself your enemy mistress . . . well, I'll not pity the man neither."

Vaela's lip twitched as she watched a raucous group making their drunken way across the yard. "No . . . but tell me, what else have you heard at the door?"

"*. . . my godmother will make her peace with it, or be forced,*" Lord Captain Van Croft muttered.

Thinking he had spoken directly to her, Emelyn woke to find herself still on the eastern road to Galecliff, with her lady's maid asleep on her shoulder, and her brother snoring across. Rubbing the tension in her neck from resting in such an attitude, Emelyn leaned Breda gently away and peered through the misted panes outside.

The night wind blew hard, whipping through the brush they passed, and just beyond, where the cliffs must plunge into oblivion over the stretching sea, she caught a flicker of light. Squinting closer she discerned it to be two lights, burning like fallen stars, bounding through the dark beside them. On a sudden the carriage door swung open, and Breda startled awake. A fearsome gale battered through the compartment, and prickling with terror Emelyn reached quickly to close it, but the door slammed shut again, stoving her knuckles.

With a terrific curse she woke Deacon, who sat up. "What's happened?"

"The wind caught the door; I don't know." Emelyn grimaced, squeezing the ache in her hand as she stared through the window. Outside was dark and deep, with no sign of the lights. Deacon laid back down, bullying his pillow.

Emelyn rubbed her knuckles to find them sticky with blood from a narrow abrasion. "Ouch . . . of all the bloody damnation—"

Deacon chuckled. "*Neath butterfly winks and softer sighs, monstrous vulgar tongue she hides . . .*"

Emelyn glared at him, employing a kerchief to clean her hand.

"How could it happen miss?" Breda asked. "Was the door loose?"

Striving not to think of it Emelyn shook her head. Much as the mysterious lights recalled those she'd seen at Hastelbrook, while walking by the cemetery on the arm of Mr. Arkwright—but surely they were no more than ghosts of the driver's lanterns, reflected in the glass.

The coach skirted the cliffs very close, though the road was smoother than it might have been. By and by the party relaxed, and her eyes drifted closed . . .

It seemed not a moment later she blinked to find herself home again, surrounded by her mother and sisters, who were shouting. Their faces were livid and strange, and despite their insistence she could little understand what they wanted. Protesting her confusion Emelyn struggled to discern their tangled voices, but she snapped awake as the carriage jostled with a sudden turn, leaving the treacherous path behind to pull between stout gateposts into the crushed shell drive of an expansive property.

The vehicle lurched to a stop, and she moved quickly to keep her brother from rolling off his bench.

"Here already?" he blurted.

Looking over the scratch Emelyn found the bleeding had stopped, and digging up her errant glove she pulled it on quickly. The door swung open suddenly again, and Van Croft offered his hand.

"Even the dullness of night cannot dim her beauty, nor the red of her hair," he said cheerfully. "My radiant Miss Morley, we have arrived."

Emelyn gathered her skirts, accepting his assistance to disembark, and the cold air off the sea struck her at once, the dark sky stretching vast and smooth overhead. Turning about she discovered a charming enclosed courtyard arranged in quadrants of square hedged gardens, each centred with statue topped fountains and benches of stone. Lined with bright pole lanterns the carriage lane halved the courtyard as it ran to a wide oaken stair rising to the house, and she looked up to see a great beam supporting the overhang of the roof, jutting from the building in Nordic style.

"Lovely," she said, pulling up the hood of her cardinal cloak against the sharp wind as she noted the stacked granite wall around the property—standing taller than a man it lent the place a sheltered castle bailey atmosphere, complete with a pavilion tower built into the wall for a clear vantage of the sea. There appeared also a prominent outbuilding across the gardens and courtyard from the manor, a substantial longhouse of stone with slant shingled roof, opposite the stables.

The wind sliced the air with volume, mingling with forlorn cries of seagulls high over the rocks, and as she raised her eyes from fire warm windows to the darkly clouded heavens her hand in her pocket seized upon the bronze coin of Saunmoor—that which she'd aggressively bartered from a disagreeable man in a seedy London shop, that which was emblazoned with the face of the queen of Saunmoor—and she wondered why she'd brought it, and if it was her fate to someday meet her, the dark immortal sovereign of Vaela's realm—the queen of the dead. There was too folded paper, beside the coin—Mr. Arkwright's letter, still tucked in her pocket. Van Croft took her arm, fishing out her hand for his grasp, and she released the letter just in time.

"Welcome to Galecliff," he said.

Hand over arm they ascended the steps to enter the grand hall, and Emelyn lowered her hood to take in the space, which arched overhead in great curved beams like the upside down bones of a ship. A heavy chandelier of dark metal hung from the rafters, its flickering light joining the glow of glass lanterns along the walls to illuminate high magnificent portraits, hung in such a way that they leaned into the room, lending a glowering aspect to their occupants—full length naval lords and their ladies over dark background or depicted with the roiling sea behind them. The dim atmosphere was tinged by a wafting damp as of mouldering wood, and surrendering her cloak to the aging attendant footman, Emelyn turned her attention to the sharply dressed couple waiting at the centre of the room.

Beside his lady, who sparkled in white, the Commodore was clad in dark blue coats centred with ivory, over storm grey breeches and shoes of black. He wore no wig, his lush greying hair quite full enough on its own, his wind-worn face bright with cheer as he stood at attention, his left arm behind his back. The lady of the house was of full and regal bearing, taller than Emelyn, with sharp features and narrow eyes. Gowned all in white and silver, her costume was embroidered with swirling patterns and lace embellishment at every opportunity. Though stern of countenance she was certainly younger than her husband, her thick bundle of hair just surrendering its ashen blonde to grey.

Deacon was escorted up the stairs to join them, and Van Croft lifted Emelyn's arm in such a way that she was obliged to give their hosts a turn. "May I present Miss Emelyn Elizabeth Morley," he announced. "These my dear, are my godparents, the Commodore and Mrs. Akehurst."

"Yes he was baptized very late," the Commodore chortled, "but how now Miss Morley, beauty of the line I declare!" and he took her hand for a bow.

Emelyn opened her mouth to respond and was surprised by his wife's sudden embrace.

"How lucky we are, to have the *Belle of Brighton* among us," Mrs. Akehurst gushed, gingerly patting her back, "a young lady so *exclusively* and exquisitely known for her beauty."

"Madam, I am honoured," Emelyn said, nonplussed at her phrasing.

"Oh you dear girl, the honour is mine," Mrs. Akehurst said, taking her arm to lead her aside. "It is so very good of you to come and see us. But tell me, can it be true that Hastelbrook keeps the largest ballroom in the county, and even a greenhouse indoors?"

"Yes, I'm afraid it is," Emelyn said. "It was my great-grandfather who adjoined it to the house with the garden nursery, which is three-storeyed glass . . ."

"Heavens but you must live like the *Golden Duke* himself!" the lady teased, speaking closely. "Of course Galecliff will never compare, though

I've heard of your penchant for daily baths—you must be pleased to learn we've a splendid little bagnio upstairs, with its own bathing stove and burnished copper tubs. Have you a bathing stove at home Miss Morley?"

"No in fact; hot water must be brought up."

"Then I shall trust you to take full advantage," the lady said, beaming at her. "Spend absolutely as *much* time there as you like; I am in earnest."

Emelyn nodded, unsure how to answer. "That is very kind . . . thank you."

"Ah the unfortunate stalwart!" the Commodore said, coming to shake Deacon's hand. "You are most welcome my good fellow."

"Your servant sir." Deacon adjusted his crutches for a bow.

The party was ushered into the drawing room, which was of similar oil timbered ceiling, though of lower height than the grand hall, with great narrow windows curtained in deep silver edged blue, and Emelyn was introduced to an alarmingly young doctor in short campaign wig over drab coats.

"Boderick Tarville, my sister's personal physician and a great credit to his profession," Van Croft hailed, slapping him on the back. "There my dear Bodie, the incomparable Miss Morley stands now before you; how do you find her?"

"*Belle of Brighton* indeed!" the doctor enthused, flashing a brass ring with a wide engraved face as he took Emelyn's hand. "Mine eyes are ope'd and I see every tale is true; but I must hear your angel's voice. Speak what you will, and I shall hang on your every word!"

Emelyn smiled. "What you will."

"Delightful!" the doctor tittered, squinting his face. "By damn Captain, you've won the Ascot here I should say; beauty and wit!"

"Don't encourage her." Van Croft winked. "She esteems herself quite high enough already."

"So, you are attendant upon his sister?" Emelyn asked of the doctor, ignoring the comment. "I'm sure he's told me nothing about her. Is she here?"

"Oh no, poor creature," Tarville said, his expression drooping with sympathy. "She does not leave the captain's manor, *Vivere Gloria*."

"Does she not?" Emelyn inquired, her curiosity piqued.

"She is of precarious constitution," the doctor sighed, his face the picture of pious sorrow, "and ever in need of my care. Lord Van Croft has kindly allowed me to quarter on his estate, the better for her convenience."

"The better to charge me assiduously," Van Croft said, and the gentlemen laughed.

■ ■

On the treacherous southern traverse through Kent, between Stevenage and the village of Knebworth, a narrow stretch of road passed from open landscape through a shaded vale overhung by sagging trees, where silent in the dark there stood a private coach-and-four. Face down in the road nearby lay a young footman, stone dead, while two surly lads rummaged through luggage trunks in the back of the carriage as an indifferent driver reposed up front, smoking with his hat off.

Inside the vehicle under the dim glow of a ceiling mounted lantern sat a pair of terrified passengers: a substantial nobleman in fine coats and bombastic wig beside a much younger woman, round-faced in pink, her tight chestnut hair pinned under a travelling bonnet. Across from them sat a rakish brigand, his flintlock pistol brandished, a gold tooth gleaming in his smile. The man was nearly handsome—ruddy of face with a backward cocked hat high on his forehead. His wide cuffed frock coat, once of a gaudy teal blue, was now faded from long use on the road.

"There my good Lord Bellgate," the highwayman said, waving the gun, "off with the shoes then."

"There's nothing in my shoes sir!" the nobleman snapped, "naught but cold stockinged feet!"

"I'll be the judge of that. Let's see those latchets off, lest I add a ball o' lead to the supper in your belly . . ."

"Damn you for a ruffian," the large gentleman groused, struggling to work off his heeled shoes. "Damn you I say!"

"In due time my bulky lord, in due time," the bandit said cheerfully, and taking up the shoes he weighed them both, discarding one to pry open the heel of the other, where from a hidden compartment he drew a pouch of coin and treble folded bills. "There we be," he said, pocketing the cash before gesturing at the woman with his firearm. "Your turn my love."

"On your humanity sir! Spare my child your aggressions," Lord

Bellgate entreated. "She is this very month to be married!"

"Is she then . . . Bit long in the tooth for matrimony ain't we?" The highwayman chuckled. "Someone caught your tail at last my sweet?"

"You're a vulgar man," she said, hiding her hands in her lap. "I'm only twenty-six."

"Maudie, do not waste your breath," her father said, glaring at their aggressor. "We are on our way to the house of Lord Lytton, a magistrate; you are wise to let us through."

The man grinned. "Your *Lord Magistrate* shall know better than to cross the likes of me."

"Then pray tell us, what is your name sir?" Bellgate demanded, his voice rising in pitch as he eyed the pistol.

"Well I suppose t'is only fitting," and the highwayman turned his hat round to reveal ten crude little carriages embroidered on the front, with room for more.

Horror dawned on their faces, and the notorious outlaw crossed his legs, the pistol leaning casually. "Willy Gladbound at your service," he said, fluffing out the tails of a blood red scarf about his waist, "and my merry lads outside." He put a hand to his ear. "What's this you say? *Don't the handsome Willy Gladbound only hunt Northumberland roads?* T'were true enough, but rather too many tongues waggin' nowadays—everyone an informer. These old Kent roads on t'other hand—cool and quiet, ripe for the pluckin' what I heard. Now miss Maudie, I'll have all that jewellery if you please . . ."

The young woman swallowed, working with shaky hands to unclasp her earrings.

Lord Bellgate was sweating. "Wait," he said. "Now look here sir, you've had your fill; leave the poor woman only her ring, and I shall see you made well at Knebworth—"

"And collared in a noose for my trouble." Gladbound's smile faded, and with a sudden motion he cracked the nobleman on the head with the butt of his gun.

"Father!" Maudie shrieked, catching hold of him as he slumped against her with a groan.

"Base common disrespect that is," Gladbound remarked, adjusting his hat. "There my girl; now the ring . . . if you please."

Maudie shook her head, and with a whimper she hid one hand behind the other, covering her mouth.

The highwayman levelled his pistol. "Don't!" he warned. "Far prettier than yourself have left this world in the attempt; if you swallow that ring my dear, I'm obliged to cut you open and have it out."

Crinkling her mouth with a sob she lowered her head, spitting the ring into her hand.

Mr. Gladbound took the bauble from her trembling fingers. "Good! Now, as we find ourselves culpable in your poor brave footman's murder, you may well be tempted to inform—"

"We will inform no one," Maudie said stiffly, quivering as she spoke.

"Then I will commiserate with my colleagues," Gladbound sighed, "and we shall determine whether to leave you warm on your feet, or cold on your backs. All right my lads! How d'you reckon we dispose of it?" There came no answer, and he licked his lips, glancing at the open window. "All right my lads?"

Outside all was quiet, the highwayman's young accomplices nowhere to be seen. Four carriage horses stood with their heads bowed, dead asleep on their feet as the coach driver sat like a statue, his pipe frozen in his hand.

A pale gentleman, long coated in black, with trailing silver hair tied behind him, stood on the back of the nearest animal, staring down at the coachman through platinum rimmed spectacles. "For twenty years my watch has slept," he said, his face devoid of expression. "But I am returned, and in the dark this way belongs to me."

"Mercy fell spirit!" the coachman stammered, visibly shaking. "The lady aboard, pure as a babe unborn she is; Take her with my compliments!"

"Her passage is paid," the vampire Lord Simeon replied, and suddenly close he clapped hands on the terrified man's head, lifting him from the bench. "Yours is wanting."

The coach jostled as he leapt to the air with his prey, sailing over the road into the woods.

A desperate shriek died on the wind, and inside the carriage Willie Gladbound sat up. "What's that then?" he puzzled, reaching for the handle.

But the carriage door snapped open, and the highwayman lurched out as though kicked by a horse. Father and daughter cried out, but the coach settled to stillness, and with timorous breath Maudie reached to pull the door closed.

Off the road into the embankment, amidst tufted thorny bushes betwixt the trees, Mr. Gladbound found himself caught between the unyielding trunk of a silver birch and the icy hand grasping his chin. In frantic terror he struggled, clawing and grabbing, but the predator's jaws seized on his throat, and the vampire lord drank deep. Tearing pain turned to dizziness, and released from the attack Gladbound collapsed, crumpling to the ground, cold and weak. Fighting for breath he rolled to his back, finding the coachman just beside him, his open eyes hazy in death.

"Ten coaches, four murders," Lord Simeon said, wiping his mouth. "Your eleventh this might have been, had I but lengthened my trip a few more days . . ."

The leaves crackled in the breeze, and Vaela slipped out of the dark beside him.

"Haunting the roads. I might have known," she said.

Lord Simeon turned to face her, she whom he had sired 200 years past—for a moment they shared each other's gaze, and the vampiress lowered her hood, her expression piqued.

"By the treachery of one of your night coachman, Penny Attridge was almost lost to me," she said. "Her father's intelligence is vital. I have disciplined the driver, and the madam who bribed him."

"Another fallen to your ledger, and with my blessing I'm sure," Lord Simeon said, nudging the groaning highwayman with his foot. "Now, this one is not long among the living. Sup quickly if you will."

Vaela crouched to examine the bodies. "There's no disguising it, you've gored their throats. Should we bear them to the sea?"

"Nay, let them lie another credit to the mythical wildcats of the British Isles."

Willy Gladbound twitched. "Demons," he gurgled, catching hold of Vaela's wrist.

The vampiress snapped away, baring her fangs with a snarl, and snatching him by the ankle she whirled him about, slapping his head against a tree.

Chuckling softly Lord Simeon adjusted his spectacles. "Though of course the wildcats are seldom known to break men's skulls against tree trunks . . .”

“His heart was rotted black,” Vaela said. “His ilk teem in the city like rats; I cannot bear them.”

Her maker watched her closely. “We do not choose our immortal gifts—to know the human heart is a capacity most rare.”

Vaela closed her eyes, as though weary of the lesson.

“Tell me,” he said. “Something has driven you to passion I think.”

“I have killed a lord for Emelyn’s sake,” Vaela said. “Must I kill his son as well? I cannot protect her during the day.”

Lord Simeon nodded slowly. “Robert Abbott is a craven reprobate; he will seek his inheritance before vengeance.”

“But more will come,” Vaela said, her eyes shining black as she crouched beside the highwayman’s corpse. “Lord Abbott was of the *Argentum Serpentis*; they want the secrets of Hastelbrook.”

“They are no threat to the vault,” he said. “Excepting the Chosen Child, no mortal will disturb its rest.”

Vaela rifled through the dead man’s pockets, coming up with several pieces of jewellery and folded bills. “And yet Lord Dramen’s gaze is fixed upon it,” she said. “My spies tell me he would prosecute trafficking in the occult for a capital crime, and cast the slaying of vampires into law. He seeks royal charter for his own society of hunters.”

“*Ever vaulting ambition o’er leaps itself to fall*,” Lord Simeon mused. “Dramen’s mortal peers will not long tolerate his zealotry.”

“You forget he holds one of our own in his power,” Vaela said, standing as she passed him a necklace, earrings and engagement band, “yet by the queen’s command . . . we are to do nothing.”

“Afaine’s fate is not ours to intrude upon,” Lord Simeon said, examining the items. “But take heart—our enemies have not yet destroyed her, by which it follows they mean to profit by her capture. She may yet escape them.”

Vaela brushed raven hair from her face, looking back at the road. “Very well, I shall *take heart* . . . And what are we to do with the unhappy travellers?”

Half recovered in the carriage, a sweating Lord Bellgate sang softly what rhymes he could conjure by heart, holding his daughter close. “*Lullaby baby bunting, your father’s gone a-hunting, to catch a rabbit for a skin, to wrap his baby bunting in . . .*”

"Enough Papa!" Maudie protested. "I'm not a child. We must discover what's happened!"

"Yes my dear of course," he said, trembling as he held her all the tighter. "I suppose I shall go and see, but of course I will, and if I do not return—"

The door opened, and reclining suddenly across from them Lord Simeon smiled. "In my eyes you find an answer of peace," he said, arresting them by the power of his gaze. "There is no pain, no alarm . . ."

Father and daughter sat very still, eyes fixed, a change coming over their faces. "Oh sir," Maudie gasped with relief. "I'm certain we've only just avoided the most awful thing . . . though I cannot remember."

"Have we shaken a wheel? Has old Toggers driven us lost in the dark?" Lord Bellgate puzzled. "The man is past his prime if ever a driver was . . ."

"Toggers, alas, has fled your service forever," the vampire said.

"Have I lost my ring?" Maudie gasped, picking at her finger.

"Your jewellery is here," and after depositing earrings and necklace in her lap Lord Simeon took her hand to slide the ring back in its place. "Now . . . let us think on Knebworth House, where Lord Lytton keeps a generous table," and reaching out he touched each of their faces. "You are distracted by nothing in all the world, but thoughts of the hospitality you will find there. Come Vaela, I find you ill-nourished, you must drink of them both."

Serene in their hypnotized state, father and daughter settled back, and the vampiress slipped into the coach, whereupon she mounted the lap of Lord Bellgate. Her lips parted, her fangs stretched to points, and nuzzling into the nobleman's neck she bit deep.

Bellgate twitched but did not resist, blinking as though lost in thought. "A grand supper awaits us, I've no doubt," he said. "Your mother selected the lime taffeta, but have we not all your spring gowns wrapped and boxed . . ."

"I do like the green," Maudie said vaguely.

"Or the sunset orange would do nicely to charm our hosts," Bellgate followed, speaking to the ceiling as the vampiress nursed at his flesh. "Lord Lytton's courtyard is enchanted with torches after dusk . . ."

Lapping to heal the wound Vaela shivered with pleasure, and wiping her lips she looked at her maker.

"Go on my dear," Simeon said, gesturing in welcome. "I insist . . .

do not deny yourself."

With a lusty sigh Vaela moved carefully over, and straddling the woman's legs she tipped back her chin to bite softly into her throat. Maudie flinched with a gasp, but after a few blinks she glanced at her father. "I was thinking to wear orange for the assembly," she said.

"Certainly my girl," Bellgate mumbled, and slumping into the corner he dropped his chin to sleep.

Lord Simeon returned coin and cash to the man's shoe, and after a few swallows Vaela licked to repair the hurt on Maudie's throat before leaning the dozing daughter against her father.

Outside Simeon woke the horses with a word, snapping the reins to set out as Vaela joined him on the driver's bench.

"Gladbound attacked with four," he said. "The surviving pair I've left mesmerized in the wood, little more than misguided boys . . . they shall set to burying the dead, and then perhaps I'll appoint them to the staff at Nonsuch House."

"These two shall arrive without footmen or driver," Vaela said, her hand over her heart. "The mystery will haunt them."

"A small price to pay for their lives."

"And what now? The euphoria of their blood only softens care. Banished from Saunmoor we remain."

"We are not banished, precisely," he said, guiding the rattling coach out from beneath the leaning trees, to leave the crooked way behind. "But I've twenty years of bookkeeping to review. Until the queen can be reasoned with, present purpose must keep our focus."

"Then I shall attend upon mine," Vaela said, and leaping off the bench she vanished in the wind.

Moments later the vampiress flashed out of her speed, the air whirling about her as she came to rest among the headstones of the Hastelbrook cemetery up the hill. The nectar of mortal blood warmed her body, and slipping behind an elder apple tree she embraced the trunk, her claws scoring the bark as she scanned the windows, listening for any sign of her mortal charge . . . and finding none.

Searching for the voice of Adam Comberland, the footman under her sway, she found him at last below stairs, his words emanating from basement quarters in the servants' hall.

"A fortnight away from my spark . . . It's too bloody long," Comby

complained.

"*Nothing for it my friend,*" a young man responded. "*But after what Miss Morley dragged you through in London, and Breda nursin' your griefs, she'll be thinking of you night and day I s'pose.*"

"*It weren't Miss Morley's fault,*" Comby said. "*She don't know the low streets as I do.*"

"*Still, she might have seen to your comfort, cash-wise, for the inconvenience of bein' set upon by the Mohocks in that alley.*"

"*Oh she did, and more than I could reasonable accept.*"

Vaela grunted with a smile, and shifting to the other side of the tree she espied a young scullery maid in the walled kitchen garden just outside the eastern door.

"Timothy!" the girl shouted, opening one of several barrels by the wall to spill a bucket of ash inside. "There's coals to see to! If you're down the hill already that'll be the devil to pay!"

The vampiress slipped closer and the maid shivered, squinting into the dark.

"Bloody slugabout, is that you?" she called, wiping her hands on her apron. "I should like a drink too mind, but some of us get on with our work."

Finding no response, the maid turned with a huff, and Vaela snatched her, pinning her to the wall. With a squeal the girl burst into tears, but stopped short as the vampiress caught her eyes, whispering gently.

"Hush, sweet girl, you shan't even remember me. Now, where has Miss Emelyn gone?"

▪ ▪

Saturday June 25th

Seated at a busy oaken desk in the basement of his London home, Fitzwilliam Arkwright poured over a ledger of business, scratching corresponding notes in a little logbook as he tallied purchase orders for the month. He wore a white shirt under grey waistcoat and charcoal breaches, cuffs unbuttoned and sleeves rolled to the elbows, his dark hair loose to his shoulders. The wine cellar was cool and quiet, pleasant for the business of numbers, with flickering ship's lanterns hanging along the walls, adding to the warm light from the hearth behind him.

Her face came to him here and again, she who had undone him, and he paused to stare through the paper, dwelling on those fierce and fleeting moments of her company, the warmth of her eyes, the touch of her lips . . . The distraction was relentless, and he found the wine of small support.

"Leave Miss Morley be," he muttered, jabbing his pen at the inkwell.

A creak from the top of the stairs caught his attention, and the familiar voice of his aging butler called down. "Lord Admiral Norris has just arrived—with some urgency sir!"

Looking at the clock to find it half-past two in the afternoon, Arkwright leapt up to don his coat. "Really? Thank you Enson, I shall be up in a trice!" he cried, tying back his hair and adjusting his cuffs.

"He is coming down sir!" Enson called back.

Heavy boot steps, punctuated by the tap of a cane sounded on the stairs, and a long wigged elder gentleman in dark red coats stepped through the arch into the cellar, nodding as Arkwright bowed before him. "Fitzwilliam Arkwright!" the admiral declared. "I'll not stand on ceremony; we've business to attend, you and I."

"Please," Arkwright gestured to the chair opposite his own, flashing around the desk to pour the admiral a glass of Madeira before taking his seat. "You will forgive the disarrangement, I keep this space for the records."

The navy lord sat, looking with distaste over the bottle-stocked shelves along the walls about him. "Whoever contrives an office in the wine cellar?"

"I cannot imagine," Arkwright said, glaring about the room.

The admiral stared at him. "I regret the intrusion, but I've just come from the office of your useless clerk, who would not cover a sneeze but by your permission."

"Better to let them breathe," Arkwright said, and finding no response he cleared his throat. "Yes my lord, what seems to be at issue?"

"Casks man, what else," the admiral retorted. "The Board of Admiralty requires you should see to your duty; we are tormented of this, these bloody black storms over the Celtic Sea, meandering as though to collect shipwrecks by direct purpose! Thirteen frigates lost, with two more dashed on the rocks at St. Agnes not a month ago."

"That is an astonishing ill fortune," Arkwright marvelled.

"Yet even *this* wrath of weather shall pass," the admiral said, "and when it does there shall be much to repair and refit."

"A new contract then," Arkwright said, closing the ledger and cracking his logbook. "We shall by all means accept your business, and my clerk should have told you the same."

"It is the delay sir," the admiral said, taking up his glass for a drink. "There's a run on casks of every size, barrels, hogsheads, tuns, and the staves to make them. I come with ready capital to Arkwright Cooperage only to be told the Royal Navy must wait like any common client."

"There is no need to wait," Arkwright said. "Much to my disappointment casks are not so difficult to make; surely one of my competitors has the room."

"They have been weighed and found wanting," the admiral snapped. "Now, the agreement that stands in my way is Morley Maritime. I strenuously suggest you put them aside."

"Ah, then it appears we have a pickle," Arkwright replied, drumming his fingers on the desk.

The admiral pursed his lips. "Morley is a sinking ship sir; surely you've heard the reports. Half a dozen frigates lost at a stroke. I should like to buy out the contract; I'll guarantee you his price for the work already done."

"My lord," Arkwright said, sitting up straighter, "you'd not ask that I cancel an order half finished? The sea lanes have grown treacherous for large and small concerns alike."

"Yet I'll wager he hasn't paid you," the admiral said, snatching his goblet for another drink.

"He is in arrears," Arkwright conceded, "but Mr. Morley works to rebuild, as would any man of good business. I'll not put him—nor any in his family to further distress over a contract."

"And can you expect him to honour it, with scarcely a ship for the cargo?"

"I don't believe he'd have us over a barrel," Arkwright said thoughtfully. "I am sorry my lord, but I can be of no further assistance to the Royal Navy in this matter, not until present business allows."

The admiral stood from his chair . "So you are intransigent," he said, knocking the floor with his cane. "You must realize I have the power to act against your charter . . . but I fear my time here has been utterly wasted."

Arkwright smacked the desk, getting to his feet. "Not entirely my lord," he replied, and turning to a cupboard on the wall, he creaked it open to fetch out a bottle of red wine, its label thin and faded. "A small consolation sir," he said, "for your steadfast support."

Admiral Norris accepted the bottle, frowning as he raised his brows. "Chateau Latour… 'ninety-six. I say, do you know me so well?"

"Give me a fortnight but one," Arkwright said. "We shall complete Morley's order and turn our whole consideration to the Royal Navy."

"Thirteen days to start?" the admiral puffed. "I don't like it."

"I shall set every man to the task, for a guarantee of one hundred hogsheads a week."

"One hundred casks a week? That is a steady clip."

"As the king's subjects we must do our part," Arkwright said.

"Yes, indeed," the admiral said. "I think you knew your game the moment I appeared," and he drew back his chair, resigning himself to sit once more. "One hundred a week . . . very well, let us draw up the terms," he said, setting the Chateau Latour gently on the desk.

Arkwright stared at the bottle, finding in the glass the same deep green of her eyes.

"Today sir, if you please," the admiral added.

"By all means," Arkwright said, snapping to attention as he took up his pen.

Chapter 19
Lost and Found

By Saturday afternoon it was clear that the Akehursts were something of an unusual couple. Of unbreakable jovial temperament, the Commodore oft expressed himself with great bursts of laughter, adding a leap from his chair or stomp of his foot where the story required it. For her part, the lady of the house glanced Emelyn's way thrice for every word she spoke to her, and over an elegant dinner of fennel soup, small birds and sirloin with blood red dressing, Mrs. Akehurst acknowledged her hardly at all, addressing herself instead to Van Croft with questions of his travels, though she tended to stare like a statue through the answers.

"The relish is delightful," Emelyn said, advantaging herself of a pause in the conversation. "So sweetly tart; is it a preserve?"

"American cranberries my dear, with sugar," Mrs. Akehurst said, forking her beef, "quite a novel fruit, grown in a bog you know. But of course they will be unknown to you."

"I do know of cranberries," Emelyn said with a smile.

Later that afternoon under the grey day Emelyn's promised tour of the park was cancelled when her hostess pled a swollen ankle. "Such exhaustive labour of foot preparing the house!" Mrs. Akehurst decried, taking Emelyn's arm with a pout. "My godson has no taste for our humble estate, but of course I am desperate to show you, from pavilion to verdure to cottages, even the old dovecote behind the pond. We've 300 nests therein for winter, though we keep seabirds, rather than pigeons."

"Fascinating," Emelyn said. "But I was thinking, perhaps I might start out on my own . . ."

"Seabirds do not ravage the turnips," Mrs. Akehurst interrupted, "as pigeons are known to do."

"I see. As for a walk . . ."

"We've stall-fed beasts for the cold months as well, but it is a small farm after all."

"And I should quite enjoy seeing it," Emelyn said, losing her patience. "I shan't walk but where you recommend, of course."

"Oh heavens I wouldn't hear of it," Mrs. Akehurst said cheerfully. "Your first excursion shall be on my arm or not at all. Perhaps tomorrow."

The young Doctor Tarville was attentive enough to Deacon, though his most flattering manners he reserved for Emelyn. Having been offered a choice between rooming upstairs and taking a more rustic bed in the longhouse across the front lawns, Deacon had opted for the latter to spare himself the long manor staircase, with a promise from the doctor that he would be attended morning and night.

Saturday wore on, and despite numerous protests of friendship from Mrs. Akehurst, Emelyn found herself spoken *of* a great deal more than *to*, and loitering in the hall that evening whilst the grand drawing room was prepared for games, it was impossible not to overhear the lady's every word.

"Doe-eyed and delicate I daresay," Mrs. Akehurst commented to the captain, "though her beauty is undeniable. I shouldn't wonder if she were only on loan from the sea. You're quite sure she means to stay?"

Van Croft laughed. "She's sister to Venus I'll not deny it," he said.

Sitting beside him for a game of whist, Emelyn added to her observations that the captain seemed nothing if not proud of the burgeoning enmity between herself and his godmother, the both of whom he'd encouraged to partner for the game, while he allied with Deacon.

"Like a bloody rose in a room all of white, Miss Morley struck me from the first," Van Croft related, nodding with respect to Deacon's play. "By the ravish of her beauty, and I daresay the snap of her tongue—which may try a fellow's patience," he added with a wink. "In fact I could say the *Belle of Brighton* nearly cost herself the pleasure of my pursuit."

"Oh did she verily!" Mrs. Akehurst burst with delight, laughing over Emelyn's reply.

"Perhaps your godson is unaccustomed," Emelyn repeated louder, "to a lady rebutting any particle of his address."

"I daresay he is," the Commodore added joyfully, standing nearby with the doctor to observe. "And if, Miss Morley, you find him much winking, he only does so to present himself at ease, in particular when he is not."

"Carefully sir," Van Croft said, a bit flushed. "Those who betray my secrets are like to find themselves over the cliff," and the company laughed again.

Play and banter continued, but Emelyn's cards were hopeless, and her brother asking always to see the last trick, by which he would perfectly memorize the cards, began to grate on her nerves.

"Oh no, Miss Morley," Mrs. Akehurst groused, watching her play. "But can it be Mr. Morley has five tricks to your none? Are you in the same family?"

"I've never been quite sure," Deacon remarked, giving the table another once over.

"My apologies," Emelyn said as the captain laughed. "My brother masters every game he plays; we may as well hold our cards the wrong way round."

After several more hands the victorious gentlemen left the table, Van Croft adjourning to the mantel with Tarville and the Commodore while Deacon opted for the cooler clime near the windows, their hostess having excused herself for some urgent matter among the staff.

"Well I daresay you've won the captain's heart," Emelyn said, coming to stand beside her brother.

"And you've lost the lady's," Deacon chuckled. "Go on then, join your gentleman. It's too cold for you here."

"I am perfectly content," she said.

The men shared a laugh over some scandalous half-whispered story, and taking leave of them Van Croft strode to meet her. "You are the guest of honour my dear, I'd not have you despair for company; there shall be additional ladies arriving soon enough."

"Additional ladies, my favourite sort," Emelyn said, and the scratch on her hand tingled as he squeezed her glove.

"I think the rustic halls of Galecliff are where I shall tame you," he said, adding a wink.

Emelyn cleared her throat. "My lord . . . if the lady of the house has not time to show me the grounds, shall I risk her wrath by asking her husband? Or perhaps you will offer in her stead, though she says you don't care for it."

"To my home at Vivere Gloria, Galecliff is nothing," he said, leaning close to confide at her, "an estate without contour, dull and flat."

"Still, I should like a walk," she said quietly, meeting his eyes.

"We shall be outside for the party of course; until then you must defer to my godmother's advice."

"Must I?" Emelyn asked, scratching her knuckles. "Is there something I'm not meant to see?"

"Now you mention it, there is an old stair descending from the gate, naught but a narrow spine of stone running all the way to the sea, against the cliffs. Many have run afoul of it, particularly in the dark."

Strangely Emelyn thought of Vaela. "Running all the way to the sea? But it must be five hundred feet from this height."

"Indeed, and the stair twice as long as that, even steep as they are. I trod them as a youth."

"So I am not to go out. But does she imagine I must fall down every stairs I encounter?"

The captain chuckled, and taking her hand he kissed it with the signature clench of his teeth, biting precisely down on the concealed wound.

Emelyn flinched with a noise, loud enough to blush, and the conversation at the mantel went quiet. "Nothing," she said quickly. "I apologize my lord; I seem to have hurt my hand."

"Have you?" Van Croft pulled off her glove before she could protest, turning her hand to study it.

The little slit was shiny with scab, though oddly black about the edges, and scowling over the cut he summoned Doctor Tarville with a whistle.

Like a faithful hound the young doctor appeared at his side, and after some examination he recommended a quick wash with a quantity of alcohol poured over the wound. "I do not hold with those who say natural earth does no more harm within than without," he said, drying her hand with a rag when the fuss was done. "Is not the skin meant to protect us? But when it is broken, we too oft find infection . . ."

"Well said sir!" the Commodore pronounced, raising his glass.

"Yes thank you," Emelyn said, wincing as Tarville dabbed the hurt, which had been provoked to a raw cherry hue by the application of brandy.

Despite appearances Van Croft was determined to tuck her

fingers into the glove and roll it up her wrist himself, which he did as Emelyn watched. For a few moments more he lingered, and she waited as he appeared bound to speak, but he cleared his throat, and with a second gentle kiss on her knuckles he left her by her brother, ushering the others back to the mantel.

Perplexed, Emelyn stared after him, rubbing her hand.

"I know that face," Deacon said as he watched her. "I think you'd rather be at home, but we're only here because the captain seeks your favour. I doubt his success, and I might protest his use of your hand . . . but you must let him try."

Emelyn nodded vaguely. "Mrs. Akehurst holds something against me, do you not think," she said, seeking distraction from the sting, and the captain's tender impertinence.

"Other than cards?" Deacon clarified. "Nonsense, what should she hold against you?"

"I'm sure I don't know."

Drinks were slow to arrive, and the men settled into pipes and cognac, moving on from strange and disturbing news at sea to the ostensibly happier topics of hunting, fishing, and war.

Having little to contribute, and less room to speak should she think of something, Emelyn wondered how she would manage so many days away from all things familiar. Sipping a bitter coffee, she stared into the crackling logs, resolved to write to Margaret at the earliest opportunity.

Now in a chair nearer the fire Deacon held the floor. "The Mohocks are the worst of the lot," he said, continuing his discourse on the violent gangs of London, "haunting the streets like a red sashed militia—robbery, kidnap, murder, recruiting where they can and pleased as Peter about it, for none dare inform on them."

"I've heard they enjoy the sponsorship of a lord," Emelyn said, recalling the grief she'd suffered at the hands of the very ruffians, and the towering Mr. Lorris, who had defended her.

The men smoked and sipped, seeming to mull it over.

"The sponsorship of a lord," Van Croft grunted. "Impossible."

"Well it's said they take thirty people a week," Deacon continued.

"I heard of the Mohocks accosting a gentlewoman and her beau in Westminster," Doctor Tarville chimed in, "making them dance by jabbing blades at their shoes!"

"But we shan't credit them with *every* mishap," the Commodore chimed in, "particularly at night. Should not the *Lurkmen* have their due?"

"The Lurkmen only take children, or so I've read," Emelyn said, stirring her coffee as the men turned to regard her, "poor foundlings off the streets, whom none shall miss . . . For all we know they're better for it."

"Good Lord!" The Commodore laughed. "Well my dear we can only pray t'isn't true."

"But are there not thousands of forgotten children about the city?" Emelyn suggested. "The charity houses do little enough; I've seen them sleeping in the streets."

"The *Lurkmen* gentlemen!" Van Croft cried, sloshing his drink with a laugh. "Miss Morley's political solution to London's pickpocket waifs. She'll be digging up old Tom Poker next. Tell us my dear, what do you hear of that old bogie?"

"I don't keep up with children's fables my lord," she said, returning his gaze.

The gentlemen resumed their jawing, and Emelyn left them to sit by the window, turning her attention to the monochrome dusk. The long day drew to its close as she watched, and the captain came to take her unmarred hand, giving it a nibbling kiss as he bid her goodnight.

"I daresay Lord Van Croft doubts I could have anything to add on any topic," Emelyn said, lifting her arms as Breda helped her into a nightdress.

"He is a nobleman miss, and a sea captain," Breda sighed, "but I'll wager you're not to be intimidated."

"And how do you find the staff?" Emelyn asked, twisting her hair. "Anything of interest or concern?"

"I've heard there's two out later than they ought," Breda said, "and the weather miss . . . it seems strange to me, the sky rolling so dark without rain."

Emelyn climbed into bed. "Well, whatever the clouds, I should like to peer from the lookout over the wall, but Mrs. Akehurst forbids I walk without her, lest I tumble into the sea."

The windows of The Honourable Magistrate Taffram Brule's long narrow office were black as shadow in the late hour. Tired and sickly, the heavy gentleman leaned to adjust a dim lantern on his desk. Footsteps sounded up the stairs, into the hall, and the door at the far end burst open. In strode a hard faced young man in fine coats and long ostentatious wig, a sword clinking on his belt.

Mr. Brule coughed into a kerchief, a horrible, double retching sound, and the young man stopped his approach, wrinkling his nose.

"By Judas man, are you contagious?" he asked, speaking through a clenched kerchief.

"Robert the Blade!" Brule waved him closer. "No by hell, not contagious . . . unless my master wills it."

"Your master? Lord Dramen?" the young man mused, eyeing what appeared to be a huge rounded heap in the back corner, draped in black as like unused furniture. "Why is it so dark, have you something to hide?"

"Nothing sir!" the magistrate declared, slapping his desk. "You've roused me for an appointment, when I'd rather be abed with a pair of nymphs . . . What is the urgency?"

"Lord Abbott, my father."

"Missing yes, not a trace." Brule nodded. "And thought dead, I very much fear."

"Yes but not *proven* dead."

"But I see you waste no time in plundering his tailor," Brule chuckled with a cough. "And the executor has paid the wig-maker bill, by the look of it."

"The *executor* be damned," Robert Abbot said with a sneer, leaning over the desk. "How am I to mount a proper search for my father without the power of the estate at my command?"

"Seven years sir. If *missing* Lord Abbott remains, that'll be seven years, before you inherit."

"So I am aware!" Robert snapped. "That is unless the body is found."

"Correct."

"But Emelyn Morley, she *will* know something of it, if anyone does."

"You imagine her a murderess?" the magistrate grunted. "Revenge upon you for cuffing her in the alley, perhaps?"

Robert adjusted his wig, straightening up. "And what else shall it be, you sickly old fool. Coincidence? My father was to invade Hastelbrook, and then he was gone."

Mr. Brule was scrubbing at a spot of ink on his hand. "The Morley estate is cursed my good fellow . . . I should keep my distance, were I you. Anyway, Miss Morley is not there."

"Where then? How do you know?"

"We have eyes and ears farther afield than you imagine. The girl has gone to the house of Galecliff, upon Beachy Head over the Channel. She is courted by Lord Van Croft."

"Is she indeed? The *Bloodhound of His Majesty's Navy* . . ." Robert stuck out his jaw to scratch his chin. "As it happens I know a pair of gentlemen—served under the captain's first mate. Perhaps I shall send them round."

Brule wheezed with a grim chuckle. "To what purpose? *Your pardon Miss Morley, but we might inquire, where you've gone and hid the corpse of one Lord Abbott?*"

"Mock me, but I'll not be waiting seven years for my estate," Robert warned, grasping his sword. "My father was about *your* business after all, serving the brotherhood, when he disappeared."

Brule coughed softly as he poured a dark liquid into a thick mug. "So it is the money, more than justice, which concerns."

"My inheritance *is* justice! And what is that liquor? It smells foul."

"Medicine sir, German mum, bitter and strong."

Robert turned up his nose. "If Miss Morley knows anything, my men will suss it out. Alas for you sir, who have been of no more help than our damnable executor."

Mr. Brule leaned back, folding his hands over his stomach. "Steady on . . . I may have some recourse in mind."

"There we are!" Robert banged his hand on the desk. "Name your price. When I have my estate, you shall be seen to."

"Ten thousand. Unless the girl coughs up the body first." Brule chuckled again.

"Ten thousand! Have you lost your block sir? I'll pay you five hundred."

"Ten thousand I think, *but,*" Brule said quickly, raising his hand, "not for my sake. You are expected to take your father's place in the order, and with that mantle comes the burden of his pledge, yet unpaid.

Ten thousand guineas for the cause . . . for Lord Dramen's *Vampire Act*, and what comes after."

With a snarling curse Robert threw up his hands, turning to pace about the room.

The magistrate watched him, his watery eyes drifting back and forth as he nursed his mum. "That's not a fifth of what capital you could move. Well sir what say you?"

The young man stopped, leaning once more over the desk. "Shall I have the estate free and clear?"

Brule wheezed with a chuckle, downing his drink and turning over the jug for another. "You shall have not only the estate, but the title, not in honorific but in earnest. My Lord Abbott."

"My Lord Abbott," Robert said, straightening up. "A handsome address . . . if ever there was. But how are we to bring it about?"

"Fabricated witnesses, evidence, and documents attesting to Lord Abbot's running afoul of the very thief-takers he meant to hire. Blood, clothes, precious effects will be discovered, sworn seen on his person the night he disappeared."

"Thief-takers. An ignoble epitaph if ever there was. And how long will it take sir?"

"Months I should think. We must be delicate."

"Months!"

"As I said, unless the girl proves of material use. But again I say, you must act with care. There is a watchful shadow over Miss Morley, unless we very much mistake."

"Leave the girl to me," Robert said impatiently. "I want you gathering this evidence as rapidly as may be done. And I've your word it will be sufficient . . . to exercise my father's will, without a body?"

"Predicated on the trifling detail that he is in fact *dead*, and nevermore to be seen."

Something shifted in the corner and Robert blanched, his eyes trained on the huge covered shape.

"Now!" Brule pronounced, startling his guest as he drew a document from one of the drawers. "You will complete this banker's draft putting 10,000 guineas to the accounts of Lord Dramen. The draft matures the moment the estate is yours."

Robert Abbott swallowed. "Yes sir, very good . . . but is that great heap *taller* than when I arrived?"

"Your eyes play tricks in the dark," Brule answered, providing a pen as he slid the document across. "I prefer the dim light you understand, since the first I tasted his blood."

"I beg your pardon?" Robert stared at him.

"Just here sir!" Brule jabbed the paper with his finger. "Your signature, if you please . . . good, and by the amount. Yes quite correct, thank you."

Robert dropped the pen on the desk, backing away. "Is that all then? Is it settled?"

"Quite settled," Brule said, excusing himself for a retching cough. "Yes . . . quite settled. Now sir, I might suggest you find your way out, and quickly."

But Robert the Blade had already fled, the door banging behind him.

With shaking hands Mr. Brule sipped his drink as the dark shape in the corner expanded, rising from a crouch to its full height, and the monstrous vampire Vorsadat turned, his pale bald head coming into view, floating in a sea of black. The vampire's wrinkled face broke into a grin, and the empty sockets of his eyes glowed as long bony fingers wrapped about the magistrate's shoulders.

"Ten thousand guineas Mr. Brule," he spoke in guttural tones. "The better to undo the queen of Saunmoor, to speak her name in the House of Lords, to plot her demise . . ."

"Yes my lord, but these things must be done properly," Brule said, rattling the liquor down his front as he sipped. "There are palms yet to grease, men of name yet to conscript to Lord Dramen's purpose."

"*Afaine*," Vorsadat murmured at his ear, "the immortal girl in your keep. It is by mortal hands she must die, to rend my queen's heart. Why does Dramen hesitate?"

"She will be destroyed, you have my word. We need but a little more time, for Dramen to conduct his experiments."

"I go to the cliffs over the sea," Vorsadat whispered, "to attend upon a little red bird. Do not disappoint my return."

The magistrate shivered as with a cold rush of wind the lantern went out, and the monster was gone.

Deep within the high boundary of Saunmoor, far beneath the citadel of Umbremar, there opened a damp and cavernous space, steeped in silence. Here Lord Simeon stood at the end of a sagging pier by the rocky shore of an underground lake, vast and dark as clouded ink. A slender mist played over the water, glinting with sourceless light, revealing strange and teeming movements beneath the surface.

Behind him the cavern wall gave way to a hollow shaft rising straight up into the underbelly of the citadel, its sides rough and textured with embedded skulls beyond count, as like an ancient well of the dead. Gazing out over the lake, Simeon marked the familiar sound of the towering shaft caving inward as a river of bones tumbled into the gap, flooding the landing until nothing remained but a dense and undulating ossuary wall, sealing the way out.

The silence grew heavier, and he squinted across into the gloom to just make out a sprawling monstrous tree, withered grey and twisted as it grew from the far barren shore, its blind branches stretching upward until they pressed the cavernous ceiling, steeped in darkness. A narrow slip of shadow was drifting closer on the lake, moving by an invisible current. Lord Simeon folded his hands, breathing deep.

"My summons was abrupt, and yet you have come, even to the Deadmere," the voice of Pazoa Qiminossa, the vampire queen of Saunmoor, rippled over the water, echoing among the stones.

"To indulge my fear of the lake," Simeon replied, "would only compromise my service to you."

A slender open boat drifted into view, dark wood inlaid with gold. Its pointed prow was capped and horned in the same precious metal, and at the stern was secured an ornate chair, in the style of a medieval Persian throne, tall and square, with intricate carvings. Seated upon the throne was the queen. Her dark umber flesh was swathed in revealing purple silk—a deep Tyrian shade of the East, with platinum rings about her neck, her slender arms bangled in clasping gold. Her face was shrouded, draped and indistinct, her raven hair long and thickly braided over her shoulder.

The boat rolled closer upon a wake of white. But as Simeon looked to the water he beheld not foam or froth, but moving hands—knuckles and fingers in their hundreds—the hands of the dead. Bleached grey as forgotten stone, they pushed the skiff forward, until it drew near the dock, and the queen gestured.

"Join me."

Simeon stepped aboard, jostling for a moment as they set out.

"My brother advises that I must be disappointed in you," she said, her voice drifting like ghosts through the veil, swimming in the air about him.

"It is not for me to say," Simeon began carefully, "that your trust in Vorsadat is misplaced, after his tenure so long at your side."

Pazoa tilted her head. "In all our history of unending night, my brother has only myself to cling to. That you should accuse him now, as he accuses you, it vexes me."

"I do not accuse him."

"After spending time in the old man's grace in Rome, you send Vaela to treat with him, against my wishes."

"The *old man*, Tredavius, is not your enemy, my queen."

Pazoa stood slowly, drifting closer, her height matching his.

"Carefully, Lord Simeon; that is a precarious reflection," she breathed. "I require the bloodstone. He keeps it from me. That makes him my enemy, and you his consort."

"Tredavius knows more of the prophecy than I," Simeon replied, staring into the anonymous drape of her veil. "But whatever this . . . affliction upon you—I submit every potential means to see it cured, must be considered. The old man bears you no ill will, he would not see your reign compromised."

"You speak freely," she said, touching his cheek with a slender claw.

Simeon swallowed. "Your dominion over Saunmoor is unquestioned," he said. "But you are threatened, my queen. Your children witness your pain, as do we."

"My pain must be nothing to you," Pazoa said, gripping into his coats. "It is only dreams, feral voices of the long dead past screeching in shrillness while I sleep . . . denying me rest."

"Yet rest you must," he insisted, "lest the dead wake to wander, breaking free of your control."

"Do you find me enervated in my own house?" she asked, holding him tighter as she pulled him close. "Would you rebuke me for misrule?"

"No, my queen, but if these attacks upon your mind continue—"

She released him, and retreating a step she sat heavily in the chair, expelling a ragged breath. "Shall I heed your counsel," she said. "A stranger—of my acquaintance but a century. Or shall I hearken to my brother, whom I have relied upon these seven hundred years."

Simeon adjusted his spectacles. "I do not seek to convince you without evidence, but only entreat you to watch him with care."

"As I watch you," she snarled, gripping the arms with bared claws.

"As it pleases you," he replied, bowing low. "And now, by your leave, I have many matters to attend."

"You have none to attend but your queen," she said coldly. "If you mean no treachery in seeking the old man's counsel, then you must convince your queen of your sincerity, here upon the Deadmere, within reach of those who at my whisper would drag you into the deeps, to your utter end."

"I very much hope we do not come to that," he said, standing rigid.

Pazoa crossed her legs, leaning back. "Then, my dear Lord Simeon, pray defend yourself from my brother's warning—avouch your good intentions before me, until I am satisfied . . . or disappointed."

* * *

Sunday June 26th

Finding the captain indisposed with the Commodore, Emelyn

wandered the halls that afternoon, yet drowsy after exhausting dreams she could not remember. Though the house glittered with all manner of artwork, crystal and finery, Galecliff manor seemed remarkably damp and drab, its thick walls bearing Mrs. Akehurst's decorous touches but reluctantly. After some while Emelyn returned to her designated apartment, which gratefully was more cheerful than the others she'd seen, not of dark wood but papered in happy blue above the wainscot, with deeper blue drapery and broad paintings of sailing vessels adorning the walls. A rocking chair of painted walnut sat in the corner. Her narrow ship's windows overlooked pruned back orchards and a charming pond forded by a footbridge. Beyond this ran the north property fence before growers' cottages and a little road spindling away down the hill for the crop fields, beside which towered the dovecote—a round brick building with little windows circling just under the roof.

After enjoying the view a few moments Emelyn reposed for a second nap, drifting off to the distant wash of the sea mingled with boastful laughter from below . . . and once again she dreamt of Hastelbrook, finding herself caught on the stairs between Sarah above and Isabelle below, who with ghostly white faces demanded she confess her secret.

Emelyn shook awake with a cry, sitting up to find her neck bedewed with sweat, and one of the staff rapping on the door.

Summoned back to the drawing room she arrived in a pretty gown of brilliant white, which she hoped to enliven her spirits, and found the gentlemen in their usual place, engrossing light and heat from the fire to leave the rest of the room rather cold. Again Van Croft came for her hand, and Emelyn watched as he kissed it with a ticklish nibble.

"I wonder my lord, if we are to wait yet *another* day to see the grounds?" she asked. "Perhaps if we only toured behind the house; the farm and cottages are charming from my window . . . unless she fears I must fall into the pond?"

"You shall see them soon enough my dear," he chuckled, bowing his leave to return to the Commodore, just as Mrs. Akehurst swept in from the hall.

"As I was explaining," the Commodore pronounced, glancing at his wife, "what wonders Queen Caroline has wrought for Hyde Park!"

"Well she ought," Doctor Tarville chirped, "left to govern us once again while dear old George scurries back to Hanover."

"Oh do speak freely gentlemen," Mrs. Akehurst said dryly, taking Emelyn's arm before she could sit down. "My dear Miss Morley, you'll forgive my neglect, but it would seem we've staff in dereliction of their posts, two in fact, disappeared altogether."

"*Disappeared?* But they've not come to misadventure?" Emelyn inquired, sparkling with interest.

"Who could say," Mrs. Akehurst replied, guiding her to sit at a small table by the books, its face demarked for chess and populated with beautiful marble pieces, one side white and the other deep crimson. Watching Emelyn take her seat at the red side, the lady installed on the chair opposite, and turning round she shouted at the sour faced elder footman dozing by the door. "Fenders, claret!"

The fellow startled to attention, approaching in short order with brimmers of Bordeaux on a silver tray, and accepting the ruby drink in exchange for her half-finished coffee Emelyn took a long sip. "Shall we have a game?"

"Chess? Oh no my dear good heavens," Mrs. Akehurst said, shooing the footman away, and without preamble she launched into a rehearsed sort of speech, declaring herself the most ardent defender of Lord Van Croft's interest, lauding him not only as the heroic saviour of her husband's life—*my Henry might have lost more than his hand,* but furthermore the most worthy example of the male sex she'd ever encountered—*fit for a princess if ever a man was!*

Certain she was meant to find herself wanting by the captain's comparison, Emelyn listened politely as cakes and tea with early ripe Cheshire cheese was brought in, and selecting a few morsels she puzzled where to set her plate, looking over the chessboard.

"On the window ledge my dear," Mrs. Akehurst said quickly, flush with a smile as she watched her. "Yes well, as I've explained he is a man with no end of prospects, and yet now we find him positively besotted, and here you are, dear creature."

Emelyn returned her smile. "Here I am."

"And of course your beauty is arresting," the lady continued, picking at her plate, "but we are wise to remember *Charms strike the sight, but merit wins the soul,* so I would impress upon you that beauty alone does not captivate a man of such stature for long."

"And I shall hope to be known for more than that," Emelyn said, striving not to be offended.

A few questions later she meant to break free and ply Doctor Tarville after his thoughts concerning Deacon, but Mrs. Akehurst tapped the board for her attention. "Your accomplishments my dear."

"My accomplishments?"

"But as the eldest daughter of a well landed squire you must be sufficiently accomplished?"

Emelyn nodded slowly, considering her safest response . . . but the onset of the wine was pleasurable, and she was determined to enjoy herself. "Shall I draw you up a list?"

Her hostess laughed. "Oh but as your steadfast ally I shall contrive the list myself; I only want that you should impress our captain, in every way."

"Very well," Emelyn relented, finding little recourse but to sip and see it through.

She was asked first of languages, and shared of her fluency in French, dabbling in German and Italian, and her study of Latin, though the lady seemed distracted by the captain's emphatic bluster by the fire.

"Latin!" Mrs. Akehurst blurted, returning her attention. "Oh but there's never a gentleman who wants to hear Latin from a lady."

"Then I shall speak it very quietly," Emelyn said, lamenting the near empty weight of her second glass.

Turning to the subject of music, Mrs. Akehurst waxed eloquent on her own wide-ranging proficiencies. Emelyn nodded agreeably, checking to find Deacon engaged with the Commodore, who'd drawn up a chair and looked to be explaining the empty cuff of his sleeve.

"I've little to recommend me at the harpsichord," Emelyn confessed, endeavouring to remember the questions. "I have no strings, nor winds, excepting a fair hand at the harp. But it is singing I like best."

"And how are you out of doors? Riding? Archery?"

"There's no greater freedom than riding," Emelyn said with a happy breath. "I've a perfect blonde Arabian with white fetlocks—Queen Bess. I've jumped and raced her all about the estate."

"Jumped and raced? Riding pillion?"

"I am not afraid to mount her astride."

Mrs. Akehurst gave a little laugh. "Astride! Shall I suppose you hunt and play cricket as well?"

"No, madam, I do not," Emelyn said, tiring of the contest, "though I am fond of archery, at which I'm an even shot, if second always to Sarah."

"Fine. And how is your needlework?"

"It could be no worse blindfolded."

"My goodness! To admit such to me is well enough, but I should make no mention of it around the captain."

"Indeed, I imagine hearing of needlework at all would knock him straight to sleep."

Unimpressed with her response Mrs. Akehurst turned to theatre and the arts, and while answering to the best of her ability, Emelyn dreamed of stealing to her room . . . where she must pen a letter to Margaret, and a response to Mr. Arkwright, before any thought of retiring.

But the lady of the house pressed onward. "And have you any painting, sculpture? How is your dancing?"

"Dear me," Emelyn said, warm with the drink, "my mother would not approve of leaving my dowry and allowance off your list."

"Oh my dear this is not an interrogation!" Mrs. Akehurst returned, laughing again. "You must understand, we navy wives are endowed with a certain frankness. But your father must have settled something upon you?"

"I cannot speak to my settlement," Emelyn said. "The estate is entailed; my sisters and I shall have nothing at all unless disposed to us by my brother, if he is . . . that is when he inherits," and she shook her head, draining her glass. "If he does not live to see it the estate must pass to a distant cousin we know scarcely at all, and whom we have rather learned to abhor."

"My but you do share freely," the lady mused.

Emelyn scowled at her glass, feeling the claret had betrayed her.

"Miss Morley, you must understand," Mrs. Akehurst said, lowering her voice, "I'm only determined that you should seek proposal from our dear captain on broader basis than personal elevation."

"Are you his mother?" Emelyn murmured under her breath, massaging her head with a long euphoric blink.

"Precious thing you are mumbling with sleep."

"I confess I am spent," Emelyn said, seizing her chance to stand with a curtsy. "I have not been sleeping my best."

"Just another moment," the lady said quickly, standing as well. "But I've one more question for you, of Hastelbrook. Can it be true you've a crypt *inside* the house, and beneath the library of all places?"

"Yes ma'am it is. But the crypt is not in use, and hasn't been for generations. The stone caskets are empty."

Mrs. Akehurst squinted with a little smile, as though trying to dismiss an unpleasant thought.

"And we keep a second kitchen upstairs, which I'm aware is quite unusual," Emelyn said, seeking to clear the air. "But it is only small, where my sisters and I might go snacks."

"Go snacks?"

"Share a morsel between meals, if one is so inclined; the kitchen was added to avail guests in the stateroom, which is also upstairs, above the small library."

"The stateroom *upstairs*? I've never heard of such a thing. But it must be rested all year."

"On the contrary, we make good use of it," Emelyn said, increasingly eager to quit her company, "my sisters for drawing or games, and sometimes I read by the windows, though I prefer the library below."

"Public rooms upstairs . . . Well your mother must run the house as she sees fit of course. Oh but I have so enjoyed our conversation," and with a beaming smile Mrs. Akehurst bid her goodnight.

Feeling a compulsion to embrace her brother Emelyn returned to the hearth, leaning down to squeeze him about the shoulders, and Deacon flushed, tapping her arm. "Yes, thank you Emie, goodnight."

"Until the silver morrow, Miss Morley," the doctor gushed, and the captain took her good hand for a gentle parting kiss.

"Goodnight my lord," Emelyn said, noting the line of his jaw in the firelight.

"I would have you know," the Commodore said, escorting her by the arm back to the grand hall, "your arrival is a ray of light in the gloom. Never has the captain attended us with so charming a friend; I should say he finds himself lucky to know you."

"You honour me sir," Emelyn said, "though I might account myself something of a disappointment to your wife."

"Now now, not a word of it," he said, patting her hand. "My Genevieve is disposed to mistrust any young lady Van Croft takes to. He lost his natural parents when he was a boy you see, a tragedy I find she is over conscious of, doting upon him like her own son, and she not fifteen years his senior!"

"Oh, I'm sorry . . . I didn't realize."

"I'll not have it temper your buoyancy," he said. "Bygones and all that."

"Commodore," she ventured, finding the opportunity could not be wasted. "Sir, I should like to confirm; you do mean to permit my brother for the party?"

"You have my word," he avowed. "Too often do those without it look down upon those who suffer disability, either by birth, or accident as is the case with your brother. I'll not stand for it in my home. What's more, the young doctor shall attend him—Tarville is a talented surgeon in his own right."

"You show Deacon great kindness," Emelyn said, feeling a happy flutter at his good will. "Would my own family fared better on that score."

"Family can be difficult," the Commodore said, stopping at the base of the stairs. "My only daughter, our Melinda, is staying now with relations in Bath, where she spends her living with a reckless dedication I'd not thought possible."

"Then she shares a fondness for purchase with my mother."

The Commodore laughed, releasing her arm with a bow. "Sleep well Miss Morley!"

"Goodnight," Emelyn replied, gliding her hand along the rail as she ascended to make for her room.

Breda took down her hair, helping her out of her clothes into a night dress, and Emelyn sat at a little writing desk by the door, removing the opal pendant Vaela had given her to lay it on the table.

"Mrs. Akehurst confirmed there are missing among the staff," she recalled aloud. "Have you heard any more of it below stairs?"

"Two footmen disappeared miss," Breda said. "But it is a danger, the house being so close to the drop, and slippery near the edge, as I heard."

"Have they likely fallen? Over the cliff?" Emelyn said, quailing to imagine it as she drew a blank sheet for writing.

"I don't know miss," Breda said, watching as Emelyn smoothed the paper. "Do you mean to respond to your Mr. Arkwright . . . tonight?"

"I do," Emelyn said, looking at her. "But you must tell me; did you read his letter?"

Breda went pink, blinking at the wall as though trying to remember.

"I'm not angry," Emelyn said, "but for your courage I'd never have seen it."

"It were none of my affair miss, I shouldn't have done; it is only . . . m'lady never stops your letters, and I was ever so curious."

"Yes, so was I," Emelyn sighed, setting herself to write.

Breda laid out a gown for the morning, and before long Emelyn had a half a dozen false starts crumpled on the floor. "I can get no further than *Dear Sir, I have only come upon your letter by the deft hands and subterfuge of my lady's maid . . .*"

"Have I committed *subterfuge?*" Breda asked with alarm.

"No, Breda, it is a compliment; I only mean you preserved it by deception."

"Yes miss, sorry miss."

The warmth of the wine began to fade, and Emelyn frowned, finding herself caught between the case for Arkwright's company, and her miserable duty to assure him such a thing was impossible.

"Perhaps tomorrow miss?"

Emelyn shook her head, and starting again she wrote quickly and truthfully as she could bear, her eyes welling at the unhappy words.

"There, it is done," she said at last, signing and sealing the finished copy. This she followed by working up a letter to her dearest friend Margaret, which brought on emotions of a different sort. Herein she regretted once more her *accident of passion* upon the hill, by which she meant kissing Mr. Arkwright under Margaret's nose, and the awful badgering she'd given her . . . *for only trying to protect me, of course, as ever I hope I would have done for you, were I in your place.* The idea that Maggie could not believe in Vaela, after Emelyn's earnest confession, was painful, but she made no mention of it, determined that a more auspicious time to address her friend's doubts would come.

"You are wrong after all, dear sweet Mags," Emelyn said, scratching the little cut on her knuckles. "It's all real . . ."

"Miss?"

"Nothing, Breda, I'm finished. If you would take them down please."

Her lady's maid obliged at once, and Emelyn sat quietly, reviewing in her mind what she'd written, until by and by Breda returned, sharing that the letters had gone out that very minute with the night post run for Eastbourne.

"Will there be anything else miss?"

"No, Breda, thank you."

Emelyn tucked herself in bed, and by a combination of wine and fatigue she was soon asleep . . .

In her dream the small dining table was lovely, bedecked in white beneath a grand *triomphe* of miniature sugar loaf statues—tiny Emelyn and her sisters dancing in a ring, with an exquisitely detailed elm tree and a white carven Deacon up high, lazing on a branch.

"Mama," Emelyn said, finding herself seated as she observed the carvings. "Is it not in poor taste, Deacon's figure depicted moments before he fell?"

Mrs. Morley and her sisters drifted into the room, taller than Emelyn remembered, their faces hazy and unimportant. "You'll stain your gloves my dearest," Mrs. Morley said. "Arms off the table."

Looking again Emelyn found the sugar statues were no longer white but red, as suddenly the table teemed with insects—fat little crawlies dark crimson in colour.

"They're only cochineals my dearest," her mother said. "Without squishing them to juice there could be no carmine red, and it is such a glorious colour."

"Eat your sugar and answer us," Sarah and Isabelle said together, looming behind her.

"I don't want any more questions," Emelyn said, "not tonight . . . I must get back to Galecliff or the captain will wonder where I've gone."

The figures of her mother and sisters began to grow, taller and wider and leaning closer, and Emelyn felt Isabelle's nails on her back, walking up her spine as oft she had done when they were children, but the sensation was creeping and unpleasant.

"Look at us Emie," Sarah and Isabelle said together.

"I won't look up," Emelyn said. "Not this time; you only mean to frighten me!"

"What slumbers beneath us Emie?" Isabelle asked. "We heard you down there, laughing and talking to the dark, when you were little."

Emelyn shook her head, watching the insects as they crawled about the feet of the statues. "You couldn't have done; you were not yet born."

"Answer us my sweet," her mother said sharply. "Is it weapon, wealth or the queen's way out? Is it only a statue, or a tomb, or something more? Does it sleep? Does it wake? What lies in the vault!"

"I don't understand your nonsense!" Emelyn retorted, and staring at the table she found two of the figurines were yet undyed by the crawling bugs. These little statues were familiar, very tall and gaunt, cloaked in carven sugar, brilliant white, and she thought at once of the hooded bust in the gallery.

The arms of the chair had twisted around her own, but with a splintering crack she broke free, and she ran. Her giant sisters moved slowly, stomping after her with cries of protest as racing across the grand hall she made for the long gallery. The doors opened before her, the familiar black cowled statue raised its head, its vast cloak spreading in welcome, and resisting the urge to look back she dashed forward, reaching out to catch hold of the figure's garment . . .

The dream broke, and with a gasp Emelyn found herself sitting up, her head swimming. Holding her face with a groan she strove to arrange her thoughts, and after clambering out of bed she rushed to the desk for pen and paper. "You must remember," she said aloud, knocking over the chair as she slapped a blank page onto the desk. "Remember . . . remember." The ink lid was stuck, but popped off with a splash, and after dipping the nib with a jab she pressed it to the paper.

'Sugar'

"Sugar? Is that all?" she flustered, staring at the word. "But there must be more . . ."

There was a light knock, and having roused from her cot in the dressing room, a sleepy Breda poked her head in. "All right miss?"

Emelyn sighed, rubbing her head. "I forgot. It's gone . . . It's not fair."

"What's gone miss?"

"The dream. Is Deacon bedded down in the longhouse?" Emelyn asked, setting the chair on its feet. "I cannot sleep."

"Yes miss, but it's nigh one o' clock."

"Very well," Emelyn replied, dropping the pen in its place. "If you would be good enough to fetch my cardinal, I want to check on him."

"Now miss?"

"Yes, Breda. Now."

Over the edge of the white chalk cliffs, sheer down five hundred feet from the house of Galecliff, a lifeless arm in torn sleeve bobbed in the shallow brine as Vaela watched, standing where the rocks met the sea. Fangs bared, she lifted to examine the second corpse of a pair, both young men in servants livery, badly broken from the fall, and not a drop of blood between them.

There came a great howl on the wind, a fell voice she took no pleasure in hearing, and with a hiss she dropped the body. Returning to the dry path against the cliffs, the vampiress bounded up a treacherous uneven stair carved to follow the juts and crags of the rock, scarce wide enough for one as it climbed from the sea all the way to the windswept grass above.

Reaching the overgrown gatepost of the estate boundary she leapt atop it, flashing along the wall as a hulking lantern eyed creature kept pace on the opposite side of the property. At the tall pavilion lookout she stopped.

"Heedless butcher, why have you come?" she whispered, knowing well the vampire Vorsadat could hear even the blood in her veins.

There was no reply, but she marked a large crouching thing upon the roof of the main house, clinging to the peak like a monstrous owl, its burning saucer eyes fixed upon her.

Vaela spoke scarcely loud enough to trouble the air. "Go back to Hastelbrook. Go back! That is your post."

With a silent spring the monster leapt from his perch, long arms wide, claws spread like daggers, and the vampiress dodged aside as he landed with crushing impact, smashing through stones like breadcrust.

Crouching with eyes black Vaela hissed, watching as the roofed pavilion sagged dangerously, its foundations compromised by the break in the wall. "Reckless madness! You will wake them all!" she snapped.

The hulking Vorsadat pawed the dust from his ancient coats, his lantern eyes extinguished leaving only blackened hollows. "Ever lugubrious lady, fear not," he said, his voice low and grating. "The sea breaks louder than I."

"Do you roam so far afield only to murder?"

In a blink he was atop the wall, half again her height as he hunched before her. "Nothing goes to waste," he said. "The dead belong to me."

"You have been collecting corpses," Vaela said darkly, retreating a step, "despite the queen's forbiddance."

Vorsadat cocked his head like a curious animal but did not answer.

"You can have no purpose here," she chided. "To watch the Chosen Child is my charge alone. You are to wait upon the vault, to listen for any sign of change."

"Your vigil should have been mine," he said, lurching closer with a ravenous grin.

Near enough to feel his carrion breath Vaela stepped back again. "Yours? I think not," she scoffed. "You have no subtlety for such things; you avail your part from a distance."

"While you pretend to mothering a child; barren in death as you were in life."

The stone cracked and the pavilion shifted again. "Emelyn is a child no longer," Vaela said, continuing her retreat along the wall as he crept closer. "Take your ravage and ruin away with you. Or should the vault betray a sound and you be not there to hear it?"

Vorsadat dragged his claws as he approached. "The vault steeps in silence," he growled. "It speaks only to the Chosen Child; the key lies within her . . . and I will have it out."

"You will not," Vaela said sharply. "By Pazoa's command she must remain unspoiled."

"My sister is unworthy to rule," he snarled, looming nearer like a pale grinning shadow. "Her time bleeds away, soaking into the ground . . . The mortals will eat her children. I will see to it."

Vaela bared claws and fangs. "It was you . . . *you* served Afaine to the hunters. You cannot imagine to go unpunished!"

"Punished shall I be?" The massive vampire twitched, and she gasped to find herself held by her throat, suspended over the cliff. The unfathomable darkness of his heart washed over her, scarred and twisted, forged in bitterness and pain from the mortal outcast he once had been, scraping his meagre existence in the frozen mountains of Red Ruthenia. But beneath this, clawing upward from the very hollow of his being, she sensed something deeper—a pure and seething hatred far older than he. Vaela could not speak, but only stare as the monster's eyes ignited in baleful fire, his thin lips curling back to lengthen cruel fangs.

"Punished by whom?" he croaked. "I have warned our queen of

your conspiracy."

"You deceive yourself!" she choked, hissing through the crush of his grip. "Something . . . is preying upon you—"

"Luckless lonely raven of Touraine," he rumbled, pulling her close, "I will break your little Miss Morley, I will have her secrets . . . and you will burn to cinders by the sea."

"You dare not touch her!" Ferociously Vaela strove against him, but unable to free herself from his grasp the vampiress could do little more than scratch. And grinning like a demon he tossed her over the edge.

With a flailing shriek she dropped, plunging like an arrow of black through the cold salt air, the night wheeling past, until after what seemed an age she crashed through the foam, striking the rocks beneath.

Gaping sightless Vaela stared into nothing, limp against the swirling currents as her broken body struggled to reknit, until a gnarled hand yanked her from the sea by the hair, the eyes of her enemy burning out of the dark. "I dare not touch her?" he snarled in mockery. "Your warning breaks late; by the tiniest scratch I have infected her dreams . . . already."

The vampiress dangled before him, coughing as she tried to speak.

"Your maker will not save you; Pazoa calls him to answer his treachery," he said brightly, shaking her with a cackle.

"Simeon is no traitor!" she spluttered. "The traitor is you!"

Vorsadat hoisted her closer, sniffing at her throat, and snapping the ring Tredavius had given her from its chain about her neck he tossed it into the sea before spinning to fling her away.

Cracking hard against the cliff Vaela collapsed to the ground, contorting in agony.

In an instant he was upon her. "The traitorous old man cannot help her—Pazoa only diminishes as I increase," he growled, eyes burning white as he crouched over her.

"You . . . cannot," Vaela rasped, blood dribbling from her lips.

Vorsadat's large, bony hand smoothed back her hair, petting her head. "Interloper," he said. "Your foreign blood drains in the sand. You have failed her," and snatching the dead footmen from the shallows he leapt into the dark, and was gone.

Chapter 20
Night Scream

Dominated by a long common room with wide bricked cooking hearth at one end, and a well stocked larder at the other, the longhouse in which Deacon quartered was well maintained and tidy, pungent with the aroma of pickled vegetables, tallow potted beef, butter and hard cheeses bundled on the shelves. Dried spices and joints of meat hung from the ceiling, and just before the fire the western wall pushed back, making way for a sunken annex where in the corner was made up a little bedroom, with a great tall cabinet opened to a box bed tucked inside its lower storey, upon which Deacon reclined in a dark robe, spreading out cards on the blanket beside him as a restless Emelyn perched on a stool to watch.

"But you do look paler," she said. "Are you sure you're quite well?"

"You mustn't keep fussing," Deacon replied, taking no notice as he turned over an example hand. "Now, there is nothing better than to anticipate which cards are still in play."

An anxious tension had settled in her chest, and unsure whether it was her brother's vaguely ailing state or something else, Emelyn stood up, coughing at the fragrant haze of smoke that hung in the air. "Can it really be necessary, an entire bowl of burning sage?"

"*To work against building up of hard waters in the lungs,*" Deacon recited, watching her pace. "Can you not keep still? Shall we cut our losses and retire?"

"I don't want to sleep," she said, looking about the room. "Something is wrong . . . How should you fall ill so soon after arriving?"

"It's nothing Emie, no more than a chill. Tarville assures me it's only that I'm too much on my feet."

"That is nonsense! I never see you but you're sitting down. I do not trust this doctor."

"Emelyn Morley not trust the doctor?" he posed, glaring at the cards as though he'd missed something. "I can hardly speak for the shock."

"I am not being difficult," she said, wrinkling her nose as she examined the little green bottle beside the tea at his bedside. "Even this medicine reeks awfully."

"Emie there is more to medicine than honey and ginger."

There came a booming crack, and a deep rolling tumble that might have been thunder, startling them both, but squinting at the windows Emelyn found no sign of rain, and little enough wind.

"Close thunder without lightning?" Deacon observed, leaning out of his bed to better see the windows. "Or perhaps we missed it."

But the tension in her chest had grown suddenly worse, stealing her breath, and quickly Emelyn took up his tea, taking generous swallows in the hope of easing her nerves.

"That's China pekoe from Twinings," he said. "I'm really rather fond of it, if you don't mind."

"Is it?" she said breathlessly, striving to distract herself. "It's very good, what's in it?"

"Honey and ginger," he replied.

Setting it down again she nearly spilled as the tightness sharpened to a heartsick pain, as though some part of herself deeply familiar was going cold, slipping away—

"Emie what's wrong?" he asked. "You are flush and distracted."

Tears welled in her eyes and Emelyn shook her head. "I don't know . . . I feel sick," she said, pressing a hand over her heart as she imagined herself but a speck of shadow, broken and helpless, soon to dissolve in a rising tide of endless light . . . and she realized all at once the fear was not her own. "Vaela!"

"I beg your pardon?"

"I'm sorry Deacon, I must go," and quickly she leaned down to kiss his brow before turning to dash out of the building.

"Emelyn, what the devil!" he called after her.

Heeding a compulsion to seek water she dashed between the cliff wall and the house, shocked to discover a massive gap in the stones—the pavilion tower she'd not yet had the chance to ascend was leaning at such an angle that it looked to collapse at any moment. Dreadful urgency spurred her on, and she rounded the ivied corner to streak past black dining room windows for the back gardens, where coming to the edge of the pond between the pear trees she stopped, watching them list in the wind oblivious, the water muttering quietly.

"Where are you!" she shouted, her eyes wet with panic, and turning again she flew back across the main courtyard, down the drive to the open front gates. Around the high gatepost nearest the cliff's edge she came to a place where the grass appeared to vanish, and creeping closer she found the start of a harrowing descent.

"The stair," she panted, appalled to find the narrow path just as Van Croft had described, open to an unfathomable drop on the one hand, with the sheer wall of the cliff on the other.

But there was nothing for it, and shedding her cloak lest it catch the wind, she folded it quickly to leave by the gatepost. With her back to the chalky stone she began to edge her way slowly down, but the strange and sympathetic ache was increasing, and so with one hand pressed to the cliff wall she quickened her pace, heart in her mouth as she hurried, until at last the rocks below drew mercifully closer, and the stair melted into a slender chalky trail.

Not ten yards distant the relentless waves crashed over the rocky shore, but the pang of horror was with her still, and squinting in the dark she picked her way along the path, searching for its source.

A small dark heap at the base of the cliff caught her eye, and she rushed to examine it.

"Vaela!"

There the vampiress lay, and turning her by the shoulder Emelyn found her pale as marble, with veins darkly visible in her face and neck. Vaela's eyes were open, milky white, her fangs bared and lips parted. Her cloak was torn and sopping, the black robe beneath no better, and there seemed persistent wounds on her arms and back, mars that showed little sign of healing.

Unable to understand, Emelyn trembled like a leaf to look at her, and before there was time to think she was digging into her wrist with a small sharp rock, hissing impatiently at the pain. The cut was deeper than she meant, alive with throbbing, but she held it close, guiding the steady trickle of blood to Vaela's mouth . . . "Vaela wake up," she said, her voice unsteady. "You cannot die, you *wake up!*"

For some moments there was no effect, and the pooling blood began to flow down Vaela's chin. Emelyn's arm grew heavy, her head light, and slumping against her she lowered her wrist, pressing the hurt between Vaela's lips. The vampiress quivered with a swallow, her eyes drifted closed, and Emelyn yelped to find herself suddenly on her back with Vaela atop her, plunging into her neck.

Emelyn gasped, startling at the attack. "Wait . . . carefully!"

The vampiress drank with little growls, growing warmer as she supped, and the pain turned to a dizzy euphoria as Emelyn lay helpless, her wrist bleeding into the ground as she clutched fistfuls of sand. "Vaela—"

Her body grew cold, and staring into the clouds she watched as the dark sky split asunder, revealing blurry golden stars that pulsed and sparkled, as though beckoning her to join them. Her vision faded to nothing, and she felt a distant jostle as Vaela leapt away from her with a shriek, crying out her name . . .

■■

Just north of London town, in the drawing room of the imposing manor of Charwell House, seated leg over knee in an upholstered armchair of French walnut, the baron Lord Dramen swallowed a bit of cake as he stirred his tea. Before him a lovely green gowned woman with high cheekbones sat by the crackling hearth at the edge of the red Persian carpet, playing the up and down strokes of her cello with somnolent beauty for her audience of one.

In silken shirt and smoking vest, a choking white cravat almost to his ears, the heavily wigged baron squinted as he sipped, rattling the teacup with a curse at the clop of heavy boots entering the room.

A young gentleman, tall and lean in riding coat and dark breeches, came to stand before him, snapping into a bow, strands of blond hanging from his face.

"Alexander my boy," Lord Dramen said, setting down his tea.

"Father, I apologize for the small hour," Alexander Dramen replied. "It could not wait until morning. I have ridden through the night chasing bad intelligence . . ."

"Miss Edenko you must excuse us," Lord Dramen said, waving his fingers as the woman stood with her cello to swish out of the room.

"First," Alexander said, "you must sort out your Mr. Grouthe, for every place he bid me search came to nothing. John Lawford's been seen neither about town nor at home for some days; your man is perfectly useless!"

"First!" Lord Dramen pointed at the floor. "First you will take your weather muddied boots off the Bokhara."

Alexander puffed his lips, stepping backward off the carpet. "Father you must hear me . . ."

"Have you any notion at all," Lord Dramen said, as with a final sip he set his teacup carefully back on the saucer, "what it costs me to hire Irma Edenko for a private concerto at such an hour? Guess carefully; she's been in the country scarcely a week."

"I'm sure it's a great deal," Alexander replied. "But there is yet no sign of Lawford, not so much as a whisper; if any harm has befallen my friend—"

"The answer is three hundred pounds," the baron said. "I confess it a trifle, a mere pittance to what our conviction of vampires and their thralls will realize. When the streets run with unholy blood they shall run also with gold."

"Yes, we have a vampire in our power—the moment is not lost on me," Alexander said, "but you must answer, Father; what do you know of Lawford's disappearance?"

Dramen frowned with distaste, dusting crumbs of cake from his hands. "Your compatriot reprobates are of no concern to me, nor should they be to you."

"Reprobates? John is loyal as any fellow could ask! He would not simply vanish of his own accord."

Standing from his chair Lord Dramen faced his son eye to eye, made taller by the tower of his wig, and with a bemused expression he stomped his foot.

Alexander puzzled at the gesture, but his response was interrupted by a terrific boom, as though something had struck the ceiling just beneath them, rattling the house.

"Do you hear that boy?" Lord Dramen inquired. "Or perhaps you'd rather dismiss the predator we keep as our guest, and turn your mind to drinking with schoolfellows and gropes for coin."

"I do not make light of the creature," Alexander contended. "But was John not a tireless agent on your behalf? Father, if you are still out of joint over his altercation at the Morley estate . . ."

"Out of joint." Lord Dramen chuckled, and striding to the marble fireplace he snatched up a poking tool from its rest by the corner, looking at it fondly. "Shall I regret curing you of inferior company?" he asked, jabbing the wheezing logs into a fury of sparks. "Dare you forget John Lawford was dispatched to Hastelbrook on *your* recommendation, where he accomplished little more than dragging my name through Grub Street!"

"And for that he apologized, redoubling his oath to the brotherhood. You cannot doubt his sincerity."

"The Argentum Serpentis does not treat with failure," Lord Dramen said. "Our enemies await any misstep."

"So I'm to forget my friend over a squabble with the Morley solicitor, and without any word of his wellbeing? Where is he, Father?"

"The priority, my boy," Dramen pronounced, "is that our demonstration of *vampirism* before king and ministers should come off smooth as a die."

"Has John's father recalled him to Germany? Then it can only be at your request."

"Yes, Germany, precisely," Lord Dramen said, clanging the poker back in its place. "There, are you quite satisfied? Or shall I cut you off, that you might relinquish your duty to the order and pursue an errant friend?"

"No, sir," Alexander said, glaring at the carpet. "You are my only means."

"The truest thing you've said to me. Now, as you have cost me exquisite moments with Miss Edenko . . . I have decided you are to be deputized."

"*Deputized?* What is that?"

"You find Mr. Grouthe *perfectly useless*," Dramen mused, "and though I grant you'll not see the man's face but through the end of a bottle, his ruthless devotion to my will is beyond question. He will show you the ropes—perhaps you might learn something after all."

"*Devotion*, Father? But I suppose it's an open secret you are patron saint of the Mohocks, of which he's a captain. Every red sash blaggard in the city knows your name."

"And you don't approve? Then you shan't object to taking his place."

"Taking his place?"

"For the dungeon watch."

"Shall I indeed?" Alexander said bitterly. "And am I expected to torture the prisoner, as does your Mr. Grouthe?"

"You may do as you like," Lord Dramen said, taking his seat again. "She is fed one part human to ten parts pig blood, by a soaked rag every hour. Miss Winter would have her ration reduced for caution, but the vampire is a harmless plaything by day, and she must retain at least strength enough for a convincing presentation."

Alexander grunted in disgust. "I hold that you should have destroyed the creature," he said, "not made her your plaything."

"Then we are fortunate you do not steer this enterprise," Dramen retorted, adjusting his cravat in the gold-veined mirror over the mantlepiece. "Now fetch the dear cellist back to me . . . and be grateful I do not ask you to bleed the pig."

■■

In a rage of sorrow a woman wailed far away, but the drear and distant sound was to Emelyn as nothing, for she sat warm and dry in the long gallery at home, her journal open across her lap. The room was changed, the walls and floor swept bare, and every exhibit vanished, save one, the black cowled statue, which standing in the centre of the floor loomed larger than she remembered. Returning to her diary she found the words appeared but briefly as she wrote them, before fading from the page. Particles of dust glimmered in the air without moving, and she wondered what her family would make of it, if this journal was all that was left . . . after she was gone.

The room was filled with a close and silent stillness, and looking up again she observed there were two statues now, heads bowed and sleeves clasped as though in supplication, while between them the floor had melted into a track of flowering garden green, leading away through the wall to a gold crested hill in a country bright with dawn. Closing her journal Emelyn stood, and coming to the deep hooded statues she touched the folded stone of their cloaks, feeling strangely that she must apologize for leaving them, even beg their forgiveness . . . but she had not the words. The garden shimmered in rich and welcoming colours as she approached—its light was glaring, though wonderfully so, and admiring the sunrise over the hill she was about to step from the edge of the marble floor into the soft green when something made her pause.

Looking down she found wet sand clenched in her fist, and within the sand a black ring on a slender chain.

A shadow moved behind her, and turning back she found the statues standing close at either hand, their presence fortifying her spirit as she beheld a knot of darkness fuming into being on the opposite wall. Like a boiling storm it swam and spread, threatening to consume the gallery. As though in reaction to this invasive presence, like autumn leaves spiralling in the wind, golden threads of light twisted about her— strength flowed to her extremities, and softly stern she heard her own voice:

"It does not end this way. You cannot abandon them. Emelyn Morley, wake up!"

With a heaving breath she opened her eyes, finding herself flat on her back, the sloshing sea water up to her ears as she lay with her head in Vaela's lap. The stars above were extinguished, covered in an endless dark churning its way to the east, and the vampiress was staring at her, frozen still, her eyes wide.

"Emelyn?"

"Vaela," Emelyn breathed, reaching to touch her face, "I think the tide is coming in."

With a splash Vaela snatched her up, leaving the cold foam of the sea behind to flash up the carven stair by the cliffs.

Emelyn clung to her tightly, her eyes shut lest she catch any sight of the drop, and seconds later she was laid down again in the windswept grass by the gatepost, her head resting on the folded cloak she'd left behind.

The vampiress dropped to kneel beside her.

"Thank you," Emelyn said, wiping her face.

Vaela was trembling, her expression fixed with shock. "I don't understand," she said, her voice small and faint as oily tears found their way to her chin.

Sitting up Emelyn embraced her, finding her soft and sedate. "It's all right . . . I'm all right," she said, and discovering sand yet clenched in her fist she shook it away.

Holding her tightly Vaela moaned with pain. "You must never forgive me."

"You were starving," Emelyn said, taking hold of her face. "I would not let you expire—you needed blood and I would do it again."

"I lost you," Vaela whispered. "I felt your heart go still—"

Emelyn took her Vaela's hand, pressing it to her collar. "You didn't," she said softly. "Feel it now. I am warm, and strong," and with a hard kiss on the cheek she released her, moving to sift through the sand she'd dropped.

Vaela shivered, staring at her. "You are warm," she repeated.

"But what happened to you?" Emelyn asked. "How did I find you in such a state?"

Vaela said nothing, slouching as she sat.

"I had a vision, or perhaps a dream," Emelyn said, squinting in the dark as she picked at the grass, "but more real than any I remember; I could swear I was at home. The house was emptier than it's ever felt, but there was an enchanted garden asserting itself into the gallery, and I was holding a clump of sand, and there was a ring, like black glass— yes! Here it is look, just like this one, but here it has a chain. I must have grabbed it before I swooned away, and so dreamt of it."

Vaela accepted the ring to study it, scowling with a grunt. "It cannot be . . ."

Emelyn flopped to her back on the ground, finding her lacerated wrist, her neck, and even the cut on her knuckles were gone without a trace. With a contented noise she indulged a long stretch. "Do you know that ring? Is it important?"

Having donned the chain around her neck Vaela fidgeted with the bauble. "It is a token of the queen's regard, given centuries ago to the eldest vampire in Britain—the *old man* as we call him, Lord Tredavius. He knew her at the very founding of Saunmoor, when she was young, newly free and coming into her power. The old man loved her, and she banished him from her kingdom."

"Why?"

"The bloodstone you keep at Hastelbrook was hers, his gift to her, but he took it away, to hide it from her sight. The prophecy warns she must never attain it, for by its possession she may divine her way into the vault, and to her doom . . ."

Emelyn sat up, her breath coming faster. "You cannot mean—"

"Do not fear," Vaela added quickly, a note of pleading in her voice. "I do not speak to burden you—the bloodstone cannot be detected by the queen nor her children, so long as it remains at Hastelbrook. It might be anywhere in the wide world for all she knows. She is as much vested in your safety as I am."

With a long exhale Emelyn laid down again. "But what is the purpose then, of the ring?"

"It is a symbol," Vaela said. "That which our queen knows the old man holds dearest of all. He would never part with it, but to return it to her must arrest her attention. She will give him the audience he desires."

Laying on her side Emelyn regarded her. "Then perhaps I was *meant* to return it to you, who could say? But how came you to the bottom of the cliff? You must tell me."

Slowly Vaela stood. "I fell," she said, "in conflict with another."

"You *fell*. From Beachy Head?" Emelyn sat up. "You're not referring to that terrible vampire with the lantern eyes? I thought I saw him . . . following the coach on our way."

"The same. He is gone now . . . I should fear his return, but when he realizes I survived, he will be cautious. He would not dare end me himself. He meant for me to burn to ash with the dawn."

Emelyn got to her feet, staring wide eyed. "Then he must never threaten you again," she said. "Have you a safe harbour somewhere? Is there aught I can do?"

"Do not fear for me, I have safe harbour," Vaela said, her expression yet heavy with sorrow. "And you are safe in the house; you must return there. I have broken your trust, and my own. I must go now; I must start again."

Emelyn took hold of Vaela's lacerated cloak, peeling it from her shoulders to drop it away. "You shan't leave like this," she said. "Here, take mine."

"I do not understand how you are revived," Vaela said. "The amount of blood you lost—"

Emelyn draped the dry crimson cloak about her. "Am I not the *Chosen Child?*" she posed. "Perhaps there are perquisites."

"What?"

"Perhaps there are benefits, to the position."

Vaela nodded with a frown. "I must go."

Emelyn adjusted the fit of the cloak, and she wiped Vaela's cheeks with her thumbs. "Your tears are black . . ."

"Yes—tears of the dead."

"Dead? No, I'll not have you speak so." Emelyn took her hand. "But are you well enough to fly, or to run—to travel as you do?"

Vaela nodded, her eyes glistening. "I am well enough."

"And you *will* accept my forgiveness," Emelyn said, holding her gaze, "you must take it with you."

"As you wish."

Grasping her shoulders Emelyn stretched to kiss her forehead, and found she could not let go. "I can't help but feel responsible," she said. "If I were not here, the monster would never have thrown you from the cliff."

Vaela shook her head, her forehead touching Emelyn's. "No, Vorsadat's mind is rotten, his treachery has been growing for some time."

"Then I must protect you from him," Emelyn said. "He cannot mean to harm me, or he'd have done . . . months ago, or years ago."

"He will not harm you in body," Vaela said, accepting her embrace. "Though he may harry your dreams—only until the queen corrects him."

"They have been strange and awful of late," Emelyn said, longing for to secret the vampiress inside, to find her some dark and comfortable place of safety.

"You must go to bed now, and hasten to healthful day," Vaela said, sliding gentle claws over Emelyn's back as she released her. "Keep your lady's maid close, when you sleep."

"She is only in the next room, in the dressing room adjacent."

"Good," Vaela replied, and with a bracing smile she vanished.

Emelyn stood quietly for some moments, feeling the ticklish wind in her hair, the cold grit of sand in her clothes, and looking to the sky she thought of the vision: the long gallery, and the towering statues that stood at her side as she faced the unfurling storm. "Whatever you are," she murmured, rubbing the place where the sharp rock had gored her wrist, "is it you I have to thank?"

Her brother was wide awake, just inside the door when she returned, and escorting him back to his little annex, she invoked the breach in the wall to excuse her abrupt departure, explaining that the noise they had heard was doubtless the breaking of stone. "I fear I stepped too close for a look," she said, "and rather lost my cardinal in the wind over the cliff."

Deacon went pale. "Dammit Emelyn! I should think you sharper than that," he chided, dropping his crutches as he retired again to the box bed.

"So should I," she said, helping his legs onto the bed. "Perhaps Mrs. Akehurst was right, and I'm not to be trusted outside."

"Well I can't imagine she anticipated the pavilion tipping into the wall . . . it must be terribly unsound," he said, stretching back on the pillow.

Monday June 27th

The image of the guardian statues, and the garden corridor leading to brilliant daylight over green hills stuck with her, and though the previous night's terrors had well faded by morning, so too had the golden warmth of her miraculous recovery. Left tender with fatigue, if whole in body, Emelyn was gratefully amenable to a request that she take her breakfast in bed, as Van Croft, the Commodore and staff were about the grounds struggling to sort out the sudden and total collapse of the overlook pavilion, which had crashed into the sea just before dawn.

"It's too dangerous my dear, rocks and great splinters of timber hether and yon," Mrs. Akehurst fussed, lurking in her doorway. "And the bulk of it over the cliff! There was too a filthy tattered cloak found outside, which I dearly hope is not yours. But am I to understand you slipped out for a walk in the dark?"

"Oh no," Emelyn said quickly, smiling as a footman squeezed by his mistress with the breakfast tray. "I was only to see Deacon; he meant to teach me a better game of whist, and then I was straight to bed."

Salt fish with eggs, bacon and parsley awaited her, and Emelyn was happy to find the very same tea Deacon had been served at his bedside.

"Well I suppose that is all very well," Mrs. Akehurst said, "but if you are determined to find yourself outside you must keep away from the gates, and come not near the breach! In fact I should insist you keep away from the grass altogether, at least until the damage may be made safe . . ."

"Quite right," Emelyn replied, hoping to see her off. "I'm sure I'll only be out with the captain, if at all," she added, hiding her mouth to chew.

∎∎∎

The Spring-Gardens at Vauxhall were a vast expanse of green park just south of the Thames from London proper. Sorted from the common rabble by a shilling's fee at the entrance, it was a place to see and be seen, attracting all manner of elegant evening society for dining in open air supper boxes, with long tables and benches organized between canvas covered uprights. The gardens featured foremost a concert of musicians: the composer George Frideric Handel presiding over some thirty men ensconced in the second story of the *orchestra*, a newly built octagonal temple stage in the centre of the park.

Tonight the crowd was thick, with over a thousand on hand to take in all manner of diversions including tours of alfresco galleries, poetry, theatre, and even puppet plays as the music resounded about them. Amongst the innumerable patrons of quality was Baron Dramen, who had taken his seat on the bench at the enviable Duke Lindsor's private table. Six bedizened ladies and ten wigged gentlemen rounded out the seating, laughing and drinking as they called out instructions to frantic table hands, who, being hungry to earn their material gratitude rushed to oblige. Availing himself of a fine brandy punch Lord Dramen spoke in hushed tones to the excitable Earl of Hampton, describing the scientific wonder of the vampire he held captive at Charwell House, and what pleasures might await the man bold enough to make her acquaintance.

"I tell you sir, her capture shall be marked as a cornerstone of history," Dramen confided, "which early investors such as yourself may advantage . . ."

Miss Winter came to the table, dressed in black, with a broad tilted bonnet and choking ivory cravat, her silver crucifix gleaming at her throat.

"My lord, if you please, a word," she said, leaning close to his ear.

Dramen smiled as he turned to address her. "My dear Miss Winter," he said quietly, "I've Hampton on the hook just now; I need only draw up the line . . ."

"I begin to doubt you take my precautions to heart," she said, holding his eyes.

Lord Dramen dabbed his mouth as he stared at her, and slapping his napkin on the table he rose from his seat. "Your pardon sir," and he turned with a bow for the young duke, who was also on his feet, at the head of the table.

"Your Grace," Dramen said. "It would seem our Miss Winter stands in want of my attention."

Duke Lindsor smiled, his face waxen and strained, giving him the look of a man strangely out of sorts in his own element. "You will speak with her of my request, I trust, before your sweet guest is moved to Bedlam," Lindsor said, waving his hand as though to permit their leave.

Arm in arm Dramen and Winter walked from the supper boxes to the wide way around the park, lined with thickly canopied trees.

"Shall I remind you this is a public grounds," Miss Winter said, looking to the starless sky. "Your attendance at night is no small risk."

Tapping his cane as they walked Lord Dramen sighed. "Handel's programme carries over our heads like the airs of the gods; the pleasure grounds thrive as never before, though I might observe the duke sweats like we've stopped his gin. Shall I trust him to remember himself?"

"He is well tangled in your web, he will hold," Miss Winter replied, brushing her hand across the jagged trunk of a sycamore as they passed. "But the poor man has lost all taste for lesser subjects. Just yesterday he confessed to the murder of a kitchen maid, but she did not satisfy him."

"I do not concern with satisfying him," Dramen said, clicking his tongue with scorn. "Thrice has he set his blade to our vampire—that must be enough. The creature cannot die before she is presented to king and court. Our victory is at hand."

Miss Winter smiled for a merry group as they passed. "Our *victory* is yet fragile my lord . . ."

"Soon all the realm will be united in our praises," Dramen replied, nodding as a painted gentleman tipped his hat, "and by their witness shall the king bestow us every honour, upon his return."

"We are by no means assured our vampire is without allies," Miss Winter warned. "You think to rest on my expertise, but I've never claimed omniscience on the subject. Only once before have I been so close to such a creature, while it lived."

"And you drove a stake of yew through its black heart," Dramen said. "Yes, Miss Winter, your dear patron Lord Crennock has oft described to me the scene. But you forget, it is ten days she has been in our power; if some malevolent force meant to set her free we'd have seen it by now."

"And if the royal family find her so tempting a curiosity as to take her from you? Or Sir Robert Walpole encourages them to it?"

Dramen tutted, jabbing his cane at the ground. "Yes I hear some call him *prime minister* now . . . but it matters not. The crown's impending crusade against the damned will live and die by the knowledge only we possess."

"Such knowledge can be taught," Miss Winter contended. "Nay my lord, for the brotherhood to ascend as you hope we must prove she is not the only one."

Continuing on they drew nigh to a miniature tent theatre, where animated puppets entertained a gathering crowd. "The vampire resists our interrogations," Lord Dramen said, chuckling at the dancing characters. "She is reticent to expose others of her race, but there remains one measure of persuasion we've yet to administer."

"You cannot mean sunlight," Miss Winter said, glancing at the show as a round periwigged puppet crashed against the doors of a little manor house, too large to get inside.

Lord Dramen tilted back for a laugh. "Are you not amused? Walpole has received the gift of Number Ten Downing Street, and fat on royal favour he cannot manage the door."

"I've little mind for puppets," she said, moving to block his view. "Only a fool would expose the vampire to sunlight; if you scorch her to death we're left nothing but empty boasts."

"Do not presume to speak as my equal," Dramen said curtly, pushing her aside with his cane. "Now, how fares your byzantine contraption of a box?"

Miss Winter pursed her lips, turning to face the show. "It will be ready to contain her by week's end."

"Bloody long wait for a thousand-guinea coffin . . ."

"Before she is ever presented at Kensington Palace we must be assured it is strong enough to hold her, even at night, lest you be remembered for butchering the royals by means of an escaped vampire."

Thunder rolled through the heavens, and Lord Dramen wrinkled his nose with distaste, offering his arm to resume their walk. "You have my every confidence of course," he said. "But even should she give us the slip, there's twenty lords who have borne her witness."

"Their testimony amounts to nothing the moment she disappears," Miss Winter said. "Sooner or later, by use or design she will meet her end. We need more."

Leaves swirled into the air along the path, the wind rising as they walked, Lord Dramen swinging his cane. "Yes, now that Bedlam is mine I should like every cell in the lower halls filled. But it's no small feat to capture a vampire."

"Then I suggest Hastelbrook," she said simply.

"Hastelbrook again? Is not the creature who murdered thereabouts the very same that now sits in my dungeon?"

"No, my lord. As we extracted her teeth for scientific inquiry I took the liberty of measuring her bite. There is another one, female, and that she should kill so near a place steeped in dark mysteries as Hastelbrook cannot be coincidence."

"Another female?" Dramen mused.

"We must place the estate under close watch, for a start."

Dramen sighed. "As we did with Sir Thaniel Gliffton, who pursued the eldest Miss Morley, or John Lawford, who was for the youngest, and the both of them now dead. Even Lord Abbott has vanished, on the eve of his attack upon Hastelbrook. Nay my dear, I think it better to let old legends lie, for now."

"*Now* is precisely the time to strike." Miss Winter held his arm tighter, "to shore up our advantage. Lord Abbott's overture was detected, and certain as we are of his demise, I am no less certain that Hastelbrook is even more valuable than we imagine."

"Then I must hope you find yourself cleverer than poor Abbott."

"We need subtlety my lord. The girl is our way in."

"What girl?"

"Emelyn Morley. I've a contact, an antiquarian, who's made quiet study of the lore of Hastelbrook his particular vice. He suspects the entire family may be under the influence of supernatural powers, Miss Morley in particular."

"Another antiquarian? And how should he avail us? That snivelling Gapplethorpe proved useless enough."

"My man brings a distinct advantage," Miss Winter said, lowering her voice. "He was boatswain of Lord Van Croft's first command, and has been entrusted to administrate on his behalf, for some affairs or other.

Van Croft is the same who now courts Miss Morley, and has taken her to Eastbourne, to meet his godparents. My man shall meet them there."

Lord Dramen grunted. "Really? Well, then you must correspond with him as you like, but do not forget we have twice meddled with Hastelbrook, and twice it came to nothing. Lord Abbott makes three men dead, in pursuit of its secrets."

"One of those by my hand, of course."

"By my hand," Dramen corrected, "and my hand was forced. You were but the instrument. My warning stands."

"And it shall not go unheeded." Miss Winter smiled. "This is why I believe pursuing Miss Morley on her own, separate from the herd, is in order."

Chapter 21
Awakening

Tuesday June 28th

The destroyed pavilion presented so grand a spectacle as to insert itself into almost every conversation, and though it was ever on her mind, by Tuesday Emelyn was quite fatigued of hearing Mrs. Akehurst, who was pleased to lament that if she'd only been listened to the creaky foundations would have been reinforced years ago. At last the Commodore was bound to answer, explaining that the damage was far more extensive than to be caused by any structural flaw, emphasizing that an outsized portion of the wall had broken apart, which prompted Mrs. Akehurst to sarcastically inquire whether he thought cannon fire more likely.

During the day under grey stormy light the men continued to work, clearing stone and debris as the captain directed them, while Emelyn sat on a window bench in the dining hall to watch—this being the brightest room in the house. It was a great wide windowed space facing the south property line, raised high enough to look out over the granite bricked wall, which was bordered by densely flowering bushes on the inside. Here she could read or journal, mustering nearly but not quite enough spirit to unpack her embroidery hoop and complete the scene Sarah had helped her with.

Van Croft moving lumber with his shirtsleeves rolled up was a sight she found not unpleasant to observe, and while he worked nearest the windows her books went increasingly neglected, though his short patience with the staff was regrettable. Meanwhile Mrs. Akehurst was ever watchful to prevent the accident of Emelyn and the captain finding themselves together unsupervised, though their hostess spent the balance of her time ruing the loss of Galecliff's beautiful lookout, and the catastrophic effect it must have on the party, which could by no means be cancelled.

For his part the Commodore was often outside with the men, while Deacon took to the library and an increasingly agitated Doctor Tarville excused himself, being unable to assist in the work of repair owing to *an unruly spasm of the hip*, which prevented him lifting objects of any significant measure.

"Excuse me, Doctor," Emelyn said, finding him lingering in the dining room after dinner. "I wanted to ask after my brother's medicine. I understand it's a receipt of nettles primrose and sea water? Except by the smell it must contain something more . . ."

"Ah, Miss Morley of course," he said, taking a generous sip of his wine. "Yes your brother's care is well in hand I assure you. The smell is a simple ferment of Atropa belladonna."

Emelyn blinked at him. "Deadly nightshade?"

"Miss Morley, you may find me unused to explaining my practice to inquisitive ladies, but in small amounts belladonna is taken to relax the muscles. Now if you will excuse me," and giving her a bow he snatched his wine from the table corner, taking his leave.

That evening Emelyn took Van Croft's arm for a tour of the house, roaming only so far as the small wood-pillared veranda at the back overlooking the gentle slope to the orchard pond. He said little, and she responded in kind, half wondering whether he might prefer his own company. But his sharp kiss on her knuckles, and a strange depth in his eyes tempted her sympathy, and she allowed him to keep her hand.

"Have they any more idea," she asked gently, "how the wall might have crumbled?"

"Hang the wall," he said, staring into the troubled pond. "There are many things of greater moment than my godparents' vanity. Your brother's health, by example. Has he no idea to walk again, as he ought to?"

"Oh," she said. "None, my lord, I'm sorry to say. That ship has long sailed."

Van Croft drew closer, and appreciative of his concern she allowed him a kiss on her cheek, tingling as he touched her.

"There you are," Mrs. Akehurst exclaimed, bursting upon them from the house. "Do be careful sir, if Miss Morley runs afoul of the debris I shall never forgive myself."

"We're not at war, Godmother," Van Croft said, squeezing Emelyn's hand before he released it. "We only came to observe the orchard over the water."

Catching Mrs. Akehurst's disapproving gaze Emelyn smiled, taking an extra step away from her gentleman.

"The pear trees are poorly this year," Mrs. Akehurst said, staring at her. "If it's fruit you seek, I must recommend the dining room."

That night her dark dreams continued, though Emelyn could little remember them, excepting the presence of bright and burning yellow eyes, and a vague notion that fleeing to the long gallery for sanctuary had ended the nightmare, prompting her to wake. In vain she came to her window to look out, but her hope for stars was dashed, as low black clouds yet smothered the world, immensely drifting overhead like a dull and vast oblivion.

Wednesday June 29ᵗʰ

Men with axes and hammers tore into the secret space where Vaela's coffin rested—they were upon her.

"The Barefoot Ghost of King Street! The she-demon is found!"

Vaela could not move, but lay with no more strength than to watch them, arms crossed at her chest, gasping as the trap in the floor was triggered. The coffin dropped, and fuming white water crashed over her, filling the open casket as it sank into the Thames beneath the bridge. A hulking shape with eyes of fire reached out to seize her from the depths, even as rays of sunlight found her flesh from above, burning with such heat as the wide rushing river could not extinguish—

And then she was falling again, plummeting from the high cliff at Beachy Head, into the shallow waves, breaking upon the rocks—and the crimson cloak was still about her—Emelyn's cloak. And then suddenly Emelyn was there to embrace her, hair fanning bright and red beneath the brine.

"I am your murderer," Vaela spoke into the water, but Emelyn only smiled as she took hold of her arms—pulling her downward through the seabed, through the rooftop and into the dark immensity of Hastelbrook, where the crypt door welcomed them in, where the deep sealed vault awaited.

"You will accept my forgiveness," Emelyn said, the memory of her words piercing the gloom.

Vaela opened her eyes with a gasp, pulling air into her lungs. The scrape of bloodthirst seized her at once, crackling through her body as she bared her fangs, breathing with noises—adjusting to her wakeful state. There was no rushing sea, no crushing rocks, no hunters, no monster, no Emelyn. The ebonwood coffin in which she reposed was safe and familiar as ever—padded in wine-red velvet, scented with orris root and benzoin, and Emelyn's gift of the red cardinal cloak wrapped tightly about her. The narrow space was dry and quiet, hidden between the walls of Lord Simeon's London lair—Nonsuch House. And crouching in the tapering dark at the head of Vaela's coffin, was Lord Simeon, her maker himself— the upper edge of his spectacles glinting faintly against the shadow of his form.

"Your nightmares deepen," he said, leaning close. "I know the monster attacked you. Shall it be *three* nights of silence? Or shall you let me in."

Vaela closed her eyes, and reaching up she found his hands, pulling them to her.

Her maker's fingertips spread against her scalp, and relaxing her mind she allowed his power—memories flooded her thoughts: the house of Galecliff, the broken wall, the burning eyes of Vorsadat, his stranglehold upon her throat, and the fall. And then there was Emelyn, stirred to action by the bond in their blood, whom Vaela, in a feral thirst, betrayed and attacked, losing all control—

"No," Simeon said, stopping abruptly. "Emelyn Morley lives. This pain is not yours to bear."

"It is *only* mine to bear," Vaela said.

Simeon sighed, rising with her hand in his as she stood. "Tell me about your dream, tonight," he said.

"I dreamt of the hunters, finding me asleep," she said, dizzy with hunger.

"Your fear of Vorsadat, which I felt, is rational," he said. "We must tread carefully. But your fear of the hunters is misplaced. The counterweights beneath have been seen to—even should intruders discover this space, the floor will be closed to them and solid, while in the deeps rushing below you would be already well concealed."

"Baron Dramen will not rest until they find us," she said.

"Children, groping in the dark."

"Do you forget Afaine?" Vaela contended, meeting the silver of his eyes. "These *children* have one of our own in their power."

"Only by Vorsadat's betrayal. And as I have told you, that the mortals have not destroyed her will prove their grave mistake."

"Let us hope." The vampiress pressed a small wooden plate, and a thin panel opened, allowing her to slip through the wall into the house.

The dark business of Fenchurch Street was awash in ghostly fog—a formless grey that hung heavy and thick about the lantern lights, casting men and women in the role of toiling ghosts as they brought in their wares and shuttered shops for the night.

In bare feet Vaela walked softly, arms at her sides, brushing close past those who yet lingered in the streets. Their mortal hearts waxed and waned within her, channelling hard-earned joy and hope, lust and fear through every touch—and from one stout man who shoved her aside to make his way into the winding alley of Paul's Head Court, she felt revenge, bloody and impending. There was *someone* at home—a codependent he would tolerate no longer—someone he would be free of, someone who must not live through the night.

Vaela turned to follow, and after thirty paces of muddy steps she took him, pressing him into the wall beneath the overhanging tenement, in a deeper pool of dark, sheltered from the peering lights. The man was shorter than she, and despite her aggression, quick to smile.

"Hullo my love!" he chuckled, squinting in the dark.

"Hello," she said, feeling the depths of the rot in his heart, even as she drank in the seductive scent of his life. By his quick temper, and need to prove against his small stature, this man had killed before.

"See to me on credit, won't you?" he breathed. "It were a special night for me; shall we square accounts in the morning?"

"You owe me nothing," Vaela said, and with her hand tight across his mouth she bit suddenly into the side of his neck, bringing all her teeth to bear. Without the spell of her eyes to calm him, the man thrashed helplessly against her, pinned as a bird in the power of a wolf, and by the wound in his neck she drank deep, leaving him with scarcely the strength to stand, when she was satisfied.

"Now exert yourself," Vaela whispered, crouching before him as he sat, rasping and moaning. She took him by the chin, smacking him to catch his eyes. "You will not murder that child," she commanded. "Not tonight, nor any night—for if you do, you will find me again, and our second meeting you will not survive."

The man whimpered with pitiful snorts, collapsing to sit, and with a swirl of her cloak, she was gone.

The Underloft tavern was closed, or so it seemed from the outside. But within the dimly lit common room, where the hearth had gone cold and long tables yet wafted the smell of ale and pipe smoke, there sat three persons upon a broad bench by the wall. These were young Penny Attridge, in a new gown of white with cream petticoats beneath her apron, and her father Thomas, who sat in his working vest and shirtsleeves, holding her hand as he examined the solitary boy some way along the bench beside them. The taproom was lit by several stout candle lanterns along the bar, their little cages casting latticed shadows on the walls, with additional candles set fresh upon each of the empty tables.

"Jack Longton," the boy said loudly, removing his hat. "Please to acquaint you sir, and your little girl."

"I'm no littler than you are," Penny put in, leaning to speak across her father.

"Thomas Attridge, master Longton," Thomas said. "This my daughter, Penny. Can it be we know the same, that is, the lady in black be it whom has requested our meeting here?"

"S'right," Jack said, flipping his hat in his hand. "That shall be mistress Vaela sir, she who works with my lord Simeon de Rhoda, he what owns the workhouse, Haderon, which you might call my office of employ."

"Do you know why she's called us here?" Penny asked.

"Can't speak to what you're doin' hereabouts," Jack said, "but I'm called for news o' what me and my boys have got up to, and what we heard."

"And what have you heard, Jack Longton?" Vaela asked, standing suddenly before them, cloaked and hooded not in black as was her custom, but a fine supple red.

"Miss Vaela!" Penny gasped, as her father quickly bowed his head.

"Penny," Vaela said, giving her a smile. "How are your lessons?"

"Exceeding well," Penny said quickly. "I study my catechism every day. And we're learning moral stories now, like about the tortoise and the hare, and the fox and the grapes."

"Very good," Vaela said. "And you, Jack. You've grown, I see."

"Thank you, mistress." Jack offered off his hat. "And you've changed your cloak, since last I seen."

"It was a gift," Vaela said, gripping the sides of it. "Now, is it true the baron Lord Dramen has taken control of the governors at Bedlam hospital? What do you hear?"

"Right you are mistress," Jack said, whistling as he shook his head. "What I heard the incurables are to be lumped all together, or expelled."

"Why?"

"What for opening new cells, mistress. There's a Doctor Waydale who works them dungeons—his boy had shoes mended at Portree's Cobbler. And my good lad Hal, Portree's son, hears tell that Lord Dramen plans to hold vampires in those dark cells, what for study and *dissectation*."

"Mr. Attridge," Vaela said, turning her black eyes upon him. "I would have all you've heard at the Devil's Inn, all to do with the vampire, she whom Dramen's brotherhood holds prisoner. Does she yet live?"

"Yes mistress," Thomas said, squeezing Penny's hand. "It is their imminent plan that the vampire is to be presented at the palace, to the king, and that fellow they call *prime minister*—Walpole."

"Yes, when?" Vaela asked.

"I don't know mistress."

Vaela looked between them. "Was there not a woman, here with you? Younger than yourself, Mr. Attridge, if only just—a woman of noble bearing. Have you seen her?"

There was silence, and Penny leaned forward to peer at Jack.

"Nay mistress," Mr. Attridge said, shaking his head.

"Not as I've seen," Jack said. "What were her name, if you please?"

"It is Lady Bradley," Vaela said. "She works for me, for us, as you do. I should like you all, being that you have earned our trust, to trust in each other. But if anyone has heard more of Dramen's vampire to be presented at court, it would be—"

"Lady Bradley!" Jack piped up. "Not of Lord Bradley, Earl of Estmarch?"

"Yes, of course," Vaela said.

Jack swallowed, gripping his hat. "Well, she's dead mistress, sorry to say."

Vaela drew in a sharp hiss, staring at him. "Dead? Are you certain?"

"Found at home she was. No word on who done it. Was she a friend to you?"

"She was my informer . . . my ears at court," Vaela said, staring vaguely.

"I'm sorry, miss Vaela," Penny said quietly, clinging to her father as she spoke.

The vampiress approached them, producing a little pouch of gold coins for Mr. Attridge, and another for Jack, who with a quick slide was beside them. "Do not be afraid," Vaela said, drawing their eyes to hers. "You are under my protection. Lady Bradley's fate has naught to do with her work for me . . . and I will find it out."

■■■

Thursday June 30ᵗʰ

The week carried on bleak as ever. Van Croft and the Commodore laboured over plans for the pavilion's reconstruction, while Mrs. Akehurst remained cold and remote, except on those scripted occasions for games or meals.

It was not until the afternoon that Emelyn caught the captain alone, just as he was leaving the Commodore's office. "Has Mrs. Akehurst a particular reason to dislike me?" she asked.

"She is only jealous of your beauty," he said, taking her hand for a kiss, "as I am of your diary—that little book that is ever engrossing your private attention. But the work shall be done soon, and then we must atone for these moments apart."

Predictably Mrs. Akehurst interrupted them, and with a bow the captain took his leave.

"Now my dearest," Mrs. Akehurst began, taking her arm to confide, "I'm certain he regrets his neglect of you, but we should be at quite a loss without his aid!"

"Oh it's no trouble," Emelyn said quickly.

"You may pine for his company, of course, but I would caution against any visible air of yearning, lest it have the opposite effect you intend."

"Mrs. Akehurst, I can assure you I am very well balanced," Emelyn said, feeling heat in her face. "I expect nothing more from the captain than natural civility."

"Oh indeed," Mrs. Akehurst replied with a smile.

Left to her own devices Emelyn soon joined her brother in the modest Galecliff library, where she perched at a corner table, while Deacon smoked in a chair by the fire. Here she found herself longing for those peaceful evenings in the small library at home, but sitting in stillness the impressions of her harrowing experience with Vaela came stronger, and with closed eyes she recalled the sight of her crumpled at the base of the cliff, blind with thirst and pale as death, until the taste of blood shocked her violently to life—

Emelyn cleared her throat, chasing away the image. "Are you feeling better?"

"A little weaker I suppose, if you must know," Deacon replied. "The doctor assures me it will pass."

Finding he looked no different than usual Emelyn sighed, returning to her journal:

> *'I am tempted, in some roundabout fashion, to inquire of the doctor how I should have survived so great a loss of blood. But how could his answer avail me?*
>
> *On two points I am resolved: that my recovery cannot be natural, and that Vaela was not its agent. Am I mad to imagine the hooded statues have a hand in my fate? Whatever they are, in my sleeping thoughts they have followed me here, but with darker dreams as well, which began the night I saw those lamplight eyes following outside the coach, and scratched my hand. But if this monster is Vaela's enemy, is he not mine as well? I only wish I apprehended more of her world, to better know the gravity of such a thing.'*

"Are we not the most remarkable creatures," Deacon said,

interrupting her pen. "Two footman vanished, twenty feet of the wall collapsed into the sea, and we whistle along as though it were always so."

"The search for those missing goes on, I'm sure. How else should we address it?" Emelyn asked.

"I've had a look at the breach," he said, knocking out his pipe, "it defies all explanation. Some of the stones were driven into the ground, some even split or scored . . . as like something crashed into them."

"A falling pavilion perhaps."

"I've accounted for that, but much of the damage must have been out of the tower's reach when it fell."

"Then perhaps it was a monster," she said, smiling at him, "or cannon fire, as Mrs. Akehurst suggests."

At this Deacon yawned, turning the page of his book, and wishing she might put to Vaela the very same questions, Emelyn stood from her chair, resolved to take a walk.

"Great heavens Miss Morley!" Mrs. Akehurst fussed, catching her at the door. "There is a wrath of high winds about, and by what clearing the men have done the gap is wider than ever! I should never forgive myself if you were extracted into the sea," and taking Emelyn's elbow she led her back to the small and windowless library. "There, I understand you've a great love of books," she said, beaming as though presenting toys to a child.

"Thank you," Emelyn sighed, untying her hat. "I should be grateful for your caution, but I won't be kept inside the whole week."

"Of course not my dear, only while the gales are dangerous."

■ ■

The broad span of London Bridge stretched some nine hundred feet across the busy rush of the night-steeped River Thames, bisecting the river over the backs of nineteen grand arches of stone. Dozens of buildings crowded the length of it, affording but breadth enough for two lanes of traffic on the narrow road that tunnelled beneath them. Shops and residences filled the teetering structures as they overflowed their foundations, hanging into the air off the sides of the bridge, supported by aged and creaking struts. Here even in the dark small hours a loose train of carts, carriages and pedestrians pressed their slow progress from one end to the other, while the river below teemed with bobbing lanterns guiding merchant skiffs and sloops about their sleepless business.

The grandest imposition on the bridge was the mysterious Nonsuch House, a profoundly decorous mansion of beam, plaster and granite. Painted in gradient gold like a captured sunrise and gleaming from onion-capped towers to columned porches four stories below, the building straddled the road with a high arch like its neighbours, welcoming the traffic to a sheltered roadway that led under the house. Its gilded windows were heavily draped and barred, excepting those of the western garret, which were thrown wide, opening from stepped gables to a grand view of the eastern river. Here a heady breeze slipped over the sill to explore the featureless room, tussling silken drapes before gliding over faded bloodstains to find a tottering man wheezing with his back to the window. Vaela held his throat, raising him just high enough that his toes scraped the floor for purchase.

A thick faced fellow with tight cropped hair and gilded blue coats, the man struggled against her grasp as she watched him.

"Please!" he implored, shrill with fear. "I never meant to stop her breath! I never meant—"

"You knew," Vaela snapped, her eyes black. "You knew by her desperate tremors . . . she was dying, but hunger blinded you."

"Hunger?!" he squeaked. "No, I loved her more than anything! I only wanted her quiet; if her husband had discovered us—"

With a squeeze of her hand Vaela cut off his voice, holding him close. "The lady you murdered was an informer, loyal to *me* . . . but perhaps you will see her again."

"Wait! I beg you!" he croaked, but yanking back his head she plunged into his throat.

Reprehensible life in the man's blood warmed her to the fingertips, and dropping to sit she pulled him into her lap, pinning his arms as she drank, until with a final shudder he began to cool.

"I nearly destroyed she whom I cherish most," she whispered at his ear, "just as you did," and wiping her mouth she rolled him away. "Enter!"

The little door to the room swung inward on oiled hinges, and two pale young men shorn of hair in black livery ambled in. Vaela stood silent, watching as they tied a bag over the man's head, locking a heavy band of metal about his neck. With a droning count of three the footmen heaved, lifting their charge by ankles and armpits.

Gathering her hair to tie it back Vaela grunted as they waddled for the door. "Leave it . . . I will take him."

Descending three flights of stairs, the body over her shoulder, the vampiress trod slowly the steps of the house she once called home, its aging walls alive with creaks and groans.

In the music room of the lower floor east she shifted a grand pastoral painting to reveal a hidden door of iron that opened to a fourth descent carved in stone. A damp draught whistled about her, and plodding carefully down to a hanging corridor beneath the bridge she came to an open hole overlooking the deep rushing current below. The corpse of the gentleman murderer hit the water with a smack, and was gone.

Returning upstairs Vaela concealed the door, dragging her nails along the wall as she ascended again, her cloak brushing the carpeted steps behind her.

The warm blush of crystal covered candles and whale oil chandeliers lit her way as she passed framed pictures commissioned by her maker: haunting and beautiful paintings of dim, quiet figures from lives now long past. At the top of the stairs the largest of these rose like a phantom, watching her from the facing wall as it had for fifteen decades, a life sized portrait of Vaela herself, painted by the renowned Italian portraitist Sofonisba Anguissola, before the house was built. Here the vampiress was depicted in a strict millstone collar over a gown of black, hair coiled tightly as she stood half behind an empty heart-back chair, her dark eyes distant and cold.

Gliding along the balcony she doubled back to approach a gold inlaid set of doors, and like animated statues a pair of vacant faced footmen pulled them open. The central room of this, the third storey, was a grandly furbished library high above the arch of the road, its wide crimson carpet dominated by a three sided desk facing her from the windows, with lofty shelves of ancient books on every wall. Seated at the desk was the vampire Lord Simeon, his long silver hair clasped behind him, his spectacles glinting by the light of a single candle. The heavy laden desk was piled with ledgers and bills, and scratching his signature with an ostrich quill Vaela's maker set the page aside to unfold a longer document.

"With mortal men enough to speculate, every investment turns to ash," he muttered, signing the paper. "The diamond mines will have to be buttoned up, lest we collapse the market . . ."

"And betray our allotted place beneath human history," Vaela recited.

Lord Simeon glanced at her with a smile. "You are my finest student."

"I am your only student."

With a smirk he set the document by. "I heard the poor fellow's excuses. Another rotten soul commended to the deeps?"

"Yes. He smothered Lady Bradley, my informer at court," she said, and detecting animal notes of mortal fear she looked to the far side of the room, where she espied three men and two women standing quite still, facing tight against the wall like dolls turned the wrong way round.

"Taste them if you like," Lord Simeon said, dipping his pen. "I've had my fill."

"No."

Her maker touched the quill to paper, but did not write. "You are restored, my dear—Miss Morley delivered you, even where I could not."

Vaela stood stock still, frowning at the desk.

"I account myself grateful to be in her debt," he declared, resuming his work, "as I am sure you are grateful for her forgiveness. Let us speak no more of it."

Vaela looked past him, staring at the dark windows. "Can a human heart forgive its own murder?"

Simeon drew another document with a sigh. "If murdered she was, murdered she would remain; you must relinquish your guilt of it."

The vampiress nodded, her brows knit with pain. "And how am I to trust myself in her presence?"

"You must *trust* the bond between you," he said. "Without it she'd never have discovered you broken upon the rocks. Emelyn Morley's regeneration defies understanding—except by allowing that whatever power imbues the vault has chosen her as its vessel."

"Shall we trust a nameless influence we cannot measure, while Vorsadat threatens her?"

"Your fear begins to smell," he said, withdrawing a folded bill to spread it on the desk. "His attack upon you both, regrettable as it was, ended in nothing; in fact one might say we owe him our gratitude."

"How?"

"Without his accusations against me I'd not have been detained,"

Lord Simeon said, "and had I come to your aid, likely both of us would have been destroyed."

Coming closer Vaela looked over his desk. "Pazoa believed your word over his? Is that why you were released?"

"Even dedicated to his protection as she is, the queen knows her brother is not well. Vorsadat has not her strength."

"Then let him suffer," Vaela said, glancing at the prisoners against the wall. "And what are these? Are your superintendents being punished?"

"Punished, yes; fallen to greed every one of them—the Haderon, the Blarney, Saint Ambrose, Bloom House and Reedwell. And what of Mother Bright's reading school—more your concern than mine, was it not?"

"I cannot speak to it," Vaela replied. "I've not been to Gravesend in many years."

"Well, we can be certain only that Hack & Humble thrives. There appears to be no shortage of demand for night coaches in the city. Alas the workhouses have all gone to seed."

"Your two decades away measures a long time by their reckoning," Vaela said, taking up one of the ledgers to crack it open.

Lord Simeon scowled, reviewing his notes. "And ever I underestimate mortal corruption. Perhaps we should sell gin—the enterprise none can bankrupt."

"*Best thirds flour?*" Vaela said, reading from the page. "Is this what they feed workhouse children? They may as well bake with sand."

"Good will and treasure wasted on personal excess. You might have looked in on them."

"I've no interest in administration," Vaela said, snapping closed the book, and flashing to the window she opened the darkened panes, peering down as a sudden gust swirled in.

"Mind the draught," Lord Simeon said, clapping a hand over his papers.

Endless clouds hung heavy in the air, and looking up Vaela inhaled the sharp breeze. "The sky is dull and dead; I would have peaceful stars, over the raw smells and sounds of London."

"We serve at the queen's pleasure," Simeon said, blowing his ink to dry. "We shall remove to Saunmoor when summoned, not before."

"The city's heart is black with fear . . . it sickens me," Vaela said, watching the steady train of wagons, their drivers slouching and lanterns burning low—a great commerce of lumber and victuals making their way over the bridge from Southwark.

Lord Simeon was beside her now, sharing the view. "Daily, how much they must consume," he said. "The thin feeding the fat."

A tiny green-eyed babe passed by underneath, swaddled in the arms of its mother, and Vaela stared, listening to its little noises. "If I had lost Emelyn . . . it would have been the end of me."

"As I recall she was but a few weeks in the world, when you imprinted upon her," Lord Simeon said. "That was a risk."

"I wanted to hold her; I did no harm," Vaela said, watching until the infant was out of sight. "A young scullery invited me in. I bid the nursemaid to sleep, and when I plucked Emelyn from her cradle she did not cry—she was only pleasant and curious."

Her maker placed a hand on her shoulder. "Once I feared you would fade beyond my reach. Now I find myself in Miss Morley's debt twice over."

Vaela's claws stretched to their limit, aching in the tips of her fingers. "I felt the end of her—the last beat of her heart echoed through me . . . It was too late, even to make her one of us."

"Your heart breaks," he said, "but it must be clear to you now, she was not yours to destroy. Let this cold quandary lie."

Vaela took a deep human breath, staring into the lights of the wagons creeping their way down the bridge.

Lord Simeon adjusted his spectacles. "I have decided the Anguissola will remain."

"Have I not suffered my portrait long enough?" Vaela scowled at him. "You promised it would be sold on your return."

"I promised to revisit the matter, which I have done, and I am resolved I'll not be parted from it. There is memory, and manifest truth in your likeness."

"What truth? I was lost, invisible, even to myself."

"It is our providence to exist uncounted, unmattered. And yet, I think were it painted tonight, the chair in your portrait would not be empty."

The wind stirred about them, and Vaela swallowed, watching the mortal procession below. "Perhaps not . . ."

Friday July 1ˢᵗ

That night Emelyn retired early, before the first of several naval officers were to arrive, and slipping into restless dreams once again she imagined Vaela had gone feral to cull the servants in their beds, leaving only the Akehursts to keep house, with a grease spattered Mrs. Akehurst shrieking herself hoarse over a turkey burned black, which she avowed Van Croft must still prefer to the meagre goose Emelyn had prepared . . .

"An ungrateful, dispassionate dilettante if ever there was; but she professes only the barest regard for you!" Mrs. Akehurst decried.

Emelyn spluttered awake and sat up, snatching the blankets close.

For a moment there was silence, until a frustrated Mrs. Akehurst spoke again, her voice rising up from below. *"Can you be insensible to the insult of bringing her here?"*

"Madam you disgrace yourself," Lord Van Croft snapped. *"I have made my choice."*

"Oh my dear Jonathan, if you would but look past her beauty! And what should you find but a distracted girl born to a declining and peculiar family, who only pursues you for want of wealth and connection—"

"It's a dream!" Emelyn declared aloud, covering her ears, and the argument below went silent.

Looking around the room she could hear nothing but the distant roar of the sea, the soft creaks of the house, and slumping her shoulders she marked the handsome bracket clock on the mantel, ticking in its case.

"Two o' clock," she muttered, lying down again. "Go to sleep."

But she could not. The clock ticked, and she occupied herself with unbraiding her hair, combing it out between her fingers. The voices came and went, and with frustrated curiosity she held her breath to listen. Sounds about the room grew strange and stretched, until suddenly she heard a terrific creak of wood, and a man snoring, followed by shuffling footsteps.

"What on earth," she marvelled, finding by and by that she could push the locus of her hearing about the house as though by sheer direction of will.

At first she caught only traces of laughter, and clenching her fists to concentrate she roamed her sense through the halls, coming upon Mrs.

Akehurst again:

"Yes, and no one could deny she makes a fine ornament, but are there not questions of her deportment, her strange and aberrant nature even as a child—"

"She will be mistress of Vivere Gloria!" Van Croft declared. *"Tomorrow I mean to honour her, and you will attend us."*

Clutching her head against a twist of dizziness Emelyn lost them, and redoubling her focus she reached out again, but the noises confounded each other; the sudden caw of a crow blared in her ears, and startling at the ensuing sounds she found herself listening to the night outside, where the wind whistled over the rooftop.

A raspy chuckle caught her attention, a guttural, grating wheeze, and she stopped her breath to hear it. There was a dry smacking of lips, and the foul voice made words. *"I hear the drum of your heart, little Miss Morley, even as you hold your breath. Are you listening?"*

Emelyn dove under the blankets, pulling them over her head. For long moments she lay very still, striving to hear nothing at all . . . until the sand in her eyelids grew heavy, and the startle of fear gave way to sleep.

Saturday July 2ⁿᵈ

She woke to Breda's hand on her shoulder, and half blind by her own hair Emelyn sat up to find the morning dim with grey.

"Must wake up miss! Mrs. Akehurst is waiting to attend you."

The basin water was cold, the brushing was brutal, and standing with closed eyes as Breda knotted up her hair, Emelyn very much hoped the final, terrible voice she'd heard had been only a nightmare. Breda finished her in a gown of ivory silk, and Emelyn donned Vaela's opal jewellery as there came a strident knock at the door.

With a look of polite surprise there stood Mrs. Akehurst, clutching in her hands a flat red box wrapped with ribbon.

"Apologies." Emelyn curtsied. "I've overslept."

"Certainly you have my dear," Mrs. Akehurst said, holding a smile. "I am to present you with this, before you join the captain in the drawing room."

"Oh I see," Emelyn said, watching as the lady snapped the lid off the box. Nestled in dark wrinkled velvet there lay a stunning silver necklace, its chain mounted with a cluster pendant of diamonds encircling a grand sapphire, and just above it a silver half-moon brooch, set with seven arcing blue stones to match.

"It's beautiful," Emelyn said, her colour rising, "but he might have waited for me to come down—I'm sorry, he needn't have troubled you."

"Upon my word you do like to apologize," the lady said, examining Emelyn's pendant and earrings. "No my dear, these poor little opals will never do. Off with them at once, and you shall wear the captain's gift."

After gingerly setting Vaela's jewellery on the desk, Emelyn sucked in a breath as the lady pulled the new chain very tight to fasten it behind her neck, adjusting the weight of it on her collar as Emelyn slipped the brooch into her pocket.

"Now you will follow me, if you please," Mrs. Akehurst said.

Captain Van Croft stood in the drawing room before the fire, dark coated over a white vest, his black hair tied smartly back. "Excellent!" he cried as the ladies approached, and anticipating his action Emelyn offered her hand for a biting kiss. "How she sparkles in silver and sapphire," he praised, admiring her necklace and its environs.

"Indeed how lovely," Mrs. Akehurst enthused, making a little curtsy as she turned to leave.

"Oh no, dear madam, you must tarry!" Van Croft said with a laugh, rushing to offer her a wide-back pleated chair arranged facing another.

The lady blinked with a smile, following his instruction, and taking Emelyn's hand he showed her to the second chair, bowing as she lowered herself to sit.

"Shall we have breakfast perhaps?" Emelyn asked hopefully, watching as Van Croft snapped at the footmen, and she felt a blush as a trio of servants entered the room with three boxes apiece, each wrapped in luxurious colours with broad ribbons and bows.

Mrs. Akehurst flinched as the boxes were set on the floor beside her, and the captain posted himself by Emelyn's chair, gesturing at the gifts. "Few ladies are ever so conscious of style as Genevieve Akehurst," he said, lifting Emelyn's hand to catch her eyes, "and she being our most generous hostess, I should like her to present my gifts to you, my dearest Miss Morley."

His teeth found her knuckles again and Emelyn swallowed. "I am startled with pleasure at your generosity," she said, "but surely your godmother has other matters to attend; would you not rather give them to me yourself?"

"Indeed, Jonathan, there's a great deal to see to," Mrs. Akehurst said, gripping the armrests to stand.

"Stay, Godmother," Van Croft said, staring her back into the chair, "and I'll have my rank from you, if you please."

"Your pardon *my lord*, of course," Mrs. Akehurst said warmly, repenting of her departure with a smile.

"Now!" the captain said, continuing to stare at her. "Who better to celebrate so many new garments than a lady who knows the fashion? Let us start with the bandbox, if you please."

The presentation of gifts that followed could not have been more awkward had Emelyn caught fire, and soon enough her cheeks were sore from smiles as she strove to put Mrs. Akehurst at ease, who, playing the role considerably better, fawned over the packages and gawped at every new garment. In the end Emelyn had five new dresses including a sharp maroon riding habit, the measuring of which the captain confessed to having obtained from her mother, with a grand sagging hat in the French style—black feathered in royal blue, alongside six pairs of gloves, one set of fur-cuffed boots, a luxurious dark sable hooded cloak, and a delicate laced shoulder wrap for the indoors.

Contriving her exit at last, Mrs. Akehurst pleaded a need to consult her husband regarding repairs to the wall, and Emelyn sat blushing over the open boxes as Van Croft took a knee beside her.

"Well, this is all very generous, my lord; absurdly so," she said, watching as footmen collected boxes and folded the garments for delivery to her room.

"Trifles. But truly the necklace sets you alight," the captain observed, and he reached for the cluster pendant at her chest as she covered it with her hand.

"Thank you, my lord, but I am rather waiting for you to explain yourself."

"And wherefore must I explain myself?" he inquired, taking her hand. "Can I not bestow as I like, upon the lady who has so captured my attention?"

"I mean you must explain *why* Mrs. Akehurst so evidently cannot abide my presence here, and why it amuses you."

"Ah, there is our Miss Morley." Van Croft grinned. "I've no doubt you could set her to rights. But you must think no more of it. My godmother will no longer misunderstand us."

"That is no answer," Emelyn flustered. "I will have the truth of it, or how shall I defend myself? Does my family give her pause?" she asked, yet unsure whether the angry voices she heard were real or dreamt.

"Ah, dear creature, no," he said, rubbing her knuckles. "Once perhaps, she endeavoured to shepherd my affections as she pleased. That is the heart of it."

"Can you mean she sought to match you with her daughter? Were you engaged to Miss Akehurst?"

"I hardly remember," he said, kissing her fingers again.

"You were!" Emelyn pulled her hand away. "How could you," she said, lowering her voice as she glanced at the footmen. "How could you lead me here with no warning?"

"Forgive me, my beautiful Miss Morley, but you'd never have come. I only wanted her to see my heart has found its rest," and taking Emelyn's hand again he bid her to stand. "Now I'd not have you crabbed of temper for lack of breakfast . . ."

Resignedly she took his arm, and together they repaired to the dining hall, where following the mouth melting scent of gingerbread Emelyn scanned the room, surprised to find Doctor Tarville the only person seated, perched on a corner chair as though he'd been sent there for punishment, nursing his wine. The long dining table was set in its customary morning place near the wall draped in white, festooned with serving trays and platters, a quartet of footmen dressed in sea green livery posted on the wall side, ready to serve.

Mrs. Akehurst was not to be seen, but the Commodore greeted them with a cheerful wide-armed welcome, begging Emelyn's leave to borrow her gentleman on a matter of confidence.

Watching him go she couldn't help allowing herself a tickle of pride over the extravagant gifts, despite the awkwardness of the event, and accepting a plate of puffy eggs from the server she closed her eyes as she forked them down, resolving to disarm Mrs. Akehurst with kindness, and rise above whatever bitterness the lady meant to cling to.

There seemed to be no one else coming for breakfast, and humming softly to herself Emelyn passed over the usual fare of seabird and kippers to marvel at a display of intricately moulded gingerbread figurines, choosing a delightful pageboy blowing his trumpet. The confection was delectable as she'd ever tasted—a honeyed mixture of cinnamon, clove, butter and nutmeg with a bite of pepper, and sighing with pleasure she looked up to find the doctor staring vacantly.

Emelyn approached him, chewing rapidly to swallow. "Hello Doctor, shall I say you look out of sorts?"

"Nothing, Miss Morley, of course," he stammered, snapping to his feet.

"But it's not to do with my brother's condition I should hope?"

"I am confident he will recover, of course," he said, moving to the table to refill his brandy. "Though whatever chill he's acquired may grow the worse before it improves. But I cannot work miracles Miss Morley; I can make no promise to restore the use of his legs."

"His legs? Oh Doctor, no one could expect such a thing. The accident was twenty odd years ago."

"Yes, yes of course," Tarville said, smiling as though it pained him. "Good morning, Miss Morley," and with a little bow he left her.

Finding herself alone once more, Emelyn had just reached the front steps, intending a walk across the drive, when she observed a heavy drab looking stagecoach just pulling up. Rolling to a stop the vehicle creaked as it settled, and a half-hearted footman stepped down from the back to fetch open the door.

There were five or six hard-faced travellers packed within, showing no sign of movement until a single slender gentleman excused himself to emerge from between them and disembark. The man appeared frozen somewhere between fifty and sixty years of age, dressed in a long closed coat of black, with a broad brimmed hat over a split collar of white to match his cuffs.

With a deep breath and sour expression he took note of Emelyn's person, snatching a pair of pince-nez off his nose to squint her over. "Madam, I greet you," he said sharply, removing his hat for a swish to reveal receding hair of stone grey, long enough to just reach his shoulders. "But you can only be Miss Emelyn Morley."

Emelyn made a curtsy. "At your service," she said, her eyes on the coach in hope of acquainting his wife.

"My name is Rosch," he said, replacing his hat so that the brim obscured his eyes, allowing his view no higher than her neckline. "I am these many years unmarried, Miss Morley. I travel alone."

"Ah, do you indeed," she said, tilting to see his face.

Handing down a trunk from the roof, the coachman returned to his seat, and the footman tossed the luggage to the ground before leaping aboard as the vehicle started away.

"I cannot imagine but the gale over the cliffs would chill a young lady, through such a gown," he said.

"Oh, yes, I mean to go up," Emelyn said, continuing to marvel at the historic oddity of his dress, which recalled actors she'd seen pretending to the austere Puritan traditions a century past. "But I suppose you are acquainted with the captain, or the Akehursts?"

"All of them, of course," he responded, a little flushed as he lifted his gaze to her eyes. "I would speak further, madam, but as I'd never expect to meet you at the first unsupervised, I must bid you good day," and with a pinch of his hat he turned to march stiff legged up the stairs as footmen from the house jogged down for his things.

Emelyn stared after him, and with a befuddled sound she turned to set off across the courtyard for the longhouse.

In his corner box bed, Deacon was deep in a fitful sleep, his face and neck dewy with sweat. Emelyn watched him for some time, until after dozing away on a nearby chair she woke suddenly from a terrible dream, and rising to leave bumped full into Captain Van Croft.

"Excuse me my lord."

"Apologies, Miss Morley; if you would walk with me," he said, offering his arm.

The sky was dark for day, though the sea air was undeniably pleasant as they walked down the drive, and Emelyn breathed deeply. "Shall we tour the grounds at last? Or is it back to the house lest I fall into the sea."

"Mrs. Akehurst forbids I should allow you near the boundary," he said. "But we shall break her rule together," and guiding her between the garden quarters he made for the outer wall by the cliffs.

Emelyn glanced at him. "I have acquainted Mr. Rosch, who's just arrived. I hope I'm not impolite, to describe his dress as unusual."

"Not at all."

"But I've never seen such a Puritan costume outside the theatre," she ventured. "How do you know him?"

"Jacob Rosch was boatswain of my first command," Van Croft said. "As true a friend as one could ask, though I'll not argue his strangeness . . . he's not just an old navy man, but a traveling minister, scholar, and self-appointed hunter of the dark."

"And what is a *hunter of the dark*?" Emelyn inquired, feeling a curious foreboding.

"Witches, demons, vampires, he seeks to unmask them all," the captain chuckled. "Oh he mourns for the days of Cromwell, but the fellow never wants for an entertaining story . . . in fact it is he you've to thank for my acquaintance."

"Really."

"But a month ago we were at the assembly rooms in Brighton Hall, where above the mantelpiece hangs the portrait of a beautiful girl, fiery red of hair, white flowers in her hands . . . *The Belle of Brighton* it is titled. T'was Rosch who solved the mystery of its lovely subject, informing me your family kept a house in town and attended assemblies there. I must have dispatched a letter to Hastelbrook that very hour."

"We sold that house ages ago," Emelyn said. "The girl in that portrait is six years younger than I."

"And you've grown to far surpass her in beauty," he said, stopping close to kiss her hand.

His mouth was level with her eyes, and she looked at him for a moment before turning to admire the lanterns along their way, already lit. The lights diffused their globe encased brilliance like watery magic over the garden hedges and statuary, as though to steal notice from the impending breach in the wall.

"I wonder do you believe in such things?" she asked. "Witches, and demons . . . or vampires."

The captain grunted. "Witches are madwomen, demons may contend for our souls, but vampires, of the literal kind? No Miss Morley. I'd as soon believe in dragons, or river sprites . . . which brings me to a point; you needn't waste breath on childhood phantasms. The *Lurkmen* you championed in the drawing room are no more real than Rosch's vampires; you do well to avoid such fribble in mixed company."

Emelyn swallowed. "But there have been first-hand accounts; I cannot imagine those who are taken by people-snatchers would dismiss them so easily . . ."

"How shall a body leave first-hand accounting, if he's been taken," Van Croft mused, and as they reached the wall he pulled her suddenly close.

"Your pardon sir!" she objected, leaning away from him.

"Even as you challenge me, you tantalize," he said, breathing at her ear. "I will not force your kiss Miss Morley, but you must allow it will happen soon," and taking her arm again he resumed their walk along the wall.

Steadying her breath Emelyn recalled her forbidden embrace with Mr. Arkwright, wondering how it would feel to risk the same with the captain, a man as different from Arkwright as night was from day. "My lord, I must have the whole truth," she said suddenly. "Was there a promise between yourself and Miss Akehurst?"

"Melinda Akehurst is an aggressive, regrettable creature," he said. "I knew her from a child. I was called to sea for some years, and was surprised on my return to find her grown a woman. Long away from the fascination of female company, I was ill-prepared for her advance."

"And you entered an engagement?"

"I knew my mistake at once, and broke it off," he said. "Her desperate attentions are nothing to me now; let us not think of her."

"I'm sure I don't know what to think," Emelyn replied, staring at the wide space in the wall as they approached, just coming into view of the pear orchard and pond behind the house, and past these the walled kitchen gardens and growers' cottages where the hill descended. "But I cannot help feeling appalled on Mrs. Akehurst's behalf," she added. "I wish you had told me."

"Do you remember the rocky island of Tresco?" he asked. "And the Troy Town maze all of pebbles, which you so adored. Was it not the only time you've been on a ship?"

"How would you know about Tresco?" she asked, surprised to find the approaching gap in the stones much wider than she remembered.

"Your father of course," he said. "You see, Miss Morley, I mean for you and I to leave directly from Hastings, Monday next, aboard my own ship. I expect fair winds; we shall have naught but the clear sea air to trouble over . . . just the pair of us, away from all of them. A day for Tresco, perhaps two."

"That is an incredible notion, sir," Emelyn said, startled at the idea, "but you must know it is impossible, that I would ever consent to such a thing."

The breach yawned before them, a broken expanse of deepest blue where the view of the sea was unrestricted, with naught but balding grass lashed by the wind before the plummet.

"A closer look perhaps?" Van Croft winked at her, and releasing her arm he marched between the stones to the edge.

Emelyn felt a nervous thrill as she rushed to catch up with him, and stepping carefully into the breach she found the ground marred and torn, with bits of stone protruding, and what looked to be little channels carved into the earth.

Van Croft scaled the near broken side, balancing atop as he looked out over the long grey of the channel.

"Be careful!" she chided, her feet tingling to see him so reckless.

"A view I have not taken; it is glorious!" he called, his voice small against the wind.

Emelyn crept closer, crossing the trampled green of the gap to inch forward until she could just peer over the edge. The drop was stupefying, an impossible plunge to white tongues of the sea lapping a miniature landscape far below, where the fallen tower had spread its shattered corpse over the rocks.

There were slashes and scores in the ground, and trembling with incautious excitement she crouched for a better look over the drop, but with a shout the captain was upon her, seizing her about the waist to pull her back.

"Where is your head?" he snapped, yanking her to face him. "That fall is two hundred yards!"

"One hundred seventy-five," she said breathlessly, "if written estimates are correct."

"Foolish, Miss Morley, damned foolish!"

Coming to grips with how close she'd come to the edge Emelyn nodded, and accepting his arm to head back she could not help noticing the frenzied beat of his heart.

"I was only curious," she said, "forgive me."

Her mind was perfectly blank as they climbed the shallow stairs to the front doors, and no sooner had they entered than the Commodore's wife burst upon them with news of an urgent letter for the captain. Kissing Emelyn's hand without biting he left the ladies in the hall, and she rubbed her knuckles, her view of his exit blocked as Mrs. Akehurst stepped before her.

"Well!" the lady pronounced. "It appears you have slipped my vigilance at last. But you are hardly dressed for the wind, Miss Morley, or perhaps you trusted my godson to keep you warm."

"It was only the briefest of walks, Mrs. Akehurst," Emelyn said.

"I've nothing to report."

The lady buckled under Emelyn's polite stare. "Well, fine. But I am told you took very little for breakfast. I do hope the fare was to your liking?"

"I did have some eggs, thank you," Emelyn said, "and the gingerbread especially was divine; I wonder where it's been hiding."

"The secret is baking over soft melted beeswax," Mrs. Akehurst said curtly, "as they do in Austria. Our cook herself is from Missau. I suppose your own cook has never been off the island?"

Emelyn smiled. "No, I suppose you're right."

Mrs. Akehurst sighed at her. "Ah well, but I fear the letter will be ill-news for the captain, and likely to put him out of sorts."

The day stretched on; the sky growing steadily darker, though the chill wind brought no rain, and after a brief nap to fortify her appetite Emelyn donned her new cloak and hat before the mirror. The voluminous slanting headpiece she did not like, and snapping it off she fastened the crescent brooch at her throat with a frown.

Returning downstairs to find the lower floor eerily empty, she requested her dinner be sent to the longhouse with that for Deacon, and finding him sitting up in good spirits she consented to a practice round of cards.

"Perhaps you should challenge Mrs. Akehurst," she grumbled, falling behind at once. "I'm certain whist is counted among her many accomplishments."

Deacon nodded thoughtfully. "Shall I remind you trump is diamonds?"

"You've run me out," she said impatiently.

Evening deepened—the outside courtyard came to life, draped with long hanging ribbons and paper shapes between the light poles, casting patterned shadows over low hedges and trimmed green. Several posts had been planted with dark tarpaulins stretched between them to cover the gap in the wall, and finding the captain still locked in the Commodore's study, Emelyn wandered among the lanterns until she was accosted again by Mrs. Akehurst, who had reimagined herself in frilly taffeta for the evening. "I must have your company my dear," she insisted, and the ladies set out for a courtyard promenade before the first of the guests were to arrive.

"No stars to be had," Emelyn observed. "But the rain holds yet."

"Yes my dear, and I hope you will forgive my directness," Mrs. Akehurst replied, "but I must apprise you of the sober news concerning the captain, as much as it is my business to tell."

"Really?" Emelyn asked, watching the golden shadows cast on the lawn as they walked.

"It appears he has suffered a sudden and tragic development in shipping," the lady said, "which I fear may compromise his attention. Alas I can say no more, but I have stridently reminded him, on your behalf, that obligations of business must never be allowed to vex one's affections."

Emelyn flushed. "Thank you madam, but that isn't necessary."

"Well, who can predict a man's heart," Mrs. Akehurst sighed, pausing near a little fountain to admire the lights. "But you mustn't be discouraged my dear; he may yet take you into his confidence."

Measuring her response Emelyn recalled the captain's description of the Akehursts' daughter. "I daresay he will."

"Well, let us hope."

"He has already spoken of things he might rather wish he'd withheld," Emelyn said, hoping her hostess might guess.

"Has he confided in you? Dear me but I hope he's not troubled you with his affairs; I must speak to him."

"Please don't."

"You must trust me, Miss Morley," Mrs. Akehurst said, squeezing her arm. "A naval captain wants a wife buoyant and fresh, free of such weighty concerns."

"I thank you for your counsel," Emelyn said. "Now I must beg your pardon to go up; I shouldn't like to be found unchanged for the party."

"Oh we still have time my dear," Mrs. Akehurst said, but Emelyn took her leave, feeling the lady's gaze at her back until the grand front doors closed behind her.

Chapter 22
Confessions

"And I'm quite sure Mrs. Akehurst only meant to delay me, that I should be caught out still in my tea dress for the party," Emelyn complained, lifting her arms as Breda assisted her into one of the new articles: a glossy gown of aquamarine, low bordered with a wide shoulder line, to be complemented by the silver sapphire necklace, while the fire of Emelyn's hair was twisted back with silver chains, and capped with hanging lace.

"Not very sporting of her miss," Breda commented, pulling to tighten as her mistress inhaled a breath.

"Has there been any more word of the missing staff?" Emelyn asked, sitting to dab her neck with lavender oil.

"No miss; all the talk is of the tower now, and the wall that were collapsed," Breda said, pulling a white heeled shoe over Emelyn's foot.

Put together at last, Emelyn drifted her fingers along the balustrade as she descended to the grand hall, finding her hosts standing with Deacon—the sour faced Mr. Rosch, Doctor Tarville, and Lord Van Croft closest the stairs, swelling with pride in a long open frock coat of deep blue over alabaster waistcoat, his dark hair gathered back with blue ribbon.

"A vision, Miss Morley!" the Commodore declared. "An absolute vision."

Ascending a few steps to meet her the captain took Emelyn's hand, pulling it to his lips. "Would I could devour you before their eyes," he said, a happy growl in his voice.

Emelyn smiled. "My grateful regards to your restraint."

"I must see to the chairs," Mrs. Akehurst said. "I fear we may run short."

"Excuse me," Emelyn said quickly, leaving Van Croft on the stairs to pursue their hostess, and catching up to her in the windowed hall beside a little indoor garden courtyard.

"Miss Morley, such a radiant colour. How may I be of service?"

"Mrs. Akehurst," Emelyn said, unsure how to phrase herself, "if you'll forgive me . . . It would seem you feel obliged to hold me at a remove, and I am sorry for it. I should have hoped we could be friends."

"Oh my dear girl," Mrs. Akehurst sighed, hand over her heart as though taken aback. "Have I treated you unfairly?"

"Not at all, of course not, as such . . . but of course if I'd ever known; if I'd ever thought of your daughter and the captain, then of course I should never have come."

"So he's confessed himself to you," the lady marvelled. "Well, we mustn't allow that the captain's broken promise to Melinda should temper our good opinion of her replacement."

"I've never aspired to be anyone's replacement," Emelyn said, rather wishing she'd let the lady count chairs.

"Oh my dear, of course not," Mrs. Akehurst said sweetly. "Now I must beg your pardon, there are arrangements to be made before the party."

Outside great beacons were lit on the gateposts to buttress the ebbing dusk, the gates were thrown wide, and a light supper of seabird and fennel soup was served in the dining room, for which Emelyn found little appetite.

Beside her sat Lord Van Croft, aggressively merry with drink as he plumbed for tales of vampires from Mr. Rosch, who soberly protested, apologizing to their hosts.

"My study is purely academic, I assure you," Rosch said. "I am but a traveling parson now. Your godson has seen fit to allow me a stipend, for some meagre administration of his affairs in Brighton."

"Nonsense!" Van Croft cried, squeezing Emelyn's hand under the table. "He's a keen sense for the corrupt this one, even in business! But you're only here for the stories old man, now go on; spin us a tale of vampires."

"How very jolly—ghost stories for our soup," Mrs. Akehurst said.

"But I'm all ears!" Doctor Tarville chirped, his good humour apparently returned to him.

"Perhaps it was creatures of the night broke the wall?" Van Croft posed, draining his wine and snapping for more.

"Well my friends," the Commodore said, a little red in the face, "let us hope there shall be no vampires at the party tonight!"

"Let us hope indeed," Mr. Rosch frowned, "for they should find Miss Morley the most tempting among us."

Emelyn forced a laugh. "And why is that, Mr. Rosch?"

"I don't mean to frighten the lady," Rosch said, looking her over, "but in the annals of supernatural report it is too oft the red haired maiden who attracts the powers of darkness—in fact, a great many accused witches are known to have been red of hair."

The others seemed to hold their breath, and Emelyn forked a bite of her bird. "Then I am heartened sir, that your study is *purely academic.*"

"The lady is not amused," Van Croft chuckled. "Come Miss Morley, you must learn to bear such silliness with good temper. And you sir, I should be clear your lectures on witches and warlocks are not to include Miss Morley."

"Naturally," Rosch replied, raising his glass.

Emelyn smiled. "The captain believes Mr. Rosch and I need defending from each other."

"You are both under my protection," Van Croft said. "Therefore let there be peace!"

"Hear hear!" the Commodore cried, raising his glass. "To our families on land!"

The captain cheered and they toasted together.

"The guests won't be long now," Mrs. Akehurst said. "I sent word to the inn they should arrive after dusk, that we might thrive in the romantic lights of the gardens . . . and the better to hide our unaccountable misfortune with the wall."

■ ■

"Loretta Louise Pleasance Pembrook," the powdered and painted Lord Crennock repeated, squinting in the dim light of the London night coach. His weathered face was cast in ghostly makeup over candy green coats and wig to match. "An awful lot of name for a penniless doxy," he remarked. "I was to unveil the Chardin in my dining room tonight; I very much hope you are certain."

Miss Winter perched on the bench across, wearing strict black to the throat, a train of dark lace hanging from the knot of her hair. "The painting can wait my lord; this opportunity is providence." she said, fingering the crucifix at her chest.

"And how did such a low creature ever find herself at Hastelbrook?"

"I'm sure I don't know, but she's been publishing her tale to every willing ear. Apparently the girl attended there an assembly, where in the dark garden maze, she maintains she was attacked, by a vampire."

Lord Crennock frowned, swaying with the jostle of the coach. "Then perhaps the little drab is only mad."

"I rather doubt the coincidence," Miss Winter said. "Our conviction that a vampire haunts Hastelbrook is hardly public. No, I'm quite sure the poor wretch has seen something."

The carriage rolled to a halt, the door opened, and Lord Crennock pressed a kerchief to his nose. "You may brave the muck on your own, my dear. I shall remain where I am."

"As you like my lord," she replied, and gathering her skirts she climbed out, stepping into the soggy street.

Flanked by two surly looking men with red sashes at their waists, Miss Winter wrinkled her nose as she studied the dingy alley off Tower Street. Tired tenement buildings creaked around her, leaning together as though to preserve their strength, while an increasing drizzle peppered the rooftops.

Finding the correct door, Miss Winter nodded and one of the men stepped forward to pound his fist upon it. "Constable calling!" he cried.

The door creaked inward and a weary looking fellow with patchy hair and grease stained shirt peered out at them. "I seen him just rush past," the man said, pointing away down the street. "Hurry now an' you shall have him!" and he shut the door on the intruder's foot, cursing as the men pushed it open, shoving him against the wall of the little entryway, no bigger than a closet.

"You're never the constables!" he shouted, struggling in obvious fear. "Bloody Mohocks, dun' I pay my protection monies?"

"Patience, Mr. Pembrook," Miss Winter said loudly, stepping into the hall to find a cramped rising stair on one side, with a short descent to a foul smelling kitchen on the other. "We know you and your wife keep a house of ill-repute."

"Reformers are ye? We keeps no such thing!" he cried, thrashing as the men held him to the wall.

"I'm not here to persecute, but to pay you, Mr. Pembrook!" Miss Winter yelled over the struggle, quieting the man at once. "Now, I believe your daughter's circumstances are reduced of late, and she's come home? We are aware she's been babbling of Hastelbrook Hall in Sussex . . . and vampires."

"Leave a poor mad girl be," the man whimpered. "Cut off from her rightful gentleman she was, he won't see her now; disappeared out of her life and she ain't been right since."

"To your great fortune I want only to speak to her," Miss Winter said, bidding the men release him. "Ten guineas sir, but you shall tell no one of our visit," and she pressed a stack of gold coins into his hand.

"We are at your service," Mr. Pembrook said with a flush.

Ducking her head for the angled ceiling, Miss Winter ascended the stairs to find a short hall with several doors, the nearest of which slammed at the sight of her. Coming to the end as directed, she pushed the door gently on its hinge, startling a young woman of abundant figure and wild curly hair who sat in a sooty linen shift on the floor of the small peaked room. Her fingers black with charcoal, Miss Pembrook stared up at her visitor from a nest of half-finished sketches.

"Hello, Miss Pembrook, I come to you as a friend. My name is Ariana Winter."

"Please ma'am," the young woman answered, "have you a message from Mr. Foster, from my Hershel?"

"No, Miss Pembrook I have not," Miss Winter said, picking her way into the room. "I understand he's broken his promise to you? Was it he who secured your invitation to Hastelbrook?"

"To everywhere ma'am! It were he what made me respectable, even while his wretched mother should rather see me dead. It's she what keeps us apart! If only he were here ma'am, he'd tell you straight . . ."

"Let us forget Mr. Foster for a moment; it is you I have come to see."

"But perhaps not his mother," the woman said miserably, smudging her forehead as she scratched it, "perhaps he's cursed as well."

"And how have you been cursed?" Miss Winter asked. "Did it

happen at Hastelbrook, at the party on June the sixth?"

"Yes!" the woman burst. "It was there I saw her . . . I saw her."

"Saw whom?"

Loretta Pembrook grabbed her head as though in pain. "The woman! The woman in black."

"The woman in black . . . have you drawn a picture?" Miss Winter inquired, looking over the odd characters and unfinished faces. "Well, perhaps not."

"I have!" Loretta said, crawling to rifle under the bed, from which she withdrew an artist's folio, tied with ribbon, and cracking it open she selected a single sheet, handing it over with care.

"Remarkable," Miss Winter breathed, staring into the coldly beautiful face of a woman draped in wild raven hair, her eyes gone over so heavily in black as to nearly tear through the paper. "Loretta speak truthfully, do you believe the woman in black to be a vampire?"

"Vampire!" Loretta gasped, bringing fistfuls of hair to her mouth. "She snatched me through the hedge, pulled me down—"

"And then?" Miss Winter pressed, her eyes wide.

The shutter banged in the wind and Loretta flinched, head down as she picked at her nails. "Supped on my blood mistress, bit into me like I were ripened fruit she did . . . but only for a moment."

"And did she speak to you? Miss Pembrook you must think," Miss Winter said, grabbing her chin. "This vampiress, did she speak to you?"

"Her voice were like an angel," Loretta Louise Pembrook whispered, smiling faintly.

"What did she say?"

"She warned me keep my tongue, but I could not. I should go mad if I did! *Emelyn Morley is under my protection*—that's what she said; she warned us to come not near the place again."

Miss Winter took a sharp breath, releasing her. "*Emelyn Morley is under my protection*," she repeated. "There, you delightful girl, you have been most instructive," she said, smiling as she folded the illustration.

"But that were my best work, you can't have it!" Loretta protested.

"It's very good. Shall we say twenty guineas?" Miss Winter asked, counting them out from the little pocket bag at her waist.

"Oh . . . oh," Miss Pembrook said, blinking as she accepted the coin.

Descending to the landing below Miss Winter nodded for the men to release their prisoner. "Your daughter's earned twenty guineas by a sketch," she said, tapping Mr. Pembrook in the face with the paper, "perhaps you've misplaced her trade. Good night Mr. Pembrook."

"By Jove, bloody well done," Lord Crennock said, examining the illustration.

"Her testimony quite approves my suspicion, and better than we could have hoped," Miss Winter said. "The vampiress that killed Philip Denlund is somehow connected to Hastelbrook, and the eldest Morley daughter is her creature."

"This must rather confirm the rumours," Lord Crennock said, staring at the sketch. "Whatever lies hidden beneath the estate, doubtless it has drawn the vampire near . . . But shall it present us an opportunity; dare we imagine to capture her?"

"Such a trap could only be set by making use of Miss Morley herself. I shall write to my contact tonight. Long has he suspected their lineage of dark dealings."

"Then let us pray something comes of it," Crennock replied with a frown, staring at the sketch, "for we have no mandate until King George and all his royal slugs bear witness . . . and I begin to fear Dramen overtaxes his prize."

"With an immortal in his power he imagines himself a god," Miss Winter sighed, "but we cannot wager our future against only one such creature, and she must not die before St. James's Palace."

"Nor afterward, not before she is locked and secure among the incurables of Bedlam. Dramen means to begin anatomizing the creatures with all haste. The Argentum Serpentis must lead this discovery, Miss Winter."

"Yes, indeed we must, and I fear the crown will take her from us."

Lord Crennock pursed his lips, folding the paper. "I see, therefore the insurance of a *second* vampire in our care would not go amiss, though any plan to make it so must be kept strictly within the brotherhood."

"In which Dramen is pleased to remind me I have no membership," Miss Winter said.

"My dear Ariana, in this Dramen is lord and master," Crennock said, leaning back in his seat. "His Mohock rogues own every night gang in the city, and it is only he among us with any connection to the hunters of Rome."

"You forget I have been to Rome," she said. "I have met the Invisible College; I have spoken to the Magister myself."

"And were afforded, I trust, overtures of respect for your accomplishments," Crennock replied. "Nevertheless, there is no future for this enterprise in England without attaching ourselves to Lord Dramen's will."

"Yes, my lord."

"But fear not—for all his arrogance, the man is sharper than to underestimate you. None else in our company have slain a vampire."

"It is true," Miss Winter said, folding her hands in her lap. "But at the risk of offending my own pride, I might remind you I slew the creature in its place of rest, during the day. The danger of confronting a vampire at night cannot be overstated."

"Then we must hope your contact comes upon Miss Morley's vampire sympathies before he parts her company," and banging his cane against the ceiling Lord Crennock frowned as the Hack & Humble night coach lurched into motion, continuing its way down the cobbled street.

■ ■

The courtyard of Galecliff spread its arms wide in welcome, and by seven o' clock a happy host had descended upon the manor. Emelyn was posted with the captain by the drawing room doors, that he might introduce her as all comers were welcomed for games and drink. Ladies and gentlemen blushed and fawned to meet them; a good many casting long looks back as they passed.

Some twenty couples were in attendance throughout, with a number of single gentlemen arriving on horseback, excepting a few of the elder fellows, such as the lurking Mr. Rosch, who stood scowling by the fender in the same closed coat and white collars, his bare forehead gleaming in the firelight between stringy strands of grey.

There commenced several long rounds of whist, in which Deacon and Van Croft partnered once more, which every opposing team learned to resent.

For her part Emelyn strove to better acquaint some of the ladies, but found Mrs. Akehurst keen to follow her, overbearing every conversation with effected flattery.

"Come now, dear beautiful Miss Morley, you must tell them about your home," Mrs. Akehurst interrupted, "but I've had it from Mr. Rosch that Hastelbrook Hall is the most *haunted* place in Sussex! Is it not true?"

"Certainly not, it's not true," Emelyn said, smiling against gasps of laughter from the others. "And I shouldn't take the word of a gentleman who purports to hunt vampires for a living . . ."

"Are there vampires at Hastelbrook?" one of them asked, her eyes wide.

"Well, of course you must all come to the midsummer ball, in August," Emelyn said quickly, addressing the group, "and you shall see for yourselves we are not haunted, quite the reverse."

"And what is the reverse of haunted?" Mrs. Akehurst asked, "blessed of Heaven perhaps?"

So it went on, until Emelyn surrendered her efforts to mingle and positioned herself so attentively close to the card playing Van Croft that Mrs. Akehurst let her be.

"They'll think I was raised by ghosts if she has her way," Emelyn muttered.

"There is no such thing as ghosts my dear," he said, laying down a card.

Feeling rather detached from the scene, Emelyn took his arm again after the game, allowing him to steer as Van Croft drank with abandon and laughed like thunder at the jokes of his naval comrades. By and by a sober faced Commodore came to whisper at him, and the two of them adjourned for a private conference.

Having eavesdropped without meaning to, Emelyn was quite sure the Commodore's whisper had been *it is confirmed,* which she could make no sense of. This she pondered over, when in something of a strange mood the captain returned, and took to sharing the private disgraces of many a navy man about the room. "Franklin Brewer," he said, pointing one out, "challenged his own brother for a young lady; lost the duel and the lady, caught a ball in the hip for his trouble, as you can see in his ridiculous gait."

"Would I find that amusing, with a brother in crutches?" Emelyn asked.

"If you're only to pout and be sour, go and join him," he said, finishing his drink.

Emelyn stared at him. "What is wrong my lord? It's clear enough something has happened. What did the Commodore say to you?"

"Only a setback of business," Van Croft said, his gaze afar off, "naught that need trouble you."

"Well, if you are abruptly penniless we must write to my mother at once," Emelyn replied, watching a chuckling group of ladies with envy.

"No, Miss Morley, not that," he said softly. "Never that . . ."

Spreading through the house like eager children, the guests had soon mastered the ground floor, marvelling at the unique maritime architecture as the Commodore expounded joyfully over his home, explaining the dark walls were panelled all in original decking, designating the portraits a tour of British naval history, and every looking glass originally of service in ship's quarters. The couple of the hour mingled about, and escorted to the open courtyard with many others in tow Emelyn was treated to a veritable parade of naval fellows, only too eager to peacock for the illustrious captain. With many a toast, and jibes over Van Croft's good fortune, the men brandished their most qualified stories, well seasoned with repetitive praises for the lady.

"They pursue your favour like they owe you their lives," she said in a quiet moment, watching as he quaffed another glass.

"Many of them do . . . though too many others I've lost," the captain said, and holding her arm tightly he strolled among the garden statuary, where they discovered Deacon standing by a discus thrower of cast bronze, speaking to a dusky young lady in silken white, her dark hair coiled under a lively bonnet.

"Mr. Morley!" Van Croft hailed, coming alive to slap Deacon on the shoulder. "You've the crow's eye for cards by damn. I must have you with me, next I face the gambling tables of Lord Admiral Norris; we'll take them all, signets to stockings!"

"My lord Van Croft," Deacon said, giving a deep nod as he adjusted on his crutches, "may I present Miss Kate Harrington, and this, Miss Harrington, is my eldest sister, Miss Emelyn Morley."

"A pleasure," Van Croft said, and "Lovely to meet you," Emelyn chimed.

"How do you do," Miss Harrington said, her face bright as she dipped for a curtsey. "I've heard nothing but praises for the pair of you I'm sure!"

"Miss Harrington's father is a shipwright, or was, by trade,"

Deacon said, rather faltering.

The young lady laughed. "Oh he'll let no misfortune put him out of work, Father is a shipwright still, good sir."

"Ah the shipwright," Van Croft said, swaying where he stood. "Your father will never want for work madam, if the number lost at sea were any indication. And your mother, she is . . ?"

"She was Jamaican," Miss Harrington answered quickly, as though expecting the question. "And you speak true my lord, Papa is never in want of a project."

"But I'll wager *Papa* spares not a thought," Van Croft carried on, "when his designs come to rest at the bottom of the ocean, all the better for business!" and he slurped his wine with a cough.

"You're drinking through your nose my lord," Deacon said, "perhaps you should sit down a while."

"Yes perhaps," Emelyn said, "if you'll excuse us."

Holding her brother's gaze Van Croft resisted her attempt to pull him away. "Sit down shall I? Is it wise to speak so to a man of quality twice your size?"

"Not if we're to run Admiral Norris out of his house," Deacon said, offering his hand.

"Right . . . good man," Van Croft puffed, shaking his hand.

The conversation continued in unsteady fashion, with the increasingly wine addled captain ranging between guffaws of laughter and bristling frowns, as though he must take offense every few minutes or fail in some duty to himself. Tiring of Van Croft's manner, and Deacon's acerbic retorts which flew just high enough to escape the captain's wrath, if not his suspicion, Emelyn extracted her gentleman at last, and they circled the gardens together in silence, passing under the flattering glow of the lights.

"My respect must be earned," he muttered after some while. "Your brother is a deft hand at whist, but he must keep better guard of his tongue."

"You've every practical advantage my lord, over all the men here," Emelyn said, verbalizing thoughts she'd rehearsed. "I should think to find you *more* patient with the world, not less. As for Deacon, you may count me over sensitive to his situation, but I'll not take your side over his."

Van Croft smirked. "*Every* practical advantage have I?"

"Is that all you heard?"

The captain chuckled, squeezing her hand on his arm. "Let us say no more of it," he said. "You have my protection Miss Morley . . . and so shall your brother, if it pleases you."

On they walked, breaking away from the others to meander down the paved path to the back of the house, coming to the reflecting pond among the pear trees, surrounded by lamp posts. Beyond the water and the orchards surrounding it gleamed a number of cottages, their windows cheerfully aglow.

"The growers' houses make a charming little village," Emelyn said, breathing deep.

Van Croft made no answer.

"You're out of sorts my lord . . . will you not speak of it to me?"

Footsteps sounded behind them and the captain turned as a tall young gentleman strode to approach.

"My dear Curry!" Van Croft crowed.

"Van Croft you old cannon!" the other said, clapping his shoulder. The fellow was handsome, if perfectly erect of posture, in blonde coats with light close cropped hair crowding beady eyes over a haughty mouth.

"Emelyn Elizabeth Morley," Van Croft presented. "*The Belle of Brighton*, for upon a time that quaint little village was lucky enough to have her."

"Ah yes, my lord captain's beautiful holdings," Mr. Curry declared, his aloof tone of voice almost musical as he took Emelyn's fingertips for a sharp bow.

"I am no more the captain's holdings than you are sir," she said.

Curry grinned. "But tell me, Miss Morley, what is it to flutter your eyes and pull the arm of the most eligible man in the empire?"

Emelyn felt a flush. "For that, you're better asking his godmother," she said, regretting it at once.

But Van Croft only laughed. "I warn you she's tongue enough for two sets of teeth," he said.

"Upon my word," Curry exclaimed, "the very snapdragon I'd hoped for." He stepped back as though to present himself, bowing sharply again, bending at the waist. "Come now, Miss Morley—what do you observe? I will have my comeuppance."

"Will you?" Emelyn said, liking him less by the moment. "Shall I say you bow like a Jumping Jack, in collar stiff enough to spare the weight of your head?"

The men laughed together, and with an awkward farewell Emelyn excused herself, unlinking Van Croft's arm only to startle as he pulled her back to him.

"Stay my dear, it does not please me that you should go," he said, holding her fast as Captain Curry shook with silent mirth, pursing his lips.

With a blush Emelyn smiled, clenching her fist between them. "Perhaps you will excuse us, Captain Curry."

"Oh dear," Curry said, and with a chuckling bow he left them.

Van Croft bristled. "I should like you to understand Miss Morley, it is not for you to dismiss my company."

"And I should like you to understand I won't be yanked about," Emelyn said, her pulse rising as she watched Captain Curry's long departing stride.

"Forgive me." Van Croft tossed away his glass, and rubbing his eyes he swayed with a chuckle.

"I believe you're drunk sir," Emelyn said, pulling away from him. "What do you expect of me? Am I to take care of you?"

The captain twitched as he stared into the dark, and he clenched his fists in such a way that she could hear his knuckles creak. "Some call life at sea the *long blue madness*," he said. "But my men are not mad . . . I'll not believe it."

"Believe *what* my lord?" she asked, shivering in the wind. "Whatever has driven you to such a state . . . you must give it air, or I will part your company and go back to the house."

"What are words but little animal noises," he said, raising her hand to kiss it. "You're not like the others, Miss Morley; you have no fear of me, and little enough respect . . . I think you would devour us all if you could."

"You're speaking nonsense," she said, her fingers tingling as he kissed them.

Van Croft grinned suddenly, releasing her hand. "Let us secret behind the curtain. I would see the drop in the dark, come!"

Before she could react he'd set off, and shouting in alarm she chased him. The erected tarps set to span the gap in the wall flapped in the wind as they approached, and she caught up just in time to seize his wrist before he reached them.

"My lord don't! If you think I'll permit you any closer the edge you've lost your mind . . ."

Shaking his head he smiled, resigning himself to the pause as they stood breathing together.

"Tell me about Tresco," she said, chasing imaginations of the harrowing fall, and Vaela's near end, from her mind. "Why should you wish to take me there, of all places?"

Freeing himself from her grasp Van Croft laughed, waving at the wall. "Tresco only to start," he said. "Beyond these walls lies the grand and terrible world Miss Morley, connected by naught but the body of the sea, the most dangerous creature under God . . . But it must be nothing to you, safe within the boundary of a woman's life."

Emelyn watched him warily. "You needn't be a man to step on a boat, my lord."

A young footman jogged to meet them, with the grateful sight of her new sable lined cloak in his hands. The lad wrapped the soft thing about her shoulders and she thanked him, fastening the brooch as Van Croft started again toward the cliff.

"I thank you again for the cloak . . . No, Jonathan, get back!" she burst, rushing to follow him as he disappeared under the tarp.

There stood the captain but a few steps from the drop, the wind twisting about him, and Emelyn lunged for his wrist just as he turned to grab her, pulling her to him.

"*Jonathan?* Am I a child Miss Morley," he growled, "that you'd command me so?"

"You're miserable with drink," she said firmly, tingling head to foot as the flapping tarps closed behind them, sealing them away from the eyes of the party. "Come back, it's not safe."

"*I* am not safe," he breathed, holding her tightly by the shoulders. "You cannot imagine the things I've done, what I've seen . . . yet even here, there is no fear in you. You imagine yourself superior to us all; you carry it like a secret."

"I'm sure I'm as frightened as you are . . . standing *here*," she said.

He was too close, his eyes lingering too long, and though she expected it the sudden press of his lips was very different than she'd imagined. The captain kissed hungrily and deep, tasting of wine, and reluctant with a noise she found herself meeting his kisses with hers, warming to the press of him, until tilting back she closed her eyes, shivering as his mouth found her neck. His lips plucked at her gently, and making fists in his coats she recalled the delirious pierce of Vaela's bite.

Squeezing her against him Van Croft kissed her chin, his hand rising to her bosom, and covering her chest she stepped back. "Nay my lord, enough! You must comport yourself . . ."

"No one can see us," he said. With bleary eyes he stared at her, and turning sharply toward the sea took a step before she could grab him.

Lunging forward she caught his arm, using all her strength to drag him back. "Jonathan Van Croft that is the last time!"

Swatting the tarps aside he followed her, and safe on the other side she released him. "You are not yourself!" she scolded, her heart pounding wildly.

The captain snapped his waistcoat, standing tall. "Your strength belies your size Miss Morley," he said. "I am affected by your concern, but I suffer only the dignity . . . the indignity of drink."

"Yes, perhaps some cold coffee—for us both," she said, touching her neck where his lips had been.

The captain gave her his arm, and escorting him round the house she walked with care, excusing them past a gaggle of his navy friends before the stairs.

"Ho there captain!" one of the men cried. "Dutch or pirates on the sea; but whom should we despise the more?"

"Neither!" Van Croft shot back as they started to climb. "Despise whatever doom makes a seaman revolt against God and nature . . ."

"By Jove a riddle, let me see!" another laughed, and Emelyn kept his arm as the captain sought to turn back.

"No, my lord," she said. "That's quite enough; you must rest."

With a grumble Van Croft turned again, ascending unsteadily at her side, and drawn by sweet smells and music she brought him to the dining room, which had been decorated with hanging naval flags over tables of sweet wines and cheese.

"That is chilled Constantina, to be paired with the Double Gloucester," Mrs. Akehurst advised, guiding her guests in their refreshment, and spotting the captain she rushed to confront them. "Just look at the pair of you, like mites on Mimolette," she said, clasping her hands.

"Am I the cheese or the mites?" Emelyn asked.

"And how do you fare captain?" the lady inquired, looking concerned. "But I hope she's not mishandled you."

Van Croft stood like a statue, his eyes far away, and after seating him in a chair Emelyn excused herself to gather a plate, finding toasted rolls with grapes and savoury blue cheese on a near table. "Have you any coffee?" she asked the footman, sensing her hostess had followed.

"The Wensleydale is excellent," Mrs. Akehurst said. "But what have you done to the poor captain? You've not badgered him for the ill news I should hope."

Emelyn raised her brows, pausing as she picked at the grapes. "Certainly not," she said, finding her strategy, "but I'm sure it's nothing."

"Nothing?" Mrs. Akehurst repeated. "Oh my spoiled dear, I've spoken to the Commodore, and I assure you it's a good deal more than nothing."

"Nonsense," Emelyn said, adding to her plate. "Lord Van Croft is a wealthy sea captain *with no end of prospects*; what can it be but a trifle of business. Anyway he means for us to sail to Tresco, which I think is lovely."

"Oh but if you only knew," Mrs. Akehurst lamented, "you should be grateful to chase any such notion from your head with horror."

"With horror?" Emelyn inquired, turning to face her. "Surely you don't mean to frighten me. I do not frighten easily madam."

"Don't you?" Mrs. Akehurst asked, taking note of the captain as he collapsed into a chair by the doors. "Well I'm sure you'll rue the asking, but let us test your stomach. Two of the captain's ships were to dock at Hastings; one the *Old Garnet*, the other called the *Anna Corona*. I believe he meant to take you to Compton Place by the sea, to meet their captains tomorrow."

"And I suppose the ships are behind their time," Emelyn said, having a nibble of cheese. "But I shan't be surprised, my father in the maritime trade as he is."

"No my dearest, they are not behind their time. They were doomed at sea, and in so dreadful a fashion as defies describing . . ."

"But you will try? Or is the tale as dull as I imagine."

"Well I hesitate to dissemble for so happily naive a person, but let us see how you handle the truth of it: it was the *Anna Corona* wrecked first, coming on full steer and every sheet to the wind, to break upon the rocks at Saint Agnes."

"Full steer?" Emelyn puzzled. "You cannot mean deliberately?"

"Quite so, for even if the crew had abandoned her, someone must have been aboard to drive her in, while the other," Mrs. Akehurst continued, lowering her voice as she glanced about them, "the *Old Garnet*, being reportedly heavier with coal than regulation should permit, went off in a great monstrous fire, scuttling herself to smithers by turning guns on her own decks."

The sky overhead rumbled in its sleep, and Emelyn cleared her throat, hiding a tremble to think of it. "But that sounds rather like a sea widow's tale . . ."

"The tragedy is confirmed," the lady said, speaking closer. "Both crews destroyed themselves to a man, a thing quite beyond comprehension, and what shall the Admiralty say to it? But as the vessels were under his command Van Croft must speak for them, and if the one is found to have been illegally laden he may stand to lose his commission."

"Then you must excuse me, madam," Emelyn said, accepting a fresh coffee to go with her plate, "and I thank you, of course, for telling me all."

Leaving her nonplussed hostess by the table she returned to coax the captain to eat, watching as he slurped from the hot mug. "Keep your eye on him," she said, addressing the near footman.

"Yes ma'am."

Pulling her cloak tighter against the wind, Emelyn returned outside, finding her brother still standing with his crutches by a tall spiralling shrubbery, engaged with Miss Harrington who appeared quite rapt.

"And how is the poor sot?" Deacon asked, smiling at his sister's approach.

"Lord Van Croft is burdened with a sudden and tragic turn of business," Emelyn said, recalling her father's own loss of ships. "He deserves our patience."

The distant clouds grumbled again, but the rain made no appearance, and as the conversation dwindled she spotted a young woman whom she knew by face, if not by name, standing by a fountain carved like an Eastern dragon amongst an exuberant group. Accepting a glass of wine from a weary footman Emelyn bid her brother farewell and arranged herself to walk slowly past the ladies.

"Oh Miss Morley!" the one she knew squawked, noting her at once. "Miss Morley! Mrs. Philip Lancourt, Jane, but we played quadrille if you remember, in Chelsea last year. Now my gentlewomen this is the

Belle of Brighton!"

Introductions followed, and after acquainting the Misses Spencer, Darlington, and Stillhouse, the latter being the youngest, and one Mrs. Oliver, Emelyn relaxed, begging their pardon for not having been sooner introduced and smiling at the flattering fuss over her gown.

"Well if I were a dressmaker I should have you painted to sell my commodities," a lively Miss Darlington said.

"But I thought . . . was the Belle of Brighton not blonde of hair?" Miss Stillhouse puzzled.

"Immodestly red I'm afraid; my apologies," Emelyn said, eliciting laughter as she sipped her wine.

"Now I was just coming to it, but have you heard," Jane Lancourt confided to the group, "the Duchess of Whitmore capsized her yacht on the water at Wadehill Place, and is drowned, can you imagine?"

"How horribly silly," the dark haired Miss Spencer grunted.

"My sister Sarah's debut was at Wadehill," Emelyn said. "The Easter ball."

"But I remember you there of course!" Mrs. Lancourt marvelled. "And now that I think of it, did I not see you first at Daulton House in 'twenty-nine, my goodness six years ago; but was it not your coming out?"

"It was."

"I remember the ball was unremarkable," Miss Spencer added sleepily, "but there was a chase on the king's road south; that was interesting."

"Yes," Emelyn said, recalling the odd event of the king's mounted guards pursuing some poor fellow past the house, lending an air of excitement to the pause between dances she'd taken with Margaret.

"And you caught the eye of Prince Frederick," Mrs. Lancourt said, beaming as she flapped her fan, "until you quarrelled outside and he would not know you . . . but we all wondered what had happened."

"I suppose I disappointed him," Emelyn said, staring into nothing as she thought of the aggressively forward Prince of Wales, and Vaela's intervention on her behalf.

Wearing a coarse leather vest over his shirtsleeves, the sandy haired Alexander Dramen stood at the top of a narrow stair plunging down into the dim light of a flickering room. From below there came the clattering sound of metal chains disturbed, and a sudden scream—a shriek of pain, angry and surprised. A man's grim laughter followed, and Alexander steeled himself to descend.

The square chamber at the bottom of the steps burst into reflections cast by a hanging lantern, creating a symphony of flickers in each of the four walls, which were plated top to bottom in mirror polished silver. Its floor grimy with stains, the room was adorned with but a single sturdy chair under the light, its legs bolted down, with a line of chalk drawn before it as though in warning. The chair faced a heavy curtain of iron and silver chains draped from hooks in the ceiling, with a secondary mesh of fine silver mail making for an inner lining, while a wide thick length of iron links ran across the floor under the curtain, completing the boundary of the quarantined space beyond—a makeshift cell, bare save for a ponderous coffin near the back wall. One of the casket's sides was split outward, the lid broken away, and beside this, sitting in the corner with head down as she embraced her knees, was what appeared to be a young woman, little more than a girl, though Alexander Dramen knew better. Deathly pale she was, without shoes or sleeves, her striped breeches and stays scandalously torn, with dried blood on her garments and in the dusky blonde of her hair, which was tied strictly back.

In the near corner of the room the broad dishevelled figure of Baron Dramen's enforcer, Mr. Grouthe, crouched before a darkly stained bucket, wringing out a rag within.

"Mr. Grouthe, has she been fed?" Alexander asked.

"You're just in time to see it done my lad," Grouthe answered, marking him with a gap-toothed grin as he stood.

Alexander watched the dripping red soaked rag. "And how do you get it back from her, when she's finished?"

"She knows she don't sup 'less we have it." Grouthe squished the rag in a hammy fist, dribbling the floor as he took a long hooked pole from its place on the wall. The pole was pointed sharp, banded and tipped with silver, which the big man made use of to part the chains, flinging the cloth through the gap. The rag slapped against the prisoner's knee, crumpling off her leg to the floor. "Well go on dearie!" Grouthe barked. "Have your suck won't you?"

The girl growled softly but did not look up. "Blood of pigs," she said, her voice creaky and thin, as one badly in need of water.

"Aye, and lucky you are to have it!"

Alexander glanced at the bucket. "Pig's blood, with human mixed, is it not?"

"Nay my lad," Grouthe replied, his eyes on the girl. "Naught but blood of swine, on Miss Winter's order."

Alexander came to speak at him closely. "The vampire can little recover from your abuses without proper feeding. The box will be secure enough; we cannot present her to court at death's door."

With mock reverence Grouthe snatched off his hat, releasing shaggy hair. "Well my lord, slit your arm and give it her lips if you like," he said, his grin creeping back. "But there were no call to whisper, that little creature can hear your eyes move."

"Of course," Alexander said, clearing his throat. "As you were Mr. Grouthe, she's my charge now."

Mr. Grouthe chortled. "Scream if you've a problem sir, and I'll see her back in her corner, though not fast enough to save your hide I'll be bound," and with a parting smirk he waved his hat, turning to hike up the stairs.

With hands behind his back Alexander waited for the stumping footsteps to reach the top. The door closed, sending the lantern light and all its sister sparks aquiver.

"I am to watch you until dawn," Alexander said, addressing the prisoner, "but you needn't fear me; I will not torment you."

The vampiress looked up, her eyes gleaming in the reflected light. Her face was sweet and fair, though streaked with what looked to be tears of black over faded white makeup, and there was a pair of red dots painted on her cheeks.

"Have you a name?" he asked, standing just behind the chalked line.

In a blink she'd snapped to her feet, startling him back as she appeared just inside the chains. The vampiress was lithe and pretty, a head shorter than he, her eyes large and blue. "You smell very like your father," she said, "you must be Alexander, the baron's boy."

"I am hardly a boy," he said, holding his position. "Twenty-one this month."

"A man then," she said, picking at the tattered ruin of her bodice.

"I would find you a cloak, for your modesty," he said, averting his eyes from her gaze, "but I dare not, lest you employ it to escape the chains."

The vampiress did not respond, and Alexander shifted where he stood, focusing on the broken coffin behind her. "Your name, or how should I address you?"

"Afaine is my answer, and my name," she said, prodding one of the hanging iron chains with her fingertip. "Now you must answer mine: is it true I'm to be presented to the king?"

Alexander blinked at her. "It is . . . after the coffin we have commissioned is delivered, tomorrow."

"But I've nothing to wear."

His eyes flicked back to hers and away again. "I find you in better spirits than I might have expected."

"Will you come closer, and greet me properly . . ."

"I will not cross the line, lest you mesmerize me with your gaze," he said, and looking at the fitted breeches on her legs he found them split with tears as was her bodice, lacerated by the work of many blades.

"Then will you jab me with the stick perhaps? It's my favourite game."

"No I will not," he said, stepping as close to the line as he dared. "I am not like Mr. Grouthe, nor the others."

"They come to me masked," she said, standing near enough to almost touch the chains. "Even caged, even helpless as I am in daylight, they are afraid."

"*I* am not afraid of you," he said, meeting her eyes, "and I regret the tortures you have suffered at their hands."

"Shall I swaddle myself in your regrets?" she posed, poking again at the barrier. "And what of your prayers? Will you pray for me?"

"I suggest . . . I suggest you drink of the rag," he said. "It must be more to you than nothing; pig's blood is still blood."

"As sewage is still water," she said. Her expression was blank, but her eyes, even wet with misery as he found them now, were bright and beautiful.

"My father would prefer you get nothing at all," he said, pausing to swallow. "He would starve you until you are soft and pliable by night as you are by day."

"Your father lies to you," she said. "I smell his deceit; I hear it in the beat of his heart when he speaks of your friend. You will never see John Lawford again."

Alexander took a sharp breath. "My father may be harsh, even misguided in his zealotry, but he is God fearing. My friend is only banished, not murdered."

The vampiress stared at him, still as a statue. "That is the lie. Your father's crusade is only for power—he would sacrifice all . . . even his children, to achieve it."

"I do not believe you," Alexander said, sadness in his voice. "Though it stirs my pity to see the evidence of your torments. It is only to prove your existence, that you are here. How old are you, immortal creature, if I may ask?"

"They took my teeth," she said, breathing suddenly deep, "and my nails, again and again. I have bled and mended, mended and bled a hundred times over. Am I not proven to the world of men?"

"Only well enough for our friends; my father wants more, though I repent of his means. Were you of no danger to us, and it within my power to release you—"

"Eighteen I am," she interrupted, "that is my age, and it has been, since toothless King James fell ill for the last time."

"But then . . . you must be a century my elder. And who is the one who made you?"

"The Dark Lady Pazoa, queen of Saunmoor, is my maker."

"The queen in the dark? So you would claim the city of the dead for a real place?"

"Certainly, Alexander . . . it is my home."

"Then how should you explain yourself, caught sleeping at the bottom of a well?"

"I've many burrows for sleep," she said, glancing at his feet. "My secret at the inn was betrayed, but my mother will set me free . . . to the destruction of all your house."

Following her gaze to the floor Alexander retreated a half step. "No one is coming for you," he said. "Locked in this cage day and night you must fail to realize it's been two weeks and more . . . Perhaps your queen is afraid."

With a snarling hiss she slashed at the chains, and he leapt back. The vampiress shrieked in anger, a fume of bloody smoke wafting from her fingers, and quickly she retreated, clutching her hand.

Alexander's heart pounded in his chest. "Perhaps my pity is weakness," he said, catching his breath. "For of all earthbound creatures none show such violence, such cruelty as vampires."

"And what of your cruelty?" she retorted, her eyes leaking black as she cradled her fingers. "Mortal men have only such power as other mortal men deign to give you. And how do you repay it, but to build towers of wealth on the bones of your lessers."

"I am not my father."

"My kind has no such defect," she continued, speaking over him. "Our power is elemental, for we are undying—we grow stronger with each passing year, while you dry out and decay."

Alexander's eyes softened as he regarded her. "But you have no power here, beautiful creature though you are," he said. "By this time tomorrow you will have been presented at court, in the Council Chamber at St. James Palace, all glory and credit to my father."

There were clomping footsteps on the floor above, and the vampiress shrank at the noise. "You *do* pity me," she implored. "You are not like the others—let me out!"

"Forgive me," he said, his face etched with sorrow. "I have no power to aid you."

The vampiress spat at the chains, and she quailed as heavy bootsteps sounded on the stairs, accompanied by a thumping knock like a cane against the floor. "Alexander, please," she whispered, her eyes glistening black. "You cannot let them take me tomorrow . . . If I am to nevermore see the stars, let my end be here, by your own hand!"

The stairs creaked, and stumping to the bottom came the imposing figure of Mr. Grouthe, his mop of hair tied back, the hooked pole in his hand. "Lord Dramen is out, attending the duke at Spring Gardens," he said, staring at the prisoner. "Lindsor grows ever more thirsty for *you* my love! What do you say to that? Does your heart swell to think of another visit?"

"We were speaking as civilized creatures," Alexander said, noting a long silver knife tucked in the man's belt. "Your assistance is not required."

Grouthe scratched his chin. "Oh aye, but she must be taught to keep her distance; see how close she stands," and with a swift motion he jabbed the silvered pole through the chains.

The weapon's point missed, but lurching away the vampiress screeched, bumping the silver mirrored wall and crouching to the floor with a hiss, her back fuming in reflected wisps of smoke.

"That will be all, Mr. Grouthe," Alexander said sharply, catching hold of the staff.

"Go on then, give her a jab ye self," Mr. Grouthe chuckled, raising a brow as he surrendered the tool. "Righteous work my lad."

The vampiress stood slowly, and Alexander took the staff, tossing it away. "I am sick to my bowels of our *righteous work*," he said. "Before she's presented to the palace we shall let her be, let her rest."

With a hearty laugh Mr. Grouthe clapped his hands. "Let her rest is it? Nay my lad, to rest does her not a mite of good; it's man's blood she wants and the same she'll not have. The tortures of the damned await her; there were no harm starting in on it now."

"I said that will be all," Alexander warned. "Does she not look to you little more than a child?"

Grouthe's humour drained away. "And how many children ye suppose she's devoured?"

"None, you fuddering fool," Afaine snapped. "The Dark Lady forbids it."

"Does she?" Grouthe chortled. "Nay my lad, she'll say anything to court our mercy, but we'll not be tempted."

"Alexander Dramen your friend is dead," the vampiress said coldly. "Ask him."

"Not another breath from you love!" Grouthe barked, smacking the chains to startle her. "Every word earns ye another snag of the hook."

"Enough!" Alexander cut in, moving to block his view of her. "You are dismissed Mr. Grouthe."

"Dismissed am I?" Grouthe said darkly, leaning down to collect the hooked staff. "You forget where you are lad; one backward step and she'll have you in her power. When day breaks you may take her any way you like, even gently if you pity the monster, but you'll not block my way, for I've a mind to punish her cheek."

"Don't go," Afaine whispered, standing close behind him. "Ask him of your friend."

Alexander clenched his fists. "Mr. Grouthe . . . is there anything you've not told me of John Lawford?"

"Bound to be shipped to Germany as I heard it," Grouthe replied, hefting the pole.

"Bound to be shipped? Near three weeks he's been missing, is he not in Germany already?"

"What do I know of it," Grouthe said, and taking an aggressive stance near the line he drove the staff through the chains, jabbing as the vampiress snarled in alarm, slipping away from it. "Put your charms to the baron's son have ye?" Grouthe posed. "You'll learn to regret it—"

The silver pointed staff prodded and lanced at her, as shifting about she avoided it, hands raised, until a long lunge prompted her to lurch left, bumping the wall with a scream.

"That's enough!" Alexander shouted, catching the staff as he snatched the silver blade from Grouthe's belt, bringing it quickly around to his throat.

Dropping the pole with a clatter the big man spluttered. "Steady my lad! I should consider now with care . . ."

"I'll have no more lies," Alexander growled, "not from you, not from my father! Answer with truth or by the brotherhood I'll open your throat over her waiting lips."

The vampiress bared her fangs, eyes wide and curious as Mr. Grouthe answered with spittle, struggling for the words. "Ask it . . . ask what you will!"

"Has my father commanded any harm come to John Lawford?"

"Surely not!" Grouthe said, gasping as the knife drew hard against his throat. "Please my lad, better to leave off . . ."

Alexander pulled the blade tighter. "Shall the son of a baron find any reprisal for killing a low wanted wretch? No sir, I will not leave off, so if you've nothing of use to admit to me—"

"Wait!" Grouthe coughed. "John Lawford were murdered, t'is true enough! But it weren't by my hand; Ariana Winter, she's the one. Lord Dramen ordered she do him gone."

Alexander's eyes went glassy, and with gritted teeth he pulled again. "Take up the staff," he ordered, allowing Mr. Grouthe to retrieve the pole. "Now raise it up, unhook the chains.

Grouthe shouted a curse. "Mad fool would you set her free? But the floor iron is bolted down; there's no takin' it up without the proper tools!"

"You'll unhook the curtain all the same, or shall I end you?"

The knife pulled and Grouthe yelped, raising the pole to catch the links where they hung from curved bolts in the ceiling. "Dammit sir, see reason!"

But the knife began to bite, and with shaky hands he obeyed, unhooking the links along the ceiling. The web of chains sagged lower and lower, until it dropped halfway down, and wheezing with a tremble he unhooked the chains from the wall.

With a splash the iron and silver curtain collapsed to the other side. Something knocked him away and Alexander sprawled to the floor. There was a scream, and rolling to his shoulder he gaped to see the large man flat on his back, as holding him pinned the vampiress nursed at his throat with happy grunts.

Clambering to his feet Alexander brandished the knife, freezing as her head clicked to regard him, wild eyes shining like fire in the reflected torchlight.

"I'm not so weak as that," she said, her voice no longer dry, but smooth and strong.

"Have I killed us both," he breathed, a weight of terror seizing in his chest as he crouched to lift the fallen silver curtain, holding it high for a shield.

Mr. Grouthe gave a piteous whimper, and shrieking in his face the vampiress sprouted her nails, cleaving into his head.

Alexander shivered as he watched—her attack found its mark again, and again, striking her prey until drenched claws carved into the stone floor beneath, and suddenly she was very close, beaming up at him with red teeth. Her grip was warm as she seized his wrist; crushing pain compelled him to drop the knife, and there was only the silver mail shimmering between them.

"Disarm yourself," she said, her eyes melting into his, round and black.

No sooner had the silver slipped from his fingers than she crashed into his chest, taking him to the ground.

With a huff the air fled his body, and she took hold of his face, watching as he fought for breath.

"Afaine," he gasped, "I will not beg your mercy . . . do what you will."

Expressionless she regarded him, and leaning down she kissed his neck.

The pain of the bite was brief, spreading to an intimate pleasure that soothed away his fear, and with a groan he embraced her, cherishing her against him.

"Shall I die now?" he murmured, gazing into the mirrored ceiling to study her, the pale girl straddling him immodestly to nurse at his throat, and he beneath her, sprawled in shadow. "Or am I to be your slave?"

Afaine withdrew her fangs to look at him. "I'm too old to play with dolls," and her tongue tickled his neck, licking to heal the wound.

Alexander watched her reflection, his eyelids growing heavy.

Shifting to face him the vampiress wrinkled her nose with an impish smile, and sticking out her tongue she let a drop of blood fall from her mouth to his. Alexander coughed, a brutal heat surging through his body; crackling darkness engulfed his senses, and his eyes fluttered closed.

Moments later he shivered awake, finding his attacker atop him still, chin on her hands as she stared at him, rising and sinking with his breath. Her demeanour was starkly changed; no longer monstrous she seemed to him sweetly serene, her natural eyes soft and blue.

"You are not fled," he said, "and I am not murdered."

Afaine nipped at the air near his face. "You vex me Alexander Dramen. I could not reach your eyes to command, and yet you set me free. Why?"

Alexander swallowed, resting his head on the floor. "Pity perhaps, or anger. I want no further part in my father's crusade; I should rather see it crumble."

Smiling against his shirt she sniffed at the fabric. "He is very lucky tonight," she said. "Lord Dramen is not at home."

"Lord Dramen be damned," he said, meeting her eyes. "Is it true you do not hunt children?"

"You've a wonderful scent . . ."

"Will you answer?"

"It is true." Afaine tickled his chest with her nails. "Childhood is all that remains of mortal magic; it is sacred."

Fastening his arms about her Alexander knit his brows. "I do not want you to go."

"Your blood is pure and strong," she said, sliding up to face him again, "I could sponge it forever, but I will not—" and she blinked as he stopped her mouth with a kiss. For a moment her tongue found his, but quickly she sat up, pressing him down by her fingertips.

"Don't go," he entreated. "Stay."

Her lip twitched, and baring her fangs she pinched one in her fingers, snapping it off with a squeal.

Alexander stared as she pressed the bloody tooth into his hand, working her tongue in her mouth.

"Why?" he asked in horror.

With a swallow her smile returned, her teeth restored. "This one I give willingly, for you to remember me."

Holding her tightly he tried to pull her closer, but she slipped from his arms like an eel, appearing by the steps.

"You have my gratitude, you silly succulent boy," she said, and in a blink she was away. The basement door split asunder, there was a crashing clatter of glass, and she was gone.

Repairing to his feet Alexander shuffled to the base of the stairs, blinking vaguely at the savaged corpse of Mr. Grouthe, and moving to the chair he dropped heavily to sit, turning the wet pointed fang in his hand. Reflected lantern lights fluttered into the distance in all directions, coming to stillness as the air settled around him, and with a long breath he leaned back, slipping the tooth in his pocket. There were frantic footsteps overhead now, and voices calling out . . . but he paid them no heed, wiping his mouth with a kerchief as he stared at the empty corner where she had been.

Chapter 23
Performance

Begged from her peers by Mrs. Akehurst with little explanation, Emelyn was obliged to follow her hostess to a small upstairs salon: an austerely decorated room with mohair papered walls and a single round window like that of a ship. Behind a pair of spidery chairs by the hearth rested a harp of grand size, draped in baize cloth to the floor like a leaning ghost, with the only other furniture being a thick rectangular table under the window.

Emelyn watched as the lady closed the door behind them. "You mean for me to prepare a song, for the harp perhaps?" she asked.

"Yes my dear the music, but this room is much too small for such a gathering," Mrs. Akehurst said. "The harpsichord in the dining room will suffice, and as you're wanting for practice I thought you might arrange yourself here before coming down."

Emelyn smiled, checking the room again. "I'm sorry madam—harpsichord? But I do not see one, and as I believe I mentioned, I play the harp."

"The room is too small my dear, were you listening?" Mrs. Akehurst moved to the table, which to Emelyn's surprise she opened, revealing it to be a box framed set of keys, with cords and hammers behind.

"Ah," Emelyn sighed, "so it is a clavichord. I thought that was a table."

"Naturally," the lady said, guiding her to sit on a stool before the keys. "It is a very keen instrument, six octaves. You shall work something out I'm sure."

Emelyn swallowed, testing one of the notes. "Mrs. Akehurst when I said I have little to recommend me at harpsichord, I might have said *very* little. I'd not wish to offend your hospitality."

"The door is closed Miss Morley, so I shall speak candidly," the lady said, standing beside her with rigid posture. "As you know my godson has suffered a great misfortune, and he is not himself. I very much fear he means to seduce you, and you mean to encourage him."

"I beg your pardon?"

"The man is clearly over his weight in wine," Mrs. Akehurst said. "For the safety of you both I must recommend you keep apart from him."

"I understand," Emelyn said warily. "I do not perceive him a danger to me, but I thank you for the advice."

"And have you any intention to follow it? Or do you think perhaps you know my godson better than I, who all but raised him."

For reasons she could not tell the image of the captain slumped in his chair despondent with drink aroused her to anger, and Emelyn scowled at the keys. His reckless advance to the edge, and their kiss in the wind over the cliffs returned to mind . . . his hands on her back, the wine taste on his lips. "Forgive me madam," she said, standing from the stool, "you may seek a rift between us, but I will not blame the captain for his wine, certainly not if what you've told me is true. And as I am only here by his invitation, to avoid him entirely would serve no one."

"Oh, Miss Morley, but I think I see you at last," the lady said, heaving as though relieved to speak words long kept inside. "You've detected his reticence, and while he is drunk you would press your *single* advantage."

Emelyn flushed. "His reticence? Have you been so long out of courtship to forget a gentleman's prerogative? Lord Van Croft is hardly the sort of man to act out of obligation; he has pursued *me* at his own aggressive convenience."

"Innocent as the dew glistened lily, of course you are," Mrs. Akehurst said hotly. "Shall I even wonder that you call him *Jonathan*."

"I don't . . ."

"You have perhaps forgotten that he is a lord?"

"Madam I invoked . . ."

"Or perhaps *my lord* is an address you find beneath you?"

"I called him Jonathan but twice," Emelyn said louder, "to arrest him staggering over the edge of the cliff. Would you rather he were dead, so long as properly addressed?"

"Are you a witch Miss Morley, to wield life-saving power over a man by repeating his Christian name?"

Finding no polite response Emelyn shook her head.

Mrs. Akehurst cleared her throat. "Well . . . we have raised our voices," she said. "I've but one more inquiry. Have you kissed my godson?"

"I am sorry madam," Emelyn said coldly, "but I will not speak to you on this or any intimate topic."

For a moment they stared at each other. "Yes of course," Mrs. Akehurst said, composing herself. "Now, shall I inform the party that the *Belle of Brighton* will not sing, finding her penchant for music overstated? Or will you contrive something to delight us?"

"Mrs. Akehurst," Emelyn said slowly, striving for calm. "I have explained to you that I play the harp; I'm not sure what you mean to gain by humiliating me—"

"Humiliating you?" Mrs. Akehurst laughed with scorn. "Oh no Miss Morley, you are far too free of speech for any hope of it. But what of Lord Van Croft's humiliation, who only jilted my daughter because he did not know his own heart. Shall I sit by while he surrenders it to you, a desperate fair of vacant fortunes and lamentable family rumoured by riddles for generations!"

"Do you mean *riddled by rumours?*"

"Whatever I meant, while you're under our roof the least you might do is play for us, lest by your refusal you bring embarrassment not only upon yourself, but upon my godson."

The lady swished out of the room, and Emelyn stood aghast for some moments, until with a curse she dropped to sit at the clavichord, finding flight as impossible as surrender.

A half hour later she'd muddled through several pages of sickly sweet music, which after making no better use of than an untrained child, she swatted from the music rest. Any notion to play for the party, particularly while the captain looked on, was violently absurd, and covering her face she laughed with a mortified whimper, startling at a light knock behind her.

There stood the Puritan gentleman Mr. Rosch, haunting the

doorway, his buckled hat in his hands. "I do beg your pardon Miss Morley," he said, taking a single step into the room. "I'd not thought to find you alone . . . but perhaps it is fortuitous."

Emelyn stood to face him. "Hello Mr. Rosch," she said, wiping frustrated moisture from her eyes. "How may I be of assistance?"

"Ah yes, we shall come to that," he said, looking her over in his accustomed way, as though she were some sort of rare or dangerous creature. "But I am sorry to understand the lady of the house and yourself have fallen out?"

"Can it be news already?"

Mr. Rosch nodded, working his mouth as though finding the words. "But that is of course not why I am here . . . I wonder if you would care to comment, on a few questions I have pondered, concerning your home."

"Yes, I understand you've told Mrs. Akehurst I live in the most haunted place in Sussex," she said shortly.

"Ah, but that is the very matter which I should invite you to clarify."

"Hastelbrook is not haunted sir," Emelyn said. "Is that clear enough?"

Rosch stepped closer. "Thank you, Miss Morley, but I do wonder what you make of the rumour, that a Mr. Philip Denlund, who was murdered just down the hill from your property . . . was done so by vampires."

Emelyn rubbed her eye. "I make nothing at all of it."

"No, I suppose not," he said, adding a heavy sigh, "though I wonder too if you cohere with accounts of a woman in black, said to have been spotted in the village that night?"

"I'm sure I don't know," Emelyn said, imagining Vaela gliding up the stairs behind him, to snatch him away and spare her the conversation.

"Really? You do not know," he said, betraying the odd twitch of a smile, as though he'd expected more.

"I can only tell you I've grown up with stranger stories than that. But they are only stories, Mr. Rosch. Now if you will excuse me, I've precious little time to learn this instrument."

"Ah the clavichord! Well selected," he said. "I am nothing at the keys, though I do cherish the strings, particularly the melancholy timbre of the viola."

"I don't suppose you've brought one with you?" she asked.

"Indeed I have; it sits in a place of honour on the bed in my room."

"I see. And is there any chance I might impose upon you, to play for my voice tonight?"

"Ah." Mr. Rosch rotated his hat in his hands. "Forgive me, Miss Morley, but at the risk of disappointing a lady's vanity, I confess to finding country ballads rather vulgar."

"Then perhaps Purcell," she said, summoning a smile. "*Evening Hymn?*"

"For a devotional of such beauty, Miss Morley, I should be delighted," he said, rubbing his chin, "and then perhaps I might speak to you further, on what dark things I must."

"Very well; we have a bargain sir," Emelyn said. "Play for my song and we shall speak of whatever you like."

"Very good," he said, bowing with a sweep of his hat.

■ ■

"No . . . NOO!"

Alexander spasmed awake, finding himself still in the chair before the fallen chains, the lantern overhead burning low. The scream had been a woman's, and a voice he knew well . . . well enough to understand she'd cried out not in fear, but with terrible anger.

There were noises above as of splinters of wood cast aside, and the clacking of a lady's boots descended the stairs. In the mirrored wall he saw her, the darkly gowned figure of Miss Winter as she crouched to examine the mutilated form of Mr. Grouthe, her expression wide with horror.

Alexander gripped the armrests. "Miss Winter," he said, speaking to her reflection, "you're looking well. Better than he at any rate . . ."

"You impossible fool!" she shrieked. "What have you done?"

"Very little . . . though it's true enough I've been a fool, and for far too long."

Miss Winter drew the knives from her gloves, and with two steps she was behind him.

Alexander did not move, except to lift his chin as her blades surrounded his throat. "The box is delivered," she said, rasping as though short of breath. "*Where* is the creature we must put inside it?"

"She is gone," he replied, smiling up at her, "and she's left me the key to your lies . . . I know you murdered John Lawford."

"Do you?" Miss Winter twitched, a madness of rage in her eyes. "So, you have released a mass-murdering demon for *spite*?"

"Not for spite. She overpowered me with charm . . . as you have."

Smiling with tension Miss Winter blinked, and the blades slipped away, tucked once more into her gloves. "You will answer to your father, not to me," she said, vibrating with anger. "And while we wait for him . . . you will tell me what happened here."

An hour later Alexander waited by the windows in the long Spartan office of his father, his freedom checked by three surly enforcers who wore sashes of red, armed each with a pistol. With six yards of bare floor between him and his father's desk, he stood facing the glass, staring down into the wide bricked courtyard at a fountain topped by marble stallions, though he saw them not, for his mind's eye was only for her—she whose bright blue eyes belied her monstrous nature, who had taken his blood, and given him of her own, leaving him naught but the desire for more.

"Do you hear me boy?!" Standing behind the mahogany fortress of his desk, the wigless baron Lord Dramen shouted like an angry general, pounding his fist, though the words were to Alexander little more than a faraway storm—rumbles and cracks as Miss Winter raised her voice in turn.

"He is enchanted still my lord!" she exclaimed, "though I cannot say whether the vampire has enthralled him completely, or if it is only the temporary effect of her attack. His answers are enigmatical."

"It does not square," Lord Dramen puffed, red faced as he caught his breath. "The ship's chain lies bolted to that floor still; how did she cross it?"

"The vampire is not a disembodied spirit," Miss Winter answered impatiently. "Cold iron is no obstacle to her; I cannot think why you went to the trouble."

"We took every precaution!" Dramen protested, the bitterness of denial in his voice. "You assured me she would never escape!"

"She did not escape my lord, she was set loose *by your son*."

Ignoring their voices Alexander watched as a large crow lighted on one of the marble stallions outside. "Where are you now, Afaine, I wonder," he murmured.

"But is the monster not weakened?" the baron spluttered, gesturing wildly. "Might we not pursue her?"

Miss Winter cackled with a derisive laugh. "Oh dear, my lord no, one does not pursue a vampire at night. We should be grateful she spared your son at all, after tearing Grouthe's face from his very skull. By his blood she will be returned to full strength. But you needn't fear; in following my guidance yourself and the other members are made safe."

"But will she not plague us for her revenge?"

"On the contrary, after such a captivity she will be desperate to flee the confines of London, and doubtless return to some dark hole, or perhaps to *Saunmoor*, if the legends are true."

Dramen swatted the air as though to dismiss the thought. "Then we've no hope to recapture her? Do you hear that boy! Do you hear the ruin you have brought upon your house?"

"It is just as she predicted," Alexander said, still gazing out the window.

Lord Dramen spat with curses, pounding the table again. "Bring him! Bring the villain here—"

Dragged by the arms Alexander was forced to kneel before the desk, his father glowering over him.

"Betrayed by my own son, blood of my blood! You will not escape my judgment boy."

"Neither shall you escape mine, Father," Alexander said darkly, raising his head. "I see you for the power mad creature you are."

"How dare you, ungrateful spawn!" Lord Dramen frothed, trembling with ire.

"I know your lies!" Alexander shouted back. "This serpent that slithers about your ankles, I know it was she murdered my friend!"

The baron frowned, catching his breath. "Miss Winter is deadlier than any serpent my lad; she is better fit to be my son than you are!"

"John Lawford never deserved such a fate!"

"John Lawford be damned!" the baron bellowed. "What is he to the revelation of immortal monsters among us?! Wicked, selfish boy, you have stymied the greatest discovery of our age! In death your friend is forgiven, but you are not."

"Punish me how you will; I only regret that I ever took part in your crusade—condemning every man or woman who stood in your way, for heresy, for witchcraft, for vampire sympathies, and with no evidence beyond your word."

"Stuff and rot!" Lord Dramen fumed. "Carelessly you stepped too close, and the vampire bewitched you—will you not *insist* it is so?"

Alexander lowered his head, sagging in the grasp of the men at his sides. "No, Father . . . I acted of my own free will, and would do so again."

At this the baron worked his jaw, sinking down to sit. "Then truly you are lost to me . . . never has such a creature been held captive, not in the history of Britannia. And now, by your action alone she is fled—a loyal captain of the Mohocks butchered in her wake!"

"And many others to follow," Miss Winter put in. "But of course setting her loose upon the unsuspecting public should carry its own punishment, even were the mindless creature of no scientific interest."

"Mindless?" Alexander repeated. "How very little you know of her."

"The *vampire* has but animal intellect," Miss Winter said quickly, "unfettered by reason, temperance or human mercy—it presents only the *appearance* of these things, to beguile. Her mind, my dear Alexander, brims with naught but the craving for human blood. And so I do say *mindless*, for even to her immortal queen our prisoner was but a pawn, a slave of darkness to be disposed of where necessity demands."

Alexander shook his head, saying nothing.

"Harken to the last female voice you will hear for some time my lad," Dramen said, a snarl on his lips.

"This animal association is of course why no ally came to her rescue," Miss Winter continued sharply. "These dark creatures have no loyalty, no memory of such structures as family or friendship—neither can they experience joy except to satiate their ravening bloodthirst."

"And yet when I showed her that *human mercy* you speak of," Alexander said, "I tempted her gratitude, not as a mindless predator, but as a kindred being . . ."

"Blasphemer, the creature's heart is stone dead as her flesh," Dramen pronounced.

"My life was spared," Alexander shot back, "which, by Miss Winter's counsel must be impossible."

"I'll have no more of this, stand him up," Lord Dramen

commanded, summoning the footman for a brandy as the enforcers lurched Alexander to his feet.

"Shall we have the box prepared my lord?" Miss Winter asked.

The baron snatched up his drink, scowling into the glass. "Indeed. I will see him atone."

"I will not fear you, Father," Alexander said, struggling to step closer to the desk. "I would sooner be locked away than serve you again."

Lord Dramen's eyes were cold, his frown set deep. "My judgment is thus," he said, clapping down the empty glass for another, "you will be sealed within the very coffin designed to contain the creature you have released. You will find it quite comfortable I'm sure, plated on three sides with silver, and embraced in heavy chains at head chest and feet, permitting only enough air to breathe. There you will reflect on your treachery until daybreak, whereupon you shall be transported to the incurables quarter . . . of Bedlam."

Alexander swallowed. "Bedlam? So I'm to be tucked out of sight for a madman."

"Lest some connection between yourself and the vampire should linger, putting your father's house in danger," Miss Winter said, giving him a smile.

With a contemptuous sniff Lord Dramen snapped his fingers. "We are finished here! Take him down . . ."

"We might have presented a vampire to the world properly, scientifically," Alexander said, struggling as the men seized him, "but you only dissected her by torture, to serve her up for profit!"

"Show him out," Dramen said, leaning back as he sipped his brandy.

"And what does it profit us in the end?" Alexander demanded, wrestling to slow his departure. "Your investors will only want more of her, but your prize is gone—your *Vampire Act* has failed!"

"Out!" Dramen roared. "Get this spiteful creature from my sight!"

"Patience my lord, do not take him to heart," Miss Winter said, squeezing the baron's shoulder as they watched Alexander disappear through the portal at last.

Lord Dramen clenched his fists on the desk, and swatting away the glass he hissed through his teeth as it shattered by the wall. "I can still feel her milk white neck in my grasp," he lamented with a groan. "And now she is gone." He gave a hard sniff, frowning as he straightened his posture. "But perhaps the Gypsy seer—that old crone aboard the floating carcass at Gravesend. Her eye is not what it was, but she may yet be of use."

"Her *eye*, my lord, is gone," Miss winter said. "To rely on Mother Bright's derelict gift would only put us in danger."

"And what should you suggest, Miss Winter?" Dramen snapped. "Even the vampire's blood, collected at your advising, is inert—useless, as though she's stolen its potency away with her!"

"Have you tasted it? That was foolish," Miss Winter said, and watching as he slumped in defeat she sighed. "But perhaps it is fortunate."

"Fortunate?"

"Educational," she said, plucking off one of her gloves by the fingers. "In the vilest possible language the creature promised her blood would never avail us, if surrendered against her will. Perhaps without a vampire's blessing . . . its blood is inert, just as you say."

"A vampire's *blessing*," he repeated, rubbing his face with a despairing growl.

"There there my lord, the eighth deadly sin is despond," Miss Winter said, offering him her bare hand. "We must not lose hope, for there may yet come a night when thirst for your son overbears her caution, and she returns to finish him."

Begrudgingly Lord Dramen took hold of her fingers. "And if she does?"

"If she does, then the hospital must be ready, an open trap contrived to catch her once more."

Lord Dramen brought her hand to his mouth. "Then I shall leave you to design it," he said, sorting her fingers to press them each to his lips, "but let her escape be kept secret, for as long as you can."

"That may prove difficult," Miss Winter said, turning her hand for the wet of his lips to explore the other side, "but we dare not forget there is another. In the wake of this catastrophe let us return our attention to Hastelbrook in earnest, and the eldest Morley daughter, whom I believe is corrupted by the same vampire that murdered Philip Denlund."

Bending her digits Lord Dramen growled as he kissed them. "Very well," he muttered, "but I will not see mistakes of the past repeated," and with a few more suckling kisses he released her.

Miss Winter sighed again, employing a kerchief to dry her hand. "Agreed my lord—the pieces are already in motion."

"Your Mr. Rosch?"

"At Eastbourne he will interrogate our subject. By every report she is a fickle, distracted sort of girl; she will be easily broken. It is by her compelled obedience we shall capture the vampire of Hastelbrook."

"So be it," he said, "but carefully. Odd and unfortunate the Morleys may be, but their advancement by Lord Van Croft's association cannot be ignored. There must be nothing to connect your man's endeavour with the house of Dramen."

"Perish the thought, my lord," Miss Winter said, and bowing her head she curtsied low, her eyes holding his.

"I should like you to myself tonight," he said, "to ease the pain of our loss."

"You must steel yourself for solitude, my lord," Miss Winter said, swishing around the desk to take her leave. "Tonight my patron requires me. He must be apprised of these developments."

Dramen puffed his lips with impatience, staring after her. "Then I say damn him."

"Lord Crennock is your wealthiest supporter my lord," Miss Winter replied as she walked, "and mine."

"Just before you go, my dear," Dramen called, pouring another brandy, "picture if you would, the skulls of traitors posted over Temple Bar—when these are the skulls of *vampires*, and the secrets of their power ours to command . . . even kings and popes will bend the knee."

Miss Winter stopped in the doorway to look back at him, grinning broadly. "Indeed my lord, I cherish the day . . . but in the meanwhile your safety is paramount. You will cleave to my advice, keeping to these walls after sunset."

"Have you not just promised the little monster has fled the city?" he asked, grunting into his drink.

"We cannot guess the number of vampires in Britain," she said. "If one of them should be drawn by revenge to catch you in the dark, it would strip you like a rush."

Lord Dramen sneered. "Perhaps if the fruit of your concern were your company?"

"Patience my lord," she replied, holding her smile. "It will be some while yet, before we all have what we want."

Miss Winter disappeared through the door, and rubbing his temples Lord Dramen erupted with a curse, swatting his second glass from the desk. With a shattering splash the floor was marred red, and the footman rushed to attend to it.

"Leave it!" Dramen barked, scaring the servant away, and turning to the windows he looked into the dark with a frown. A light mist played against the panes, like spirits floating in the lantern light, and it began to rain.

■■

Chairs scraped as the assemblage settled in, murmuring with interest as Emelyn curtsied before the harpsichord, espying Lord Van Croft on his feet, lurking in the far doorway to the hall, looking rather weak in the eyes as he nursed his mug. Mr. Rosch stood at her side, viola under his chin and bow at the ready. The crowd murmured softly, and Emelyn stopped her breath with a smile to find Mrs. Akehurst rushing to her side, clapping as she approached.

"This is not what we agreed to my dear . . ."

"I agreed to nothing," Emelyn said, gazing happily about the room. "But I shall be singing Henry Purcell, *Evening Hymn*, while Mr. Rosch plays," and turning to Rosch, "if you'll take the music gently—legato, if you please—I'll keep the melody above it."

Mrs. Akehurst flushed, smiling as she cleared her throat. "That is a very familiar piece Miss Morley, with long and exalted notes; I can hardly recommend—"

"Thank you," Emelyn said, welcoming her to rejoin the audience.

A hush fell over the crowd, Mr. Rosch plied the first notes on his instrument and Mrs. Akehurst found her seat as Emelyn inhaled deeply, clasping her hands at her waist. Lord Van Croft met her eyes, and she began to sing. The first wordless rise of her voice resounded about the room, and those yet standing turned with rapt attention, all save her brother, whom she found watching Miss Harrington, as Miss Harrington watched the performance.

"Now that the sun hath veiled his light, And bid the world good night—"

Glasses were raised, gloved fingers pressed together in admiration, and the listeners grew utterly silent for the music.

The song continued, and at *"To the soft bed my body I dispose,"* Emelyn glanced accidently at the captain. He ambled nearer as though entranced, and amending her gaze she settled on a quizzical pair of navy gentlemen, who stood in the back with pinched expressions, either of nerves or distaste.

With a final *Hallelujah*, Emelyn let the piece drift to silence, then dipped low as the audience erupted in whistling applause.

"Again by thunder, again!" A young man cried, standing from his chair as several others joined.

Mrs. Akehurst applauded with the rest, a look of reluctant appreciation on her face, and the assembled guests stood clapping as three footmen filed in with new trays of beer and Bordeaux.

With fresh libations all around the company's expectant focus returned to Emelyn, and nodding to Mr. Rosch she lifted her chin for the encore.

Finishing high and strong for the second time, she curtsied for the ovation, thanking Mr. Rosch as several of the younger fellows rushed to regale her with praises. "I say madam!" and "Damnably fine!" the men enthused, crowding closer until Van Croft flushed them away.

Taking her hand, the captain pressed a long kiss to her knuckles. "Your voice graces us like doves falling from heaven . . ."

Puzzling at the metaphor Emelyn smiled. "Thank you my lord," she said, noting Mrs. Akehurst standing from her chair, "but I require a word with our hostess, if you'll pardon me a moment."

The men took up a raucous chorus of sea shanties, and slipping through the room Emelyn tracked her quarry to the neglected windows.

"Most ably sung," Mrs. Akehurst said, leaning to squint at the covered gap in the wall. "I should have expected rhapsodic reports of your talent to be exaggerated. I find they were not."

"Mrs. Akehurst," Emelyn said, feeling an exuberance of charity after her performance, "I regret our conversation upstairs . . . I will not begrudge a godmother's protective nature, but I heartily promise you, I had no mercenary design in coming here."

"Apologies, Miss Morley, whatever obstacle I see to his inclination, it was unbecoming to discuss with you. You could not know his history here, though his reason for inviting you was clearly to upend it."

"Well, let us hope that's not the *only* reason," Emelyn said, her good humour threatening to dissolve. "I am sorry for whatever has come between the captain and your daughter, but I have only this week learned she was in being."

"Yes of course," Mrs. Akehurst said quickly. "In my defence I have been more than a little distracted; mysteriously your arrival has coincided with a number of calamities. These are abruptly trying times for the estate."

"The wall, yes of course," Emelyn said. "And is there no word of the missing footmen?"

"No in fact, and now there are three—a young maid disappeared just this evening. And of course there is the ruin of the tower, which is sure to be talked of across the county."

"Well, I shouldn't like to be thought a bad omen," Emelyn said lightly, trying to catch her eyes. "Of course if there's anything I might do, you have but to ask."

Mrs. Akehurst cleared her throat, blotting her eye with the kerchief. "Lord Van Croft earlier requested your company to the roof walk. That, I daresay, is what you should do."

"How lovely, but not alone surely."

"You shan't be alone, Miss Morley, my godson will be with you. Good evening."

No sooner had Mrs. Akehurst nodded her goodbye than Emelyn felt the soft midnight cloak return to her shoulders.

"Come now, Miss Morley," Van Croft said, reaching around her to fasten the brooch at her neck, "you've never been to Galecliff until you've seen the captain's walk. You needn't fear—the lights have been seen to. We shall be perfectly visible from the courtyard."

Emelyn watched Mrs. Akehurst drift away with a sigh. "Why did you tell her I called out your Christian name? I only thought you in danger, I meant no disrespect—screaming *my lord* seemed absurd."

"Peace, Miss Morley," he said, speaking close as he stood behind her. "She has mistranslated . . . I told her I must never hear my Christian name again, unless it be repeated by your angel's voice."

"I see," Emelyn said, feeling a warm tickle as he adjusted the cloak about her, "so let this be a lesson to us; compliments passed through your godmother are bound to spoil."

Van Croft chuckled, short and heartily. "Agreed."

Ascending to the second floor they made their way to a narrow stair which mounted to a small landing. Here the way turned again for a steeper climb terminating in an angled door overhead, and swinging the portal outward the captain guided her up, taking her hand as Emelyn emerged onto the roof.

The small rectangular walk was enclosed with elegant iron railings, dim lanterns posted at each corner, and as her eyes adjusted Emelyn found the view arresting: a broad surrounding scape of darkened, tree peppered hills that marched to the edge of the southern cliffs, giving way to the deep vast of the sea beyond. Overhead the immeasurable dome of the sky slept in blankets of grey, and peering down the slope of the roof she espied the courtyard, alive with party lights and little moving figures.

A chill gust slipped about them, and she pulled the cloak tighter, walking to the corner. "It's beautiful," she said, inhaling the blustery salt air as Van Croft came to stand just behind her. "But we are not in fact visible from the gardens my lord, it is too high and too dark . . ."

"It is," he conceded, his nose at her ear. "But I've not brought you here for their benefit."

"And why have you brought me here?" she asked. "To trick me again?"

"I have never tricked you, Miss Morley."

"You certainly did," she contended, "when at Hastelbrook you put my family out of the room, not to propose, but to toy with me. Or have you forgotten?"

The captain pressed closer, and her ear prickled at the touch of his lips.

"Your liberties have run out, my lord," she said, turning to face him.

"Dearest Miss Morley . . . shall you repent of my kiss now, where earlier you took such pleasure?"

"A surprise of passion," she said, avoiding his eyes.

The captain nodded, feigning a retreat, and she startled as he snatched her in his arms, pressing his mouth to hers. At first she resisted, affronted at his agency, but a heated urge rose within her and she grabbed him, returning his kisses with force. Trading lusty breath they kissed and kissed again, until his hands came to her neck and she broke his grasp, backing into the corner.

"No my lord we cannot; there is no promise between us, and I've protests you must answer."

"Oh come, Miss Melinda Akehurst is your protest, a vulgar wilful girl who carves out her felicities by deception. Forget her."

"Forget her? What happened between you reflects upon us," Emelyn said. "Mrs. Akehurst will publish me for a heartless acquisitive, seeking to snatch the man she all but raised from under her nose."

"Really, Miss Morley, you must learn to discount the opinions of those smaller than yourself."

"I suppose for a man, and of rank and wealth that is easily done," Emelyn said. "But I've not your advantages—it is my reputation in the balance, not yours."

"And what of Galecliff, and the reputation of our hosts?" he asked, taking her fingers to remove her glove. "We arrive to find their hospitality in tatters; servants in open revolt, the property wall crumbling around us."

"What are you doing?"

"Hush now," he said, and discarding the glove into the wind he slipped an alarmingly extravagant ring on her finger, a band of etched white gold mounted with clustered emeralds—a ponderous diamond gleaming in its centre. "The emeralds to match your eyes."

Taken aback Emelyn blushed. "I see," she said. "But you needn't throw away my things . . . That's two gloves you've lost me."

"And many more before I'm through," he said wryly, dropping to his knee as she stared at him. "Emelyn Elizabeth Morley," he continued, breathing deep. "I must have you, in every way. Grant me your promise, and be kept always under my protection, to share with me a most fruitful life of bliss."

"Wait, please," she said, her hand sweating as he held it.

"My dear Emelyn, I have gone to great trouble and expense," he went on. "I have fought for you like a lion, overthrowing every objection against yourself and your family. Will you hesitate?"

"My lord, sir, the ring is magnificent, but if you intend to ask, could we not wait until we are away, for the sake of appearance?"

"Appearance!" the captain burst with a laugh, hopping to his feet. "You shall be created viscountess *and* baroness by our union. Is that not *appearance* enough? Or are my titles disagreeable to you?"

"No, my lord, of course," she said with a flush. "But to entertain your offer in the house of one whose daughter you've jilted, after her use of me—our hostess will spread it about as my revenge upon her; she'll paint me for a spiteful succubus."

Van Croft laughed again, shaking his head. "Your imaginings will be the death of you," he said, lifting her hand to kiss the ring. "Genevieve Akehurst has no power over us—she is a hopeless harridan who never accepted that I should choose for myself. For years have I suffered her counsel, her calls, her letters . . . By this ring, my sweetest darling, we shall silence her together."

Emelyn watched his eyes. "But I was not her enemy until you made me so. Please my lord, my family is beleaguered by gossip enough as it is."

"Are you refusing me?" he asked, his expression hardening.

"No. I don't know," she said quickly, finding the moment nothing like she'd ever imagined. "No my lord . . . I am not refusing you, but can you not wait, at least until we are gone from here?"

"Your silly sensitive heart, how I adore it," he said, pulling her close. "Kiss me, Miss Morley, and I will consider the matter . . . but let the ring stand."

Emelyn turned to absorb his kiss on her cheek, panging with conflicted desire. "The *ring* is the matter my lord; everyone will see it for what it is."

"Then select a different finger," he said, nuzzling under her ear. "One kiss Miss Morley."

Looming against her he was too much, and not enough. "One kiss," she breathed. "And after I should like to be alone, for a few moments . . . in the peaceful dark."

Without hesitation he grabbed her chin to press her lips, kissing aggressively as he pushed her into the corner. Time and again she responded, finding an unbridled desire to overbear him, or be overborne herself . . . and heaving for air she turned her head as he continued, kissing his way from her chin down her neck. His mouth brought soft heat to her flesh, and with a groan she allowed him further than she meant, looking to the deep restless clouds as he snapped off her cloak, administering his kiss upon the restricted swell of her bust—

"You must know," he said, pecking at the cleave of her bosom as he tested the defence of her bodice, "I would kill a dozen men for you . . . you have only to ask."

Closing her eyes at the fierce and forbidden sensations Emelyn creased her brows. "And what use have I for that?"

Embracing her tightly the gentleman's fingers loosened the laces at her back, and it seemed every fibre within her hummed in response, recalling the heightened sensitivity in her body the night she'd lain freezing with fever, wrestling within herself as Vaela's blood overpowered her own—increasing both her senses, and her passions. But tonight the bloodsick was long past—breathless hunger threatened her most intimate boundaries, and she gasped as his hand caught hold of her thigh. "No sir, you must stop," she entreated, chasing his hand from her skirts.

Van Croft relented, redoubling his effort against her bodice; her stays surrendered to his attack and he pulled them down, his rough hands finding her bare beneath.

His caress was wildly ticklish at first, and she twitched with a giggle, but the sensation grew quickly captivating, her flesh responding with pleasure, and she clutched hard at the railings, arching back. Shining in the glow the peak of her breast slipped its guardian fabric, and Van Croft advantaged himself, tending her with succulent kisses as she heaved against him, until his hand tested her skirts again and she protested, freeing herself from his grasp with some effort.

The captain tried to collect her, but ducking his arm she retreated along the rail. "No, thank you," she panted, "that is quite . . . that is quite enough."

With a long sigh he bowed his head, and catching her breath she looked down to find her skin glistening wet in the low light, her bodice scandalously compromised. The captain stared at her, and rounding her shoulders she turned away to study the damage.

"Have you left a mark?" she flustered, finding an irritated spot on her chest.

"Only the tiniest brand of my deepest love, that Cupid should know who you belong to."

"Really sir," she said, working to repair her modesty. "Your deepest love, already?"

"Deepest devotion then, if you prefer," he said, standing just behind her. "What is a worthy marriage after all, if not mutual barter of advantage? I have been too long out of heart Miss Morley . . . You will deliver me from despond and secure my legacy, while I preserve your family from ignoble collapse, and raise them to better society."

"How vibrantly romantic," Emelyn spoke over her shoulder, feeling not a little athirst and unsatisfied. "Now I'll thank you to tighten the laces you've ruined."

The captain obliged, and she pulled at her stays to fix the front as he laced her up the back.

"I can manage from here on my own," she said, waiting to fasten the brooch as he wrapped the cloak about her shoulders.

"Do you hear the music," he said, turning her gently to face him. "We must satisfy expectation Miss Morley, a dance or three, what say you?"

Emelyn smiled at him. "The mark of your teeth forbids me any such exercise. Go on if you please, I shall have those moments alone now."

"I might beg your forgiveness for the bite," he said, taking her hand for a parting kiss, "but my teeth have never tasted sweeter meat."

"Your *teeth* have never tasted anything, my lord," she said, watching as he returned to open the slanted door for the stairs, and disappeared within.

The door clicked closed, the soft rise of music played on the wind, and Emelyn leaned into the rail, gazing up to the churning wash of the sky. She did not blink but only stared, feeling soft and tantalized at the lingering sense of his touch. At a sudden shiver she prickled all over, and watching the cheerful hubbub in the courtyard she began to wonder of her future life, and whether Jonathan Van Croft should be the man she gave everything to . . . but then must he not have *all* her secrets, even Vaela?

Thoughts of Mr. Arkwright returned unbidden, and she closed her eyes with a blushing breath, curious to imagine if it had been he instead of the captain. But the moment passed with a sigh, and checking herself again she discovered the red mark on her bosom had faded. Testing the skin she found the irritation gone, and was just turning to descend through the door when she was arrested by the sight of what looked to be a great broad owl, or perhaps a man hunching like one, across the courtyard upon the roof of the longhouse, with round eyes burning white. The being was of impossible size, as though it must surely be closer than the distance between them, while the diminutive figures below continued their ambling in perfect lantern-lit ignorance. Looking again she found the giant shadow had vanished, leaving no trace but the rising terrified beat of her heart.

"Just behind you, little red," came a chillingly familiar voice, growling with the wet scent of death.

Broad dagger-clawed hands reached out of the darkness around her, and turning as though in a dream Emelyn beheld the monstrous man's burning eyes very close—

Chapter 24
Nightfall

Footsteps shuffled about her, alarmed voices shouted, and faintly Emelyn heard them, though she was somewhere far away, or nowhere at all. The world had vanished; her feet found no surface, her eyes no light, as though she were suspended in a deep and sensationless fluid, a vast nothingness too substantial to let her fall but too airy to touch.

In the distance ahead of her the burning eyes reappeared, beckoning like hopeful candles, and pawing at the darkness she swam to meet them, desperate for a way out . . .

"He'll never escape them," Margaret said, her voice piercing the dark.

Fresh floral scents tickled her nose, and Emelyn woke with a start, finding herself outside under a bright sun, in a wide paved courtyard between the wings of a grandly familiar house. She stood at a veranda railing supported by ornate balusters of stone, overlooking an open view of the country road running south along the Thames. In a gown of daffodil Margaret was there just beside her, but younger . . . she couldn't have been more than sixteen.

"This is a dream," Emelyn said, blinking to find herself wrapped in an elegant gown of soft silvered white.

Men and women were gathered around them, watching the road with rapt attention, and following their eyes she discovered a chase in progress. And what a chase it was: a single dark gentleman on a heavy laden black steed, high in his saddle and riding hard to flee what appeared to be two dozen mounted soldiers of the king's guard. The soldiers were thirty yards behind and closing fast.

"His stallion is flagging Emie, do you see," Margaret said, her eyes wide with excitement. "Is he a highwayman?"

"I remember this," Emelyn said, the sweet scents of a particular autumn afternoon coming back to her. She was outside Daulton House on the day of her debut, just past her seventeenth birthday, on October the 28th, 1729. And yet, this time it was different, for the gentleman pursued was one she knew—Mr. Lorris, the captain of the Lurkmen, who had come to her rescue in London, when Robert the Blade and his Mohock brigands had set upon her.

The soldiers would surely overtake him, but Mr. Lorris took no notice, and as Emelyn watched he displayed a most daring trick, snatching something from his pocket and slipping halfway round the horse's neck, slowing it for but a moment to reach its muzzle. He righted himself quickly, and the horse lapped at its nose, shivering to the withers. The soldiers were almost upon him, but as they drew pistols the fleeing steed recovered its pace, and lowering its head the beast consumed the dusty road with widening strides, bolting ahead of them like a shot from a cannon.

"What?" Margaret gaped, grabbing Emelyn's wrist. "Did you see that? How on earth did he manage it?"

"Vampire blood," Emelyn said, surprised to think of it. "He must have carried some—given it to the horse," and she watched as the soldiers buckled into confusion, their animals twisting in protest as their quarry flashed away down the road, far out of reach. "That is Mr. Lorris, who saved us, Comby and I, in St. Giles."

Margaret stared at her. "That hasn't happened yet, Emie," she said, "Now, shall we not enjoy the party as it was? Let us go inside . . ."

"I suppose," Emelyn said, her thoughts coming slowly as though befogged by some intractable force. "But then, I am dreaming, I must be."

"Certainly not," Margaret said happily, taking her hand.

Uneasiness clenched in her chest, but the environment was compelling, the scene so beautifully complete, that by the time they'd reached the doors Emelyn was doubting even her doubt. "I usually cannot see my feet in dreams," she observed. "But we have done all of this before; I know it . . ."

Margaret stopped, clenching her lips as though to shore up her patience. "Emelyn it's not a dream; we've danced each with many partners already, don't you remember? You argued with that insufferable Miss Blinnley and we came outside, and now we must make up the time we've lost; we must drink and dance all the more!"

"Yes, I suppose we must," Emelyn said, feeling her eyes go wet as she looked at her friend. "But Mags do I not owe you an apology? Did we not argue? Arkwright kissed me at Dhorings Park, and you separated us, and I was wrathful . . . but it's all slipping away."

With a bracing grasp of her shoulders Margaret kissed her cheek. "Oh Emie, what shall it matter; I'm quite sure you have my forgiveness."

No sooner had they stepped inside than a footman flashed to meet them, offering glasses of sparkling wine. Accepting the drink Emelyn marvelled at the grandeur of the space as they moved aside from the doors, posting themselves under a towering peppermint myrtle tree, which sprouting from an ornate vase grew in oddly perfect symmetry to its twin on the other side. Looking up Emelyn found the vaulted ceiling was painted with a swirling ocean fresco depicting the deadly spiral of Charybdis, complete with ships caught in its wake, and the fresco was moving.

"Doomed to sail ever closer the centre," someone said, *"down down into the drowning dark; will their fate be yours, Miss Morley?"*

Emelyn turned to look but saw no one, and Margaret clinked her glass. "I see Miss Blinnley giving you the eye," she confided with a giggle.

Lamenting to find her drink already empty Emelyn frowned, recalling an unpleasant exchange. "If Urania Blinnley calls my hair orange again," she heard herself exclaim, "I shall smack her where she spits."

"And if Mr. Montrose asks me for a second dance, I shall have nothing left to wish for," Margaret said, rising on her toes to peer about the room.

They parted company for one dance after another, and Emelyn took a second drink, meeting Maggie at their designated space by the myrtles, while outside the last light of dusk seeped away. Sipping her wine Margaret waxed cheerfully on the good fortune of their first ball. "We could not ask for better *venue*; not so deep in the country to be lost, nor near enough the city to be smothered . . ."

But Emelyn's attention was fixed on the windows, for outside there had appeared a pale woman in black, staring back at her. Standing alone at the far edge of the drive between parked carriages, the stranger's face was cold and distinct, her posture perfectly still, almost as though she were a lifelike sculpture painted for the occasion.

"What an unusual person," Emelyn said, pointing. "Look Mags, I might swear she stares at us."

Margaret interrupted herself to look, but the woman was gone. "There should be no one out there now Emie, the footmen are all inside, or in town."

Emelyn sighed, finding a young man across the room dancing his eyebrows at her. "Oh look, Mr. Bredhill wants another turn."

"He's only toasting you Em; raise your glass or he will persist."

"It's bad form to toast empty—"

"Well he shan't know you're empty from over there."

With a resigned smile Emelyn raised her spent drink, before tilting it back for the last drop, and finding no staff about to collect her glass she tucked it into the plant.

"There you are my dearest!" a radiantly gowned Mrs. Morley cried, rescuing Emelyn's glass to bestow it upon a passing tray. "The prince himself is arrived, and the ladies whisper he has come to meet *you*. Quickly now!"

Led by her elbow Emelyn obeyed, surprised at the rush. "Are we running away lest he catch us?"

"He *must* invite you to dance," her mother said, ignoring the comment, "and you will not be nervous, though he is widely known to be handsome, and wonderfully popular," she added. "The court of Prince Frederick is all the talk, exceeding that of his father in every way."

"I'm not likely to be invited to court Mama."

A great host had assembled on the floor, and guided through the crowd Emelyn blushed as her mother squeezed her to the forefront. "You are yet shorter than the other girls my dearest," Mrs. Morley said, "we must arrange you here."

"Yes Mama, all right." Emelyn looked to the top of the grandly splayed stairs to observe wigged attendants bent at the waist, flanking the doors with a bow as a young gentleman of severe expression made his entrance.

"You know every step," her mother said, squeezing her hand. "You are sure to enamour him of your beauty and proficiency, but remember *soft* laughter my dearest, and soft opinions. You mustn't belabour him."

"Belabour him?" Emelyn puzzled.

"Hush," Mrs. Morley commanded, directing her attention back to the front.

The resplendent prince regarded his audience with a good natured frown. He was handsome, if not strikingly so, with a fastidious wig long in the back and wide shouldered coats of white with gold embellishment, with a broad and decorated sash. The red faced crier at his side turned sharply to call out:

"His Royal Highness, son and heir of King George II, Frederick Prince of Wales and Great Britain, Earl of Chester, Duke of Cornwall and Rothesay, Duke of Edinburgh, Marquess of the Isle of Ely, Earl of Eltham, Protector of Hastelbrook, Viscount of Launceston, Baron of Snaudon, and of Renfrew, Lord of the Islands and Steward of Scotland and anointed Knight of the most Noble Order of the Garter."

The assemblage bowed as he descended the stairs, and Emelyn dipped in a low curtsy. "Protector of Hastelbrook?" she whispered. "Mama, did you hear that?"

"Do not look up," Mrs. Morley hissed, "he approaches."

Emelyn swallowed, studying the gleam in the rose marble floor as she waited.

"And who is this breathtaking creature coiffed in red?" The prince asked, stopping before her.

Rising with her mother Emelyn smiled, meeting his eyes.

"Your Royal Highness," Mrs. Morley said, "may I present my eldest daughter, Emelyn Elizabeth Morley, who makes her debut tonight, having just this week turned seventeen, on the twenty-fourth. We are honoured beyond words, to find Your Highness in attendance."

"The *Belle of Bright*on in being," he said. "Then the honour is mine, if she will but grace me with a dance."

He offered his arm and Emelyn took it, looking at her mother, who ushered her forward with a surreptitious gesture.

They danced the rigadoon, and Emelyn found his company easy, though when he asked first what it was to live in so notorious a house as Hastelbrook she responded by talking of music. They danced a second, more rigorous than the first, and after acquitting themselves to applause he complained of the heat, pleading a need for the air. "There must be a gross of hot candles," he said, wiping his forehead with distaste, "and one sweating body for each, just as gross."

At this Emelyn giggled, accepting his arm, and she wondered if after their walk they would dance again, and perhaps again after that.

Then perhaps if she found spirit enough to amuse him, as she did her friends, he would call upon Hastelbrook, and how bedazzled her mother should be for it . . .

Like a great cooling breath the night air greeted them, and happily she hopped from the lowest step to the pavers.

"I'm sure you've never met a prince, Miss Morley," he said, smiling as they strode from the house. "I should guess you burn with questions; you must give them air."

"Has Your Highness ever been to war?" she asked at once.

"I am twenty-three in January," he said. "Too young to have seen war of any account. Nor shall I, if this sluggish peace continues."

On they walked, and he kept her arm until they stopped by a wide fountain of stacked cherubs blowing their horns. Emelyn stared into the pool as the prince stared at her.

"But tell me, Miss Morley," he said, tickling the hair at her ear with a twirl of his finger, "what sort of creature are you precisely, beside one to ensnare a poor fellow by his eyes?"

Scratching her ear she smiled, watching the little stone figures as the water cascaded over them, darkly smearing their faces. "I confess I've imagined myself as any number of creatures, Your Highness," she said.

"Never mind," he said amusedly. "I will share with you that I've written a play, a comedy. It shall strike my critics like a wet glove."

"I do like comedies," she said.

The prince waved his hand as though dispelling the topic. "Let us speak of your home—Hastelbrook, that mysterious citadel of curiosities."

"I'm sure I don't know what you mean," she said, feeling strangely that something was different this time.

"It is satire, Miss Morley, satire. But I've a mind to dedicate it to yourself, should you condescend to accompany me to the opening."

"Of your play?"

"Of Hastelbrook, Miss Morley. There is a secret deep inside, and we must crack it open."

"We must what?" she asked, feeling a flutter of confusion.

"Now I wonder," he continued, resuming their stroll, "if you've heard it is *very* good luck for a young lady to have a kiss at her debut."

"I've only heard that from yourself sir, and just now."

With a chuckle he stopped to take her hands. "I find you inspire a careless joy in my tongue," he said, and lifting her hand he kissed her glove. "Therefore pray do not abridge yourself, but speak as we were equals. What do you want Miss Morley? Do you not want the immortal treasure that lies buried beneath your home?"

"What *treasure* Your Highness? I'm sure I don't know what you mean."

"Tell me what you want, Miss Morley," he repeated sharply, squeezing her hands.

It seemed the very air had grown hazy, and with the distant sense of recalling her own words, she obliged him as best she could, sharing that her mother carried great expectations of marriage to her advantage, "though for me, I must have more than simply to match for good sense," she said, and marking his attentive gaze she continued breathlessly, explaining how she imagined meeting a gentleman of heroic humanity, with whom she would fall into the warmest glow of love—perhaps even a prince, who would adore her family as his own, and lift her from the little arenas of her life, requiring her by his side for every manner of adventure.

A snort of laughter escaped his lips, and the prince covered his mouth.

Blushing at the interruption Emelyn cleared her throat. "Do I amuse you, Your Highness?"

"Your beauty is unequalled in my acquaintance," he said, calming himself with a sigh, "but your pedigree, Miss Morley, surely you understand, is enigmatical on the best of days."

"Enigmatical?" she repeated, her smile fading.

Prince Frederick glanced about them, pulling gently to guide her on, toward the darker side of the open drive. "I am sympathetic of course," he said, speaking low. "One does not choose one's family."

"Am I meant to find something wrong with my family?"

"Not at all; forgive me," he said, his chuckle almost musical, "but it is rather in the common knowledge that your house was built by a madman."

Emelyn scowled as they walked. "Is it?"

"Oh come Miss Morley, is Hastelbrook not properly famous for the same—complete with every rumour of ghosts and secret catacombs, and buried treasure."

"No, Highness, we should be known for the largest ballroom in Sussex, and the largest indoor gardens, with even banana trees—"

"Banana trees, yes of course. But the house is not the end of your family's strangeness—there is too the matter of your father's crippled son, a great misfortune to your society I'm sure."

Her eyes warmed with anger, and looking back at the house Emelyn felt a pressing urge to retrieve her arm and leave him, but seeming to sense her displeasure the prince held her fast.

"Wait, dear creature, do not quail at my words" he said, pausing at the edge of the light where grey pavers gave way to the shadowy garden verge. "They are but harmless repetitions of what's generally known, spoken without malice."

Unable to amend her frown Emelyn stared straight ahead. "Would you be so good as to walk me back, Your Highness."

"Nonsense," he said, cracking a grin. "Miss Morley let us not argue. You've yet to hear my offer, which I think you shall find more than apt to wash away unhappy words."

Cautiously curious she watched as he took her hands again.

The prince breathed deep, taking a pause. "Like the risen sun the radiant Miss Morley makes her debut," he said, "and like a tragic comedy, I leave for Hanover tomorrow. While I'm away word of the fire haired beauty at Daulton House will only spread, and on my return you shall have a hundred suitors."

Emelyn felt a blush. "No, I'm sure you're wrong . . ."

"One hundred, Miss Morley, and not a penny less! But it will not do you understand, it simply will not do. In fact I am prepared to lay my very heart at your feet, to prevent it."

Emelyn's hands had begun to sweat, but he held them tight. "Is this a proposal, Your Highness?" she asked.

"Indeed my dear girl, of a sort," he said, his face the picture of earnest longing. "I propose an exchange of wonders; in trade for your companionship I will create myself your truest advocate and admirer. You and your family shall rise in every estimation; under my protection scandal shall be unknown to you."

"Scandal?" There was a knot in her stomach, and Emelyn reclaimed her hands. "Forgive me sir, but I think I understand you, and that is not what I want."

"There can be no status more envied among women," he said softly, leaning close, "than to be kept by the Prince of Wales. You and yours shall want for nothing—"

"Pauper Prince Freddy," a soft woman's voice spoke behind him.

The prince turned with a start, and Emelyn gasped, finding the same darkly hooded woman she'd seen from the windows, standing not ten paces away. Coldly beautiful she was, of pale skin and sharp features, her eyes hidden in shadow, with raven hair spilling loose from the depths of her cowl.

"A curious vagabond," Prince Frederick said loudly. "I suggest you seek your own society madam, behind the inn perhaps. Or should you prefer I call up the guard?"

It was as though Emelyn had blinked and missed something, for the woman was suddenly close; tall as the prince she was, arm outstretched as she grasped his chin, her eyes wide and black. Frederick's shoulders drooped, and like a doll on a hook he stared vacantly, his gaze locked on hers.

"Little prince of disappointments," the woman said, "go back to the house; practice your desperate cravings on the silly fish you find there. Your part in her story is done."

His expression sullen, the prince bowed with a snap, taking his leave without so much as a backward glance.

At once terrified and intrigued, Emelyn swallowed. "Hello madam."

"Hello little one."

A thousand questions tangled within her, and Emelyn cleared her throat. "How do you call the prince a pauper?"

"He's wasted his living, all his lascivious luxuries turned to debt. But we mustn't speak here."

Emelyn opened her mouth to respond, but something snatched her. Daulton House and all its little lights bolted away in the dark, the wind stung her eyes, and she cried out to find herself returned to her feet some great way off, by the weathered wall of a decrepit outbuilding half reclaimed by nature.

Standing before her the woman in black lowered her hood, and Emelyn found in the pierce of her gaze an unmistakable warmth, a silent reassurance almost familiar.

For a long moment they regarded each other. "Who are you?" Emelyn asked.

"My name is Vaela," the woman said.

Emelyn blinked with a curtsy, abruptly certain the woman was not mortal as she was, but something more, something unnatural. Strangely there was no fear in the conviction, only a deep and yearning curiosity. "I suppose I'm to thank you . . . for casting a spell on the prince."

Vaela reached out, brushing Emelyn's cheek with her nails. "I am not magic," she said. "I am flesh, and blood, and yours I must taste at last. You are ready."

"Am I?" Emelyn's heart was in her mouth, but she held her ground, her skin prickling with expectancy as the vampiress embraced her. Cold lips found her neck beneath the ear, and at a sharp sting she flinched, but the pain of it washed quickly away, consumed in a deep hum of pleasure as her eyes drifted closed.

A moment later the connection was broken.

"Is that all?" Emelyn said, touching her neck to find no sign of injury. "But that was easy."

"Yes," Vaela replied, picking at the petals as she turned a white musk rose in her fingers.

Emelyn shifted where she sat, and finding sprigs of chasteberry flowers within reach she plucked one to play with. The party was far away, her mother doubtless desperate to find her, but feeling as perfectly sedate as she ever had, she cared not. "Have we met before?" she asked, tickling herself with the flower. "I cannot imagine how I know you, and yet, it were as though I always have."

"Time and again we meet, and always you forget me as a dream," Vaela said, "and so you shall, until you are strong enough to remember."

"Forgive me . . . my lady Vaela, but something is wrong. Has not all of this happened before?"

One petal remained on her rose, and with a little flourish the vampiress plucked it out, discarding the bare yellow nibs that remained. "As a little girl you once tottered down the secret stairs to the family crypt beneath your house, through the hidden door in the library shelves. Do you remember it?"

Emelyn met her eyes, finding in Vaela's gaze a great affection, though behind it there seemed to burn an eerie light, like distant torches.

The vampiress sat up straighter, taking Emelyn's flower to cast it aside. "You were alone, and became locked inside. At the bottom of those stairs you spoke to the darkness—you asked the dark its name, and how did it answer?"

"I don't remember," Emelyn said, feeling a sudden uncertainty, as though the very world around her was poised to change. "I was but four years of age . . ."

Vaela rose like a phantom, standing before her. "When you were born the seal in stone turned, but the door below did not open, and for twenty-three years it has lain silent . . . You are the Chosen Child—the vault must share its secrets only with you."

Using the shed for support Emelyn got to her feet. "The vault?" she puzzled, striving to recall events she knew well had not yet taken place. "But we never spoke of it here—"

"The key is within you," Vaela said, her face draped in shadow, her voice cold, "it must be. Dear Emelyn, you must let me in; you must teach me what lies beneath."

A nauseous warning clenched in her stomach, and Emelyn backed away from her. "This is wrong," she breathed, looking about her. "This is not what happened . . . this *is* a dream."

Deep in the hood only Vaela's eyes were visible, pinpoints burning in the dark. "Have I not been gentle with you?" she asked. "And still you resist . . . You are wasting our time little one; you must unburden yourself. Speak to me of the vault, tell me what it whispers!"

"You are not Vaela," Emelyn murmured.

The vampiress growled in a watery, sick sort of way, and the sound changed, breaking into a deep dreadful chuckle as her cloak expanded, taking on a hunched and massive shape. The hood peeled back, and the pale balding crown of the vampire Vorsadat emerged, his visage wide and ossified, cruel lips cracking in a smile under empty eyes.

Overhead the clouds surged and twisted, crackling with lightning etched blue. A vast hole opened in the heavens like the mouth of Charybdis, and breathless Emelyn staggered back, the wind lashing about her. With splintering protest the shed tore from its foundations, streaking apart into the sky. Leaves and trees followed after, rent from their roots as the landscape buckled in all directions, and too frightened to speak she turned to flee, finding the beacon of Hastelbrook ahead of her as though she'd willed it into being.

"You will let me in!" Vorsadat bellowed, his voice booming in the air. "Or wake nevermore!"

Dashing through the gardens she tore up the hill, reaching the stairs to the gazebo, where grabbing her skirts she began to climb. But with a single bound he closed the distance, and she shrieked as the massive vampire crashed through stone, toppling pillars and roof to ruin as he landed ahead of her. Turning again she retreated, but long iron-hard fingers caught the back of her head, pulling her down.

"Do you know where you are?" he asked, baring his teeth near her face. "This is not your home."

"Wake up!" Emelyn pleaded.

"Your little captain abandoned you, and upon the roof I took you," the monster continued. "I breathed my blood into your mouth . . . I am within you Miss Morley; you are mine!"

"Vaela!" Emelyn screamed, struggling as he pressed her down.

"What is Vaela but a failed suicide?" he mused, his voice growing soft. "You preserved her wretched life, but she cannot help you. For eight hundred years have I preyed upon dreams, and yours will be your prison. Now, look—"

The crushing dark gave way before her eyes, and though she felt the ground beneath her still, it was as though she were staring through the ceiling, looking down upon herself in bed, in her little room at Galecliff. Her face was pale, her eyes half open, but dead and vacant. Beside her sat Doctor Tarville, sweating with obvious fear as Lord Van Croft leaned over him. There too was Breda, hands at her mouth, and Mrs. Akehurst with her husband the Commodore, while Mr. Rosch looked on with grim fascination . . .

The terrible voice returned, disturbing the hair at her ear. "The key is within you," Vorsadat whispered. "Let me in Miss Morley . . . show me what lies beneath, or languish alone, here in the dark, forever."

Emelyn felt a whimper. "No . . . it's only a dream."

"Your last dream," the monster growled. "In the world outside you shall wither away, a senseless valetudinary fed and cleaned in her bed, until, in their mercy your family allow your decease, and the mind and memory of Emelyn Morley dissolve within me. Give me what I want!"

Like encroaching tendrils a madness of fear closed in. "I don't know how," she pleaded.

"You lie to protect it; search your mind—"

Memories of childhood flashed violently before her, and for a moment she could feel the cold stone of the crypt beneath, as though its impressions were being pulled from her thoughts by force.

And then it stopped. All sensation ceased, excepting a faint notion of something else deep inside, like a kernel of light resisting the darkness. The tendrils of fear recoiled at its presence, and with a long exhausted breath she grew still, her eyes wide and unfocused. "But this is not your dream . . . it's *mine*," she said, hot tears tickling her cheeks.

The ground began to boil, and the massive vampire yanked her to her feet like a toy, even as the liquid surface turned to a flood. "Clever child," he growled, the sharpened yellow of his grin stretching broad. "Take us where you will."

With a crash the liquid broke upon them like a wave, and Emelyn escaped him, twisting under the current. The spark of light was beneath her now, and spearing her hands through the murk she dove deep to swim for it as the monster pursued, slashing and tumbling after. Her fingers breached a rippling edge, and breaking through the ceiling she splashed to the floor, rising warm and drenched to find herself in the long gallery of Hastelbrook, with the hooded statue staring her in the face. Grasping the stone she felt at once the call of its memory . . . *home*.

With a thundering crash Vorsadat landed behind her, his hollow eyes red with hellish light as she turned to face him.

"No more games," he growled, and raising claws like daggers he lurched forward, but as Emelyn flinched the checkered marble suddenly extended beneath him, upsetting his balance as the far wall stretched into the distance, dragging him away. Atremble with hope she watched . . . and fighting against the current her enemy started back, tearing through the tiles on all fours, gaining ground.

Emelyn backed into the cowled statue, surprised to find it melting to the floor in response. Coming alive the tar-like liquid poured into the air, building ever upward to solid forms, until she was flanked—as in her dream below the cliffs—by a pair of towering hooded figures, cloaked as a midnight sky bereft of stars.

The enraged vampire bellowed, and the shock of his will rippled through the hall, cracking the walls and crashing like a wave in her mind. As a puppet on invisible strings she was compelled forward, yielding one agonizing step after another as moment by moment the ache to surrender came stronger . . . and from somewhere inside her a rebellious spark rose to meet it. With a last vital effort she arrested herself, a heavy foulness surging up from her throat, and with a wretched sound she collapsed. On hands and knees her back arched painfully, her stomach revolted, and gaping at the floor she vomited up a molten oily smoke—the ichor dragged from her mouth into the open air, twisting into nothing as her body purged it away.

Wild with rage Vorsadat gave a bestial howl, loping claws splitting marble as he bounded closer, but the infection of his power was gone, and rising to her feet Emelyn wiped her face, inhaling a mighty breath.

"GET OUT!" she screamed.

The cloaked figures bowed together, their cowls vibrating with a low harmonic tone—a sonorous union of instrument and voice to shake the very earth. In the waking world it might have deafened her, but calmly she watched as the note blasted the vampire off his feet. From its vast distance the far wall of the gallery came hurtling back. The doors opened wide to an empty oblivion, and screeching in desperate fury Vorsadat sprang forward, claws outstretched to reach her, but the portal overtook him and he flailed backward at impossible speed, fading to a speck in the immeasurable dark. The doors slammed closed, and the long gallery settled to stillness.

Turning back Emelyn found the hooded statue returned to its place, and closing her eyes she leaned gratefully against it. "Now," she whispered, addressing the stone, "I must wake up."

Monday July 4ᵗʰ

The world changed, and she began to feel herself flat on her back, sweating into the bedsheets, the sour taste of bile growing in her jaws.

"She's shaking man, do something damn you!" Van Croft shouted.

"I'm at my wit's end!" Doctor Tarville pleaded. *"I can do no more than I have. But if we turn her over and roll up her shift, perhaps a clyster of tobacco . . ."*

"I will permit no such indignity!" the captain snapped. *"Do you not see how she struggles? The fever is breaking man!"*

Emelyn gasped awake, rolling to her side, and with her mouth just clear of the bedstead she retched. An oily black foulness splashed to the floor, and twisting back she collapsed again, heaving with exhausted breath, her ribs aching, her senses raw. Slowly she blinked, finding the canopied bed surrounded by blurry figures, the young doctor leaning closest, his eyes large as saucers.

"Wipe her lips you buffoon!" Van Croft ordered, his image looming near.

The doctor obliged, dabbing Emelyn's mouth with a towel, and there came a collective exhale as the witnesses moaned with relief, murmuring amongst themselves.

"Her colour returns. Miss Morley can you hear me?" Doctor Tarville asked gently, his words blaring in her head.

"Don't yell," Emelyn said, her voice creaking as she rubbed her eyes.

"You've been in a most terrible state," the doctor said, handing the bowl of blackened water to Breda, who took it away, "all night and day we feared the worst—"

"All night and day," Emelyn repeated, trying to work it out.

"The hour is late, well after dusk. It is Monday the fourth."

The throbbing weariness in her body began to fade and Emelyn sat up, accepting a clean cloth to wipe her face. Like darkness fleeing over the threshold of a brightening room, the confounding nightmare slunk away, and looking down she found herself wearing a sheer white shift under a red robe, spattered with black about her open collar, her hair loose over her shoulder.

Doctor Tarville offered a glass of water, which she took at once, drinking deep. Beside him was Mr. Rosch, wearing a narrow one-eyed scowl as he studied her, with an unnerved Van Croft on the other side, while Mrs. Akehurst and her husband stood by the foot of the bed.

"Welcome back my dear," the Commodore said, clapping the footboard with a bracing frown. "Nothing like a good purge to set one to rights!"

Emelyn drained the glass, wiping her mouth. "What's happened? I cannot remember."

"You must have taken a fall, descending the stairs from the roof," the doctor said, raising a nervous finger. "You were found in a deep state of unconscious, with symptoms most disconcerting."

"Let us come to the point; is she contagious, Doctor?" Mrs. Akehurst asked impatiently.

"Everyone out!" Van Croft burst, startling the company, and badgering them to the door he closed it behind them with force.

Left alone with him Emelyn clutched the blanket to her chest, watching as he paced by the foot of the bed. "Who undressed me, untied my hair?" she asked. "Was it you?"

"Don't be absurd," he said, still pacing. "It was your maid—she claims that when you are unwell you prefer your hair loose."

"Yes."

"And what proof have you, that letting it down should benefit your health?"

"Is this what you want to talk about?" Emelyn asked. "But I am very tired, my lord. I feel I've just escaped . . . from a most terrible dream."

Van Croft hissed as he breathed, crossing the room again. "The doctor discovered in your effects vials of medicine—stoppered and marked by the day. Are they intended for you?"

"Has Tarville gone through my things?"

"Answer the question, Miss Morley."

Emelyn yawned with a noise. "They're potions I had of Doctor Bayten at home, which I've no need of, though my mother insisted I bring them."

Van Croft stopped to glare at her. "Have you not embarrassed me enough without this deception?"

"What deception?" she asked, surprised to find the wild beat of his heart audible across the room.

"You have fallen suddenly and alarmingly ill, and for the second time in a month, by Rosch's account."

"My medical history is none of Rosch's affair," Emelyn said, rubbing her eyes again.

"But it *is* my affair!" Van Croft snapped, pacing again. "Can you explain yourself, Miss Morley? Have you some aberration of health you would conceal from me?"

"No, my lord, I have not," she said, tying back her hair.

"Yet moments ago you lay still as a corpse, only to wake casting up bile, black as pitch!"

Emelyn leaned against the headboard, holding the neck of her robe. "My lord, if you're only here to berate me, you may continue outside, on your own."

The captain did not answer, but stood rigid with fists clenched, until with a flourish he withdrew a familiar object from his pocket. "And what is this?" he asked, presenting the bronze coin of Saunmoor.

A charge of nerves made her sit up, and she cleared her throat. "It's a struck medal isn't it. I had it of an antiquarian, in London, if you must know."

"*Per sanguinem reginae,*" Van Croft quoted, scowling at the obverse side of the coin. "*By the blood of the queen.* And this face is meant to be the queen—of what?"

"Of Saunmoor, I suppose," she said, striving to appear unbothered. "I'll have it back, if you please."

"And the reverse," he continued, "*In oculo umbremaris.* Is this to say *In the eye of Umbremar?* Can you explain it, Miss Morley?"

Emelyn swallowed, hoping banal honesty would disarm him. "Do you know the legend of Saunmoor, sir? Umbremar is the vampire queen's castle, if you believe the folklore."

"The *vampire queen* of Saunmoor?" His face was unreadable, but tense, and she suddenly feared he meant to keep it.

"Mr. Gapplethorpe sells all manner of odd and curious things," she said. "There's nothing to it, my lord. Now, please, may I have it back."

"Then why should you bring it here?"

Emelyn shook her head, holding out her hand. "Shall I keep you abreast—a man I've known not a month—on my every caprice?"

"We are to be married!"

"Are we?" she said sharply. "I'll have my coin sir, please."

Van Croft frowned with effected boredom, tossing it back to her. "You do well to make no mention of such a thing, around Rosch."

"Yes, of course," she replied, nerves cooling as she slipped the coin under her pillow.

Van Croft wiped his hand on his coat, as though glad to be rid of it. "I would speak of your brother," he said.

"Very well?"

"Bodie finds himself confounded by the riddle of his legs, and though I'd yet hoped the salt air would do your brother good—I'm told you have stopped his medicine."

"*That* medicine smelled of poison," Emelyn said, "and what can you mean *the riddle of his legs?* There is no riddle, my lord. Deacon broke his knees in a fall. He's been in such a way since I was an infant."

Van Croft fussed with his cuff. "Bodie tells me there is evidence of scars, in the ulcering around his knees—past infections that should have been fatal long ago, but rather healed, each in their turn. Rosch is keen to suspect the unnatural—even the unholy. Can you speak to what treatment has preserved your brother's life?"

"I've no idea sir. This would be the first I've heard such a thing."

The captain raised his chin. "Would it indeed?"

"Yes, my lord. Or do you mean to suspect me of something?"

"Miss Morley, if I am to take you fully under my concern, your comportment must live above reproach!" he said hotly. "You must shun the very appearance of blasphemy, intemperance or immodesty. I cannot elevate your society if you forget yourself, do you understand?"

Bitterly stung Emelyn twisted the ring off her finger. "I believe I understand perfectly," she said, tossing it on the blanket. "You are determined to belittle and mistrust me—it is plain that I never should have come here."

Startled at her action, Van Croft knelt by the bed, seizing her wrist. "Don't be a fool," he said, kissing her hand.

"No thank you, my lord—I'd like you out of my room," she said, retrieving her hand only for him to seize it again.

The captain pressed his forehead to her knuckles, hiding his face. "No dammit . . . forgive me," he said, a tremble of fear in his voice.

Emelyn puzzled at him. "I'll not be lambasted for falling ill, nor for *bewitching* my brother, or whatever you think I've done," she said. "Now if you please, I should like to change out of this mess. Goodbye, my lord."

Van Croft shook his head, keeping her hand. "No. Hang the others, put them from your mind. All I ask—you must swear to me that you are not ill, that you do not suffer from that which lies beyond my protection."

Struck to see him so unnerved she turned her hand in his grasp, touching his face. "You needn't fear for me," she said. "I'm feeling very well recovered. If there were any more I could tell you, I would."

The captain shook his head. "My concerns are . . . inarticulate," he grumbled, standing to collect himself with a sniff. "I will accept your word that you are well, in which case we must look to the future, lest you forget I have proposed, and you have accepted."

"Well, no, my lord, you pushed a ring on my finger and congratulated yourself. Have we not settled to revisit the matter at some other place and time, away from here?"

"You're not a child, Miss Morley," he said, plucking the ring from the bed. "In wearing an engagement ring a lady understands herself to be engaged."

"I was attacked! I had meant to take it off—"

"Attacked?"

A stab of memory made her gasp, and for the briefest moment

she recalled a horrible face, as different from the captain's as the cratered moon: a monstrous presence leering over her, long fingers in her mouth as cold blood found her tongue, but quickly as it came the memory faded. "I wasn't—no, I was! Ah, it's nothing," she stammered. "I meant if I hadn't fallen on the stairs."

"You are yet hysterical," he lamented. "I will recall the doctor. We needn't celebrate tonight."

"We needn't celebrate at all, my lord; you've given me much to think about," and with a huff she slipped from the far side of the bed to stand by the wall, crossing her arms. "Goodnight."

"Is this the gratitude I am to expect?" he asked, rounding the bed to confront her. "Am I to be left foundering in purgatory, without your consent?"

"My lord, if you please!" Emelyn said sharply. "I am exhausted."

The captain reached for her hands, which she refused, swatting as he tried again, until with a lunge he caught her about the waist, turning to heave her onto the bed.

"Stop!" she shouted, bouncing away from him to curl up against the headboard. "Please go."

"I will not," he said, breathing hard. "Not until I've completed my suit . . ."

Emelyn buried her face in her knees. "Then I will disappoint you. I mean to take a bath, and forget where I am."

The bed moved with his weight and she blinked to find him arranging himself against the headboard beside her.

"What are you doing?" she marvelled. "Shall I flee my own room to escape you?"

The captain folded his hands in his lap. "You must do as you like."

The clock ticked as they sat, and she stared at the wall, pretending herself alone.

"You ask me not to fear," he said after some while, his eyes gleaming in the candlelight, "but I've lost two ships and eight dozen men, Miss Morley, by some *impossible* tragedy. The admiralty will demand an inquest; it may be that I stand to lose my commission."

"I am sorry for your ships," she said stiffly.

He closed his eyes. "I cannot lose you as well. It sickens me, that I left you alone—that I could not protect you from this curse . . . from whatever it was befell you."

Emelyn sat quietly, searching for an answer, but a sound of footsteps approached in the hall, and she looked to the door as the latch turned. Mrs. Akehurst's sharp eyes peered inside, and snatching it from its base Van Croft hurled the bedside candle, startling the lady to retreat as it shattered against the slamming door.

Surprised at the violence Emelyn squelched an inconvenient urge to laugh. "They might have excused us!" she exclaimed, "me for a sick patient and you for taking care, but not now she's seen us both on the bed—it's indecent my lord, you must leave!"

Van Croft made an impatient noise. "You might have quit the bed yourself, yet you're still here."

"It's my bed!"

"Your bed is six hours by coach."

Emelyn groaned, rubbing her face. "You understand she's seen the ring, and who do you think she'll blame? Not you sir, the man she loves like a son. Whatever spark of credit remained to me is gone, especially now."

"I don't want your credit, Miss Morley, I want you," he said.

"And sure as my hair is red she will write to everyone she knows," Emelyn added, "including my mother, to disparage me."

Van Croft cleared his throat, his hand drifting back to hers. "No, dearest Emelyn, I will not see you disparaged. Grant yourself to me, and I will drive the wolves before us. I am worthy of you, surely you see that."

"Do I?"

He started to speak, and stopped.

Emelyn joined him in silence, letting her eyes drift closed.

"I have never found myself in such a state," he said softly. "I lash out, when it is you in all the world, whom I would be tender with . . . If you find me anathema to your well-being, truly, I will take my leave."

"Anathema to my well-being?" Emelyn repeated, glancing at him sidelong. "Well, you're here now. I suppose the damage is done."

Van Croft chuckled, evidently encouraged. "My only charge then, Miss Morley, is that if there be any truth to Tarville's concerns, or Rosch's superstitions—anything they might fasten to, let me not be caught unaware, but confess here and now, that I might protect you."

"And what do you think I have to confess?" she asked, imagining for a fleeting moment the absurdity of sharing Vaela, "that I'm secretly ill, or a witch, or a madwoman? But I am none of these, my lord."

"Then allow me to ease your burden, to deliver your family from their ignominy," he said, turning fully to face her, taking her hand.

Her vision softened, and it were as though the portal to parts unknown he might be to her, was now illumined by a raw and weary hope: to redeem at last her family's fortunes, to insulate her life from the Roschs and Akehursts of the world . . . and perhaps to find some joy in it herself, perhaps even mutual affection, after all.

"Accept my offer Miss Morley."

Emelyn met his gaze.

"Marry me," he said.

"You're a brute," she replied, her hand tingling in his grasp.

"But shall I be *your* brute?"

Tears prickled her eyes, and she chuckled softly, looking at their hands.

"Do not doubt you have the power to preserve us both," he said, adjusting himself to properly kneel. "Let every whisper against us— against you and yours, be undone. Let every fear for the future of Hastelbrook die in this room."

Emelyn wiped her eye. "Very well," she said, allowing him to slide the ring back on her finger, "I will marry you, though I cannot promise it will conduce to our happiness."

"Then let happiness be what we make of it." He grinned, and taking her under the arms pulled her close, kissing her jaw as she turned her head.

"No, sir." She grimaced. "There's foulness on my smock have you forgotten? I smell of death."

"You smell of blood," he corrected. "I couldn't give a damn," and turning her chin he kissed her.

Emelyn accepted the salute of his lips, and for some moments there was naught but the sound of their kisses, until recalling their conjunction on the roof she began to sweat, rousing a familiar thirst. "No, I am not dressed!" she protested, pulling away as she crossed her arms for modesty.

The captain chewed his lip, watching as she backed into the headboard. "It's not yet eleven," he said, "there is time for dancing yet, if you're well enough."

"I cannot say; I will come down when I am ready. Now please let me be."

Van Croft winked at her, a charged gleam in his eye as he dismounted the bed. "Then I go before you, Miss Morley, to muzzle the wolves," and with a sharp bow he took his leave, shutting the door behind him.

Sitting on the edge of the bed Emelyn stared for some while at the ring, half smiling.

The familiar and fortifying sense of Vaela drew suddenly close, and she shivered with a gasp, turning to the windows. The windy current of night blew gently across the panes. "Vaela," she said, twisting the ring on her finger, "the Bloodhound of His Majesty's Navy is in love with me. I wonder what the world will say to that," and falling backward she pointed her firsts for a long stretch, clenching her eyes. "Breda!"

A recuperative regimen was organized at once, and with a saucer of gingerbread figurines on the stool beside her she was soon undressed and luxuriating in the foam of a hot bath, while the copper bathing stove in the corner puffed fragrant steam, promising reinforcements should the water begin to cool.

With a happy groan Emelyn settled back. "Yes, Lord Van Croft has asked," she said, amused at Breda's obvious impatience for the answer, "and I have accepted him. So it would appear my search is over," and with a vague smile she selected a cookie.

■ ■

Standing on the peaked roof of the longhouse, Vaela lowered her crimson hood to survey the deep troubled sky. Below her the dwindling post lights of the garden courtyard were being relit—determined footmen striving with their torches against a rising wind off the sea. The windows of the Nordic house of Galecliff shone with active candles, and searching them over she found the square panes of an upstairs room befogged by the steam of hot bathwater. Inhaling deeply the vampiress smelled Emelyn's hair, slick with washing, the wet on her skin, lavender oil in the soapsuds—

"The clouds are strange," a male voice spoke from the air, and Vaela turned to find a gathering darkness taking humanoid shape, until the vampire Morion, eldest sired by the queen, stood beside her, in black cloak and great coat, high collared to his chin, his ebon hair to one side.

"Morion," Vaela said. "Something has happened—Vorsadat was here, and is fled; he set upon her, I am sure of it. And yet she is safe—she is in the bath, eating gingerbread. I cannot account for it."

"Pazoa felt the echo of his aggression," Morion said. "What precisely has he done?"

With a soft snarl Vaela bared her fangs. "He infected her, or so he made claim. By the power of his blood he must have invaded her mind, her dreams. Surely our queen will censure him now?"

"It would take all her strength of will, to call him home. This she will not do, unless his betrayal is proved beyond doubt."

Vaela pulled the black ring off its chain. "Then it is time she call all allies to her. By this ring she is meant to understand the sincerity of Tredavius. He asks only for an audience."

Morion accepted the ring, turning it in his hand as he scowled at the house. "Gingerbread," he grunted. "How could she have repelled the monster's attack?"

"She is the Chosen Child," Vaela said, marking the sweet bakery scent wafting from the house. "Perhaps the vault itself has protected her, where I could not. But it is not finished . . ."

"How?"

"By the bond of our blood, I feel the monster is not gone from her—not entirely. Not yet."

"Then you must watch her all the closer," Morion said, staring at the house. "We cannot tell when the door to the vault will reveal its secret, nor dare we guess . . . how much time the queen has left, before her will falters."

"If anyone might shore her up, it is Tredavius," she said. "She must permit his return."

"Though he keeps the bloodstone jewel from her?"

"That is for her protection. Emelyn must enter the vault—the queen cannot, not until the prophecy is understood to its completion. But I fear for her . . . I fear Vorsadat will return."

"He dare not," Morion said. "I will not be far—he will not risk confronting me, now that his game is up."

"I would take heart to hear your mother the queen means to punish him," Vaela said.

"I cannot promise," he said, turning the ring in his fingers, "but you will take heart in this: our little acrobat has escaped her human captors."

Vaela's eyes flashed as she looked at him. "Afaine has escaped?"

"She has, Pazoa has felt it."

The bathing room window glimmered, and the vampiress closed her eyes with relief, listening as the maid filled a bowl to rinse Emelyn's hair.

"As for Vorsadat," Morion continued, "I will see that your charge is made safe, until he repents of his rebellion. But you must make no mention of my presence here."

"And what of Lord Simeon and myself?" Vaela asked. "Will the queen dither between friends while her brother's treachery threatens us all?"

"My mother is in pain," Morion answered. "You shall wait upon her when you are called, not before," and with a sigh of breath the vampire lord's body twisted into vapor, slashing away on the wind.

■■■

"But you really are feeling better miss?" Breda troubled, sitting behind the tub as she rinsed Emelyn's hair in a basin.

"Yes, I believe I am. I am feeling . . . I feel strong," Emelyn said, speaking to the ceiling.

"Well I'm that happy miss," Breda said, squeezing the water out of her hair. "It frightened me to see you in such a state."

Emelyn stared into nothing, unable to recall more than shadows, though there seemed here and again a slight chill beneath her skin—easy enough to excuse in a bath. There was nothing for it now but to relax, and so she enjoyed the twisting tussles against her scalp, reaching to select another of the gingerbread figures. "Look, a lovely hackney coach," she said, holding up the treat.

"Yes miss," Breda said, unfolding several linen towels.

"But did I say anything, while I was unconscious?"

"Perhaps, once or twice, but it were hard to make out the words."

Taking a bite from the little wheel Emelyn chewed slowly, savouring the buttery spice of it. "I'm certain I had the most terrible dream, as I have every night for some time now . . . yet I'm just as certain it's over. The dreams are gone, at least."

"I'm glad to hear it miss, with everyone so concerned as they were."

Emelyn nodded, chewing thickly. "And I suppose after the captain put them all out of my room, you must have heard them talking."

"I heard not a thing miss," Breda said, wrapping the linen about her hair to tie it.

"Well, I wish I knew what they were saying now," Emelyn said, taking another bite, and she froze at half a chew, recalling the sound of Mrs. Akehurst's voice through the floor, and how she had directed her sense to hear it. Vaela was as good as her word, for what could it have been, but the power in her blood.

Breda took no notice, shifting to employ a little brush on her mistress's nails.

Swallowing the morsel Emelyn steadied her breath, striving to listen to the house.

The bathwater trickled and brinked, the nail brush swept noisily, and she pushed her awareness downward, managing after some effort to drive it through the floor beneath them.

"*. . . and when the candles are changed,*" a woman said, "*the mistress is most particular on this point, every new wick shall be blackened; let them burn to the count of twenty, that they appear used. Poor Henrietta never forgot a candle, before she disappeared—*"

Having pushed her senses too far below stairs, Emelyn refocused, and curious to hear from the second night of party, she swam her awareness into the crowded dining room, where almost at once she caught the unmistakable lamentations of Mrs. Akehurst—

"*. . . such a reckless passion; he needn't have reacted so! Of course I should be as happy for their union as anyone, indiscretions notwithstanding! But her mother had three daughters to only one sickly boy; is Jonathan not aware she will bear him naught but a bevy of fire haired girls?*"

"*There my dear, you take it too hard,*" the Commodore said. "*Who the captain settles upon is not ours to advise; we should wish Miss Morley a swift recovery.*"

"I should guess your response to Mr. Arkwright has reached him miss," Breda said, making conversation.

"Yes, perhaps it has," Emelyn said, stinging at the reminder of her letter, which she rather feared he must find cold and callous. But the world had changed; she was engaged now . . . And of course in forgetting the pleasure of Mr. Arkwright's company, with his rich and ready laugh, she must forget too his deep hazel eyes, and the intoxicating scent of him, which she'd committed to her journal.

The voices below came in waves, offering ample distraction.

"She must know something old fellow," a young man declared, *"t'was her house after all, that Abbott meant to ransack. Should the Bell of Brighton be party to his undoing?"*

Emelyn sat up, startling her maid.

"Emelyn Morley, the Belle of Brighton? Succubus of Sussex more like," some other gentleman declared. *"I'll wager Van Croft never stood a chance."*

"Yet tonight the captain's prize avoids the party," a younger put in. *"But I declare there's no finer pair of baby's rations in the county—"*

"Baby's rations?" Emelyn blurted.

"Miss?" Breda blushed, staring at her.

"Nothing; it was earlier . . . I thought I overheard," Emelyn said quickly. "Is that how navy men speak to each other?"

"Aye miss, but they should remember themselves in company."

Curious of the name *Abbott,* and how it should be connected to kidnap, Emelyn redoubled her focus to listen, finding at first the gravelly tones of Mr. Rosch . . .

"A lifetime sir," he said, speaking low as though in confidence. *"Before our acquaintance, before the navy, I had made the study of Hastelbrook history my chief concern; the woods thereabout have been haunted for a century, if the old tales are to be believed."*

"Old tales are, by their very nature, not to be believed," Van Croft answered.

"But you must see these disasters bear a terrible weight of coincidence," Rosch argued, *"to whit, I've had an illuminating letter from a colleague of the hunt, confirming that bestial murder not a quarter mile from your lady's home."*

"I am quite refreshed," Emelyn declared, interrupting the voices. "Help me up, before I've pickled myself."

Wrapped in warm linens she ran on tiptoes to her quarters, where she was reassembled in a low toned gown of green to match her eyes, hair coiled back beneath a hanging scarf, and quite devoid of patience for Mrs. Akehurst's passive aggressions she peeled off her gloves, opting to boldly present the captain's ring, which sparkled emerald and white in the mirror.

"No gloves miss?"

"No gloves Breda, not tonight. The party is small enough, and I daresay Van Croft will support the choice."

"Congratulations again miss, it's a beautiful diamond," Breda noted, presenting her a narrow ribboned box.

"Yes it is," Emelyn said, and after staring at the reflected ring for a moment she opened the box to find a gilt fan of pastoral green.

Gliding downstairs the urge to test her powers returned, and halfway to the lower floor she paused to listen, tunnelling her auditory sense through the wall and into the crowd, seeking the objectionable voices from earlier . . .

"Note you the tawny woman by the mantel? But who can she be, to smile on Deacon Morley so."

"Perhaps she's an actress," the younger voice snickered. *"Pretty I might judge, for a mulatta."*

"No one else will have him," the first man said. *"Mark the poor sod, sagging into his sticks like a gouty sailor; I should say he's scarcely half a man."*

"Miss Morley's half brother then," the youth quipped, and they laughed together.

Abashed to hear them Emelyn finished her descent, finding a familiar white gloved footman in copper livery at the bottom of the stairs, the heavy jowled Fenders.

"Beggin' your pardon miss," he said, "Lord Van Croft is about the grounds with Doctor Tarville, and bids you wait here to attend him."

Emelyn smiled. "Well, you must tell him you did your best," and passing him by she turned to make her way to the party, nearly colliding with Mr. Rosch as he appeared from a narrow side hall.

"Ah, Miss Morley, but I am heartily astonished to see you so much improved!"

"Mr. Rosch," she greeted with a nod. "Hello. Excuse me."

"But you are scarcely risen from bed," he said, stepping in her path, "and the music frightfully lively; you dare not imagine the unchaste gyrations of dancing."

Emelyn pursed her lips. "Is that your opinion of dancing, Mr. Rosch? But perhaps you yearn for the days of the Commonwealth."

For a moment his face seemed to register a deep disgust. "I daresay in sober hearts the pursuit of virtue must be alive today as it was then."

"Yes of course," she said, "but this being the *eighteenth* century we do rather enjoy music, and dancing, and even Christmas, sir. Now if you will excuse me."

"Carry on, Miss Morley, we will meet again soon," he said, and with the hint of a nod she swept around him, passing through the dining room doors.

Once inside she found the space awash in the orange candle glow of a hundred lights merrily bestrewn about the walls, chairs cleared away as harpsichord and violins guided many naval gentlemen and their partners on the floor. Deacon leaned on his crutches by the rustic fireplace at the west end, looking tired but content, with the same cheerful Miss Harrington at his side.

Searching over the assembly Emelyn found the men she'd overheard at the far side of the room by the windows. Though they were a pair to whom she'd been introduced, she'd forgotten their names almost at once, and peering over the edge of her fan she found them murmuring at each other, staring at her brother with contempt.

"What has four legs and no fortune," the shorter one snickered. He was a youth of perhaps eighteen, stocky of build with narrow eyes under bulbous hair.

"Deacon Morley, if the rumours are true," the other responded, a taller nasal sort of fellow wigged in silver. *"But look now, there she is. We must put it to her, but carefully."*

"Oh dear," the younger said. *"Is it the pretty dumpling shop at last?"*

Emelyn was on her way, cutting between the dancers to reach them.

"Dumpling shop?" Emelyn repeated, lowering her fan as she drew near. "Well, I do not say *gentlemen,* as I see no evidence of such, but it would seem you are insensible to how loudly you are speaking."

"My dear, the lovely Miss Morley," the elder man stammered with a bow. "Harry Deckland, I'm sure you remember. But I fear you may have misheard; we've not had the pleasure of a proper conversation . . ."

"Oh there's no pleasure to be had there," she replied. "Now I could not help but hear you speaking of someone named Abbott. Am I correct? But I was attacked by a person of just that name, in London, some two odd weeks ago."

The men swallowed together.

"Well?" Emelyn stared at them, blinking politely.

"It is, well, you see, Miss Morley," Mr. Deckland said with a flush.

"What do I see?"

"Lord Abbott has gone missing, Miss Morley," the younger man said. "As to the attack, but I suppose you mean to accuse his son, Robert."

"No, sir," she said. "There is no point accusing now—it is a name I had quite forgot until you shouted it. I do not ask that you desist, but if you must continue these unfortunate ejaculations, I would request you do so in smaller voices," and bobbing with a smile she turned to leave the way she came, pausing by a dessert table to hear the epilogue.

"Good Lord Freddy," Mr. Deckland exclaimed. *"We'll learn nothing of Abbott's fate now. She's shot our chances at a stroke."*

"But how could she have heard? You don't suppose she'll tell the captain . . ."

"We must pray she does not. And you might have warned me my voice carried so, you know I've been sick."

Emelyn touched her lips with a laugh, watching as the ashen gentlemen sifted through the crowd to scurry outside. Pleased with her victory she took a glass of Rhenish wine, letting her fan hang by a loop on her wrist, and she was just considering another gingerbread when the lady of the house appeared at her side.

"Here she is, blessedly returned to us!" Mrs. Akehurst cheered. "But to see a young lady so taken with sickness, and then to recover so abruptly, it does beggar belief."

Perusing the choices Emelyn smiled, revelling in the newfound mastery of her auditory sense. "Well I may *appear* to you recovered, but I'm left with a most unnatural craving for gingerbread."

"Well, I'm glad to see you make light of it." Mrs. Akehurst performed a chuckle. "But do you know, Miss Morley, before the arrival of the captain's scholarly friend Rosch, I'd never have given the unholy practice of *witchcraft* a moment's pause, and yet after so many mysteries, your illness among them—"

"Yes madam! As you say, to get the better of the malady so quickly," Emelyn said, narrowing her choice to one of three favourites, "if *unholy witchcraft* were involved, it must either have been a very good witch, or a very bad one."

"A God fearing person might hesitate to mock so dark a subject," Mrs. Akehurst said, her pulse notably elevated.

"A lesson you've had from Mr. Rosch, I suppose," Emelyn said, examining a delightfully carved gingerbread smithy, complete with little anvil and bellows, "though—I believe it was in the broadsheets some months ago—to accuse a body of witchcraft is illegal, per the Witchcraft Act, if I'm not mistaken."

The lady smiled with some effort. "Oh I'd never call a redhead young woman a witch, Miss Morley, though I might marvel at your sorcerous power over my godson. No sooner does he bestow you the ring, but he's hurling furniture at me like a demon."

Emelyn sucked in her lips, measuring her response. "The captain is a man of his own mind; perhaps your efforts to put him off only excited his passion."

The lady puffed with a noise. "And what of your passion? Shall I blame myself Miss Morley, that whilst a guest in my home you allow him to prepossess you so completely? Did it never occur to you to withhold your answer?"

"I did try madam, but he would not be deterred," Emelyn said, settling on a cheerfully carven biscuit of a girl on a swing, kicking her feet.

"And to wear the ring so *openly*," Mrs. Akehurst fussed. "If I were your mother I might call it brazen."

"If *you* were my mother I think I'd have your blessing," Emelyn said, unable to resist.

"Jonathan Van Croft and our Melinda had been intended since she was a girl!" the lady hissed, standing very close. "Oh but you *did try* to dissuade him, yes of course you *did try*."

After a slow sip of her wine Emelyn set it on the table. "Mrs. Akehurst, if you've anything *new* to accuse me of, I'm on tenterhooks to hear it."

Trembling with ire the lady selected a coiled dragon from among the gingerbread. "Well . . . if I *were* a woman of superstition, I quail to think how I should even comport myself in your presence."

And have you comported yourself? Emelyn thought to ask, but marvelling at her opponent's rapid heartbeat, she swallowed the words. "Mrs. Akehurst," she said, "am I really so objectionable? What on earth has Mr. Rosch said to you?"

"It is not your person, but your arrival, Miss Morley, to which I object. You stand a living omen among us, heralding disaster at every turn!"

"To what *disaster* can you be referring?" Emelyn asked, her own pulse rising. "But you cannot think to blame me for the missing staff, nor *my own* illness, nor the broken wall. But does Mr. Rosch suggest I've some connection to these things?"

"Lower your voice! I will not be disrespected in my own house," Mrs. Akehurst chided, smiling as several others took notice.

Withering sarcasm fought for release, but Emelyn resisted, biting off the swinging girl's feet with a snap.

"There, let us have peace," Mrs. Akehurst said, summoning her composure. "Now, Jonathan speaks to me of taking you to Paris, has he mentioned it?"

"He has not."

Mrs. Akehurst looked her over, pursing with disdain. "I understand you are not well travelled, so it may interest you to know that in *France* red hair and green eyes are no mark of beauty, but considered quite regrettable."

Emelyn took another bite, taking the kneecaps, and covering her mouth to chew she lamented a few crumbs down her bodice. "Perhaps then Parisians will know to flee before my powers," she said thickly.

"How I *do* pity your dear mother," Mrs. Akehurst said, smiling with teeth, "to be lumbered with a daughter of such nimble impertinence."

Emelyn swallowed, and sipped her wine again. "I'm sure she pities herself for the same reason."

"How proud you must be, of taking your high little road," Mrs. Akehurst said. "You imagine the captain obliged to deliver every joy you deserve, but I warn you, Miss Morley—"

"Madam," Emelyn interrupted, "I am all out of humour. If we continue you shall find me an unequal partner."

Mrs. Akehurst's smile turned sour. "Very well, as we cannot speak without acerbity, I suppose there's nothing left but to wait for the captain to bridle you," and snapping the gingerbread dragon in twain she turned to leave. "Good evening, Miss Morley."

Red faced Emelyn discovered everyone nearby pretending not to have heard, and leaving her plate she set out for the only oasis in the room, finding her brother with his companion still by the broad mantel.

"Congratulations, Miss Morley!" Miss Harrington enthused, gawking at the ring upon her approach.

"Yes well done," Deacon said stiffly. "A great victory for the Morley legacy. Perhaps we'll keep the house and all."

Emelyn smiled with effort, and she was about to request his

solitary company when an unaccountable chill shivered through her, and she was obliged to catch her breath.

"It occurs to me, Miss Morley," Miss Harrington said, "that you can know so little about me; how you must wonder," and she proceeded to expound on her life in Eastbourne, on her mother's decease, the brother she cherished, who clerked for a magistrate in Tenfield, and her father's affairs of ship building. "Papa is always about, on props incident to his lameness, but they are no obstacle to him . . . It is through my father that I know the Commodore, who is like an uncle to me, and then your brother and I discovered a great love of stories in common, especially the political."

"Pope, Swift, Dryden, and she knows of old Isaac Bickerstaff would you believe it?" Deacon put in.

"We've every issue of *The Tatler* at home," Miss Harrington said cheerfully, "it's ever so diverting, to suppose which gossip was real and which invented."

"She read Moll Flanders as a girl," Deacon added, "just as you did, Emie."

"Yes, and I was sentenced to eating alone for a week," Emelyn said, dredging up the memory.

"But that is too harsh!" Miss Harrington exclaimed. "Is it so saucy a novel as that?"

"It is, and I was nine," Emelyn said vaguely, staring into the mirror over the mantel, which leaning from the wall lent a rising angle to the reflected crowd. The chill returned, and she'd a sudden flickering vision of dancing in a darkly grand ballroom, the tallest she'd ever imagined, with walls draped in black and mirrors running the length of the ceiling.

"My sister often smuggled books in her petticoats," Deacon said. "Of course the old bookseller always knew. Emie, are you still with us?"

Emelyn startled, finding her eyes had been closed. "Miss Harrington, you're an absolute treasure," she said, taking her hand. "But I wonder if I might steal my brother for a moment."

The young lady curtsied a bright goodbye. "Oh heavens, of course."

"*Miss Harrington, you're an absolute treasure,*" Deacon repeated, mocking her voice. "Yes, Emie, I do like her, what of it. You needn't caution me."

"I wasn't going to caution you—"

"Of course, I realize the greater part of her fascination is that disability I share with her father."

"You snob," Emelyn said, feeling a snap of emotion. "It's obvious she's taken with you, and I should say you with her. But I'm not fond of your belittling us in her company; our financial fortunes are none of her affair."

"All right, Emie, I apologize," he said, puzzling at her. "It's nothing to go wet in the eyes about; are you sure you're all right? Should you not be upstairs resting?"

"I'm perfectly well," Emelyn said. "As well as can be expected, for one attending a party hosted by her enemy."

Deacon took her hand to look at the ring. "Mrs. Akehurst shall be far behind you soon enough. I'm only surprised at how rapidly the captain obtained you."

"Perhaps you should rather be surprised at how rapidly I obtained *him*," Emelyn said, and glancing over the other couples it seemed every eye was turned their way. "There is not enough air in this room, shall we walk?"

"No thank you."

"But why is it so cold?" she asked, rubbing her arms.

"It's not cold, Emie. Any closer the fire and you'll catch it."

"Well there can be nothing more expected of us here," Emelyn said. "I should like to go home. May I ask you to be ready in the morning?"

"Tomorrow morning? Emie we've been here scarcely a week. The Commodore means to deliver Miss Harrington home after the fortnight; he assures me we're welcome to stay on, at least until then."

"The fortnight!" Emelyn exclaimed, a vague nausea growing within her. "No, Deacon, I couldn't possibly . . . I absolutely cannot."

"Very well if you cannot manage another week, the least you might do is explain why we must leave."

"We're not welcome here," she said, her head coldly swimming, "and I fear for your health."

"*My* health? Nonsense. Why should we be suddenly unwelcome? Because you took ill? As no stranger to sickbeds, I can assure you retching on the linens is small beer."

Emelyn clenched her jaws, striving not to shiver. "Then answer me this—has our own Doctor Bayten ever warned you that your infections should be unlikely to heal?"

"Several times a year, and yet here I stand."

"Has he? But I don't think . . . I do not think Tarville has your best interest at heart," she said, and watching the mirror she caught sight of Mrs. Akehurst by the harpsichord with several other ladies, watching her with displeasure.

"See how she stares at us," Emelyn said, "*the Morley problem . . .* I'm sure she'd open a hole beneath us to take care of it, if she could."

Deacon chuckled, glancing at their hostess. "The match is made Emie, barring you change your mind. It's out of her power."

Emelyn shook her head, and taking offense to the unabashed gaze of Mrs. Akehurst and her cronies, she succumbed to the temptation to eavesdrop . . .

"*—she has abandoned her modesty,*" Mrs. Akehurst complained, "*see how she flashes that ring in our faces, parading herself with as censurable an air as she pleases.*"

"*Well perhaps Mr. Rosch is correct; I for one am not convinced her advantage of beauty can be natural,*" said a lady in black whom Emelyn did not know.

"*We must pray ladies, for the captain's strength,*" Mrs. Akehurst said. "*Beside her unholy attractions, after so miraculous a recovery, I shouldn't wonder if she invented the illness first to last, or drank some foul thing to bring it about, only to stir his sympathies and torture my poor godson.*"

Emelyn gaped. "Can she *really* hate me so?"

"What?" Deacon puzzled.

"*Men are simple creatures,*" one of the other ladies spoke up. "*I'm not ashamed to confess my husband keeps a girl in Chesilhurst, by whose attentions I happily see less of him. Perhaps, if your godson availed himself of that which Miss Morley seems so keen to bestow, he might find marriage altogether unnecessary.*"

With white knuckles Emelyn squeezed the mantel, and there welled up within her a monstrous thirst to revenge herself upon them, to slash the makeup from their faces and bite their flesh, to clamp down with all the might in her jaws, until their hateful voices were silent . . .

Deacon snapped at one of the footman. "Water! Fetch it at once. Emie, what's wrong? Do you hear me?"

"Yes please." Emelyn nodded, horrified at the violent stirrings, and closing her eyes she pressed her forehead to the icy marble, suing with herself for calmer thoughts . . . She recalled the captain's touch, his firm embrace against her undress, the tickle of his mouth on her body . . .

A groan escaped her lips and Deacon cleared his throat loudly, foisting the glass upon her.

Emelyn shook her head, taking the cup with both hands to drink it down, and spluttering with a cough she returned it, focusing her mind's eye on the journey home, where she would ensconce in the small library, relaxing on the window bench to watch the wind tease over the garden walls, but it was no use—there was a voice, just at the edge of her perception, a gravelly horrible voice, speaking over itself like scratches in her mind. She thought of the burning eyes—lust and wrath tangled inside her, fighting for release. Desperately she yearned for the balm of Vaela's company, but she wanted to scream, to rend her clothes, to drag the bilious Mrs. Akehurst by the hair, or to find the captain alone—to command he finish what he'd started.

"No . . . go away," she pleaded, and compelled to open her eyes she froze, gazing into the high tilted mirror. In its merry reflection, there among the revellers stood an intruder. Unnaturally tall, as though the chandelier had been draped to the floor in black, the faceless hooded figure towered over the oblivious dancers.

Spinning round to look she caught no sign of it, but turning back again she found the figure still in the glass, hunched forward as though to stare at her, the haunting sight of it most welcome in some inexpressible way, and blinking at her own reflection she discovered the great ruby bloodstone adorning her neck.

Reaching to touch the pendant she was struck by a sudden warmth of fatigue, nearly losing her balance.

Deacon grabbed her arm, but his alarmed questions were lost as the atmosphere of the room changed. Luminous halos bloomed around the candles, pulsing into the air as though each flame breathed with life, and every scent turned to smouldering cinders as all sound grew irksome and difficult. It seemed she could hear the movement of every tongue in speech, crinkling lips and swallowing throats, but the words were unintelligible; the dancing couples shuffled on graceless feet, the music clinked and scraped, and the wall clock boomed like a gong.

The towering cloaked figure moved in the glass, and Emelyn gasped to see its reflection lean down to embrace her, enveloping her body in ebon folds—there came over her a bright and crystalline sensation, as though all her skin sparkled with light, and the cold within her melted away. The room righted itself with a snap, and she caught her balance, finding the air warm and natural once more.

"Emie, are you all right?" her brother repeated.

The figure in the mirror was gone, the captain's silver necklace adorned the throat of her reflection as before. "It's over," she breathed, feeling unaccountably confident that the last grasp of the nightmare had passed. "I need air, Deacon, excuse me," and leaving him a kiss on the cheek she retreated to the hall, making her way through the front doors and down the stairs into the lantern lit night.

Chapter 25
Machinations

Overhead the endless charcoal sky swam to the east, dragging with it an icy wind. A few couples yet braved the heady breeze, walking among the garden quadrants in the flagging torchlight as Emelyn reached the courtyard. But the wind was biting, and she'd just turned back for her new cloak when she discovered Van Croft's tall narrow eyed friend, the young Captain Curry, making his way to meet her. The gentleman was changed into fine coats of grey, and smelled so strongly of jasmine she wondered if he hadn't spilled something.

"Captain Curry," she said, finding the very garment she sought in his hands.

"The air is unseasonably cold Miss Morley, you'll catch your death," he said, draping the soft lined cloak about her shoulders.

Shivering into her comfort Emelyn pulled it close. "Thank you. I meant for a walk while the weather holds."

"Then perhaps I might avail myself of your gratitude, to join you."

With a soft sigh she pulled up her hood as they set out. "Is Lord Van Croft still about with the doctor?"

"Indeed he is, and none too happy. He's declared the poor fellow *of less use than empty shoes* on the matter of your sudden illness."

"I cannot speak to that," she said. "I remember very little."

"Well, perhaps the less said of it the better," he said. "Though I am gratified to find even such a tribulation is powerless to dim your beauty."

Emelyn smiled small, looking over the textured stones of the drive before them.

"And might I add," Curry added, looking to the sky, "that to find so lovely a jewel in Sussex—Miss Morley, I am not a man given to flights of jealousy, but in Van Croft's case I must make an exception."

Emelyn did not respond, and for twenty paces they walked in silence.

Captain Curry studied the heavens with a grimace. "I've never seen such a sky," he said. "Black to bursting yet narry a drop of rain . . ."

Emelyn nodded, her eyes trained on the gate.

"Ah, but I should tell you," he continued, "Van Croft means to dismiss Tarville and hire a better, to consult after your health."

"Does he? Then I will disappoint him; I've had quite enough of doctors."

"That may be, but I'm sure the party could not help noticing your distemper by the mantel."

"A spell of dizziness, hardly worth mentioning," Emelyn said. "In truth, Captain Curry, I shall be poor sport for conversation just now; I think you'd rather return to the house."

"By thunder, how forthright. I do tire of cowed conventional speaking, in fact I deplore it—especially from a lady."

"And from yourself, apparently."

Curry laughed. "I say, old Van Croft really has the luck of the devil . . . to have caught you first."

"If only luck were enough."

"Your pardon, Miss Morley," he said, stopping to give her a bow. "I will hinder you no further, but only tell me, does such brave beauty run in your family? Have you a pretty sister perhaps?"

"I have two," Emelyn said. "Good evening sir," and leaving him with a curtsy she resumed her way to the gates, stopping at the bars to look back. Glimmering in the torchlight the strict square gardens and shadows strolling among them seemed like a distant dream, the high peaked eminence of the house almost sinister, its many window eyes glowing dimly in the dark.

Satisfied that Captain Curry had returned whence he came, and that the guardian footmen would scarcely notice her at such a distance, she slipped through the gate and rounded the gatepost for the outside of the wall, finding again the craggy stair hidden against the cliff, which wormed its slow way down to the wave breaking rocks far below. Standing but ten paces from the drop it were as though the black sea surrounded her; shrill wind whished up the stair like wailing ghosts, and gazing about her she waited, feeling a sure and watchful sense that the vampiress was near.

"Vaela," she said aloud, "are you there?"

Continuing on she picked her way to the edge of the scrubbed grass, where beleaguered green surrendered to smooth worn rock before plunging over the cliff. "You must hear me," she said, speaking into the dark. "Something has happened—something more than the bloodsick. Will you not appear?"

There was no sound but the gale off the sea, and looking around again she startled to find the vampiress but a few steps away, hooded in the crimson cloak Emelyn had given her.

"Do not stand so near the edge," Vaela said.

The salient sense of her was inviting and needful as ever, and Emelyn longed to seize her, to smother all trepidation in her cold embrace, but she resisted. "Something has happened to me," she said, "I fell ill last night, and on recovering there came the most horrible urges, and I'd the strangest waking dream; the noises were all wrong and I saw something . . . a figure in the mirror."

"Hush," Vaela said, suddenly close, her fingers at Emelyn's lips. "Let me look at you."

The vampiress took hold of her, sniffing at her neck as Emelyn stood stiffly, tingling all over. "I am raw to my fibres," she said, "hollow and relieved all at once; I must know what happened to me."

"You were set upon," Vaela said, dragging languid nails around Emelyn's waist as she slipped behind her, "but you bear no mark of the attack. By some means I cannot describe . . . you cast him out, completely."

"Cast him out?" Emelyn repeated, an icy charge running through her. "The man with the burning eyes? But it *was* he, it must have been. I could swear I saw him, following us here, just beyond the coach lights."

"Vorsadat, brother to the queen," Vaela said, holding Emelyn's shoulders as she spoke to her back. "He is fled now, but his attack upon you is known; the queen must recall him to answer."

"I tasted blood when I woke," Emelyn bewailed, turning to face her. "I cast up the most horrible foulness . . . Has he poisoned me? But how could I survive an attack from such a creature?"

"He did not seek to harm you in body, but to enslave your mind," Vaela said. "Vorsadat has great power over dreams. No mortal could resist him . . . and yet you have. You are wholly cleansed of his influence, or I would sense it within you."

"But whatever he's done, is it finished? Only moments ago I had the most terrible, passionate thoughts, even murderous! I feared I would lose control . . ."

"And now?"

"Now . . ." Seeking within herself, Emelyn found no shadow, but only her deliberate thoughts, with little sensation in body but a tremble against the cold wind, and the sharp scent of churning brine far below. "Well, it seems even its residue is no more," she said. "But I witnessed *something*—something in the mirror, something that was not there, a towering cloaked figure which, until now, I've only ever seen in my sleep. Its reflection embraced me, and I was restored."

The vampiress did not respond, her eyes dark as midnight glass, and feeling it was time at last to expound on her dreams, Emelyn did so, describing first the statue in the long gallery at home, and how oft it would manifest with its twin, as haunting shrouded giants, their faces hidden, their intentions obscure, though always the sight of them was welcome.

The sea air whistled over the tufted ground, and Vaela stared at her. "Did they come to you in your dream, when Vorsadat held you in his power?"

"They might have done . . . though there's nothing left of it, naught but a feeling. But what are they? Why do I see them?"

"I have no answer," Vaela said. "I can only guess them to be connected to the vault. Many centuries ago, long before the house was ever built, a pair of such statues stood over the buried door . . . But if they bring you comfort, perhaps they are a force to protect you, as I am."

"Then I am at a loss once more," Emelyn said. "You understand I've no one in whom to confide these things, none but yourself—she who only appears to me at night."

"Yes," Vaela said, taking her hand. "But during the day I dream just as you might, while I sleep."

Emelyn clenched her hand, finding Vaela's touch like ice. "While you rest, cold and still as a corpse in its coffin?"

Vaela smiled. "Sometimes I twitch."

Emelyn shook her head. "And now I am engaged to be married. Shall I carry these dark secrets forever?"

"You are engaged," Vaela said, lifting her finger to study the ring. "Do you love Captain Van Croft?"

"I don't know . . . but I think not. But perhaps I shall learn to. It was nothing like how I ever imagined it would be, but I am resolved it is good. I will not see my family brought to ruin."

Vaela's face was inscrutable. "You must shepherd your own heart," she said. "What is material now is that Vorsadat's watch over the vault is ended—so it falls to you, to listen and learn of it what you can. The door will not be forced."

"To listen—and risk voices and conversations I've no business hearing? Yes Vaela, your blood has awakened my senses, just as you promised. It is diverting and strange, and terrifying."

"If you don't wish to hear the company, don't listen," Vaela said. "But have you noted your other senses as well? They will all increase, even your strength."

Emelyn pinched the ring on her finger. "I have never asked for such things."

"My blood flourishes within you," Vaela said softly. "Why would you wish to be less than you are?"

"I don't mean to be ungrateful. But if these urges come upon me again—how shall I trust myself against such *temptations*? You would not understand, for you have the mastery of your power."

"Dare you speak of temptation?" Vaela grabbed her by the arms. "You cannot conceive of it. I thrive at your very scent, pang after the life that throbs in your veins. The hunger I contend with would break you."

Emelyn stared at her, and through her touch she sensed beneath the seductive balm of Vaela's presence there lurked great conflict—pure protective instinct, and guarded affection, the both of these striving against something deeper—a predatory longing, gnawing and relentless.

"Vaela, of course I cannot measure it—what it is to be vampire. Forgive me."

Vaela released her slowly, retreating a step. "When I was born to darkness," she said, "I would have devoured my own family, to slake for a single night this immortal thirst, had not my maker prevented it. He taught me the discipline of restraint, until I could acquit my need on those who deserved to be culled . . . those who are rotten."

"But you are so cold. Have you not fed tonight?" Emelyn shivered, huddling in her cloak as the wind lashed again.

"I have not," Vaela said, her shoulders stooping. "But I will nevermore harm you, not even for the sapid purity of your blood, which I cherish above all things."

"Vaela, it was my choice to feed you, you must accept that. I want us to be as we were."

"No, little one. The discipline I honed for so long . . . is broken; I must start anew."

Emelyn stepped closer, seizing the brooch at Vaela's throat, on pretence of adjusting it. "You were at the *end*," she said. "But you are no less important to me, than I must be to you. Give me your eyes. Do you hear me?"

Vaela nodded, her eyelids heavy, the tips of her fangs just visible between her lips.

"I cannot imagine that I shall prove any material use against the vault," Emelyn said, straightening Vaela's brooch again. "The door, if there is such a thing, is only a slab of stone. Yet I will trust in the prophecy, of which you tell me I am a part, because I trust in you. You must understand—as you long to drink from me, so do I long to nurture you," and drawing near enough to be bitten she presented her throat, fixing her gaze on the sky.

"Emelyn," Vaela hissed softly, baring her fangs.

"Drink," Emelyn insisted, tingling in anticipation.

The vampiress embraced her, and Emelyn pulled herself tightly close, as like a sharpened shadow Vaela bit into her throat, purring with unbridled hunger.

Emelyn gasped. Supple waves of pleasure spread like fingers of heat through her body, washing away the half remembered horror of their previous encounter at the base of the cliffs . . . Thunder grumbled far away, and gazing into the black tumbling heavens she could not help imagining what should follow if the vampiress lost control again, overtaxing all restraint to drain her until the end. Left by the wayside, serene in stillness, she might be found under the clear lens of day, eyes open to the last image of her killer, her gown of silk stained red . . .

But the vampiress held her life in trust, and as Vaela licked to heal the wound Emelyn held her warmly, thriving on the bond between them.

Vaela's finger touched her lips, and the spice of vampire blood twisted through her like fire. With a sigh Emelyn settled softly against her, and drifted to sleep.

■ ■

Beneath the mountain fortress of Saunmoor, where the winding river divided the city of the dead, one of its branches split away, descending into hidden darkness. By the light of a dozen torches, at the bottom of a flooded stair worn smooth, the water joined a long rectangular pool, flowing the length before plunging through narrow clefts to cascade ever farther down, tumbling at last into the black lake far below. Splitting the flow of the current before the pool's vanishing edge stood the second of the six thrones of Saunmoor, deepest in the earth but one, rising like a hand of sharp cornered stone, its fingers embedded in the ceiling.

Alone in the room, waiting in silence, the dark queen Pazoa sat upon the throne just above the waterline, her body wrapped ankles to shrouded face in winding gossamer white, a spired crown of iron resting on her brow, her voluminous plaited hair falling like shadow behind her. Her face was but thinly veiled—dark eyes and dark lips accented in deeper shade, her bronzy shoulders bedecked in gem encrusted gold, her fingers set with ancient rings. The flowing water rose almost to her knees, and with bare feet adorned in gilded chains she crossed her legs, watching the cascading stair through the wide mouth of the far wall as her claws— painted white as her garments, ticked against the stone.

Like a knot of darkness in the rushing foam, a ponderous form tumbled down the waterfall stair to crash into the pool, and the torches went out. The queen's cold lips parted and she sat up, gripping the armrests as the monstrous vampire Vorsadat bobbed up from the depths. Half submerged, the hulking creature swam toward her, the great hunch of his back just breaking the surface. The pool glowed suddenly bright with the beam of his eyes, their burning light drawing nearer until the ashen hill of his hairless pate rose before her, his expression wide with toothy mirth.

"Sister, Mother . . . my queen," he said, resting his chin on her knees as the ghostly glow in his eyes faded to empty sockets.

The queen's fingers touched his cheeks, moving over the hard contours of his skull, and bending close she bared slender fangs, biting into his scalp.

A runnel of blood seeped to his eye socket, and she kissed his head, cupping water in her palm to wash away the mark.

"Why do you call so loud?" he asked, his voice watery and deep, black bile dribbling from his lips.

"Sadat," Pazoa said, smoothing the water from his face. "My brother, my sweet suffering poet . . . By what miserable misguidance have you broken my law?"

The monster clicked his teeth, "The Chosen Child deceives us. She *knows* what lies beneath; she will claim its power for her own, while we sit and wait for dead stone to speak."

"There is madness on your breath," the queen said. "You attacked the Chosen Child, and threatened Vaela with destruction. Your action has only confirmed her unhappy report."

"Lies my queen . . . The little raven is not to be trusted; she would steal the child away from you. I seek only your glory."

The queen held his face. "The old man's ring is returned to me, that which I gifted him long ago," she said. "He begs my audience, to return to the fold, while you have betrayed me. Your charge was to watch the Morley estate, to listen to the earth—nothing more."

"I have listened enough!" he barked, his broad hands grasping her legs. "There comes no sound from the deeps since Emelyn Morley's birth. The stone does not move, yet she attended it as a child—she slipped down to the crypt, she spoke, and the vault whispered in response, beyond even my ability to hear. She must reveal to us what lies beneath!"

The queen leaned closer. "What lies beneath is our redemption. I have dreamt it—not only power, but an end to this secret persecution we share . . . but the steps of our path must be deliberate. I will have the bloodstone again, and the Chosen Child will show us the way."

"Without testing and tasting the child is wasted!"

"Consider, brother, I might have thrown you to the Deadmere for your rebellion," she said, holding him tightly, "to watch the anthropophagi consume you like starved eels."

Vorsadat grinned wide. "Yet I am here, safe at your knee, with nothing betwixt me, and thee."

Finding the wrinkled sockets of his empty eyes she rested her thumbs within them, keeping his head still. "I have called you to the drowning throne in forgiveness, for by some preternatural exercise your attack on our precious mortal was resisted, and you have done her no harm. Can you explain to me how it happened?"

"Something . . . *other*. A force of blinding sound, pushing and pressing; but let us take her, let us examine her, let us unmask it!"

"No," Pazoa said. "You are compromised. Our little mortal has resisted you, and more. I feel her trace, like thorns dragging in your mind. What a curious success of things it is . . . to find you the object of *her* infection."

Vorsadat caught her arms with a growl, pulling them away from his face. "Our little mortal is not my debility but yours," he rumbled. "The storm approaches, and with it the end of your reign."

"I tire of your chimerical heresies," she said, coaxing her wrists from his grasp. "The prophecy will be my ascension! Place your insatiate faith in *me*, little brother, lest you forget—before they took your mortal eyes, it was I who discovered you, who interceded on behalf of a poor sickly outcast—a wretched poet at death's door. Without my initiative Malphaegios would never have found you."

"You dare speak his name," Vorsadat rumbled, licking his teeth. "He created me eternal, and *you* took him from me. You raised me on the ichor of pitchbark trees, on the meat of the dead, distorting and contorting . . ."

"I gave you back your suffering," she said, her voice bemused. "After a lifetime of illness, you could not abide your painless immortal frame; have you forgotten? The blood of the dead gave you back what *he* took from you, as the sap of the haunted trees made you stronger."

Vorsadat rumbled. "*His* power is true strength—by his power I will see you broken."

Pazoa's lip twitched. "The twice dead do not return," she said, petting his head. "This agony we share is but a test; the deep roots of Saunmoor call an abyssal curse to prove us both, and by the vault of Hastelbrook shall we be redeemed."

"My queen speaks fantasies, for she has not the key," he grumbled, gripping the arms of the throne. "It is not the spirits of Saunmoor, but *our father* who walks in your nightmares; he gathers strength over the sea, and for vengeance he comes, through me!"

The queen opened her mouth to speak, but with spread fingers the monster stabbed his dagger claws through her ribs, and she shuddered with a gasp, spitting flecks of blood in his face as she grabbed his wrists.

"You will sleep now, sister," he breathed, digging deeper, his face close to hers as she trembled, her mouth wide.

"How *dare* you," Pazoa seethed softly, leaning back in the throne as she pulled his fingers—black with blood—from her body, and with a scream of rage she lashed him. Startled at her attack the monster buckled away, tumbling backward into the pool. The water clouded red, and the queen was standing on the throne, the twisted white of her slashed gown blooming with crimson stain, though in a breath her wounds collapsed, shrinking to restore smooth umber skin beneath torn silk.

Vorsadat launched to the side of the pool with a howl, the shredded hang of his face melting upward until it healed in place.

"Do you find me so wretched, so depleted," she shouted, her voice resounding about the walls, "that you would defy me openly—your queen, your *mother* these seven hundred years—"

"You are not my mother!" he hissed. "Your essays of pain, your experiments upon me will be no more!" and with a keening bellow he launched at her, reaping claws bared.

Pounding and hacking he scored but faint scratches against the empty throne, and heaving with eyes of fire he turned to behold the queen reappeared by the far edge of the pool, floating over the water like a phantom.

"You will put off this impotent wrath!" she charged, reaching out, "return to our grace . . . let me protect you—from this and every illusion that haunts you, let me create you stronger!"

"As you are strong?" he spat. "You would twist me to the end, as you ended our father, robbing me of his shadow! But he is returned; his vengeance fills the darkling sky."

"Our maker is dust!" she shrieked in anger, her voice cracking the stone. "His ashes moulder at the bottom of the sea. You and I alone survive him—the work we have begun must be finished!"

Vorsadat crouched on the chair, gnashing his teeth at her. "Then dredge the black lake yourself, drink from the cursed trees if you dare; I am your slave no more."

"Ever have I sheltered you," she said gently, drifting toward him over the water, "from the vile oppressions of the continent, from the pious faithful and their obdurate pursuit . . . You must fight this apparition within you; do not surrender yourself to delusions."

Vorsadat clicked his claws, lowering himself to sit as his gaze flashed bright. "No, dear sister, I shall pretend you dead as stone, until our father renders it so."

The monster tensed to spring, but with a piercing wail she was upon him, the sound of her cry burrowing into his skull as a consuming terror filled the room. Pazoa's veil was stripped away, her hair lashing like a storm, dark veins throbbing in her flesh as she crushed him into the throne. "Will you forsake your queen at the last," she demanded, "after so long at my side?"

Tensing in her embrace the monster shuddered with growls. "I am not yours . . ."

The queen clasped the sides of his head. "Surely as I know your tragic face, I sense the conflict within you," and pulling him close she pressed a long kiss on his forehead. "Heed my voice . . . let it soothe the monster away."

A cruel grin spread on his face. "Your angelic tones compel me no longer," and clashing his claws to spear her body between them he gored his own arms as she vanished, slipping out of the air some distance away to hover once more over the pool, her eyes wide and dark.

Vorsadat clacked his claws, swiping away the blood. "The darkness comes for you; Saunmoor will be his!"

"Deluded, pitiful creature," she said miserably, "you have wounded my heart."

"I will see your heart brought to dust!" he snapped, gnashing his teeth.

"If that is your will, little *Lord Cumberstone*," she said, her voice breaking with sadness. "Blood of my blood, the demons of your imagination have cost you my love. Go back to write your venal verses . . . and *be you banished*."

The queen's arms shot forward, her grasping claws twisting in the air, and a crushing impulse seized his body, as though his very bones betrayed him. The hulking vampire screeched as the force of it dragged him away from her, rolling him heels over head up the rushing ramp to the river. The water raged and choked, swirling about him as images of grass and stone flowed together, high walls surged into the sky overhead, breaking apart to melt into trees; the village lights winked out, the land rose to meet him, and the city of Saunmoor disappeared, leaving him moored in a misted field, surrounded by silent black shouldered forest.

Pazoa's words rose from the ground with a tremor. "Nevermore shall you return, nor approach the vault, nor vex the Chosen Child, lest I feed your fractious flesh to the lake, while I weep for your sacrifice from the shore . . ."

. . . .

At the sound of hushed male voices Emelyn began to wake.

"I say Freddy is it a young lady there by the door? Why it's our testy termagant alone, and deep in her cups, or I'm a fool."

"Huzzah!" the younger man cheered with surprise. *"But shall we smile as fortune does, and continue the quest?"*

Much ado sounded in the distance, coach wheels on the drive mingled with laughing farewells, and rousing slowly Emelyn discovered herself standing, propped against the darkened door to the longhouse between thick shrubberies. A pair of familiar, if unsavoury gentlemen stood before her.

"I say, Miss Morley, are you quite well?" the younger asked, drawing improperly close. "But it is only I, your friend Freddy, and Mr. Deckland. I wonder if you might have another thought, concerning dear old Lord Abbott?"

"Why is there no music," Emelyn mumbled, wrinkling her nose at the bergamot musk of his perfume.

"The party is over sweet lady, your lord is at his wit's end to find you—all but fears you've gone over the cliff."

The older fellow chuckled nervously. "Now, Freddy, she's no common maid; we must be gentle with the captain's prize."

"Oh but there's none more *gentle* than I sir," Freddy responded, his eyes only for Emelyn.

"But perhaps we should fetch him to her."

"Nay sir, not before *Robert the Blade* is satisfied as to the fate of his father. Then we shall be off, and her lord *Bloodhound* none the wiser."

The embrace of the vampiress was still with her, the dizzy rapture of Vaela's blood like a restless power crackling in her skin, and Emelyn touched her throat to find it warm and ticklish where she'd been bitten.

Grinning brightly the near lad spoke again. "She is bewitched with drink, just as you say. Come, let us ply her."

Emelyn squinted to focus, watching him as he watched her. "You should go away with your friend," she breathed.

"We've done as well as may be expected," Mr. Deckland sounded, a nervous timbre in his voice. "The captain will find her soon enough, I'm quite sure."

Freddy waved him off. "Lord Abbott, Miss Morley, what has become of him? I know you hear me, dear beautiful creature . . ."

"Go away," she repeated, leaning against the door.

"Nay, you must permit our protection," he said, taking her hand. "For you to be here alone, at the edge of so wide and dark a courtyard, where none can see—"

"I am perfectly safe in the dark," she said, coming to herself. "Now, if you will excuse me."

The excitable Freddy blocked her way. "Sweet Miss Morley, if you would answer but one question more, let it be this—would you not prefer the taste of a fellow young and fresh, to your stuffed lord," and pushing her against the door he pressed close.

Emelyn turned her head away from him.

"There," he murmured, "if you will speak not of Lord Abbott, you must bestow me some small congress for a consolation."

"Please, Miss Morley, see reason," Deckland said quickly, drawing closer. "A *Peer of the Realm* has gone missing. Your ancestral home was his object. But surely you know something of his disappearance?"

"Speak," Freddy enjoined, "but do not cry out, Miss Morley, or it shall go the worse for you."

Emelyn scowled into the dark, feeling oddly detached as she absorbed the press of his kiss on her cheek. His were aggressive, and catching one wrist she chased the other as he dug into her skirts. "Freddy? Freddy, stop it," she said sternly.

Mr. Deckland shielded the sight of them, protesting weakly as his young friend continued the attack, and turning her hips to block his insistent grasp Emelyn inhaled to scream, but at a sudden vengeful curiosity she thought better of it, and abandoning her defence she seized one roaming hand in both of hers. Half freed of her meddling Freddy grappled at her legs as he panted against her, and gripping down on the hand she had caught, she squeezed with all her might.

With an audible crack the bones collapsed, and stifling an animal sound he tore himself away from her, crashing through his friend and landing on his seat with a cry.

"Jezebel!" Freddy shrieked, his eyes aglisten as Deckland seized him under the arms to pull him up.

With motley effort the wounded man struggled to stand. "I'll have her eyes!"

"No Freddy! Away, or it's the death of us!"

The scene that followed was strange as it was amusing—amidst the departing hubbub Freddy's terrified elder stammered excuses to any who would listen, dragging his friend along, whom he insisted was only drunk, and had cried out to no one in particular. Emelyn pulled up her hood, and catching sight of a rapidly moving figure she found Van Croft barrelling toward her, stuttering his approach to puzzle at the unhappy gentlemen, who pretending not to see him fled across the drive, one supporting the other.

"Good God, Miss Morley, where have you been?"

"I only went for a walk," she said, sensing the alarmed beat of his heart even before he reached her.

The captain's eyes were soft with worry. "Your brother has collapsed," he said.

"What?"

"Come with me, quickly."

The state room was through a deep set door off the main hall, a red walled space near every inch covered in portraits, with marble busts matching the white gleam of the mantel. Under the illuminating gaze of a great many candles Deacon lay covered in blankets on a crimson sofa before the fire, his eyes half open and face pale with sweat. Around him hovered a group of familiar figures: Mrs. Akehurst, her husband, Captain Curry and Mr. Rosch, with the doctor on one knee closest to Deacon, and a tearful Miss Harrington beside Breda, who busied herself pouring a pitcher of hot water over a towel in a bowl.

All were speaking together, and it was hastily explained that Deacon had fallen in the parlour after some complaint of dizziness, for which he'd been given a medicinal cordial which the doctor meant to steady him.

"But his condition has only worsened," a waxy faced Doctor Tarville lamented, blinking slowly as he spoke.

Aghast at her brother's so rapid decline, Emelyn stood rigidly silent, until catching notes of the same stench she'd earlier smelled in his medicine she was obliged to speak. "He collapsed after your tonic, Doctor, or before? Was it the belladonna? What precisely did you give him?"

"A simple distillation of verdigris and soda, dissolved in wine to induce a purge," the doctor said, one eye half closed as he took the hot rag to wipe Deacon's mouth.

"*Verdigrease?*" Emelyn clarified. "The green rot from tarnished metal? Can that be a medicine?"

"It is a mild poison, Miss Morley, of course," Mr. Rosch put in, "but used only for an emetic; it does not remain in the stomach."

"Precisely good my Rosch sir," the doctor grunted, his words stinking of brandy.

"Are you drunk?" Van Croft and Emelyn said together, and the captain yanked the doctor to his feet by the arm.

Bitter argument ensued, but hearing them not, Emelyn knelt beside the couch, squeezing her brother's hand to find it cold. "His breathing is too shallow," she said. "Doctor! Did he expel or not?"

"He did," Tarville said, burping into his collar. "There's nothing for but to wait Miss—to wait for the fever to break, Miss Morley."

An unthinkable fear tempted her to panic, but steely faced Emelyn rose to her feet, glancing at the windows. "Let me alone with him, if you please, everyone."

"Yes perhaps we should give them the room," Mrs. Akehurst said at once.

Van Croft squeezed Emelyn's shoulder, and all took their leave save the doctor, who for some minutes paced about, refilling his brandy by a silver tray of toast and jam as Emelyn sat with her brother, finding him too delirious to speak.

"Mr. Tarville, I think you're wasted here. I should like you to step outside," she said, her heart pounding.

The doctor leaned on the table with his fingers in the jelly. "Well, I would help if I would, if I could, but it's up to nature now," he said, tucking his chin for a belch. "Not every promise made is a promise—not every promise made may be kept."

"What promise?"

"But I promised the captain, to cure . . . to cure the embarrassment of such a relation," he slurred, waving his hand. "The night breeze is rude brace to society—to sobriety, rather. I think I shall have a walk. But perhaps whatever witchcraft, that preserved him against his ulcers . . . will save him now," and he chortled heartily, turning to totter his way out.

Emelyn watched his exit, and after shutting the door behind him she fetched a chair to wedge under the handle. Deacon groaned softly, and racing across the room she unlocked the turnbuckles to throw open the window panes, pushing them as wide as she could reach.

"Vaela!" she called with what volume she dared, casting her name into the umbral orchard behind the house. "Vaela you must hear me; please come in!"

The wind whistled in response, giving her goose pimples, but among the pear trees circling the black pond no familiar shadow appeared.

"I know it was you," Emelyn pleaded, leaning over the sill. "What else could explain Deacon's scarring and recovery, all these years, but your blood! Will you not come to him now, when he needs it most?"

The door latch rattled, the captain called from outside the room, and she rushed back, moving the chair to pull it open.

"Tarville's a drunken fool," he said, donning a cocked hat, his face grave. "I am for the Two Brothers inn, they're as likely to have a doctor as not; if there's none to be had I'll ride to Eastbourne. I shall leave Captain Curry at your service—you may rely on him."

Emelyn nodded, her eyes welling. "Wait, my lord, can it be true the doctor promised you—that he promised you to cure the *embarrassment* of my brother?"

"I've seen many a man die before his time," the captain said. "I want only that Mr. Morley should recover," and snapping for a bow he turned away, pausing as she caught his hand.

"Wait . . . but *did* Tarville make such a promise? Did you ask it of him?"

"Nay, Miss Morley, I asked only that he *live up to his oath*."

Feeling less confident in his answer than she might have liked Emelyn startled as he grabbed her, but through his tight embrace she sensed the sympathetic beat of his heart, and closing her eyes she returned his kiss.

Their lips parted, the captain touched his hat, and taking his leave he marched past the others, who loitered in the hall, conferring amongst themselves.

"Oh my dear girl, if there's anything we might do," Mrs. Akehurst said, her lamentable face disappearing as Emelyn slammed the door.

With the chair propped again she returned to her brother's side, and sitting on the floor took his hand, staring hopefully at the open window. Deacon's heart thumped but faintly, his breath coming short, and rolling his eyes he turned his head.

"Emie? I was worried for you . . ."

"Miss Morley, perhaps I might be of some use?" Mr. Rosch called from outside.

"No, thank you Mr. Rosch, your prayers must be enough," she called back, and leaping up she fetched some water, tipping a pewter cup to her brother's lips.

Deacon swallowed with a cough, spotting his collar with blood. "The doctor is a tell-tale," he rasped. "I know why you want to leave. But what sort of man is Van Croft, to bring you to the home of a lady he's engaged and broken off with . . ."

"Don't worry about that now," Emelyn said, blinking water from her eyes as she wiped the blood from his lips.

Deacon smiled faintly. "If you should like us to depart . . . in the morning, I am quite at my leisure to do so."

Kneeling beside him she held his hand tightly. "All I want is that you rest, and recover," she said, listening through the wall for those outside the room . . .

"But it's plain as plaster Mr. Morley's case was always desperate," Mrs. Akehurst said. *"Perhaps among her many accomplishments she fancies herself a doctor?"*

"As I have avowed, there is a darkness attending that family, Miss Morley herself, in particular," Rosch warned. *"It was in fact while showing off for the infant sister he so adored, that her brother lamed himself as a child."*

"Well I only hope the poor fellow doesn't expire in our stateroom," Mrs. Akehurst said. *"Perhaps a solemn prayer, Mr. Rosch, if you would be good enough to lead us."*

Emelyn swallowed hard, and squeezing her brother's hand she found his eyes closed. "You are strong Deacon," she insisted, swiping her cheeks. "You will not leave me . . ."

Outside a hard sea wind galloped over the tarps bandaging the broken wall as Doctor Tarville fussed them out of his way to pass through, taking a few brave steps nearer the cliff's edge. "O dearest my captain, what say you to my promise now!" he cried into the air, swinging his arm as he downed the last of his drink. "Never in my life have I stooped so low . . . but there's more than one way to cook an egg!" and tossing his cup to the abyss he startled to find a woman darkly hooded in red just behind him.

Her eyes gleamed like silver, she hissed with bared fangs, and a shrieking young doctor lost his balance, teetering over the edge as she caught his wrist.

"Pull me up!" he cried, flailing as he precariously leaned.

"The storm is coming," she said, speaking over the gale as she plucked the brass ring from his finger.

"Keep it!" he shouted desperately. "Whatever you like! You must pull me up! Help me!"

"As you helped Deacon Morley?" she posed, turning the ring in her fingers as she loosened her hold on his wrist. "Your insignificant heart is rotten . . ."

"Wait! Mercy I beg you!" he blubbered. "I tried to heal him, on my life I did! But it was only a matter of time!"

"And so you thought to hasten his death with poison, to spare your master a crippled brother by marriage."

"The captain would have stopped my livelihood, denied me to his estate, to his sister do you understand?" Tarville pleaded. "But his request was impossible—I cannot heal Mr. Morley; no one can! I had no choice, don't you see!"

"You did—you chose poison," she said, and with a snarl she pulled him just close enough to plunge her fangs in his wrist.

The doctor cursed in terror, struggling for balance as she drank of him. "Spare me!" he cried. "Release me and I shall reverse what harm I've done; on my soul I swear it! If you care for Deacon Morley, you must spare me!"

"This is not for him," Vaela said, licking her teeth.

Before Tarville could answer her claws opened, and with a scream of horror he fell, the chalk cliffs streaking past like lightning . . .

A swirl of wind extinguished the candles, casting long shadows about the stateroom from the dimming fire, and advantaging herself of the invitation Vaela appeared by the sofa. Lowering her hood, she bent to clasp Deacon Morley's cold face, finding Emelyn on the floor slouched against him, breathing soft and slow.

Vaela bit into her finger, and turning her hand let a few drops of blood fall to Deacon's lips, covering his mouth as his eyes fluttered open. "Sleep," she whispered, "sleep, and forget."

With a shudder he obliged, his chest expanding with unlaboured breath, and moving to Emelyn the vampiress knelt beside her, taking a pillow to lay her slowly on the floor. Undoing tightly bound twists of Emelyn's hair she drew it out with her claws, letting it down.

"Dream gently," Vaela said, stroking her cheek.

The wind outside increased, the deep sky rumbled, and softly she began to sing. *"Oranges and lemons, ring ye bells at St. Clements. When will you pay me, ring ye bells of Old Bailey. When I am rich, ring ye bells at Fleetditch . . ."*

There was a clap of thunder and the vampiress looked to the windows as Emelyn twitched in her sleep. *"You* are the key we seek . . . you must be," Vaela whispered, staring down at her with eyes full and black. "I feel it in your heart, truly the vault has chosen you. Goodnight, little one."

With a sleeping sigh Emelyn rolled to her side, laying an arm over Vaela's leg, but the vampiress slipped away like a ghost, and coming to the door she removed the chair to set it aside before flashing to the window, where she hopped through, closing the panes behind her, and with one last look she vanished into the dark.

Chapter 26
The Storm

Tuesday July 5ᵗʰ

Bounding over soft forest ground the hulking vampire Vorsadat ran on all fours, and Emelyn found herself trapped behind his eyes, unable to break her witness as he dashed through the forest, seething and muttering. The smell of rain was on the wind, the grey shrouded dawn soon to come, and crashing through the rotting trunk of a fallen tree she watched as her massive host raised dagger claws to the sky before heaving down, tearing into the ground. A blur of grasping spidery hands churned up roots and dirt until a great hole was burrowed, and the monster dropped within, reaching to gather the ruined tree about the mouth of the pit before tumbling over to dig further, tearing ever deeper into the earth, through rock and clay until even the scent of the air above could not reach him. There the creature stopped in the close and sightless dark, snarling miserably to himself twenty yards beneath the forest floor, as clasping his face with long fingers he settled to wait out the lethal gaze of day . . .

Peals of thunder clattered through the house and Emelyn woke, finding herself huddled under a blanket on the floor, long hair wrapped about her face. A deadening roar filled the air, the sound of hard rain driven mad in the wind, and she sat up with a jolt, brushing to clear her vision. "Deacon!"

Her brother lay just where she'd left him, blinking at her as he rested a book on his chest, his eyes sharp and clear. "Hurricane shakes the very walls," he said, "but for Emelyn Morley *O gentle sleep! Nature's soft nurse* . . . until half past nine."

"Are you well!" she gasped, finding his colour restored, and rising to her knees she embraced him, laying her head under his chin.

"I began to wonder if you'd ever wake," he said, patting her back. "What do they say, six hours' sleep for a man, seven for a woman, eight for a fool?"

"Yes you're quite yourself," she muttered, holding him tightly. "But did anyone come last night, or was it you gave me pillow and cover?"

Deacon fussed with her hair. "I woke to the wrath of nature well before dawn, and found you covered already."

"I could not hear the storm," she said, sitting back on her heels to drag fingers over her forehead, gathering her hair to twist it tight, "though I'd the strangest dream . . . as like I were a monster, feeling the creature's very thoughts; it was grotesque."

Deacon shrugged as he watched her. "I can't remember the last I saw your hair down . . . but it's pretty; you needn't be embarrassed."

"I'm not embarrassed," she said, working to tie it smaller.

"But I suppose you're concerned for who might have popped in while my sister snored on the floor like a dog?" and he laughed as she smacked his shoulder.

"I stayed the night to watch over you," she said, tossing pillow and blanket on the sofa.

"Well you were not to be roused," he said. "Mr. Rosch put hartshorn salts right under your nose, and still you slept."

Mortified at the image Emelyn frowned. "Mr. Rosch . . . I will be glad to be away from him. I was determined we should be well on the road by now."

"*Hope springs eternal in the human breast,*" Deacon said, returning to his book. "At least we're warm and dry. Apparently Tarville staggered outside last night, the mad fool, and hasn't turned up since. Poor sot must be drenched to the bowels by now . . ."

Emelyn grunted, imagining the drunken doctor aquiver under the eaves, his coat over his head. "And what of Van Croft? Was he not to fetch us another physician, perhaps a sober one?"

"No sign of him. But don't trouble; I expect he's faced worse at sea."

"Yes I suppose."

"But Emelyn, I've been mulling it over," Deacon said, struggling to sit up, "and can you really mean to marry him? Shall such an aggressive satire of a lord be the man to tame you?"

"We are better matched than you think," she said, "and there is more to him than arrogance; I've seen it."

"I'm sure you have, when he cajoled you to the roof perhaps. But I'd not be much of a chaperone for concealing my displeasure of it."

Emelyn said nothing, helping wedge a pillow behind his back.

"I might almost say you've behaved wantonly. But you cannot love him?"

"Do you mean to protect me?" she inquired, "because I am feeling attacked."

"I know you Emie; your romantic caprices never last but there's some twist in the third act."

"My life is not a play," she said, looking to the relentless rain as it volleyed against the windows. "And our need is dire, as you so freely expressed to Miss Harrington."

"Oh come now; that *Emelyn Morley* could settle for anything less than the beating heart of love . . . well I might have expected tears of sacrifice and rending of garments at least."

"You misjudge the captain, and myself," she said curtly, rising to her feet. "I'll not be crying over my engagement, much as it would please you."

A clash of thunder shivered its way down the walls, and as Emelyn moved to the windows she was surprised with dismay to find the morning light drowned behind clouds nearly black. Deluge fumed over the land like the sky's last breath, water pulverizing the ground. Gale force winds bent the unhappy trees, and through the blur she could just make out the roiling pond, full to bursting. One of the trees cracked, toppling in collapse, and she put her hand on the glass, eyes wide at the sight of it.

"Emie, in case the house should come down upon us," Deacon said, peering at her over the back of the sofa, "you should know I never enjoyed making you cry, I only loved to console you when you did."

"I know," Emelyn said, glancing back at him. "And sometimes I pretended, just for that."

Deacon chuckled, settling back with a sigh. "Well then, I hope your captain doesn't drown, at least not before you've a sporting chance to fall in love with him."

Thunder shocked again, and Emelyn watched the rain bursting over the grass like watery cannon fire, joined now by heavier, darker drops that bounced as they landed, clinking and snapping over the building. "It's hailstones now," she said, resolved to imagine Van Croft sheltered and safe, as surely he must be . . .

"Perhaps Mrs. Akehurst will blame you for the weather as well," Deacon mused.

Lightning split the sky, fanning through the dark in rivers of light. "She's welcome to it," Emelyn said, "her opinion of me can hardly fall any lower."

"Oh I think you underestimate the lady. Mr. Rosch has her ear, and he the most superstitious man I've ever heard put tongue to teeth."

"What has he said to her?" she asked, turning to look at him.

A resounding boom shook through the house, and Deacon spasmed with irritation. "Mind the noise will you!" he flustered, turning the page of his book.

There was a knock at the door, and Breda burst into the room. "Oh thank goodness miss, you're awake! Captain Curry ventured out after the doctor, it's over an hour and he's not returned!"

"He's gone out? In this weather?" Emelyn asked. "And is Lord Van Croft still abroad?"

"He is miss, sorry to say," Breda said. "The others are in the dining room, we've been watching with hope from the windows—but if you should like to steal upstairs to change, now would be best."

Returning to the sofa Emelyn leaned down to kiss her brother's head, and following her lady's maid she paused by the door. "And you're quite well on your own? There's naught that you need?"

"I've had two breakfasts already," Deacon noted, minding his book.

Hastily brushed, rinsed and changed into a fresh mantua of dove silk Emelyn found what remained of the dwindling company huddled in the dimly lit dining room, squinting through high windows into the driving rain. Mr. Rosch, the Commodore and Mrs. Akehurst stood beside Miss Harrington, with a pair of ladies Emelyn remembered from their gossiping reflections in the mirror over the mantel: an older woman in mourning blacks beside a younger, smaller dowdy, gowned in green under an engulfing hat.

Partaking in a mug of coffee and some buttered toast Emelyn quietly greeted Miss Harrington, who nodded with a nervous smile.

"It's as though night has circled back round to strangle the day," the Commodore grumbled, holding his trembling wife by the shoulders.

"Nothing good will come of it; it isn't natural," the woman in green asserted, speaking from the depths of her bonnet.

A web of lightning burned through the clouds, and Mr. Rosch swept off his hat. "We are naught but tar and timber against the wrath of heaven . . . Our Lord Almighty does not neglect in making display of his displeasure."

"Or perhaps it's only a storm," Emelyn said, taking a bite of toast.

"Or perhaps again it is not," Rosch rejoined. "But perhaps it is the projection of evil, for I am reminded *no storm ever raged but first in the hearts of men,* and I am compelled to add, women."

The ladies murmured fearfully, thunder rumbled over the land, vibrating the glass, and Miss Harrington clasped Emelyn's arm. "How the plants thrash under the hailstones," she said, her eyes wide with excitement, "but the roof will hold."

At a splitting crack of lightning Emelyn blinked, squeezing her hand. "Will it?"

"These rafters are fashioned from the hull of a ship," Miss Harrington said, betraying a shiver as there came another cacophonous boom. "We're perfectly safe—I'm quite sure, though I confess I've never seen such weather in all my life."

"But where is Captain Curry?" Mrs. Akehurst troubled, hand over her heart. "Whatever hope could he find searching in such a tempest?"

No sooner had the words been spoken than a footman rushed into the room, announcing Curry's return, and abandoning the windows the company crowded to the front hall. For a few drafty moments the outer doors banged in the wind before the beleaguered footmen heaved them closed, and there stood Captain Curry, his face and clothes utterly drenched, favouring one foot as he leaned on Fenders' shoulder.

"Forgive the delay! Turned my ankle in the damnable rain," he complained, wincing as he was assisted to a chair by the wall, into which he collapsed with a groan.

"Did you find the doctor?" Mrs. Akehurst asked, clenching her hands beneath her chin.

"It is as we feared, the very worst," Curry lamented, pausing for breath as he employed a kerchief to dry his face.

The party murmured in disbelief, and the Commodore snapped for the footmen to relight those lanterns the intruding wind had blown out. "Courage my dear," he said, holding his wife's arm.

"I had no trace of him on the grounds, and so drew my suspicion to the gap in the wall," Curry explained, wincing as a sullen Fenders removed his boot. "I crawled to the edge, a foolish hazard in such a gale, and peering below I espied the white fleck of coats against bare rock. There is a dead man at the bottom to be sure . . . it can only be Boderick Tarville."

The assemblage gasped in horror as Mrs. Akehurst covered her mouth. "Heaven preserve us!"

Emelyn stood very still, feeling a touch of shame to find little remorse for the drunken doctor, though she could not help envisioning the horror it must have been to experience such a plunge from the cliffs.

Voices were raised, and after much travail the Commodore called for the party to move, to gather away from the windows in a central salon under the stoutest chimney.

The hard driving hail increased, candles flickered as the walls moaned, and Emelyn stood aside as three huffing footmen struggled past bearing the covered harp down the hall.

Mr. Rosch came to stand beside her, narrowing his eyes at the ceiling. "*O fevered strife of Hell, high Heaven o'er Earth betwixt, where mortal chessmen dwell, on battle lines affixed,*" he recited. "I wonder, Miss Morley, have you ever witnessed a reckoning to so blacken the sky?"

"A reckoning? I have not sir . . . But I should expect this *fevered strife of Hell* to blow over by the afternoon."

"How freely we scorn the firmament, peering upward from our wretched state," Mr. Rosch said, giving her a tight smile, "until divine thunder crashes, and the dew of clarity shines upon every pious brow—"

"Do you enjoy the storm Mr. Rosch?" Emelyn asked, finding him stranger by the moment.

"Nay madam, but perhaps the hour is upon us. If you would care to join me, to speak privately on matters incident to these events."

Sparing her the need to respond the Commodore came bustling down the hall ahead of the ladies, eager for her attention. "We are all prepared! You will indulge us Miss Morley? I daresay music at such a time should be most welcome diversion."

"But something reverent, I would urge," Rosch interjected, "to be followed by prayer, and reflection."

"Certainly sir, quite right," the Commodore said, nodding vigorously.

Lightning exploded somewhere nearby, and the ladies cried out.

"Of course I should be happy to play," Emelyn said quickly, feeling a tingle in her scalp.

Behind a bolt locking door the salon in question was a small affair, a quiet lavender coloured room for Mrs. Akehurst to entertain, wherein were displayed her most cherished collections: table service of famille rose china, exotic bird painted delftware and treasures of jewellery she never wore, mounted in cases. The north end of the space was dominated by a welcoming marble hearth, deep and strong, with the covered harp in the centre of the floor between a soft ivory settee and the fireplace, surrounded by spindly chairs that appeared almost too delicate for sitting. An ornate longcase clock stood in the corner of the room beside a golden tasselled daybed, to which Deacon was guided with the assistance of Miss Harrington.

The lady of the house was proud to present the lavender wallpapering, done in Chinese floral pattern over the wainscot, with numerous pastoral scenes hung about the room, celebrating every season in turn, though with narry a glimpse of water between them. "And the tower clock is an original Tompion," she presented, "worth upward of 200 guineas."

Emelyn found the instrument she was to play to be a beautiful seven pedal harp of maple wood, with intricate scrolling over the pillar and etched flora rising along the soundbox. Perching on the stool she waited as brandy was served from a warming cupboard above the mantel.

Mrs. Akehurst's friends were formally introduced—the elderly widow in black as a Mrs. Warring, proud to know herself as Van Croft's aunt, though there was no relation, and the smaller woman in shapeless green was Miss Beedle of Eastbourne, a respectable spinster.

Tickering over the roof the hail continued, rattling harder or softer with the gusting rain. Mrs. Akehurst took a place next to her husband, sitting bolt upright as the others found their chairs; Captain Curry being provided a gout stool for his swollen ankle.

"And what shall you give us?" Mrs. Akehurst asked, blinking rapidly.

"Minuet in G Major," Emelyn said loudly, finding the piece as needful as it was ridiculous.

"Handel, just the thing!" the Commodore blurted, rubbing his hands together.

Emelyn set her fingers and—competing with nature's fury—she plucked the first happy notes, coaxing from the strings as much sound as she could muster.

"This lamentable torrent, like an army marching over the roof!" the elderly Mrs. Warring said, addressing her friend, who nodded.

"I daresay it's more cheery if we focus upon the music," Miss Harrington suggested.

The harp strummed on, sharply at odds with the storm. Emelyn thought again of the doctor's fate—very much hoping he'd been undone by his own inebriated folly, rather than vampire attack.

From somewhere distant there came the sound of shattering glass, and the assembly startled as Emelyn pressed the strings to quiet them.

"Now, I'm sure it's only the longhouse," the Commodore announced, standing to address the room. "The western windows have run afoul of the weather, and not for the first time I can tell you."

Mrs. Akehurst stood beside her husband. "We shall put Nathaniel to the repairs. Excellent at the working of wood he is . . . yes very good."

"Nathaniel is no longer with us my dear," the Commodore corrected quietly, assisting his wife back into her chair. "There we are, sit you down again."

For some while Emelyn played, until so distracted was her audience by the crush of the storm there seemed no further point in pretending. Nervous conversation struggled against the noise, and she missed a good deal of what was said, until the ladies shifted their places to sit closer to the fire, while the gentlemen settled nearer the back by Deacon, excepting Mr. Rosch, who surprised the party by bowing and taking his leave without a word.

The sputtering fire did little to combat the gloom, though Fenders engaged it with violence, jabbing forth great heaps of sparks as Emelyn sat watching. Recalling the fortress walls of Hastelbrook, built to an immensity of thickness, she was comforted to picture Sarah and Isabelle in the easeful drawing room, playing games while their mother knit, their father sitting with his nose in the broadsheets, well safe from the howling storm.

Mrs. Akehurst appeared suddenly at her side, leaning close. "If you would be good enough to follow me Miss Morley, your confidence shan't go amiss . . ."

"Certainly," Emelyn said, grateful for the distraction.

Once in the darkened hall she was encouraged by her hostess to continue to the Commodore's private study, with Mrs. Akehurst promising to join her directly. Curious to discover it, Emelyn did as she was bade, finding the masculine office a cozy, if cluttered affair, lit by oil lanterns in wall sconces, with one upon the Commodore's desk. Tall fronded plants accented a crowded table between high shelves of books, with towering drapes of midnight blue hung in the corners of the windowless room. Drifting to explore she found maps and charts spread about or rolled in their cases, with ship's plans on easels, stark naval portraits about the walls and framed medals of valour. And beside one of these, on a writing table atop a stack of heavy books, there was what appeared to be a slender human skull, worn round and smooth—very old it looked, almost as though it were made of wood. There were too pointed teeth both above and below, as like the canine fangs of a vampire, though considerably shorter, and ungraceful, she thought, to those she had witnessed in Vaela.

Eyes wide Emelyn handled the object, finding it weighted by metal, likely lead, filling the cranial cavity. Turning its face, she was just examining the teeth when she started, finding the lady of the house staring from the doorway.

"That ghastly thing is none of yours, dear," Mrs. Akehurst said, coming to take the skull and return it to its place.

"Apologies," Emelyn said quickly. "What is it, may I ask?"

"It belongs to Mr. Rosch—that should be all one needs to know of it. Now, please sit—the service will be along directly."

"Thank you," Emelyn said, accepting Mrs. Akehurst's direction to a sofa thick with animal hide upholstery, adjacent the low fire.

"Do you know, Miss Morley," the lady began, taking a delicate seat opposite, "my godson has been a part of this household since the tender age of eleven; fate was unkind to the parents of his birth."

"It must have been hard—"

"He was a determined boy who came up very strong—in the Royal Navy by fourteen, he was created viscount and baron not six years later, owing to his extraordinary mettle at the Battle of Avola."

"Yes, I read of it," Emelyn said. "He destroyed three enemy frigates, by fire."

Mrs. Akehurst smiled with pursed lips, pulling a kerchief to dab her neck as toasted cakes were brought in, with Brie de Meaux and mulberry preserves, beside biscuits and hot coffee against the cold.

"And since that time," Mrs. Akehurst continued, selecting a biscuit, "though scarcely exerting himself, he's captured many a fawning beauty, while being himself captured by none—until just now."

"Thank you, madam," Emelyn said, offering a warm smile.

"But strange, is it not?" Mrs. Akehurst posed, "that love may work her seduction upon even the strongest of men, in the most unlikely of circumstances."

Emelyn nodded, certain the lady's words were meant to insult her, and for some while they partook in silence. The storm raged on, though blessedly softened by the central location of the Commodore's study. Nevertheless, Mrs. Akehurst appeared to grow increasingly anxious.

"The hail has stopped, that is something at least," Emelyn suggested, wondering to see her so pale.

"Yes."

Lightning cracked again, and they sighed together. Emelyn dipped a biscuit in her coffee. "I think you will be pleased to hear," she ventured, "that I mean for us to depart, the moment the weather breaks."

"I suppose you speak for the four of you, my godson inclusive?" Mrs. Akehurst asked, "though as we've had no trace of him it begs the question, is he safe?"

"But I can't imagine otherwise," Emelyn said. "He must be waiting out the rain, warm and dry in Eastbourne, if he is not at the Two Brothers."

"Let us hope." The lady effected a smile, rising to her feet as Emelyn did the same. "Nay, Miss Morley, please sit—tarry a moment, if you will."

"Very well." Emelyn took her seat again, watching as her hostess moved to the door, and paused.

"You understand, I must protect him," Mrs. Akehurst said, looking back with a strangeness in her eyes. "I will not allow your fall to be his," and opening the door she slipped outside, closing it quickly behind her.

Aghast at her words Emelyn jumped to her feet, marking the sound of keys. "Mrs. Akehurst?" she called, and setting down her plate she rushed to the door, finding it locked. "Mrs. Akehurst!" she shouted, banging on the door.

"*They think they shall be heard for their much speaking,*" came a man's voice from behind her. "But none will hear you over the storm, Miss Morley."

Emelyn turned with a gasp as he appeared from behind the corner curtain, swishing it aside.

"Mr. Rosch!"

If not for his Puritan uniform she might not have recognized the man—gone was his saturnine glower, replaced with a glowing self-satisfaction. His buttoned black coat was adorned now with a strict white collar under his chin, his broad brimmed hat low on his brow, and he wore wide cuffed dark gloves, one of which rested on the pearl haft of a dagger at his belt. "You agreed to speak with me, of what dark things we must," he said, giving her a bow.

Emelyn flushed. "Nay, sir, I'll not speak to you here alone. I demand you open this door at once."

"Mark these books upon the table!" Rosch exclaimed, indicating the stacked volumes beneath the skull. "*Cases of Conscience Concerning Evil Spirits, Wonders of the Invisible World, Saducismus Triumphatus,* and *The Malleus Maleficarum.* Can you guess their purpose?"

Emelyn shook her head vaguely, astounded to find herself in such a situation.

"They are for the detecting of witches, Miss Morley."

Mortified dread rose in her breast. "What is this? Do you mean to accuse me, Mr. Rosch?"

A boom of thunder rattled through the walls, and with a wry grin he spread his arms. "*Base profane her virgin heat! Many a man of lordly name would succumb to her entreat, masculine moth to female flame, in carnal ash to fall again!* You will forgive the subterfuge, Miss Morley, but such a case as yours requires delicacy—"

"I have no *case,* sir," Emelyn protested. "Van Croft might have your head for such a prank!"

"I have known the man longer than you've been alive," Rosch

snapped. "There is nothing he loathes, Miss Morley, so much as superstition. When he apprehends your claim to unholy powers—"

"Unholy powers?" she interrupted. "Are you mad? Let me out!"

"Peace my dear," Rosch said, a thin smile on his lips. "I do not threaten to ruin you—rather, I mean to save you."

"To save me," she balked, vibrating with anger as she turned to bang the door again. "Anyone!"

"Nay, Miss Morley, they cannot hear you. The others are locked in the salon, for their safety, as you are locked here with me."

"I am not, I refuse," she said sharply, tugging at the door. "You cannot think to keep me here."

"You see," he said casually, drawing his finger over the crown of the skull as he watched her, "I knew you for a caution of vanity from the very first—but a young lady so *express* of attractions, should not be taken with the immodest fashion of nakedness about the neck."

Thunder boomed over their heads in the distant sky, and Emelyn released the latch, turning slowly to face him. "What do you *want* from me, Mr. Rosch?"

"Your confession, Miss Morley. You will confess in writing to seducing the captain, and to your unholy fraternity with forces of darkness."

"*Forces of darkness?*" Her anger melted to disbelief, and disbelief to fear. "I have nothing to confess, sir! I do not traffic in the supernatural, and I have seduced no one."

"You have seduced no one?" Mr. Rosch gripped the haft of his dagger, stepping closer. "Heaven has blessed you in face and figure, Miss Morley—you cannot be unconscious of the languishing looks you inspire, of the spell you have cast over my old friend."

Emelyn marvelled at him. "I can no more help my face and figure than you can help *yours*, sir. And I do not cast spells—the captain is his own man, but perhaps I am here because your lust has run away with you."

Snatching off his hat Rosch set it on the table before reaching a gloved hand into his pocket, which he withdrew to cast a folded scrap of paper at her feet. "Lust? Nay, over me the apple of lust has no power. But long have I suspected your fall . . . Now I have the truth of it."

There was a cold judgment in his eyes, as though he looked upon a murderess sentenced to hang. "Read it, Miss Morley," he said. "And then you are free to go."

"And what is it?" she asked, fighting a deep and rising alarm.

"Aloud, if you please." Mr. Rosch smiled sweetly, his mouth drawn tight.

Keeping her eyes upon him she crouched, and fetching the paper stood up to unfold it. "*She who watches me,*" she began, and froze, her heart in her mouth. "Have you invaded my private diary?"

"You were careless, Miss Morley, to take no better care of it," he said, placing a hand on his chest. "Only then I will set you at liberty."

Tension coiled within her. "You understand this text is *private,*" she said. "It's a fantasy, Mr. Rosch, a caprice. Nothing more."

"To the end, Miss Morley."

Her neck was sweating, but standing rigid Emelyn continued: "*She who watches me from the darkness is . . . a living vampire, which I believe in my heart I have always known.* Really sir, that is quite enough."

Mr. Rosch examined his hat on the table, frowning as he turned the buckle. "Read on."

Heart pounding, Emelyn raised her brows, determined to find him a fool. "Very well sir, let us continue. *Her name is Vaela Audette de Masseine, and it was she who,*" she paused, "*who murdered Philip Denlund. This revelation should terrify but I feel nothing for the man, brute that he was.*" Here she stopped. "I will read no more of this. There is no such person, of course, she is only—"

"*Vaela took of my blood again tonight,*" he said, reciting her words, "*and in a wondrous heightened moment I tasted hers; but she maintains the bond between us is strengthened every year.*"

Emelyn dropped the paper. "Let us have no more fictions," she said, quivering with disgust to hear Vaela's name on his lips. "You have conspired with our hostess, but this game is done—"

"Tell me!" he cried, "does this vampire spirit appear to you always as a woman? Or perhaps as a great black dog—such a form as the daughters of Lucifer are known to take. For it is by her influence that these evil omens attend you."

"*What* evil omens?" Emelyn retorted.

The storm surged over the house, but somewhere high above, beneath the consuming clouds, the sun yet burned in the daylight sky. Vaela would be taking her sleep of the dead, and could be of no help to her now—the thought was desperate as it was maddening.

"Since your arrival," Rosch said, "four innocent lives have been lost, the property wall lies broken, as though by inexplicable attack, you fall to unnatural illness, and then the storm—days of black skies and no rain, and now, the wrath of heaven looses itself upon us!"

"You blame me for these things?" she said, challenging his gaze. "And yet *you* arrived only shortly after myself. Shall I have your confession as well?"

She heard the blow as much as felt it, a jarring knock as gloved knuckles caught her hard across the face, and she staggered with a noise, the side of her head furious with pain.

"You play for time," he said, adjusting his glove with deliberate calm. "Unrepentant slave to darkness, perhaps the sting of violence will reach you, where words cannot."

Emelyn wiped the blood from her mouth, straightening up to face him, her eyes wet.

"There," he said, "at last you understand," and seizing her by the arm he pulled her closer. "You will sign, and I shall keep these unfortunate revelations a secret pact between us—conditional on your cooperation."

"What cooperation?" she asked numbly, speaking against the ache as he guided her forcefully to the table.

"You will help us capture the creature to which you are in thrall."

Emelyn sat at his behest, head throbbing as she looked with bleary eyes over the papers before her. "I should like to read it first," she said thickly, "what I am to sign."

"By all means," he replied, turning over the page for her perusal:

> *I, Emelyn Elizabeth Morley, in full lucidity of mind do attest to the facts herein:*
>
> *I duly concede the coincidence of my arrival at the estate of Galecliff on Beachy Head, with the following events.*
>
> **In the first:** *the disappearance and presumed death of three members of staff.*
>
> **In the second:** *the inexplicable destruction of a pavilion tower on the estate, including partial collapse of the boundary wall.*
>
> **In the third:** *the descent of a most wrathful storm, worse than any in this company have witnessed, which itself followed the heels of a sudden freezing fever in my person, which set me muttering and screaming in delirium, expelling black bile and crying out the name of my secret tormentor.*

Swallowing hard she looked up at him, accepting the quill pen he offered.

'In the fourth: *I confess to witnessing the unsuccessful attempt of Doctor Boderick Tarville, a gentleman, to cure the state of ill health incumbent upon my brother, which incited me to a sisterly wrath before which the doctor fled, he being found only after his untimely death.'*

"Really sir," she said miserably, "shall you blame me even for that?"

"Go on, Miss Morley," Rosch replied, tapping the paper, "this last out loud, if you please."

Emelyn cleared her throat. "*I further confess to describing in my own hand one Vaela Audette de Masseine, whom I attest to be both an ally and bloodthirsty creature of the dark,*" here she paused to close her eyes against the growing pain in her head, steeling herself to continue, "*who preying upon the living for sustenance did murder one Philip Denlund at Hastelbrook, my home. I further confess to explaining a connexion or 'bond' between myself and the vampire, by blood shared each with each, which I maintain has given rise to an increased acuity in my mortal senses.*

Duly witnessed and signed,

Emelyn dragged her eyes from the impossible words, her pen hovering as she glanced at the skull.

"Ah, this!" Rosch exclaimed with cheer, as though a treasure long forgot had been brought to mind. "The *Skull of Udora*—she might have been a vampire thrall, or only a sympathizer, but she imagined herself a drinker of blood—she filed her teeth, just here."

"I see."

"She murdered a child, Miss Morley," he said, his expression going cold, "and found herself executed by fire, in 1627, Bavaria."

Emelyn's stomach clenched, her heart beating hard as she stared at the object. "You mean it to frighten me," she said. "But if aught you've told me tonight is true, perhaps it will do me good. May I touch it?"

"Yes, very well," he said. "There, feel the weight of it, the cranial echo of one damned, Miss Morley—do not let her fate be yours."

Emelyn swallowed, turning the heavy thing in her hands.

"This wood-like texture is a natural patina," he said proudly, "consumed in fire only to rehearse her eternal damnation—"

Here his words failed, for Emelyn stood suddenly, and with a hard swing she cracked the heavy skull against his head. Rosch staggered with a grunt, and unsheathing his dagger he swung wildly. Emelyn gasped, retreating a step as the blade nicked her shoulder, leaving a narrow split. With a gurgle he crashed into one of the cases to lean, eyelids fluttering as blood bloomed in his forehead, and with a groan he turned to collapse, crashing face down like a puppet sheered of its strings.

There was blood upon the skull, and Emelyn dropped it, her fingers tingling. She crouched, seizing her aggressor by the shoulder, and with a soft and desperate prayer she turned him over. There was a matted and growing bruise about his eye, but an insensible sound escaped his lips, and her heart leapt.

"You live, Mr. Rosch," she breathed. "I am sorry, sir . . . but I cannot regret. I will not abide you should threaten her."

Digging into his pockets she found not only further pages he'd copied from her journal, but a second accusatory letter, wherein he described her bewitching of Lord Van Croft, with a list of observations for evidence, the personal nature of which made her blush with a fury. Beneath these papers was a little key, and this she took with his dagger, resolved the weapon could by no means be left within his reach.

Fearing the pages must be hidden off her person, she moved to the darkest corner of the room, and tucked them between the covers of *The War of Succession*, a heavy-bound book filed with others of its kind, on a dusty shelf. To those documents she added Mr. Arkwright's letter, which had lived still in her pocket, guarded by the enigmatical coin of Saunmoor. With the papers hidden, she dashed across the room to fumble the key into the lock. The bolt turned, and with dagger in hand she shifted into the hallway, shutting it quickly to lock behind her—when she was startled by a shrill cry.

"Mrs. Akehurst!" Emelyn panted, finding the woman staring in wide eyed terror, "whatever you've done, it is forgiven—now you must help me!"

"Murderess . . . you've murdered him!" the lady bewailed, and with a shriek she ran.

"Wait!" Emelyn cried, catching a ring of keys as Mrs. Akehurst turned to fling them at her.

"Come not near me!" the lady shrieked.

Emelyn pursued her to the front doors, where her quarry pulled them open to dash outside into the driving darkness.

"No!" Emelyn shouted, but she could go no farther, and stopped to lean in the doorway as pain turned to dizziness, the hallway tilting around her. For some moments she stood there unsteadily, until with a furious groan she turned to dash back down the hall, making for the locked salon.

A great roll of thunder shook the house, and after taking some time to locate the correct key she barged into the room, finding stunned faces. Captain Curry sat for quadrille with the Misses Beedle and Harrington and Mrs. Warring, while the Commodore and her brother stood by with their drinks.

"Miss Morley, good Lord!" The Commodore cried. "What on earth has happened?"

Dagger and keys dropped with a clatter. "You're playing cards!" Emelyn exclaimed, affronted tears warming her eyes. "Is nothing amiss? Did you never realize you were locked inside?"

There was a flurry of movement and she was surrounded by all, though her brother only stared, pale with disbelief.

Too rattled to resist, Emelyn allowed herself to be fussed into a chair at the table. The cards were swept away and Breda with Miss Harrington set upon her, staunching the cut on her shoulder and wetting a kerchief to dab her face. Wincing at their attentions Emelyn struggled to explain what had happened, being as charitable as she could manage for the part Mrs. Akehurst had played. "And now she's run outside through the front doors, as like she were afraid of me . . ."

"Dear madwoman! Whatever could have possessed her?!" the Commodore cried, hastening from the room.

"If only we'd a doctor!" the widow Mrs. Warring put in, watching as Breda dabbed Emelyn's bruised cheek with a kerchief dipped in brandy.

"I'm all right," Emelyn said, hand pressed to her heart as it knocked in her chest.

Having retrieved Rosch's weapon, a stone faced Deacon turned it in his hand. "If unconscious, the man must be bound and secured before he wakes," he said.

"Quite right," Curry replied. "I never trusted the scamp; he's no sporting parson, neither fishes nor hunts nor rides—"

At this Emelyn moaned with a painful laugh.

"And his talk of *vampires*," Curry continued. "Ever there is a darkness of suspicion about him—I only wish we'd seen the danger."

"You will excuse us, sister," Deacon said, halfway to the door.

Curry bowed his leave, the men departed, and Emelyn slumped in her chair, withering under the ladies' questions.

"Why ever should he target *you*, dear creature?" Mrs. Warring posed.

"You weren't to somehow provoke him?" Miss Beedle asked.

"Surely not," Miss Harrington put in, "mad as dog froth, that man."

"But why Miss Morley in particular?" Miss Beedle persisted.

"He finds her a servant of *Lucifer*, if you were listening," Mrs. Warring huffed.

The questions continued, and Emelyn answered truthfully as she dared, until Miss Harrington put a stop to it.

"That's quite enough. We must let her alone now, if you please."

Offering another round of sympathies, Mrs. Warring with the green bonneted Miss Beedle left the room, followed by Breda for fresh towels, and the roaring storm held sway once more.

Emelyn stared through the glass into the dark, reliving the knock of the leaden skull against Mr. Rosch's face, and wondering what must come next.

"My sweet Lord . . . the indefensible brute," Miss Harrington muttered, checking her wounded shoulder again. "The law will have him."

The aching side of Emelyn's head had begun to quiet, and wiping her eyes she sat up straighter. "Would I could forget him this instant," she said.

"Of course." Miss Harrington sat beside her, eyes glistening with anger. "How Lord Van Croft should ever allow such a monster among us, but it is impossible!"

Emelyn shook her head gently. "I hope they fetch Mrs. Akehurst back inside."

In the hallway shouting had ensued, words rising over the onslaught of the weather—

"*Dammit man you will go to her!*" the Commodore ordered. "*I am wasted here; the war saw to that. Now get you to the pond!*"

"By the seat of my back I will not sir," Fenders rebuffed. *"And you'll find none below stairs what'll do it, not after three of us gone missing. Drag her back 'eself, and best hurry before she's off the bridge!"*

Emelyn shared a look with Miss Harrington, and rushing into the hall together they found the other ladies, catching just sight of the Commodore as he stormed after the fleeing footman.

"What's going on?" Emelyn asked. "Is it Mrs. Akehurst?"

"Come and see!" Miss Beedle called, leading them to the stateroom, wherein Deacon had first been laid on the sofa after his collapse.

Together they crowded the windows at the back of the room, and Emelyn gasped, for there through layered curtains of rain she could just make out Mrs. Akehurst like a tattered shawl in the wind, having reached the centre of the bridge over the rushing pond, which fumed and boiled so high it looked to overcome her at any moment.

"She does not swim!" Miss Harrington bewailed.

"The fiend is secure enough for now," Deacon called in the hallway. *"Is your wife not returned?"*

"Damned ungrateful rats I'll see every one of them out!" the Commodore bellowed. *"The footmen are worthless; I must go for her myself!"*

A sudden conviction overcame her, and without a word Emelyn bolted, racing down the hall to overtake him.

"Wait sir! I cannot allow you should go on your own," she said breathlessly, catching him by the arm.

"I beg your pardon, Miss Morley, but neither Curry nor your brother are in any state . . ."

"I will go."

"Never my dear! I doubt not your bravery, but for a young lady in such a squall—"

"I can swim well enough," she interrupted, "if it comes to it."

The Commodore spluttered in protest, but she was already away, through the doors and out into the open arms of the storm.

The trek around the house was softer and wetter than she might have hoped—rushing mud swallowing her ankles at every step as the pelting rain swept close. Trudging along the wall for meagre shelter she reached the rear east corner, where through the deluge she saw the pear trees leaning dangerously in the wind. The pond had exploded beyond its borders to swirl about their trunks, its rising foam nearly level with the narrow bridge across.

Pausing for a courageous breath Emelyn launched from the shelter of the eaves, splashing to the foot of the bridge. There in the streaming centre Mrs. Akehurst clung to the rail, and looking up shrieked at the sight of her, slipping on the watery planks as she backed away.

"You must come with me, it isn't safe!" Emelyn called, reaching out as she held against the wind, making her slow approach.

"Have you murdered Mr. Rosch with your witchcraft?" Mrs. Akehurst shouted back. "As you ended the doctor for displeasing you; but how many more must die!"

Emelyn squinted through the water. "I am no witch and I've murdered no one! Please, I'm only trying to help you!"

"Spare my daughter, spare my godson!" the lady implored. "You've won Miss Morley; I charge you to accept my life for theirs!"

"Stop this *madness!*" Emelyn yelled.

Mrs. Akehurst did not answer, but looking to the sky gave a miserable wail and threw herself over the railing.

Screaming in shock, Emelyn watched as the lady's white dress folded into the churning deep, and rushing to the middle of the bridge she hesitated for but a moment, before diving in after.

With a crash the icy water accepted her, the swirling current pulling in all directions. Her petticoats sank with deadening weight, and she surged into the open air with a cough, searching desperately about her. There was no sign of the woman near the frothing surface, and turning over she dove downward, fumbling into a hand several feet below. Going deeper Emelyn caught her under the chin, and wrapping an arm about her she kicked and clawed for progress, rising slowly until her fingers found the air again, where seething with the effort she swam, striving to keep her charge's face above the waterline.

The rain pummelled about them, and with choking swallows Emelyn thrashed her way to the nearest foot of the bridge, dragging Mrs. Akehurst behind, until finding purchase by the stout corner post she was able to touch.

Crawling onto the waterlogged ground she pulled her companion under the shoulders, and against the weight of sopping garments she laid her down to look her over. Mrs. Akehurst gagged and retched, before growing still, and hissing with effort Emelyn lifted her from the ground.

Struggling forward in the lacerating rain she was surprised the weight of her burden was not greater, though the wet wind threatened to topple them both.

The back kitchen doors were nearest, and they burst open as she approached, the Commodore sloshing outside to meet them.

"Foolish girl, Lord bless you!" he cried.

Miss Harrington was there just inside, and put herself to swift use helping the sopping trio out of the weather as Curry and Deacon, who looked on, shouted for brandy and blankets.

Emelyn wheezed for breath, struggling to make words. "I don't know . . . Has she swallowed water? Is she breathing?"

"She breathes miss! She is not drowned!" a tearful Breda declared, watching the Commodore hold his wife as she cast up what she'd swallowed.

After making use of the kitchen basin to cough up a good deal of water herself, Emelyn was helped upstairs to her room, where by the time she'd peeled out of her clothes she found the cut at her shoulder had staunched, while the ache in her head from Rosch's attack was all but depleted. Robed and wrapped in engulfing linens to dry, she insisted on attending the woman she'd rescued, and followed the others to sit beside her as Mrs. Akehurst was bundled into her own bed.

Mrs. Warring and Miss Beedle stood with clasped hands, muttering prayers by the footboard, while Miss Harrington ordered the misadventurous women another round of hot spirits for their nerves. As though in response to their defeat of the pond the storm seemed to be ebbing, and enjoying the quieter atmosphere Emelyn sipped her drink, listening as the ladies talked in hushed tones.

The Commodore returned, and it was quickly explained that Mr. Rosch, secured to a chair in the study, had regained consciousness, and that Deacon and Captain Curry had set upon him, demanding a full accounting of himself.

"He will deny everything," Emelyn said, shivering as Breda wrapped another blanket around her shoulders.

Pacing about the room the Commodore stopped to stamp his foot. "Let him try! When Van Croft returns he will answer for the villain, or earn my contempt."

Mrs. Akehurst suddenly stirred, struggling to sit up. "Out if you please, all of you," she said, her voice dry.

The Commodore kissed his wife's hand, and thanking Emelyn again he gestured for the others to follow as he took his leave.

"Not you, Miss Morley," the lady said.

Returning to her seat Emelyn bundled herself again, and for a time there was silence between them.

The rain washed in waves against the windows, but softer now. "I will never forgive myself," Mrs. Akehurst said at last, her eyes shining.

Emelyn turned the cup in her hands. "I can't imagine what Rosch must have told you. Clearly he deceived us both."

Mrs. Akehurst shook her head. "No my dear, do not pity me, for I've no excuse," she said, attempting a smile. "I have denigrated you at every turn . . . I wanted to trust him, and I put you in danger."

"I'm sorry if I frightened you downstairs; I couldn't very well leave the man his weapon."

Mrs. Akehurst gave a miserable laugh. "Seeing you bloodied with his blade in your hand—in that moment I believed every evil report; I thought you a witch, and that you'd killed him."

Emelyn sniffed with a nod. "I do regret my part in our quarrel," she said, "but I can tell you conclusively, I am not a witch."

"No, Miss Morley, you are not a witch," the lady sighed. "But I have been a coward. I wanted the captain's heart for my daughter, but he's given it to you, and so what have I done, but persist as your enemy?"

"Please, don't exert yourself," Emelyn said, not a little moved at her contrition. "All is forgiven."

"And to think you should risk your life for mine," Mrs. Akehurst continued, stoic against her tears, "when you might have stayed warm and dry, and been rid of my hateful notions forever—"

Emelyn stood, shedding a layer to sit on the bed and clasp her hand. "I'd not stand by and watch you drown yourself over a superstition," she said. "As to our disagreement, I do understand. If a gentleman broke it off with me, and proposed to another woman at Hastelbrook, my mother would never give him the end of it."

Mrs. Akehurst chuckled softly, looking at their hands. "You are too charitable, Miss Morley," she said, wiping her eyes. "But you are the better choice. My daughter has little love for Galecliff—she wastes every penny we provide her."

"I'm sorry to hear it," Emelyn said, reminded again of home. "But if you blame her in any part, for losing Van Croft's heart I mean, I am certain she feels that. Perhaps if you forgive her—"

"Oh dear." Mrs. Akehurst sniffed. "Miss Morley you may be wiser than what's good for you."

"Well, I should like there to be peace between us," Emelyn said, giving her a weary smile.

Mrs. Akehurst squeezed her hand. "What signifies now, is that you are Jonathan's betrothed. I daresay you will find him steadfast and true as any man, even aggressively so. But I suppose, after you are married, you must forbid him to see us. He will agree of course; it is no less than we deserve."

Emelyn swallowed, blinking at fresh tears. "You're wrong madam, I will exhort him to forgive you, as I must."

Mrs. Akehurst pursed her lips, dabbing her eyes. "These dark events that have attended your visit, they frighten me, I'll not pretend otherwise . . . but you cannot be the cause, and I am sick with shame for my part in accusing you."

"The coincidence is unsettling, the only point whereupon Rosch and I agree," Emelyn said, and thinking of the monstrous man with the burning eyes, she braced for the question. "But is it certain, the footmen have met their deaths?"

"I was at first hopeful they might have run away together, but without their purses, or even boots for the road? Nay my dear, Nathaniel and Jack, and our poor scullery Henrietta, who went after them . . . gone. There's nothing left now but the unhappy task of writing to their families. As for the poor doctor's fall from the cliff, I shall let my godson see to his affairs."

Emelyn nodded, finding nothing more to say.

"I would only advise, regarding your engagement," Mrs. Akehurst added, "that after observing you more closely than I had any right, I do wonder whether you might truly come to love him, for though he pretends he needs it not, I know that he does."

Emelyn nodded again, feeling a lump in her throat. "In all honesty our brief courtship has been something of a whirlwind. He is very proud, but I'll not deny my regard for him has grown, even to my own surprise. I cannot promise we should be a perfect match, but I will try with all my heart . . . and I should like your blessing."

"Oh, my dear girl," Mrs. Akehurst said, and the ladies shared an embrace.

Chapter 27
Judgment

Leaving Mrs. Akehurst to rest Emelyn repaired to her room, where sitting at the writing desk she stared at little round portraits on the wall, though she did not see them. The harrowing plunge into icy water had so shocked her senses that Mr. Rosch's ambush seemed almost unreal by comparison, and yet she'd the inescapable feeling a terrible reckoning must come of it.

Her compromised journal lay open across her lap, and resting her hands upon it she fixed her tired eyes on the inkwell, wondering what Mr. Rosch must have said to Deacon and Captain Curry, and they to him.

Her head nodded, the swoon of sleep creeping in, and she thought of Vaela, imagining the vampiress stood just beside her . . .

"*I am here,*" Vaela said.

Emelyn sat very still, striving to sense her presence. "Are you here in being? Or do I only imagine it—"

"*You are asleep. If I could come to you now, if I could destroy your enemies in daylight, I would.*"

"I was foolish to write of you in my journal," Emelyn repined, finding the room shifting and insubstantial. "I've exposed you—he has violated our secret."

"*Grant him no such power,*" Vaela replied, clasping her shoulder. "*Mr. Rosch cannot stay at Galecliff forever; perhaps when he leaves I shall make his acquaintance.*"

"He not only believes—he fancies himself a hunter," Emelyn said. "He has studied your kind, with all your supernatural ways; he will not be easy to catch," and she closed her eyes as Vaela kissed the top of her head.

"I cannot linger, your dream is delicate."

The door creaked open, and Emelyn jerked awake, finding herself still in the chair.

"Beggin' your pardon miss," Breda said. "I wanted to look in, to see if there were aught you needed?"

"Where are the others?" Emelyn asked. "Shall I come down?"

"The gentlemen confer in the dining room, but you are requested to remain upstairs with the other ladies, to rest if you're able."

"I'm too exhausted for sleep," Emelyn said, closing her journal. "But I suppose there's no word from Lord Van Croft?"

"Nay miss, sorry to say."

"Thank you."

Her lady's maid disappeared, and with haste Emelyn locked the door before sprawling herself on the carpet, one ear down to listen. Drawing her hearing downward through the floor, she soon found voices:

"She would condescend to testify against him this very minute," the Commodore declared, *"but I'll not see my Genevieve's good name besmirched for an accomplice; she was in no right state and only deceived by terror."*

"Carefully sir," Deacon said, a hard edge to his voice. *"Even much to her regret, your wife has abetted a villain, or this travesty could never have taken place."*

"Gentlemen please," Captain Curry put in, *"let there be no talk of setting the man free. I should sooner call him out for pistols. He must stand trial for these crimes, long in the planning."*

"Our prisoner is a fox," Deacon said. *"Put to a jury he will air his conspiracies. He will cite evidence, and exercise the benefit of clergy if he can. My sister has been through enough. I will not put her to further indignity."*

"Quite right," the Commodore said. *"Any trial could go the worse for Miss Morley, particularly if the coincidence of these dark and horrible events is brought to bear."*

"You're not suggesting there's any merit to Rosch's accusations?" Deacon checked.

"Of course not; tripe and nonsense. What I suggest is we keep the villain locked where he is. When Lord Van Croft returns he must advise us on the disposal of this unfortunate matter."

"And answer for the man he calls friend," Deacon said darkly.

Envisioning Mr. Rosch bound to a chair in the study Emelyn suddenly feared for the documents she'd hidden, and slipping from her room she rushed to the stairs to ease her way softly down.

There were no footman to be seen, and finding the study door yet unlocked she drifted it open to peer inside.

Mr. Rosch was asleep at the back of the room, his head bound in linen over the wound, his chin lolling on his chest. Creeping closer Emelyn found his arms were secured about the back of the chair, knotted together in sturdy rope. The bookshelves seemed undisturbed, and finding *The War of Succession* where she'd left it, she was just pulling down the heavy volume when at a wheezing chuckle she turned quickly to face him.

"Ah, Miss Morley, you've come back, and for a book no less, how banal," Rosch said, displaying the bruised gleam of a swollen eye as he made some effort to regard her. "But now that you are here, I should like to tender my apology."

"Would you?"

"Indeed madam, I should not have lived to so ripe an age without knowing when I am beaten. I think it were best for all concerned, that we put this sordid business behind us."

With an angry flush Emelyn clasped the book to her chest. "I think you rather mean that your assault should go unpunished. But tell me Mr. Rosch, can it be possible that you've come to some remorse?"

There was a twinkle of self-satisfaction in his eye. "Remorse? Nay, in the trade of violence we are equals." He shook his head. "But now, truly, I know you for a witch. How else to explain your unholy pact—by your own hand in thrall to the vampiress, and yet so uncommonly lucid. Has the creature seduced you to damnation, Miss Morley, or is it rather that *you* have seduced her?"

"That is the very worst apology I've ever heard," she said, turning to leave.

"*Give them according to the wickedness of their endeavours!*" he declared. "I will be released, Miss Morley, lest every dark rumour of yourself, your home and your family be laid bare before a jury. I know too of your *country handsome* Mr. Arkwright," he added, just as she reached the door.

Emelyn froze, standing with her back to him.

"You've scented a page of your journal by his perfume. What would Van Croft make of that I wonder?"

Emelyn shook her head. "You would be wise, sir, to forget my journal and everything in it."

"Ah, you've not burned it?" he asked quickly. "No . . . it is precious to you. Good! But I do not deny that I've injured you, and you put paid to that, before your cowardly brother added injury to insult. A brave man, crippled under God, but happy to correct an enemy helpless—"

"My brother defends whose he loves!" Emelyn retorted, speaking over him. "After what you've done, do you imagine deserving any consideration of fairness?"

"Oh, the magistracy will find our case *most* compelling," he snapped back at her.

Her hand was on the latch, but she turned again and walked quickly to face him, leaning close. "Has it not occurred to you, Mr. Rosch, that if your suspicions of me are correct, in how much danger have you placed yourself?"

The witch hunter swallowed, and she marked a flicker of fear in his eyes, but he smiled. "I am of the *elect*, Miss Morley. I will go to my rest unburdened, to be greeted by lily fields and streets of gold. *You* will sink through the mud at your end, to the eternal lake of brimstone, to fire and darkness."

"Fire *and* darkness?" she posed, straightening up. "Goodbye, Mr. Rosch."

Returning to the door with her book she was startled when it began to open from the other side, revealing a surprised Deacon.

"Emie, what in blazes?"

"I'm just leaving, I only wanted to see that he was secure."

"He shan't escape bowline knots in a hurry, but you should be upstairs—"

Emelyn brushed past him. "Excuse me."

"Mr. Morley, Miss Morley!" Rosch pronounced, seizing their attention. "Let me see the time is now half past noon. As regards my impending release—"

"That has not been decided sir," Deacon shot back as Emelyn paused in the doorway.

"What release?" she asked.

"As regards my impending release," Rosch repeated, "I am prepared to take whatever vehicle is afforded me. My men await at the

Two Brothers, and I must depart from thence in time to reach Horsham before dusk. Let us part our separate ways, and I shall pursue my charges against Miss Morley no further."

"And what of her charges against you?" Deacon demanded, stumping toward him.

"Deacon," Emelyn said, "the drawing room, please. We must say no more in front of him."

"Yes," Deacon replied, staring at Mr. Rosch, "the drawing room. Go on Emie, I'll join you directly."

Thunder yet shook through the sky, and swishing into the drawing room Emelyn sat herself at the chess table by the windows, the same over which she'd been interrogated for her accomplishments by Mrs. Akehurst. The image of Mr. Rosch battered in defeat, yet smugly defiant expecting his release, was unsettling. But to imagine Lord Van Croft's wrath in her defence was a welcome distraction, and she found herself dearly hoping the captain had come safely through the storm.

"There's nothing more to be done," she muttered, setting the large book on the window ledge as she looked out over the beleaguered gardens. The storm continued to wash and trample the hedgerows, but in the distant sky there shone a brightening edge of daylight.

At the sound of Deacon's approach her eyelids fluttered, and she sat up.

"Emie, are you falling asleep?"

"No, it's only the rain."

"You've been through enough," he fussed, leaning on his crutches as he stopped by the table. "I daresay none of us have slept well under such weather; you should go up."

Emelyn shook her head. "What did you say to him? But you must realize everything that man says is a lie."

"Yes . . . of course it is," Deacon replied, lowering himself to sit. "Nevertheless, as I am your chaperone, miserable job though I've made of it, you must tell me precisely what happened in that room."

"I already have. Mr. Rosch is a hidebound Puritan lunatic."

"But he made no attempt—that is, you would swear he did not try to force himself upon you."

"No sir, he did not," she said, blinking at the sound of sudden thunder, yet closer than she liked. "If he'd attempted it, I think I'd have left behind not an unconscious aggressor, but a corpse."

Lightning cracked again, flickering over the chess board. "Just as well you did not," Deacon said. "But still, I am at a loss to explain how my bookish sister should overpower a seasoned man of war so armed."

"By surprise, Deacon," she said, adjusting one of the pieces.

Deacon frowned, plucking the red queen from the board. "You might have killed the man, and this you followed by nearly drowning yourself in the pond . . . to save his conspirator. When you spoke ill of her I should have listened; I must despise her now."

"No, she's apologized and sincerely, with remorse," Emelyn said, "unlike the villain we are bound to set loose."

"You understand that to take him up on charges, to platform him before a magistrate—"

"Would only threaten my reputation, and my engagement, and our family," Emelyn said. "Yes, Mr. Morley, I understand perfectly."

Squeezing the queen in his hand Deacon flexed his jaws, as though striving to contain himself. "It is unjust," he said. "But to flee him, only to make reckless flight into the storm—"

"Is that what possesses you?" she asked. "The pond? I am a strong swimmer, Deacon, you know this. I could not let her drown!"

Her brother examined the chess piece, his expression stoic, though she could feel the distressed beat of his pulse through the table.

"My injuries are slight, and I am not compromised," she said, though her eyes welled as she spoke. "I only wonder that Rosch ever spoke to me civilly, while planning all the while such an attack."

"Don't think of it," Deacon said gently. "Perhaps we could pitch him over the cliffs, after all."

Emelyn smiled, feeling vaguely ill. "We will do no such thing, and he knows it. His injuries will heal, and he must go unpunished."

"But his accusation, it cannot be true," Deacon said, leaning forward, "that you claim fraternity with unholy forces, in your own hand?"

"Of course not. I've a fertile imagination, I always have, just as I've always assumed a person's diary is not for public consumption."

Deacon released her hand, leaning back. "The journal must be destroyed, of course. But he claims it is only part of the evidence he has against you."

"Does he indeed." Emelyn turned to open the book, rifling through the pages. "Let us discover it shall we?"

"Is that *The War of Succession?*" Deacon puzzled, watching as she flipped to the place the documents were secreted.

"Ah, here it is," she said, passing one of the papers across. "A list of what nonsense Rosch meant me to confess to. Shall my bookish brother find it a danger to me?"

Unfolding the page Deacon raised his brows. "Are these his detractions? Then I could scarcely imagine his praises."

Rolling her eyes Emelyn crumpled the quotation from her journal that Rosch had forced her to read, and closing the book she took up what she thought to be Arkwright's letter, gasping to find it was the very page she'd meant to hand over.

"In fact he may just be in love with you," Deacon said. "*I have never breathed a more natural air than I found walking at your side*—dear me."

Blushing wildly Emelyn shook the paper at him. "Stop! This is the one; that in your hand is from Mr. Arkwright. I'll have it please."

With a bemused expression her brother traded the pages. "But Arkwright can have no idea you're *affianced*, unless you've written to tell him?"

"Yes, I've written to him," she said stiffly, folding the letter to stuff in her pocket. "And with cold candour I'm certain Mama would be proud of. Now what of Rosch's abhorrent words?"

Snapping open the paper Deacon creased his brows to read.

"You must forget whatever he says of my journal," she said. "But what of the rest? Are his accusations meet for blackmail, even now?"

Deacon looked it over, nodding with a frown. "A mountain laboured, and a mouse was born."

Emelyn grunted. "Really? So there should be nothing to worry me?"

Employing his crutches her brother stood from the chair with a sigh. "No Emie, I should say he only meant to scare you. I might have come up with a better list myself."

"What does that mean?"

Deacon picked up the red queen again. "Oh you've always been strange," he said, "but if my sister had power over the weather I should berate her failing to share it."

"And what of the rest?"

"You mean that he blames you for the missing and the dead? He might as well accuse himself for all the evidence he presents. Of course it's no surprise that he denounces your power over Van Croft, who's publicly berated him in your defence. But I've seen how the captain looks at you; your enchantment over him needs no witchcraft for the casting."

Emelyn breathed deep. "I will burn the document, but he could just as easily contrive another. Is it certain he will not threaten me again?"

"Blackmail needs secrecy; his violence against you is in the common knowledge now," Deacon said, walking to the fireplace. "Though I wonder at his aim, should he have succeeded. Whatever could he think to gain by it?"

Collecting the hateful list she stood from the table. "He professes himself a scholar of Hastelbrook. Perhaps he seeks the treasure we keep buried beneath the house."

Deacon groaned. "Well," he said, watching as she tossed the unsigned confession into the fire with the crumpled words from her journal, "you must be in the room when your gentleman returns, otherwise I fear Van Croft might end the poor wretch."

Emelyn nodded, and for a time they stood silently, Deacon shifting and glaring as though there were something he was reluctant to voice.

Crackling with sparks the fire settled. Outside the rain tremored over the windows, smearing the garden view.

"Emelyn," he said at last, his eyes glistening as he watched the flames. "Who is Vaela?"

"Vaela?" Emelyn repeated, finding it a strange sensation to speak her name in company. "Deacon, she is only a story, a fancy of imagination. I've been dreaming of her since I was a child."

"I see . . . And in your imagination, is she a vampire?"

"She is," Emelyn replied, watching him as he watched the fire. "And she protects me."

"A vampire who protects you," he said, his expression incredulous. "But I suppose that answers your obsession with the dark."

Emelyn cleared her throat. "What does it matter."

For a moment they stared at the hearth. "It would appear Mr. Rosch believes in Vaela," he said, "he believes that she is real. Do you?"

"Of course not."

"But as a hypothetical proposition, as you say she protects you—if she *were* real, she would certainly find him her enemy."

"I suppose she would, if she were, which she is not. And I'll not burn my journal over it."

There was a distance in his eyes, and leaning on his crutches he took her hand, placing the red queen in her palm and folding her fingers around it. "*Imagine* whatever you like," he said, "but if you do not burn your diary, please take better care of it."

Emelyn toyed with the chess piece. "I will, of course."

Deacon stood tall to stretch. "Did you know," he said, smiling as he spoke, "Van Croft employed Doctor Tarville for his knowledge of animal physick, as well as human?"

"No, I did not."

"He's treated the Commodore's horses; I've had a look through his potions. I'm no doctor, but the science fascinates."

"Does it indeed," Emelyn said. "And what's brought this on?"

"I do wonder, did Tarville fall from the cliff by his own carelessness, or by some other means."

"What other means? Deacon, you must understand, any talk of Vaela, or any other *character* I might have written about—"

"I shall take it to my grave," he said at once.

Emelyn swallowed. "Good," she said, tucking the red queen in her pocket as there came the sound of footsteps in the hall.

"Beggin' your pardons sir, miss," Fenders said from the doorway. "The ladies are returned downstairs, and Mrs. Akehurst should like us to carry on with what regular respectability we might; dinner is to be served and your attendance urgent requested."

"Some good news at last," Deacon said, consulting his pocket watch.

Following the footman, the Morleys made their way to the dining room, joining a solemn gathering. Mrs. Akehurst presided at one end of the long table, which had been restored to the centre of the room with every effort put to its presentation: upon white linens draped to the floor rested crystal-stemmed candlesticks, with a flowering centrepiece of blue germander ensconced in China oranges.

"*The lips of an immoral woman be sweet as honey!*" Rosch cried, reciting an aggressive psalm from his study prison, "*but bitter as poison at the end!*"

Ignoring the outburst Emelyn took her place between her brother and Miss Harrington, across from Captain Curry, who was himself betwixt the widow Mrs. Warring and Miss Beedle, while the Commodore sat at the other end, opposite his wife.

Sympathetic glances were cast her way, and Emelyn focused on the table as the first course was furnished: cow-heel soup, a pickled sprat sallet with olives, and a pungent holobert pie—stewed codfish in a wheaten crust.

Emelyn scraped the dull white soup with her spoon as the party tucked in. "Mrs. Akehurst, I hope you're feeling very much better," she said, breaking the silence.

"Thank you, my dear Miss Morley; I declare I've never been so close to oblivion," the lady responded, "not as I felt sinking under that cold water. But to endure one's own resurrection . . . it is no small thing."

"And he shall bring upon them their own iniquity!"

"Ignore the ruffian, if you please," the Commodore instructed, slurping heartily at his soup.

Captain Curry dropped his fork, huffing with displeasure. "If I'd not turned my damnable ankle," he said. "Miss Morley if you should come to any discomfiture for your unselfish action, even the slightest chill, I should never forgive myself."

"Hear ye the brave effector," Deacon murmured, sipping his drink.

Emelyn pinched her brother's leg. "I appreciate the care, Captain Curry," she said, "but I assure you I am well recovered."

There was quiet again, broken only by the employment of utensils, and more tired than hungry Emelyn demonstrated as much appetite as she could muster, picking the olives out of her salad. The soup bowls were collected, the pie dwindled, and it was not until a resounding boom of thunder that anyone spoke again.

"For pity's sake let us not be cowed—let there be conversation!" Mrs. Akehurst fussed at last.

"Perhaps if we talk of polite and usual things, and forget these miserable events," the widow Warring suggested.

"Hear hear!" the Commodore said, raising his glass. "Come, Mr. Morley, are you for king or parliament? Blue or buff?"

"The Whigs dream of anarchy," Deacon said, wiping his mouth, "the Tories dream of Caesar; I must love them both the same."

"That is his established answer," Emelyn said, cutting one of the larger olives to make it last.

"Let them be blotted out of the book of the living, and not be written with the righteous!" Rosch shouted, his voice coming more clearly than before.

"I say has someone left his door open?" Miss Harrington complained, and the Commodore snapped at the footmen.

"Gentleman, and ladies!" Deacon announced with a smile, though there was unmistakable tension in his face. "I wonder if I might distract you—but have you ever heard how alchemists of old discovered the receipt for creating rats?"

"Rats?" the over-bonneted Miss Beedle repeated. "If there's one creature I shouldn't like to hear more of . . ."

The men chuckled, and Deacon held his smile. "It was quite simple," he continued, "one takes an old horse blanket, damp with sweat, spreads it somewhere dark and cool, and applies atop it cracked barley."

"And in three days, you will find rats there!" the Commodore said with a laugh.

"One cannot *create* rats," Miss Harrington said.

"No indeed, Miss Harrington," Deacon replied, "except perhaps by creating the conditions for their discovery. Now, by interrogation I have discerned that among Mr. Rosch's delusions, it is his irrational fear of the dark, that I find most striking. So frightened is he of doom by supernatural terrors that he travels only by day. He would not so much as stroll his own gardens at night."

"What are you doing?" Emelyn whispered at him.

Deacon laid down his spoon. "By way of revenge, I propose a ripe trick," he said, addressing the table. "Let us bring about the condition of his fear. Rosch demands release in time to reach Horsham by dusk—he will not leave otherwise. So, I say we agree to it, but that he should be given the slowest nags you have, that he might find himself delayed on the road—"

"But that would bring no effect sir," the Commodore said. "He will change both coach and horses at the Two Brothers, and mine shall be returned to me."

"Ah, yes of course," Deacon said, nodding gravely. "Pity."

"For the smartest man I know, you are speaking nonsense," Emelyn said softly, but Deacon only shrugged.

Sombre silence returned, and it might have found no relief but for the appearance of an enormous badger ham, set down with herb buttered squabs, mince pies and pith pudding.

"Beautiful viands! Just the thing," the Commodore said cheerfully as they set to it.

"Miss Morley, you must nourish yourself," Mrs. Akehurst said, serving a generous bite of each on a new plate. "You've et hardly a thing; there we are."

The plate was passed down, and Emelyn smiled politely as Deacon set it before her. "Thank you," she said, finding her stomach in no better mood.

By and by Miss Beedle took a second helping of pudding. "My dear cousin but the pudding is divine," she fawned. "Pray tell me how is it made?"

"*—they perish at the rebuke of thy countenance!*" Rosch called out.

"Ox marrow!" Mrs. Akehurst all but shouted, "with goat's cream and flour, almonds, eggs, and spice-rolled sugar dates of African palm."

Finding risible absurdity in the situation Emelyn dabbed her mouth, smiling into her napkin.

"I declare, Miss Morley is not distressed by his denouncements, but amused," Captain Curry marvelled, toasting her with reverence, "the most fearless young lady I know!"

"Yes, I'm surprised she's lived as long as she has," Deacon said.

Thunder grumbled over their heads, and Mrs. Akehurst snapped her napkin. "How it sours the stomach to consider setting the vile deceiver loose."

"Let us not think of it, not yet," the Commodore said. "I take heart, that Miss Morley is uncommonly strong, for one who has endured so much."

"Am I?" Emelyn was watching the return of daylight as it crept over the grounds, revealing the scrubbed gleam of white stone and flowering plants along the wall. "But I wouldn't know how to compare it," she said, thinking of Vaela.

There was no further outburst from the witch hunter, and free of interruption the party was served brimmers of frothy lemon syllabub for dessert.

Dispatching the tangy treat quickly Emelyn gave her glass to the footman, checking the windows again to find the growing sky soft with fog.

"Now, let us settle the affair over smoke and sherry!" the Commodore announced, clattering the last of his syllabub out of the glass.

Mrs. Akehurst stood from the table. "Come ladies, we shall leave our gentlemen to speak of the villain's fate."

Settled in the drawing room on opposing couches, the women discoursed around her as Emelyn stared into the fire, weary of the topic and responding only when obliged. Miss Harrington expressed a passionate gratitude that things had not gone very much worse, with Mrs. Akehurst chiming in agreement, though the widow Mrs. Warring differed. "Dare we underestimate the fanatic?" she tutted. "Surely a man of such vain apparitions as Mr. Rosch will be thinking even now of his revenge."

But Mrs. Akehurst only laughed, encouraging the others to be at their ease. The conversation continued, and feeling she'd little to share Emelyn sat and listened, nursing a glass of madeira. Her eyelids sued for rest, and it seemed the room began to smell of damp earth, close and raw as the confines of a deep delved pit, wherein the monstrous vampire Vorsadat slumbered uneasily, twitching like an old man in the throes of death, yet hidden from his immortal fear—the burning eye of daylight.

"Miss Morley?"

Emelyn shivered awake, finding Miss Harrington had perched beside her, her expression pained with concern. "Miss Morley, I cannot imagine," she began, "that is I meant to speak to you earlier," and clearing her throat she shook her head. "Of course I've never been accused of witchcraft, though I have been ill-used, for my complexion, for my parentage . . . But you seem so reserved, and I thought surely she struggles awfully; so if you should need a willing ear, you must know I would never betray your confidence."

The young lady's eyes gleamed, and Emelyn nodded. "Thank you, Miss Harrington."

"Kate, please."

"Kate. Thank you, but I am not struggling awfully; I cannot say Mr. Rosch played me false. On the contrary his dark suspicion was upon me from the first, though little I saw it. There's naught to do now but wait. The men must decide what to do with him."

"But did he not threaten to ruin you, or worse—by your injuries I cannot but wonder, did the villain threaten to murder you indeed? Were you not terrified?"

"I suppose I must have been," Emelyn said, though at the memory of the witch hunter's attack—the blow across her face, the bite of his dagger on her arm—she felt nothing. "I feel no depth of hatred for the man, but I do wonder, has he accused others before me? Rotten as he has proved himself, perhaps the world should be happier without him."

"Miss Morley, if you're set on bloody revenge, how may I help?" Miss Harrington giggled, her smile fading at Emelyn's expression. "But, you're not in earnest. Are you in earnest?"

Emelyn leaned to fetch her glass from the little table. "The truth is I don't much care what becomes of Mr. Rosch," she said, staring into the blood red depths of her drink.

Miss Harrington wondered at her with a chuckle. "Well then, I daresay you don't need my counsel, but perhaps I rather need yours. I do find your brother's company diverting—refreshing I should say. Only, I rather fear he might mistake me."

Emelyn watched her. "You'd not have your acquaintance mistaken for charity."

"Precisely," Miss Harrington said, grabbing her wrist. "But considering he is in body burdened the same as my father, the parallel cannot be avoided."

"My brother is very proud," Emelyn said, "and he's never had such a friend . . . but you are genuine—we both see it I'm sure," and thinking suddenly of Margaret she felt a pang of kinship, wondering how the three of them would get on. "Miss Harrington, would you condescend to call on me at Hastelbrook?"

"Oh, Miss Morley, I would be delighted."

The comradery continued thus, Emelyn learning Miss Harrington was one year younger than herself, and that her father, like Mr. Morley, had suffered an unaccountable loss on the western sea, which had put some considerable strain on the family.

The other ladies had grown quiet again, but the dour mood could not hold them as at last the heavens shifted from dark grey to a brilliant afternoon blue, bringing the room to life.

Miss Harrington was soon engaged with Miss Beedle, who was excited to share a receipt for summer preserves she'd lately learned, while Mrs. Akehurst invited Mrs. Warring to tour the grounds, and see what cuttings might be saved.

"The rose beds I've great confidence in," she said, "though I fear the hollyhock and sweet pea shall be a total loss."

Emelyn took the opportunity to summon her focus, to listen again through the walls, though she'd only time to hear Fenders inexplicably promise someone *the task is worth twenty-five guineas*, before the Commodore burst into the room, rosy with drink.

"We have reached our decision, good my ladies."

Mr. Rosch had signed a document confessing his action, to be held in trust, lest he think to pursue the matter further. He was to be released within the hour.

Though partially expected, the news came hard, and Emelyn poured herself another glass, feeling suddenly nauseous. "So it's done," she said.

The Commodore nodded sombrely. "Our youngest footman, Wallace, will attend the blaggard in the small coach as far as the inn. The danger is over my dear, and I pray the house may breathe again."

"Excuse me, I think I shall have a rest," Emelyn said.

Wanting nothing more than to be alone, she slipped upstairs to sink into her bed, and it seemed her eyes had scarcely closed when she opened them at a knock, finding more than two hours had passed.

"Come in," she said, watching as eggs, sausage and buttered bread was brought to her bedside, apparently at Mrs. Akehurst's direction as Emelyn had taken so little at dinner.

"I'm to tell thee miss, that Mr. Rosch has doubtless reached the inn," Fenders said, standing stiffly, "and he shall be well on his way to Horsham now."

"Thank you, Fenders," Emelyn replied, relishing the scent and hoping food would settle her.

After swallowing every bite she took a relaxing wash and changed into one of her new gowns, a clutching and confident mantua of green and white, before making her way downstairs and outside. Descending to the courtyard she found that the beleaguered gardens, though sparkling green after the rains, were but a skeletal shadow of what they had been. Like violently bestrewn chips of paint, thousands of petals frosted the grounds, once fastidious trees were bent or cracked, hedges trampled, and even many of the statues had been toppled over. Nevertheless the storm was done, the open sky liberated from black walled clouds that blew away now far to the east.

The unmistakable sound of an approaching vehicle drifted on the air from the road, and hiking her skirts she wasted no time to the gate, feeling a great relief to just espy a coach-and-four cresting the bare hill some way off. Leaving the wall behind she hastened to meet it, and was surprised to find Van Croft himself riding post on the lead horse, wearing new coats of gold edged cream, his hair tied back and a sparkle in his eye.

"Miss Morley!" he cried, bringing the team to a stop and leaping down.

"Shall I find you riding post?" she marvelled.

The captain did not answer, but startled her as he seized her waist, lifting her for a spin. "How it restores to see you, well and undefeated by the weather!" he exclaimed, setting her down. "How is your brother? Say not that I am too late . . ."

"Deacon is perfectly well, he is fine, much better," she bumbled, "no worse than when we arrived."

"He is better? Has the drunken doctor come to his senses?"

"Not at all," Emelyn answered before she could think. "But my lord much has happened—"

Grinning with hungry delight the captain grabbed her again, leaning for her lips.

"Wait!" She pushed against him. "You must hear me—"

"In a moment, my perfect darling," he interrupted, catching her hand to kiss it. "If Deacon is well, I am glad, but another opinion would not go amiss. I've brought the practitioner I promised; I found him cowering in Eastbourne, sheltered with a tailor of some repute. A willing doctor and new frock coat in the bargain! What say you to that?"

A bulbous wigged man in yellow coats, surely the doctor in question, clambered out of the coach.

Emelyn watched as Van Croft bit her knuckles. "I say . . . congratulations. But my lord, before you arrive we *must* speak of Mr. Rosch."

"Oh what's the stale trotter done now," he said, gripping her shoulders with intensity. "Dear beautiful Miss Morley, but I have news of my own; my commission is safe! The Admiralty shall find no evidence of crimes against charter now."

"What crimes?"

Squeezing her tightly his smile broadened. "My sweet, you shall never command merchant vessels, so you needn't understand; suffice to say only a fool pays every bill of custom, and all questions of load or bearing are put to rest, for the men who lost my ships are proved mad as March hares, come to no fate but that of their own making."

"My lord please, you must listen; Mr. Rosch—"

"But the captain of the *Old Garnet* survived!" Van Croft carried forth, brandishing a letter from his pocket. "I have here all that is left of him, signed by his own hand, and meant to explain the disaster, but oh, the balmiest Bedlam idiot could not contrive such a tale."

"Jonathan—"

"By this I am rendered blameless in every particular! Whether it was conspiracy, or as I suspect some strange malady at sea."

Emelyn tried again—their raised voices clashed, but the captain was louder, and succumbing to the urge, she slapped him.

They stared at each other, and with a wince he rubbed his face, working his jaw. "My lady strikes true . . . I hope she will explain herself."

"I apologize," she said, her hand tingling. "You would not listen."

"Is this the contest you seek?" he breathed, seizing her close with a fire in his eyes. "Shall we roll your dress greener?" and with a growl he pressed his lips to hers.

Though incensed, her body responded, a familiar hunger caught her up, but at the sight of their gawking witness she turned her head away. "Can your convenient doctor make no better use of himself?" she asked, stiff in the captain's arms.

"Back in the coach, Mr. Gainsford, up you get!" Van Croft barked, and the flushed gentleman rushed to climb aboard.

Emelyn covered her face, waiting until the coach door had closed. "Send him on . . . and we must talk."

The captain's smile wavered. "Come now, Miss Morley . . . My dear Emelyn, what's wrong? What's happened?"

"Send the carriage on."

The captain did as requested, instructing the driver to resume his seat, and smacking one of the horses to get them going.

"Mr. Rosch attacked me," she said, watching as the coach rattled on ahead of them. "He struck me, and accused me for a witch. I defended myself, and escaped. He was restrained, but we were obliged to release him. He is gone my lord."

The captain cursed with shock, stepping back.

Emelyn put up her hands. "To make any great matter of it would only bring gossip and scandal; he signed a document confessing himself, before he was freed."

Van Croft's shock required several repetitions of the sordid tale for answer, until with a frustrated noise he bid her cease, and arm in arm they walked quietly together.

"I'm sorry for your ship's captain," she offered. "He must have suffered a great deal."

"His suffering is over; he was not to live long," Van Croft said, holding her hand, and she felt in his touch a familiar fear, which reflected in his eyes was not unlike the rage of terror he'd expressed when she awoke from the monster's attack. On an impulse she brought his hand to her mouth and kissed it, and availing herself of the silence she proceeded to explain at length all that she dared—beginning with Doctor Tarville's untimely end.

"Dammit Bodie!" the captain decried. "And there is no doubt?"

"Captain Curry witnessed the body on the rocks below," she said, going on to describe all that she could guess of Rosch's hold over Mrs. Akehurst, which would have led the lady to drown herself, but for Emelyn's intervention.

"Miss Morley, that's quite enough . . . How could you have been so reckless?"

"Reckless? I could not let her die for spite, not with her opinion of me so horribly wrong headed."

"It was foolhardy," he snapped, keeping her arm tightly. "You are not to risk yourself for that woman."

"You misjudge your godmother, we have forgiven each other," Emelyn said. "There is peace between us, and Mr. Rosch no longer haunts the estate. And you are returned," she added.

"You worried for me," Van Croft said, eyeing her sidelong, and stopping their walk before the high gates of Galecliff he glared at the sky. "But in attacking you Rosch has humiliated me. How could they allow such a thing? Now I am obliged to hunt him down, and compel him to answer."

Emelyn shook her head. "No, not for my sake," she said, feeling suddenly at odds with the relentless daylight about them. But perhaps tonight, or some night yet to come, Vaela might answer Mr. Rosch in her stead. For now, there was nothing to be done.

"There, I see the villain has left his mark," Van Croft grumbled, examining closely her face and neck.

"It's not bad," she said, tickling pleasantly at his touch, and pulling him by the hand she led him a few steps along the wall, that it should block sight of them from the house.

"Dusk will soon be upon us," he said, raising an eyebrow, "and you've no chaperone to protect you here, Miss Morley."

"I think I've proven I can protect myself well enough," she said, allowing him to draw her closer.

"Long have Rosch's holy pretentions amused me," he said, leaning his head against hers. "It is my failure, that I brought him upon you."

Emelyn blinked, tingling as he kissed her forehead.

"Perhaps for tonight he lives," Van Croft breathed, kissing her cheek, "but I make no promise not to hunt the villain down, in future."

"I shan't speak to the future," she said, giving him her eyes. "Nor shall I forgive him."

The captain smirked, and grasping her tightly his lips met hers.

■■

The hazy light of early evening fogged the windows as a drab stagecoach rattled over the ruts, making its way north to join the long road to London. Inside sat Mr. Rosch, a silver lined collar about his neck, a large thumb-worn crucifix clasped in his lap. His hat was at his side, his bruised face weary with displeasure. Across from him sat an unremarkable younger man, pursed of expression in faded coats and the wig of a clerk.

"Twelve guineas to buy off the passengers," the man said, chewing a knot of bread as he spoke. "More than you paid me sir . . ."

"I would not have the unwashed public on the roof of my carriage," Rosch said. "We must move at speed, Mr. Snell; yourself and the driver are paid handsomely enough, more than you're worth."

"Right you are of course," Mr. Snell responded, swallowing down his bite. "Only I might take our apparent haste, and your damaged countenance to mean the situation is changed, and for the worse. Danger costs money sir."

"We are in no danger," Rosch said curtly. "Nor shall we be, once I am safely deposited at the door of Justice Tarbrough."

"And he'll take up the case shall he? Your failed gambit against the eldest Miss Morley notwithstanding?"

Rosch was digging in his pocket. "You are a simpleton," he said. "My *gambit* came off better than I could have hoped. Long has Hastelbrook festered in darkness, and now, that mercenary harlot is proved the centre of it."

"Have you got a letter for me then?"

"Yes damn you, it's here somewhere . . . ah." Drawing a tightly folded packet from the depths of his pocket Mr. Rosch sorted and passed half of it across. "With excerpts from the girl's own diary. Praise the angels, I made copies," he said gravely, returning the secondary pages to his pocket. "When we reach Horsham I shall reveal Miss Morley's self-incriminations to the magistrate, and you shall hire the night coach to London. I dare not trust that missive to the post."

"Aye sir, understood," Snell said, turning the letter in his hand. "And whereabouts am I to deliver?"

"To none other, but directly into the hands of *Miss Ariana Winter*, in care of the Marquess of Crennock, at his hall house in Hanover Square."

Mr. Snell smiled, tucking the letter gingerly into his pocket. "There's a lady you speak of with high trust, sir. Counts herself among the Argentum Serpentis now does she?"

"Miss Winter of the brotherhood?" Rosch clarified, rubbing the crucifix again. "Certainly not; nor am I, not as yet. But she is their most worthy satellite—Lord Crennock's ward, orphaned since girlhood. It was vampires, sir, who took her family."

Snell choked on his bread, blinking with fist at his mouth. "Took them sir?"

Rosch sneered at his discomfort. "Murdered in their beds."

"And thereby her value to you, for an informer?" Mr. Snell caught his breath, coughing again.

"She is no common informer," Rosch said wistfully. "Miss Winter has acquainted the same august order Lord Dramen seeks to impress— the Invisible College—even their provost, *the man with blue skin*."

"Blue skin sir?"

"They say he takes silver dust with his meals, to protect him from the touch of evil. Blue skin an artifact of that dangerous choice."

The coach wobbled, losing speed, but the driver barked at his team, and they resumed as they were.

"And what is the gentlelady Winter meant to do by your letter, sir?" Snell asked.

"The Morley girl's connection to Lord Van Croft must be severed," Rosch said, lifting the crucifix to return it to its place about his neck. "Miss Winter shall prepare our move against the estate, while I apply myself to dissolving the engagement—I will teach Van Croft his error."

"Not easily done, by what you've said of it—Miss Morley got her hooks in him well and deep don't she?"

"I've left word behind at the Two Brothers," Rosch continued. "Van Croft will know where to find me, and there I shall cool his heels with the proof of this . . . demon loving witch," he added, patting his pocket.

Snell snatched another bite of his bread. "And if the order should succeed," he posed, his eyes glittering, "that is, in turning over the old Morley crypt for treasure, dare I suppose those of us loyal to the cause might be remembered?"

"Hastelbrook is a troubled place," Rosch said, grabbing the wall for support as the carriage jostled again. "I cannot speak to the treasure, but the greater glory shall be to capture she who haunts it. *Vaela.* In this I'd thought to compel Miss Morley's aid, but by some unholy luck she resisted." He glanced at the windows with a sigh. "And yet, I am undeterred."

"You've a plan sir, I can smell it." Mr. Snell grinned.

Rosch curled his lip, adjusting his gloves. "When Van Croft is off the board, good Mr. Snell, Miss Morley will have no protection, and find herself obliged to bait the trap. Then, when the monster is caught, I shall invoke the Witchcraft Act, to send our violent fire-haired Jezebel where she belongs."

"Bedlam." Mr. Snell cackled, popping the last of the bread in his mouth.

"Of course it is made illegal to accuse a body of supernatural powers," Rosch said thoughtfully, "but no *less* illegal to claim them for oneself—and this she has done, by her own hand."

"Clever trap that is."

The carriage suddenly slowed, and Mr. Rosch lurched forward with a curse. "Deuce take you!" he yelled, fighting the latch to open the door. "Where is our speed?"

"Apologies!" the driver called back. "The team is slogging sir—what's come over them I can't rightly say."

Rosch clenched the crucifix. "I care not what's come over them, I care not if you lash them red as Saint Bart! We will make Horsham before dusk!"

"Certainly sir!"

But the coach wagged as though the horses were unsure of the road, their pace continued to slow, and by and by the vehicle came to a halt.

Mr. Rosch banged the door open, and barking his displeasure he leapt down. A shouting match ensued, while Mr. Snell toyed with the letter from his pocket.

"Nodding with sleep one and all?!" Rosch bellowed outside. *"It will not do sir! Ten guineas you've been paid, above and beyond your right fare."*

The shouting drew closer and with a twitch of his fingers Snell tucked the letter away.

Rosch pulled open the door. "We are sabotaged," he snarled, climbing into his seat. "The sun is all but set, and we are dead in the road. The animals have been poisoned, or drugged, by something of strength enough to render them senseless," and locking the door he produced a decanter from beneath the seat, which upon uncorking he splashed liberally on the windows.

"Shall I ask what you're doing sir?"

"Water of baptism, for we are obliged to wait," Rosch answered, dropping the decanter and tightening his collar. "Minutes, hours, I cannot tell. But stalled in the road we are not safe; if you've any holy icon about you, now is the time to produce it. They dare not touch men protected by sacred vestments."

"They sir? Are we in danger here?"

Mr. Rosch opened his mouth to respond, but put a finger to his lips. It seemed a stillness had come over the carriage; the noises outside had stopped. *"Sufficient unto the day is the evil thereof,"* he muttered, and brandishing the cross at the dark window he called out. "Come thee, soulless damned! Come monster, come *vampire*, you shall have no power here!"

The silence deepened, and Mr. Snell set the last bite of his bread gently beside him, wheezing with fright. "Do we stay sir? Do we flee?"

"Hush!" Rosch hissed, closing the curtains. "The living earth is cowed to silence—the creature draws near," and startling his companion he shouted again. "By the shadow in my heart I know thy foul presence! Away unnatural demon, away with thee! Or present thyself in atonement, and I shall press the sign of the lamb into thy forehead, and release thy damned spirit to the inferno that awaits thee!"

"There should be none outside but a driver well-armed," Mr. Snell suggested, his face pale, "and four animals dead on their feet, by the sound of it."

Spitting with anger Rosch shushed him again, just as there came a dreadful sound—the whining scrape of something scratching the glass, and with a crash the door broke inward. Pale hands snatched his ankles, and shrieking like a child Mr. Rosch was pulled from the coach into the dark.

For a moment Mr. Snell could hear nothing but his own heartbeat, and fumbling at the lock he unbarred the other door, kicking it open to clamber out, whereupon he called up, only to find the driver's seat empty. The horses stood shifting and sullen, nuzzling the stubbled grass, and he'd just turned for the road when a shadowy woman snatched him from behind. Her fangs found his throat, balance failed him, and whimpering curses he pawed at her icy shoulders as she latched upon him, bearing him to the ground.

Mr. Rosch came to, lying some thirty paces from the road. Struggling to his feet he fled, barrelling through the underbrush, his insides white with fear. Vine and bramble gave way, breaking at last into a starlit clearing, where wheezing for breath he paused, his face prickling with sweat, before dashing across the open. Fishing a silver implement from his pocket he risked a look back, catching glimpse of a slender shadow, low to the ground like an animal, bounding from the woods.

He redoubled his pace, but the shadow flickered closer, and it was upon him. Cold hands caught his nape, pulling him backward to the ground, and his attacker was astride him, pale fingers grabbing his chin. Raven hair tickled his face, and the vampiress bent close, her eyes black as caverns. "Mr. Rosch, I presume."

"Vaela," he rasped. "I knew you would come."

Her gaze bore into him, but resisting the pull of it he turned the implement in his hand. "Tell me," he breathed, protruding a small silver blade from his fist, "is Miss Morley your slave, or is it rather . . . that you are hers."

Vaela sat up, brandishing her teeth in a smile. "Feeble, foolish little man." Her finger touched his forehead. "Emelyn is my heart, and I am her protector."

Rosch sneered. "*Your heart* . . . Walking corpse athirst for blood, your heart is dead." His arm twitched, and the blade plunged into her thigh, driving deep. The vampiress yelped in surprise, grabbing his throat, but the silver collar fumed at her touch, burning her hand, and throwing herself away from him she screamed, staggering backward.

Mr. Rosch scrambled to his feet, holding forth the crucifix. "Away monster . . . away demon! You have no power here!"

She hissed at him, he turned to run, and leaning on one foot Vaela watched, her face sharp with pain as her quarry dashed for the other side of the clearing. Her claws receded as her hands, cracked and singed, slowly restored themselves, and gripping the little wooden handle she pulled the silver blade from her leg with a shriek, casting it aside.

Dropping to kneel she clutched the terrible ache until its smouldering ceased, the agony subsided, and the wound closed. For a moment she rested, and pulling strands from her mouth she tied back the wildness of her hair, rising with dignity. The taste of him was on the air, like a dim tongue of light betraying his path, and baring her fangs she bolted after it.

Alerted to the crash of pursuit Rosch turned to wave his icon about him, but saw no one. Clawed hands caught his back, lunging him into a tree, and with a crack the world winked out—

"Your will is strong," Vaela said.

With a spasm he opened his eyes, finding himself deeper in the wood, flat on his back. His collar was torn away, his body clammy with weakness, his breath coming shallow.

The vampiress stood above him, employing his kerchief to wipe the blood from her lips. "You have threatened she who is most sacred to me," she said. "I thought to put out your rotten heart with my foot, but you are not so evil Mr. Rosch, as you are ignorant—your righteous convictions twisted. Not enough to save you, but it would seem you have found an advocate."

"Advocate," Rosch repeated, his voice barely a whisper.

There was another figure now, shorter than she, standing close in the moonlight. The figure crouched, presenting the face of a man, elder and sharp featured, with a trimmed beard and moustache peppered with grey. He wore a monocle over the lighter of his eyes, while the other gleamed black as volcanic glass.

"Mr. Rosch, it is a pleasure," he said, his voice an eloquent monotone. "My name is Tredavius, and I have been permitted to make better use of you, than food for the worms."

"Vile damned," Rosch whispered, rattling with fear in the vampire's gaze.

Tredavius twitched his moustache. "From one scholar to another, your study of Hastelbrook intrigues me . . . I have tasted your blood, and I do find it promising."

"Take him if you must, and go," Vaela said. "But do not forget his transgressions. He must never threaten her again."

The vampire lord looked up. "Oh my dear, his part against you both is done. He shall belong to me now, until the end."

"By the throne of Saint Peter, away with you," Rosch wheezed. "To the black abyss where you must rot!"

"Certainly, Mr. Rosch." Tredavius smiled upon him. "But not without you."

There came a desperate wail as the vampire snatched his prey from the ground, and with a stir of leaves they were gone.

■■

Van Croft's long-looked-for return was merry, if strained, and it was only with some effort that Emelyn convinced him to accept Mrs. Akehurst's apology for abetting Mr. Rosch—this made the more convincing by the lady's tears over the state of her precious gardens. Bitter over Rosch's liberation, Deacon's appeal to leave the very moment Van Croft arrived was denied, and the wrathful captain ordered the men to the dining room to excuse how the whole household should have failed to protect Miss Morley.

"I'm as guilty as any of you, but I was not here!" he declared. "I will have it gentlemen, every detail."

Once more the ladies were flushed upstairs, and locked in her room Emelyn sat in the window, observing the watery sunset as it dissolved in painted clouds. She could think of nothing but home, and leaning in the corner with her feet on the bench she nodded off, until falling night had unfurled its wings to the horizon, and she woke.

She pressed her hands to the glass, peering over the dark gardens in hope, but no shadow stirred.

"Vaela," she whispered.

There were stern male voices downstairs, though she could catch only phrases, and quitting the bench she sprawled herself on the floor, the better to eavesdrop.

"I looked in her eyes and promised she might rely on you!" Van Croft charged.

"I've no excuse sir," Captain Curry said quietly. *"If I'd not injured myself hounding after that fool doctor—"*

"We all failed her," Deacon interjected, his voice scarcely audible. *"What's done is done . . . what matters now is to see her safely home."*

Straining to focus, her head grew light, and having missed the Commodore's response Emelyn squinted, pressing her ear to the floor.

"Jacob Rosch will not forget the insult of her attack, nor the indignity of his capture," Van Croft warned. *"I worry that he may be working with others—"*

Not another word was spoken that she could hear, for Emelyn had drifted away, swooning into the depths of a dream. There came an insistent sound of knocking, and she found herself somewhere else entirely—trapped again behind the eyes of the monster, the vampire Vorsadat. In a dimly lit space he perched on a high stool like a king of vultures, scratching lines in a wide open book on the raised desk before him. The shelf cluttered chamber was cold and damp, betraying itself for a low room somewhere along the river bank. Her host turned on his perch, and strewn on the floor she beheld a tangled gathering of corpses, ashen white in the faint lantern glow, their bodies frosted with liberal qualities of lime against the stench of their decay.

The knock had come from a little door at the far side of the room, and creaking it open a rotund wigged gentleman peered inside. He was pasty and moist of appearance, as like a sick patient out of bed. With one foot in the room he raised his hand to shield himself as the monster's eyes flashed, illuminating the intruder in hellish light.

"Magistrate Brule," Vorsadat rumbled, his voice low and guttural. *"I have not called for you."*

"My dark lord, I come bearing gifts, one with hair of flaxen gold, the other caramel rich and sweet," the man responded, guiding a comely wide-eyed blonde to step before him into the room, and pulling with effort he struggled to bring another over the threshold. *"Inside Miss Kinsin! One hundred guineas you've been promised!"*

"I won't sir, I won't!" came a young woman's voice, high with distress. *"That cellar niffs of death it does; stop! I won't!"*

The man lurched as though after a frightened animal, and with a broad grin the monstrous vampire chuckled, returning to his book.

"Damn your eyes woman!" the magistrate shouted. *"I'll drag you to the reformers, do you hear me?"* But whoever it was had scampered off.

"Let the harlot away," Vorsadat muttered, recording illegible words on the page with his pen. *"One morsel is good as another."*

"All right then," the blonde said bravely, *"I'll set eyes on those guineas afore I take another step."*

For a moment there was silence, and Magistrate Brule seized her shoulders. *"Steady my lass,"* he said, *"he won't be a moment . . ."*

The girl opened her mouth to answer, and vanished with a cry. She reappeared in the darkened far corner, caught in the monster's grasp, his spidery hand covering her face, and the massive vampire bared grisly fangs, fastening his jaws to her throat.

Emelyn felt a flinch, and striving against the horror of it she tried to wake, but the scene only smeared, rebuilding itself moments later as Vorsadat tossed the woman's lifeless form onto the heap, snatching a bin from the shelves to salt her with quicklime.

"What do you require Mr. Brule?" he asked, pulling a stained kerchief from his ancient coat to wipe the blood from his face.

"Forgive me my lord, I only wanted," the magistrate spluttered, *"I wanted to beg your help, on behalf of Lord Dramen, who is aggrieved by the escape of his immortal captive. But I am certain a dark lord of such venerable power as yourself, surely you might track her, the same she-vampire you so generously guided us to capture in Crawley—"*

In a flicker of movement Vorsadat seized the man by the arms, lifting him like the weight of air. Bloody teeth gnashed close. *"Your foolish master allowed her escape,"* the massive vampire hissed, pressing him to the wall. *"He will stir in humiliation until I am satisfied."*

"Yes, yes of course!" Brule rasped, shaking with fear. *"But then, in your boundless mercy, you will find her again . . . you will return her to us?"*

"The city is her cage," Vorsadat said, snapping his jaws before the man's nose, *"she cannot leave by land nor water but I drag her back. The little baron will have her again, and when he has milked her of use, she must be destroyed."*

There were noises, voices somewhere near, and Emelyn felt herself falling out of the scene, slipping down into darkness, where guided by towering shadows she was led gently back, back to Galecliff, back to her room.

"God's wounds Miss Morley, what are you doing?"

Emelyn grunted awake, still prostrate on the floor, and wiping her mouth she repaired to sitting, finding a perplexed Lord Van Croft standing over her. "I was just . . . I lost a pin," she stammered, accepting his help to her feet.

"You lost a pin?"

The dream danced away, fading into shadows, and Emelyn breathed deep, composing herself. "Never mind. Have you finished your conference?"

"Did you find it?" he asked, puzzling at her.

"Find what?"

"The pin."

"Forget the pin, my lord. What's happened; are we to disembark at last?"

"We have discoursed," he said, taking her hands for kisses. "Doctor Gainsford was useless of course; we shall leave the poor fellow at the inn on our departure, but brandy was served and pipes fired, and consensus reached."

"And?"

The captain smiled. "I have accepted your advice, and your brother's caution . . . for now. I will permit Rosch his freedom. So failing to punish him by my own hands, I broke a candelabrum in his effigy."

"Charming," Emelyn said, leaving him to go to the mirror. "And when are we to leave?"

"Your brother insists it must be tonight, though the hour is very late."

"It's six hours home," she said, examining the yellowing bruise on her cheek. "We should reach Hastelbrook by dawn."

"You must know I could not have restrained myself," he said, embracing her from behind, "had you betrayed even the slightest fear of him . . . You have some strength in you, Miss Morley, but if Rosch in any manner threatens you in future, I shall hunt him down, and murder him in the dark."

"Then let us hope he knows better," she said, covering his hands with hers, "but you are correct that I will not fear him, by day or night."

"Brave girl," Van Croft breathed, gently kissing the sore on her shoulder. "Perhaps I see now, why he thought you a witch."

Her flesh tingled and she closed her eyes. "If I were a witch he'd never have escaped . . . But as I am not, let us think of him no more."

Chapter 28
Consequences

Midnight Tuesday July 5ᵗʰ

In the Liberty of Westminster, just adjacent the City of London, Covent Garden park sat green and sharp between tall townhome buildings. Nestled in the corner amongst them the house marked number six gave way to neatly ordered kitchen gardens behind, enclosed by a private wall. The wrought iron rear gate opened from the street behind to a cobbled path running to meet the columned porch, above which the bedroom window of Fitzwilliam Arkwright flickered by the light of a restless candle.

His untied shirt damp with sweat, Mr. Arkwright stood in breeches and bare feet before the narrow wall-mounted mirror, his dark hair loose and unkempt. His eyes shone bleary in the low light, and raising the candle he pressed his fingers to his neck, looking closely.

"There again, were it a memory we should find a mark," he said firmly. "It's naught but a dream old fellow. You stopped through Crawley, the Hotel George, you took in a show, witnessed a pretty juggling acrobat, and then . . . the stable. But there is no *vampire* . . . there cannot be."

There came a light knock at the door, and he moved to a mounted basin, setting down the candle to splash his face, spluttering in the cold water.

"Really sir, you must take some supper!" the housekeeper's voice called. "It's two weeks now—you're ever shut up in your room. Enson is here, and right concerned; so are we all. I'll be sending for Mr. Mercer tomorrow, and the doctor mind!"

"Thank you, Mrs. Delfrey, that won't be necessary," Arkwright called back, drying his face.

"Please sir," she implored. "Will you not speak to what has distressed you so?"

"Whatever it is will keep till morning; you should be in bed, the pair of you," he said, pouring another gin at his desk.

"There's a letter for you sir," the voice of the aged butler put in, "from a lady sir, Morley."

Smiling bitterly Arkwright took a long swig. "Yes Enson, shots fired and hit, from Miss Morley's mother. I was careless to leave it on the floor; you may dispose of it."

"Not that sir, I mean there's another, arrived by the late post this evening. From Miss Emelyn Morley herself, by way of Eastbourne."

The door flew open with a bang, and Arkwright snatched the paper, startling them both.

"Oh dear, are you quite well sir?" the starkly dressed Mrs. Delfrey fussed.

"Tell me, have you ever dreamt a thing so real, so terrible," Arkwright posed, turning the letter in his hands, "that you forgot the whole of it upon waking . . . only for its memory to return sharp as a blow?"

"Can't say I ever have sir," Enson replied as the housekeeper shook her head.

"This letter is real," Arkwright breathed, shaking it, "but can it be more real than what I recall of that night? For it refuses to be accounted a dream. But if not a dream, it is a memory false, and where then has it come from?"

"You're speaking nonsense, if you'll pardon my sayin' it," Mrs. Delfrey tutted, "and with the gin on your breath. You need food sir, and you need sleep! I've a mind to summon the doctor this very minute."

"Right you are Mrs. Delfrey!" Arkwright interjected, admiring the delicate hand of the letter's address. "Send up some supper if you would; anything will do . . . I'll take it here. And then rest, you have my word."

The closing door muted their response, and crossing the room to his desk he broke the seal, taking a great breath before unfolding the pages to read softly aloud:

'*Sir,*

As this is my fifth or sixth attempt to undertake a response to your letter, which only came to my hands by the deft subterfuge of my lady's maid, I hope you will forgive the sincerities I am bound to express, however indelicate.'

Arkwright paused to finish his drink. "Indelicate in my favour, might I hope," he said, reading on:

'*To begin I should convey that if you were but party to the conversations in my head, you'd have heard already a great many apologies for my lubricious advance at Dhorings Park. I would have kissed you, Mr. Arkwright, and your gallant action to disguise my impropriety as your own I have not forgotten. Your letter means to absolve me of any need to account for my behaviour, but this is not acceptable to me, and so I shall explain myself as far as I am able:*
My life has been subject to certain development of forces, beginning well before that day, the effect of which has been to lurch my experience to such prospects as I could scarcely describe, and which no sober listener would believe. My lapse of boundary and modesty that day was indefensible, but I can assure you, at least, that I suffer no question of illness, mental or otherwise, and have committed no other sin against the common order of society than our salutation on the hill. It is a protection for us both that I expound on this no further.'

Scratching his forehead Arkwright scowled at the page. "My dear Miss Morley, what on earth has happened . . ."

'*As to the sentiments expressed in your letter, the truth is I am so lately drawn to courage over constraint, that I will freely own to finding your company as natural a balm to me as you hold mine was to you, and that it has brightened my spirit to acquaint a gentleman of wit and warmth who allows me for who I am. Alas, I cannot for the necessity of my family cast off the duty before me, and so it is with all aggravated honesty I must withdraw my invitation to Hastelbrook, as well as discourage any pursuit of romantic purpose between us.*'

Dropping heavily he sat on the bed, staring at the wall a moment before braving the end of it.

'In closing I can only say, though I am to forbid any further advance of your acquaintance, I will never forget the tender glimpses between us, and shall ever remember you for a most worthy gentleman, as I subscribe myself always,
Your humble servant and friend, Emelyn Morley'

His eyes gleaming, Mr. Arkwright did not stir for some time, but sat reviewing the downhearted words, until he found himself standing again, unsure what to do next. The paper drifted to the floor, and after pouring another drink he walked to the windows, gazing out over the dark street.

"Mrs. Delfrey's coffyn pie sir, and quarter chicken," a footman called, knocking lightly.

Accepting the tray to a side table by the bed, Arkwright cracked open the high sided pastry, but set down his fork, opting instead for the chicken, which after a single cold bite he abandoned. The panes rattled in the wind, and mindful of his drink he went to creak open the windows, stepping gingerly out onto the high roof of the columned porch, which he found bestrewn with leaves and soot. A hazy fog had settled over the lamplights, reducing them to weary sparks, while only a few late carriages crackled along the wide road, their drivers hunched like old crows.

There came the peal of a great bell, clanging in its steeple several streets beyond, and walking to the edge of the roof Arkwright raised his glass to the sound. "Emelyn Elizabeth Morley," he spoke into the dark, "whatever your secret, it matters not . . . I shall never care for another, as I do for you. Your health!" and bringing the glass to his lips he tilted it back.

■ ■

"I should deplore to see you off like thieves in the night," Mrs. Akehurst lamented, "but I quite understand."

Emelyn thanked her, and foregoing a hat she followed her trunks to meet the gathered company outside. Footman Wallace had returned with the Commodore's coach, just in time to board Van Croft's own for the journey to Hastelbrook.

"You must visit me at home," Emelyn requested of a tearful Miss Harrington by the steps. "I shall hold you to it."

Miss Harrington nodded vigorously. "I will write to you tomorrow," she promised, and smiling at Deacon she allowed him to kiss her hand.

Mrs. Akehurst was overcome, and after a brief and breathless farewell she presented Emelyn with a letter. "For your dear mother," she said, dabbing her eyes with a kerchief.

Emelyn accepted it slowly. "Of course, but nothing *too* diverting I should hope?"

"Not a word of it, except passing reference to your courage, which you must allow me. But I do hope Miss Morley, that you shall remember Galecliff for more than a monument of horror."

Her eyes wet Emelyn chuckled, taking her in an embrace. "I expect you shall have peace again, with the lot of us removed."

The lady of the house turned back for the stairs, and was replaced at once by Captain Curry, who approaching gingerly on his ankle took Emelyn's hand for a kiss. "In times of war we draw closer," he said. "Until next we meet, I shall think on your pretty sisters."

"Far be it from me to forbid you," she said, giving him a smile.

Thoughts of home came stronger by the moment, and feeling a certain camaraderie after all they'd endured together she was compelled to offer parting embraces even to the widow Mrs. Warring and to Miss Beedle, the latter of whom sighed dramatically under her bonnet. "You've been ever so strong my dear, you have much to recommend you."

"And you," Emelyn said, realizing she knew nothing at all about the lady.

The Commodore took his turn, clasping her with his good arm, after which he insisted she take something to remember them by, which must be of her own choosing. "Whatever you like my dear, providing it be small enough for you to carry!"

Emelyn nodded with a blush. "Thank you, but I suppose I've taken something already, if only by absence of mind," and reaching into her pocket she produced the red queen from the chessboard.

"Oh yes I see, a chess piece, and the queen!" he puzzled with a laugh. "How very particular."

"Or anything else," she said quickly, offering it back.

"Absolutely not, it is fated to be," he said with a frown. "I shall have another commissioned, and until then, by the little queen who is missing we shall remember you."

"Thank you again, for your kindness," she said.

The carriage was loaded, Breda opting to ride in the back with Wallace that Emelyn might have more room to share with her brother, and the moment for their departure came at last. Deacon was helped into the coach before her, and taking Van Croft's hand she prepared to board, pausing as he pulled her back to him.

"My patience to make you mine is short," he said closely, "though I concede it were best to put these unfortunate matters well behind us. Still, I shall permit no more than three months delay, Miss Morley, before the marriage banns."

Emelyn nodded, feeling curiously numb to imagine the ceremony, her mother red faced with joy, her sisters dazzled and jealous, her father unbelieving until the moment the license was signed, and Deacon . . .

The captain kissed her knuckles with lingering pressure. "By Rosch's conspiracy we've had no dancing, no toast and hardly a congratulations," he said. "Damn the cannons I will kiss you Miss Morley, before we set out."

There were gasps behind him, but she met the press of his lips with hers, kissing him thrice before turning away. "Very good," she said, feeling a flush. "Now we must get on."

Van Croft held her hands. "But before we do, you must satisfy a curiosity," he said softly, "for it is one of my favourite rumours of Hastelbrook—"

"What rumour is that?"

"In the last years of his life, while your great-grandfather expanded the estate like a madman, is it true he never slept?"

"Is it true you saved a sinking ship by plugging the leak with a polypus fish?"

"Of course not."

"Of course not," she said.

Van Croft chuckled, and lifting her hand he helped her into the coach. "Rest if you can. If there is aught that you need, you have only to knock above you!" and giving her a long look he closed the door, before climbing aboard himself.

The carriage rattled up to speed, and peering from the window Emelyn waved goodbye to the others.

Deacon stretched out on the bench across. "We might have allowed extra time for that kiss," he said, giving her the eye as he prepared his pillow for a lie down.

Emelyn knocked his foot with hers, watching as the lights of the drive winked past, and soon the lamps of Galecliff were behind them, the coach lanterns blinking at the long dark ahead. Soft night pressed upon the windows, and she kicked off her heeled mules to stretch her legs, digging her feet under Deacon's shoulder.

"Oh, her majesty's feet of course," he said, making great show of adjusting to accommodate them.

"Thank you," she said, noting a glisten of sweat on his brow. "Are you feeling quite well?"

"Never better," he answered, squinting at his pocket watch.

Emelyn stared at him for a moment, and crossing her arms she closed her eyes.

■ ■

At the crossroads of Castle and King streets, in the north London parish of Shoreditch, a charity performance at the weather worn Gramble theatre had been paused for heckling. A carousing crowd threw things at the drawn curtain from the standing pit—little more than bare-trampled dirt before the stage—as others joined in from raised walks at either side, with wealthier patrons shouting complaints from those few high boxes in repair enough to accommodate them. Yet braving the discourtesy, a group of brightly coloured musicians held forth in the corner of the stage; flute, drum and coiled horn played the score, while a few of the penny ante public linked arms to dance along. Women selling oranges cried out their wares, loose children chased to and fro, and from a stuffed balcony in the back those who knew the play best sang out lyrics to the music. Beside the musicians, just before the seam of the curtain, stood a solitary official crying his news into the noise.

"At this hour I am bound to report . . . I am bound to report I say, tonight's comedy, Saint Helen of Troy, has raised thirty-four pounds ten, in charity for the

storm—alms in particular for those unfortunate souls of St Pancras parish, flooded out by the rising reek of Fleet ditch."

Amongst the many close dozens in attendance, a tall and slender young man, lately of the Crawley stage's Painted Players, loitered near a laughing group of night working women, who stood fans to their noses, enjoying the chaos. Presenting above his actor's station, the young man wore a short tail wig, cuffs and cravat of hard-washed white, buff yellow coats and an expression of pursed gentility as he hovered closer to the ladies, his eyes for their pockets.

The corner of a gilt-edged handkerchief caught his attention, and with deft fingers he turned past, snapping it up.

"We are obliged to clear out at one o'clock sharp!" the man on stage called, adjusting his hat as some object or another flew past. *"If you should like the conclusion of our brave amusement, I bid you settle! And for our freelookers in the pit, the clerk's officers will gladly engage you. Any size contribution would be most—"*

But the speaker was interrupted, catching the worst of a hurled potato; the musicians bounced on their toes, playing a crescendo, and the assemblage cheered as more vegetables followed the first, scaring the man back through the curtain.

Advantaging himself of the distraction the dandy actor swiped a second silken kerchief to stuff in his pocket, retreating into the crowd.

"Mr. Blanchett," a female voice spoke, and he quickened his pace, but a young lady's hand caught his wrist, her grip cold and strong.

"Lorne!"

"Mistress Afaine!" he gasped, turning to find her, the petite vampiress, clad in a man's frock coat over lacerated breeches and stays, her neck and garments spotted with blood, the paint on her face smeared away.

The vampiress dragged him to a filthy corner beneath stairs that rose to the sagging walkway above, and there she snatched his wrist to her mouth, biting deep.

Lorne flinched with a wince. *"Ma petite immortelle* . . . What has happened?" he asked, holding her close as she drank. "We thought you'd abandoned us."

His head grew light, the noise of the crowd began to fade, and repairing the mark of the bite she leaned against him. "I was taken, held prisoner . . . and worse. You must shelter me."

"Shelter you?" he muttered, his eyelids drooping. "Nay mistress, we no longer live below; the Painted Players are scattered, evicted one and all."

Afaine pressed him to the wall with a snarl. "What nonsense is this?"

"The reformers," he breathed. "Not three weeks ago they came; you were not here to defend us."

"I was captured! I've escaped, and now I am hunted."

"*Hunted?* By what power could the immortal Afinda Faine be hunted?"

"My betrayer is among the eldest of us," she whispered, clenching tightly his open coat. "I cannot get out; he will not suffer me to leave the city."

"Hunted by your own kind?" Lorne swallowed, his expression wide with fear. "But what of your mother the dark queen, your brothers and sisters of the night? Why should you come to me?"

"They have abandoned me," she said, tearing his lapels in her grip.

The actor gave a piteous groan, trying to extract her hands from his clothing. "Dear mistress, there should be two hundred people in this very room—you might charm any one of them; bid them take you home."

"I cannot," she hissed, holding him firmly in place. "Without willing and lucid invitation there is no sanctuary, and I will charm no one in such a state."

"But surely—"

"You were the cleverest among us," she said, standing on her toes to speak close at him. "It was you tied my noose for *La Femme Déchue;* you knew me for what I was before any of them."

"I was a boy. No mortal actress could survive such a trick."

"You know me, dear Lorne—help me!"

"It freezes my heart to find you so wretched," he bemoaned, "but I will sleep in a doorway tonight; I am of no use to you."

Afaine sank to her heels, her eyes shining black. "Little master Blanchett . . . who once smelled like a princess, wearing Orris, jasmine and Bulgarose," she said, flickering a smile, "when we filled every space, when you dressed in ermine and gold, as you did the night I tailored our steps for the king, when Charleston Noddie drank Haut-Brionne as I milked his shoulder, do you remember?"

"Of course I remember," Lorne said quietly, his eyes glistening.

"Those days will come again, but you must hide me now!"

Lorne frowned, and sagging into the wall he slid down to sit. "No *ma petite*, no more routs nor riots, no more tricks; my days of stagecraft are done."

Afaine stared down at him. "*Pauvre petit monsieur.* For twelve years we trod the boards together, and now in my need I find you drunk on self-pity."

"I've nicked two fine muckenders tonight," he said, producing the kerchiefs. "I shall unstitch the monograms and fetch a shilling for each. One more night of cheese and chocolate . . . for the great Christophe Lorne Blanchett."

The actor swooned away, his chin slumped to his chest, and crouching before him the vampiress bit her lip to draw blood, before pressing a kiss on his mouth. With a jolt he awoke, inhaling a tremendous breath.

"When last have you eaten?" she asked.

"This morning I'd a fine milk porridge, courtesy of the parish."

Slipping the heavy coat from her shoulders she tore into the pockets, digging out a man's folded purse. "There must be a hundred guineas there," she said, dropping the coat to the floor. "Enough for chocolate."

Grabbing the wall for support Lorne got to his feet, and accepting the gift he searched it through with greedy fingers, finding bills and coin. "Tears of merciful heaven! How should I ever repay such a sum?"

"My teeth itch me so," she said vaguely, and pinching one of her fangs between thumb and forefinger, she snapped it off with a squeal.

Surprised with horror Lorne coughed, and taking his hand she pressed the bloody tooth in his palm. "I've no more strength to run," she breathed. "Keep this about you, and when it turns to dust, you will know I am gone."

"Gone? No, never!"

"I will not be dragged back to them—I will force the monster to end me first."

The vampiress turned away from him, but he caught her arm. "Wait, and consider!" he protested. "Surely there is someone . . . Of all those you've beguiled, someone of succour, even by his own free will!"

Afaine twitched, looking at his hand on her wrist. "I have not the power you think," she said wearily. "Their tortures broke me. Every living creature I've glamoured, every mortal I bade forget . . . none will help me now. Like dimming stars in my mind, I could not hold onto them. One and all they will remember me for what I am, to their horror."

"Not horror, not all! Surely they must have questions, questions desperate for answer. You need only find *one* more curious than afraid—just as I was."

The vampiress knit her brows as though considering, her eyes widened, and with a sudden grin she vanished, leaving him alone in the crowd.

"Emie . . . Emie wake up."

With a snort Emelyn awoke. "What is it? Why have we stopped?"

Deacon was lighting the lantern over their heads. "It would appear there's something in the road. I heard the captain shouting."

The lantern glowed to life, flickering about them, and Emelyn creaked with a yawn, wishing she could remember her dream, which she was sure had been pleasant. "A tree branch likely," she said, "downed in the storm."

With a click the door opened, and there stood Van Croft, a pistol in his hand. "There's been an accident," he said gravely, "a stagecoach just off the shoulder, badly damaged. We might have passed it by but for a man in our path. He's set a fire in the road, burning timbers without explanation. Stay where you are."

Emelyn put on her shoes as the door closed, and quickly she reached for the latch, but Deacon blocked her arm. "No, Emie!"

"Are you not curious?" she asked.

"Did you hear a word the captain just said?"

"Deacon, if there's been an accident I'm sure the man only needs our help; excuse me."

But her brother caught her wrist, and she saw in the dim light a wildness of fear in his eyes. "There should be no one on the road at this hour," he said.

"And yet here we are," she replied, and snapping her arm from his grasp she opened the door.

The sky was bright with stars, but darkness lay heavy about the rutted road, encroaching against the meagre light of the carriage lanterns, one of which had broken free to float some little way ahead, borne by Van Croft as he approached a hearty looking fire, set in the road just as he said. Off to the side a stagecoach was clearly visible, dark and still—by sight and scent marooned for some hours without horses.

Drawing near Emelyn found its door had been smashed, splintered inward as though by great force, the window half shattered.

"Miss Morley, I told you to wait," Van Croft said sharply, walking briskly back to her.

"And I've opted not to," she said, looking past him at the man in question, a drably coated person without wig or visible hair, who stood staring into the flames of his fire, his watery eyes unblinking.

"Back in the carriage," the captain said, "you'll be in good company."

"What do you think has happened?" she asked, panging with curiosity, if grateful she did not recognize the man. "Was it highwaymen?"

"The low roads make poor sport for a highwayman at night," Van Croft said, taking hold of her elbow to guide her back.

"But is that the driver? Where are the horses? Is there no one else in the coach?"

"You will take your seat," he said. "I shall clear the fellow and his fire off the road and we'll be on our way."

Holding a pistol himself their own driver stood as they returned, and stopping to pull open the door Van Croft gestured for Emelyn to climb aboard.

This she did with a sigh, moving past her staring brother to the opposite door, which she softly unlatched to climb out again.

"What? Emie, don't be a fool!" Deacon chided, his voice cut off as she closed the door.

The captain was crunching along the stones back to the man in the road, and slipping around the rear of the carriage Emelyn gestured for Wallace and Breda to keep quiet, before moving swiftly across the road to the shoulder, where she aimed for the darkened far side of the derelict stagecoach.

The door hung open on its hinge, and stepping up gingerly she peered inside. The cabin was empty, apart from debris from the broken door on the other side. Scintillating in the window the fire's glow called her attention to lines carved in the glass, as though they'd been scratched by the claws of an animal. With quick breath she clambered inside, brushing off the seat for a perch, and her eyes fell at once upon a familiar buckled hat left on the bench.

Her heart raced, and suddenly she laughed, covering her mouth with a gasp. "Vaela . . . what have you done," she murmured, recalling Deacon's cryptic plan to delay Rosch's coach until dark. Taking up the hat she prepared to disembark, but paused, listening for the captain's voice outside.

"*Then wherefore should you set the fire, to what purpose?*" Van Croft asked.

"*To follow my lady's instruction, to block the road, and forget,*" came the answer. The man's voice had a sort of tragically bemused cadence, as though he scarcely believed his own words.

"*My lady is no one, she is the dark.*"

Van Croft cursed. "*Did you not say a passenger was taken, taken where and by whom?*"

"*The driver is fled, the scholar is taken. But I am not to name him, so long as I live.*"

"*Dammit man speak sense; by whom were you attacked?*" Van Croft flustered. "*And who is this lady you speak of?*"

There was no reply. The hat grew heavy in her hand, and Emelyn found herself wishing the man had thrown it on his fire.

"You're lucky he didn't see you," Deacon said, frowning as she climbed quietly back into the coach, and pulled the door to.

"Deacon," she said slowly, placing the hat beside her, "Mr. Rosch left with ample time to reach Horsham before nightfall . . . but it would appear he never arrived. I don't suppose you've any idea what happened?"

Her brother's eyes were wide as saucers, and inhaling quickly he leaned to grab the hat.

"What did you do?" she asked, watching him closely.

"By heaven, have the rats found their barley?" Her brother's face was half affrighted, half amused. "I broke with Fenders, I paid him to assign the task to his subordinate . . . footman Wallace. Fifty guineas I paid them—all that I brought."

Emelyn nodded slowly. "You paid them . . . for what, exactly?"

"Wallace was equipped with one of Doctor Tarville's potions, a slow sedative for the animals—to be administered after Rosch changed horses at the inn."

"You had the horses drugged, that he would be delayed?"

Deacon sat very still, his eyes unblinking.

"Deacon?"

With deliberate care he passed the hat back to her. "We cannot be found with it," he said, "not after the man has been murdered. Others will know he was aboard that coach; it will come out."

Finding the thought quite abrupt Emelyn swallowed. "We cannot be sure he is murdered—I saw no sign of a body, nor was there blood."

Deacon was staring as though seeing her for the first time. "The door is smashed Emie; I could espy it from here. You must return the hat, now. We dare not be caught with it."

Climbing down once more Emelyn crossed the road quickly, finding it coldly surreal to imagine herself and her brother party to murder. Peering around the coach Vaela's words came back to her: *if I could destroy your enemies in daylight, I would.* And now, it would appear by Deacon's help, she had.

Finding the man in the road of little use, Van Croft had employed himself to kick out the fire, scattering the kindled timbers as his witness only stood and stared. The stranded carriage's door yet hung open on the wooded side, and leaning in Emelyn left the hat on the bench where she'd found it.

After waiting for the coach to block the captain's sight of her, she snuck back across, and managed to slip into her seat, just closing the door when Van Croft opened the other.

"We shall be on our way now," he said.

"Who is the man in the road? Why did he set the fire?" Emelyn asked.

"His name is Snell, and he's a fool. He's determined to remain here until daylight and make his way to the town on foot. And I shall leave him to it."

The door closed, and Emelyn settled back in her seat with a yawn, hoping to soothe her brother's nerves.

Deacon gave a strange little laugh. "Can you really be so composed?"

"I'm sure it was highwaymen," Emelyn replied, adjusting the curtain by the window, "or perhaps some enemy of Mr. Rosch."

"Mr. Rosch was a traveling parson, how many enemies do you suppose he's made?"

"Based on what I know of him, I should think quite a few," Emelyn said, crossing her arms as the coach started out again. "But I hope you don't expect me to be sorry for him."

Deacon shook his head. "Of course not; neither shall I be sorry for him, though I only ever thought to scare the villain, for what he did to you."

"You could never have known he would come to mischief," she said, glancing out the dark window. "He may be fled into the wood for all we know."

"Really Emelyn . . . is that all?"

"What more do you want?" she asked, adjusting her comfort. "There's nothing for it now."

Deacon was staring at her. "Is there not? But I am compelled to ask, Sister, how long you mean to go on pretending?"

"Pretending what?"

"Pretending *Vaela* is not real."

■ ■

Standing atop the porch, at the edge of the roof overlooking the kitchen gardens, Mr. Arkwright checked his glass for gin, and finding it empty he let it fall, watching as it shattered on the stones of the walk below. The wind brushed cool and close, he closed his eyes, and was just thinking to return to his room when a voice behind him chilled his blood.

"I was like you once," she said, "young and heartsick, when my heart beat still."

Turning at once he found her standing by the window, the young she-vampire he'd seen juggling pears at the George Hotel, whom but two weeks past had been no more than a shadow in the back of his mind, a riddle without answer . . . until the memory of her attack had suddenly returned—abrupt and unwelcome.

"It's you," he said, standing agog.

"It is I, Afinda Faine," she said, giving him a curtsy. "I've not forgotten your charity—you meant to free from the bawdy stage, for fifty guineas. Might we speak inside?"

The haunted, grinning girl from that night in Crawley made stark contrast to the tattered miserable figure standing before him. Her lithe form was clad as before in tight breaches and sleeveless vest over her stays, but drenched and foul, her bound up hair matted with blood, her torn habiliments so deeply stained they might have been the clothes of a corpse.

"I know you for a murderess, who attacked me in the stables," he said.

The young vampiress drew close. "I only tasted you," she said. "Of course I could drink you to dust right now if I liked, but surely you have questions, Fitzwilliam Arkwright. I will answer them. Shall we go in?"

Her presence was at once alluring and repulsive, and he struggled for a response. "Then my first is why, why have you returned to me?"

"Handsome sir," she said, walking her fingers up his chest. "I remembered your kindness. I only wish to talk."

He could not recall returning to his room, but it seemed only a moment later he stood by the foot of the bed, and with a trembling hand gestured for her to enter.

No sooner had he done so than she sprang through the window, pinning him to the wall, her fangs at his neck . . . but the bite did not come. "Ah well, we needn't rush," she sighed. "You've earned some consideration, giving me shelter of your own free will."

"You appear to me stinking of the river, drenched once more in innocent blood."

"That silver merchant was hardly innocent, an odious little man whom none shall miss," she said. "And the blood you see is my own. I've only come to you for sanctuary, for London is my prison. Now have you questions, or not?"

"What do you know of Emelyn Morley?" he asked stiffly. "What do you want with her?"

"I want nothing with her."

"She writes that her life has been subject to *forces* beyond her control, and offers no explanation. In Crawley you lamented that I *knew* her. Is it you who oppresses her?"

"Not I sir. She is sacred to my mother the queen, and protected. Without Miss Morley the vault beneath Hastelbrook cannot be opened."

"The queen . . . of vampires," he said, struggling to master his nerves. "The vault . . . But can that old rumour of Hastelbrook be true?"

"Of course it's true, what a question."

Arkwright swallowed. "Very well . . . but this is naught to do with me. How long should I expect you to impose?"

At this she fell silent, and with such stillness that he might have mistaken her for a statue, until a little grin played on her lips, and her eyes brimmed with dark oily tears. "We have no scent," she said quietly, "yet he smells the grime, the blood, the river in my clothes. I smell him too, for the nuance of scent is my particular gift . . . I smell the dust in his old coats, but even with such warning, I cannot escape him."

"Escape *whom*?"

With a deep breath her smile broadened, and she met his eyes as though staring into a dream. "There is a kind of peacefulness, in surrender, is there not?"

Arkwright blinked at her. "Will you answer my question?" he asked. "How long must you stay? And who is this enemy you speak of; is my house in danger?"

"For a mortal, to espy him is death." Her eyes were soft. "Your scent led me to you, just as it would for him," she said, gliding her hands up his shoulders, "but fear not . . . he cares nothing for your house, nor for you, and you will not know me long."

Arkwright wet his lips, and he shivered as she sniffed at his throat. "Then I wonder what use you could have of me; surely the river would afford your escape. Even a bloodhound could not track you beneath the water."

"No," she breathed, toying with his collar. "My pursuer can sense even the heat of my body, which blooms when I feed and cools when I thirst . . . He hears my every sound, neither could I outswim him."

"So I am to hide you, a vampire, from your own kind . . . until daybreak? And what then?"

"There is no *what then*," she said with a snarl, splitting open his shirt. "I cannot run, and to wait here until dawn would put me in your power. That I will not do, never again. Neither shall I go to my death unsatisfied," and baring her fangs she bit into his chest.

The pain lanced deep, surging out of him as she swallowed, and with a desperate instinct he slugged her in the belly. The vampiress buckled with a huff, and bringing all the force he could muster he struck again, knocking her head back as he landed a straight fist to her face. Afaine staggered, clapping a hand to her mouth, and Arkwright swung again, but cold fingers caught him by the neck, and he was flung away, crashing into the desk to topple it over.

Landing hard behind the upturned furniture, his legs over the top, he moaned as a splitting ache lit through his ribs, and now she was standing over him, blinking as she touched her nose.

Arkwright raised his hand to keep her at bay. "A moment, if you please," he rasped.

"You buck like a mule," she said with a sniff, wiping blood from her nostril and looking at her fingers.

Catching his breath he rubbed his neck. "I've another question," he wheezed, flinching as she crouched to stare at him. "At the George, when first you attacked me," he ventured, "you said you were not to. You were ordered to leave me be . . ."

Afaine smiled red. "Until the vault is unlocked Miss Morley is not to be harmed nor hindered. This boon extends to those in her orbit, but it doesn't matter now."

Dragging himself away from her he made use of the windowsill to stand, and was just reaching for the fallen decanter of gin when she snatched it up.

"Sealed well enough not to spill," she said, setting two glasses on the ledge beside him and pulling the cork. "One last drink, before we meet our fate."

His eyes darted about the room as she poured, his breath coming quickly, and accepting the glass he watched as she took her drink in one, swishing for several seconds before spitting it with a noise.

"Juniper never tastes as it smells," she coughed, wiping her lips, "and I've tried them all."

Arkwright nodded, and with a quick movement he splashed his drink in her face, but only sloshed the air as she disappeared, catching him from behind about the chest. With a cackle she tossed him onto the bed like a sack, and he coughed as she landed atop him, straddling his waist, her hand over his mouth.

"Compose yourself!" she hissed. "Someone is coming . . . tell them away, or I will murder them all."

There came a knock, and the voice of the butler. "Mr. Arkwright sir, we heard a crash; are you quite all right?"

Afaine released his mouth and quickly covered it again. "And if you mean to revoke my invitation, I will haunt this place until I've ended every one of you."

Swallowing hard Arkwright nodded, taking her hand to pull it down. "Thank you Enson!" he called back, his voice cracking. "It's nothing, just a bit of carelessness, none hurt but my pride."

"Very good sir, and the porter barrels are delivered, oak parched and sealed. The lads apologize for the late hour. Shall I have them to the cellar sir?"

"The cellar, quite right!" Arkwright answered. "That will be all Enson, thank you."

Afaine brushed his neck with her claws. "Now you need only relax, and I shall be as gentle as I may . . . like putting a baby to sleep."

Kissing her way down she found the mark of her previous bite, and Arkwright cleared his throat. "Wait . . ."

"No more waiting," she said, baring her fangs.

"I can get you out."

The vampiress snorted softly. "Hush now—perhaps you'll wake in Heaven."

"You mean to surrender," he said quickly, "but I will not. I know a way—I can smuggle you out of the city."

Tapping her fingers on his chest she grinned up at him, her eyes hard. "How?"

"In the beer," he breathed. "The barrels are wax and grain sealed—if you can keep your breath long enough to be submerged."

"We live on blood . . . not air."

"Then you should be insulated against the motion, the noise, even your scent," Arkwright said, heart hammering as he spoke. "Neither of us need die tonight," and he flinched as her tongue tickled him again, until the wound of the bite closed and healed.

For some moments she did not move, but sniffed and laid her face against him, and softly she made a sound, like a whimpering sigh. "But I was resolved to lie on your roof and watch the sunrise—"

"If you'd prefer to burn to ashes," he said, "that is easier still."

With a happy grunt she hopped from the bed, appearing by the wash basin, where she set to cleaning her arms and neck with liberal splashes.

"The dray and barrels are in the cellar," he said, wincing as he stood carefully.

Afaine dried her face in a fresh linen. "Then perhaps I shall owe you a debt," she said. "That makes two now, in the city," and turning to face him she cocked her head. "One need not murder good sheep for their wool . . . I'd not have thought to end you, had I any hope. I'm sure you understand."

"I don't *understand* any of this," he said, tying his shirt against the rip down its centre. "But if that is an apology I accept; now let me be assured the halls are empty, before you follow me down . . ."

The basement of number six Covent Garden was comprised of two connected rooms, one for tools and horse furniture, while the other was employed as a cellar for wine, beer and dry stores. Here an unhitched two-horse cart waited before wide locked doors, with casks, tuns and hogsheads arranged by the wall, heavy full and long settled into their places.

Finding one of the new porter barrels Arkwright was just rocking it toward the dray when the vampiress snatched it up, hopping into the cart with the barrel on her back.

"Easy there!" he warned, grimacing as she slid it down, setting it on its end.

"Shall I pull out the lid?" she asked.

"No, you'll only break it," he said, selecting tools from a near table. "I must loosen the hoops and pry in the head."

"I know how barrels work," she said, sitting atop it.

"Do you?"

A minute later found him in the cart, chiselling out the steel hoops with a few delicate bangs, before prying down the edge of the head to rotate and twist it out. With a terrific splash she hopped feet first into the beer, knees bent close as she submerged, before bursting up again.

"It tastes of cold urine," she spluttered, wiping her face.

"I assure you it does not," he said, frowning as he looked over the barrel. "That's heavy hops and dark malt; at tenpence a quart you're swimming in the finest porter brewed in the county. Of course no one will drink it now."

"Urine," she repeated, lowering herself down as he held the lid over her head, but up to her nose she paused, popping up once more.

"Sit down," he said. "There's no point to this exercise unless I seal you in, and I should very much like to see that sunrise myself."

"I'll not leave my debt to you unanswered . . ."

"Then perhaps you might heal my memory, that I should forget, forever, that such supernatural darkness ever found me."

"That I cannot do," she said, splashing him. "There has always been darkness, just as there's always been light to chase it away."

"And how does a man get on," he asked, wiping his face on his sleeve, "knowing vampires walk the earth."

"Daylight dispels even the fear of us," she said, slumping back down again, "and there are worse things in the world than we—"

"Then pray keep them to yourself," he said, rotating the barrel head in his hands. "Your debt is paid, now sit—all the way down."

Afaine rested her arms on the rim. "I heard the end of your unhappy letter from Miss Morley, perhaps I might offer you hope."

"My dearest hope is that your kind keep away from her," he said. "I've subjected her to scandal enough already; I will never be of her society."

The vampiress splashed again. "You'll sacrifice a barrel of fine porter to smuggle a vampire out of the city; society does not know you. Neither does it know her . . . so perhaps you needn't abandon your heart."

"Or perhaps Mrs. Delfrey's coffyn pie has gone off," he said, preparing to seal her up, "and I shall blessedly wake to find all of this but a ridiculous dream."

The vampiress reached out to touch him on the nose. "You had only a bite of chicken, you never tasted the pie," she said, and folding her arms she sunk beneath the surface.

Arkwright clenched his eyes, and summoning his nerve he covered the top, before knocking the barrel head in place. "Dear God have mercy on a fool," he said.

Chapter 29
Home

Wednesday July 6th

Eager stars twinkled over the grey landscape all around, spread happily vast to fill the sky after the blinding weather. The carriage rumbled on, and Emelyn's brother prodded her with questions, to which she responded in a dozen different ways, though none of them aloud. *Vorsadat's watch over the vault is ended—so it falls to you* . . . After what felt like a month away from home Vaela's words both unnerved and excited, but to argue the question of vampires with her brother, with Rosch's interrogation yet fresh in her mind, seemed a pernicious exercise.

"Will you not answer?" Deacon repeated. "Emie, this is not some salacious novel you can hide under your pillow."

The passing trees were yet heavy with rainwater, and Emelyn watched as little droplets negotiated their way to the bottom of the window pane. "Must we speak of it all night? One disappearance is hardly proof of vampires."

"Is that all you have to say, after everything that's happened? Shall I remind you Rosch is the *fifth* to go missing, likely murdered, in a fortnight, and taken precisely in what manner he feared; you cannot deny the evidence."

Half wondering whether she could stare a hole in the glass, Emelyn adjusted in her seat, saying nothing.

"I'd never have believed it myself," Deacon continued, "but there is no other way—this woman, *Vaela,* of whom you've dreamt all your life, *must* exist in being. She is out there in the dark, haunting your steps . . ."

"Whatever she is," Emelyn said, "she is my secret to keep, and I will not surrender her. I told you she protects me."

Her brother sank slowly back in his seat. "So the rumours are true—we are haunted, the lot of us," and he gave a lamentable laugh. "Do you know there are villages on the continent that bury their dead with sickle blades about their necks, that they must decapitate themselves, should they rise as vampires."

Emelyn leaned in the corner, covering her mouth for a yawn. "You mustn't believe everything you read."

"Vampires do not *protect* the living," he said. "The role of protecting you falls to us, your family, as it always has."

"As when you locked me in the crypt as a child?"

"Oh, you might as well know now . . . that never happened."

"Of course it happened, I remember it distinctly," she said, finding the memory hazy, though there was no fear in it.

"You remember what's always been told to you," Deacon said, "but I never locked you in. Have you never wondered why you've been forbidden those stairs ever since? You locked *yourself* in."

"Did I bar the door, at four years of age?"

"Yes in fact—you must have done. You were hours, Emie. Your candle had long gone out, and yet we heard your little voice clear as a bell. You were speaking, and laughing, as though in conversation with someone we could not hear."

"I was playing, Deacon, and there *was* light. I remember lights overhead; the lanterns must have been lit."

"No, Emelyn, you were alone in the dark. Mama could not abide word of it getting out, so the blame was put to me."

Emelyn scowled, adjusting her pillow as the childhood impression returned: playing on the floor, a great shadow bending over her, and the crypt aglow with golden light like falling stars.

"Well I'm here now," she said. "I must have come out eventually."

"Emelyn, was there someone with you in the crypt? Was it Vaela?"

"No, she has never been in the crypt. And I've nothing more to say of it."

"You've nothing more to say of it," he droned. "And if some dark night we should find you upon the grounds drained of blood, and this conversation is all I have to work it out?"

"That is not my fate."

"And what is your fate?"

"It is more than to marry Lord Van Croft, and run a household," she said. "Of that I am certain."

The road was better now, the carriage grinding along behind the briskly trotting team, and still she could hear the frantic beat of his heart, trembling through the air between them.

"Not that I should begrudge having a kingdom of my own, after living under Mama's iron will," she said, hoping to lighten his mood.

"A kingdom of your own," he grunted softly. "The captain will rule you Emie; you shan't pay calls nor keep a friend but by his whim. You'll wear what he likes, and read what he approves."

Emelyn smiled at him. "I *shall* visit home when I like. I shall wear what I like, read what I like and entertain *whom* I like."

Deacon shook his head, his face tense with worry, and shifting across she sat next to him, her hand on his leg. "You only fear to lose me, but you mustn't," she said, "neither to vampires, nor the captain. And we are not haunted; Vaela will not harm me, nor any of us."

"All those nights you slipped away," he said, squeezing her hand, "I never imagined there was anything to it, not like this."

"There is no danger, Deacon, not from her."

Her brother groaned, as though struggling with himself. "I suppose, if she wanted to harm you . . . she'd have done. Yet here you are alive and well, as far as I can measure."

"Every drop of blood accounted for."

"But Emie, how am I to understand it? For what purpose should a living *vampire* choose you? Why does she protect you?"

Reluctant to broach what little she knew of the mysterious prophecy, Emelyn touched the window, imagining Vaela's fingertips just on the other side mirroring her own. "I can say only that we are bonded; she is dear to me."

Deacon started to speak but grew silent as the carriage rolled to a sudden stop, and Emelyn peered out to find scattered clouds had dampened the stars. A light rain began to speckle the glass, the coach creaked and shifted as someone climbed down, and the door opened.

"Miss Morley," Van Croft said, removing his hat, "the wind is chill and the rain returns, might your lady's maid climb aboard?"

"By all means," Emelyn said, allowing him her hand as he stepped up to kiss it, pinching with his teeth. "Ouch!" she blurted.

"Forgive me," he said quickly, rubbing her knuckle as though he'd surprised himself.

Breda was helped inside and they set out once more; the road being rockier now, bumping along beneath them as with obvious frustration Deacon pivoted his objections from Vaela to Van Croft, while by the inadequate light of the hanging lantern Breda pretended to read.

"The man has no sense of his environment," Deacon marvelled. "One does not kiss with one's teeth."

"I don't mind, I find it amusing," Emelyn replied, rubbing her hand as she imagined the captain trying her neck.

The wind had increased, pinning leaves against the windows here and again, and Deacon muttered to himself, fussing out his book for another try.

"You know, I should quite like to see the crypt again," Emelyn said at last. "I suspect you know where the key might be found."

"Absolutely not," he said, squinting at the page.

"Well, if you're determined to scruple over it I shall apply to Papa; being his favourite I like my chances."

She waited for his reaction, but there came a terrific bump; the lantern knocked into the ceiling, and the three of them cried out, bracing as the coach rocked dangerously, threatening to capsize.

"Lean!" Emelyn shouted, prompting them to scramble for the high side, and the coach dropped heavily back to its wheels, settling at a steep angle.

"Hills of Calvary!" Deacon swore. "What's happened?"

"I'll check with the driver miss," Breda said quickly, and before either of them could object she'd slipped out, closing the door behind her as the opposite side opened.

Once more it was the captain, snarling as though to complete a string of curses. "The wheel's bedevilled in a slough; we'll set her right by and by. Wait here if you please."

"Should we not get out, to lighten the load?" Emelyn asked.

"There's mud, you foolish girl," Van Croft snapped, closing the door.

"Thank you!" Deacon shouted back, turning to lie down along the bench.

Emelyn watched as he engaged the pillow, stretching out as he could. "You cannot mean to sleep now," she said.

"After your confession my mind is turned to mush," he said, shifting his position. "Even the dead could not sleep on this rutted piss trough of a road, therefore I will avail myself while we're stopped."

Though the raised voices of Van Croft, Wallace and their driver came clear, Emelyn could see little through the glass. "It's silly to wait," she said, "when I might be of assistance."

"There's three strong men and a maid outside," Deacon said, laying an arm over his eyes, "if they need *your* help we're lost."

A rain damp Breda soon returned, and for what seemed an hour they bided their time as the men hustled to dig out the stuck wheel. Emelyn grew drowsy, and she was soon settled into her corner, head drooping with sleep.

■ ■

In the marshy Brixtane woods an hour south of London, Mr. Arkwright pulled his beer laden dray cart off the road. The night was frosted by dim starlight through the trees, and clutching the reins he sat quietly, listening as crickets and nightingales sang out their natural music.

Climbing into the back he stood among the barrels, scanning the dark road behind them, and with a determined breath he took up his tools, knocking open the head of the heaviest.

With a splash Afaine stood up, shivering like a dog and stretching her jaws.

"We're three miles south of the city," Arkwright said. "I can only pray the monster will not find your scent about me on my return."

The vampiress smiled, wiping her eyes. "He will not; we'd never have slipped away otherwise," she said. "He needn't watch the house closely—he imagined to sense me leaving the area; he must believe me there still."

"I pray you're right," Arkwright replied, and he gasped a protest as she took up the barrel, hopping from the cart into the grass.

He shouted after her, urging caution, but in a blink she had darted into the wood and let it fly, smashing the container against a standing rock. "That barrel is notched and marked!" he called. "I should have preferred it not be traced back to me; unless every stave is collected—"

But in a flash the shattered bits of wood were deposited into the cart, the metal hoops following after.

"You might have simply poured it out," he observed.

Afaine vanished, startling him as she appeared again very close. "To break it was more fun," she said. "Now go home Mr. Arkwright, and do not give up on your heart. I shan't forget what you've done for me."

"Nor I, alas," he said, and he grunted as she caught him about the neck, pressing a kiss upon his lips, though there was scarcely time to realize it before she was gone, vanished like a breath of wind.

Arkwright wiped his mouth on his sleeve, and willing himself to action he crouched to collect and stack the broken wood, covering it with a tarp. The horses snorted softly, and returning to the driver's seat he called and snapped to turn the cart around.

"Emelyn Elizabeth Morley," he said at last, speaking wistfully into the dark, "I wonder . . . do we share now the same secret?" and lashing the reins he set off for home.

■■

Where the wide night-dark Thames reached half a mile across, there by the sleeping docks loomed the *Caracalla*, a once grand ship in His Majesty's service, the late King George I. Long since decommissioned, the black and gold frigate had been hulked at Gravesend, downriver from London, nigh a century ago—shorn of masts, sails and rudder, it served as a floating charity school for poor youth of the parish, though it had been without students for some months now. Anchored by myriad chains and ropes, the ship slept against the banks, shifting in the last windy dregs of what had been a ferocious and unaccountable storm—reduced now to a black band of deeper night in the distant sky.

On the steady slope rising away from the river, the village houses were clustered close, with one higher and broader than the rest, and there on the peak of its roof stood Vaela, ebon hooded and cloaked, her garment snapping in the wind off the water. Beside her, not perched on the edge as she, but with one foot on the crest and one on the slope, stood a man clad all in black, from boots to frock coat to faceless mask and three-cornered hat—captain of the Lurkmen, Mr. Lorris.

"I hear no children's voices," Vaela said, watching the boat as it listed, "what has become of the school?"

"Mother Bright teaches no more," Mr. Lorris replied, "she has been employed by the Argentum Serpentis—that Rosicrucian brotherhood of hunters. She consults with them only."

"The baron's order spreads its reach." Vaela frowned. "Foolishly, she must have published her gift, or they'd never have found her."

"I have brought what you requested," he said, producing a small vial of a viscous black substance. "This is the last of it."

"More than enough to tempt her," Vaela said.

"What is your command?" Mr. Lorris asked, returning the vial to his pocket as he looked back toward the ship.

"My invitation of long standing has been revoked. You must board, and speak with her, until I am welcome," Vaela said, her eyes glinting silver.

Upon the old ship only a single lantern burned above decks, its light carried by a grim faced man in striped breaches and vest, his head scarfed in red. Stumping across the planks he paused to look over the rail in the direction of the village, before resuming his patrol.

Just below his sight, the captain of the Lurkmen caught one of the thicker moorings, and silent as serpents he climbed, until reaching the deck he rolled beneath the rail and stood.

"Your gaming debts are forgiven," Mr. Lorris said, just loud enough to be heard.

The man turned sharply to look, raising a bosun's pipe to his mouth, though he sounded no alarm. "What's that then; who are you?" he demanded in hissing whisper. "How'd ye know of my debts?"

"Fortunate guess," Lorris replied, and with a silver lion's head cane he swatted the whistle from his lips. The cane caught the man beneath the arm as he sought for his pistol, and Mr. Lorris spun him about, putting boot to his backside to shove him overboard.

Swooping from the dock Vaela snatched the man from the air, bounding off the side of the ship to land on the shore, where she fell upon him with a snarl, latching to his throat . . .

Mr. Lorris dropped the lantern into the drink, which snuffed with a hiss, and marking quick steps up the stairs from the quarter deck, he turned to find a second sentry, larger than the first, with roping muscles and gnarled hands.

The man clutched a torch and pistol. "Take your last breath thief!" He sneered, aiming the gun just as the hurtling cane cracked him in the face, freeing the weapon from his grasp.

Mr. Lorris dove into a roll, catching the firearm before it landed as the bleeding man drew a knife from his belt.

But Lorris was on his feet, pointing the pistol.

Staring down the barrel the man froze, dropping the blade. "Go on then, take your shot. My brothers will wear your teeth . . ."

Mr. Lorris tucked the gun in his belt. "Too much noise, you understand," he said, removing his hat.

The man relaxed with a chuckle, and with the hat over his fist Lorris struck him, catching him full in the teeth to knock him senseless.

Boots dragged across the deck, and the fellow was slipped over the side. Again there was no splash, but only the rustle of wind as Vaela claimed her second prize.

Lit by the clashing light of a dozen hanging lanterns, the captain's quarters was a substantial open room, with library walls and a lavish bed alcoved to one side, concealed by crimson curtains half closed. Sumptuous bolster pillowed couches furnished the room while each of the hanging lights anchored red and gold drapery to the ceiling, leaving it to sag in rounded billows over the room. From each lantern dangled woven talismans and globes of glass filled with water, while under the gaze of aft windows, on a riser from the floor rested a stained oaken desk, where in the tall captain's chair sat a withered Romani woman robed in purple and green, her tawny skin wrinkled as battle worn leather, white hair gathered under a twisted scarf as she hunched between candles before a spread of cards, yet to be turned. Her eyes shone brilliant crystal blue, if clouded with age, her wrists and neck jangling with gold as she flipped the first card, producing the knave of clubs.

Pulling open the doors Mr. Lorris stood in the portal, and knocking the floor with his cane he swept off his hat for a bow. "Mother Bright," he pronounced, lowering his mask to regard her, "or should you prefer your given name, Ruxandra Petulengro. It has been some while."

The lanterns swayed as the ship creaked, and across the room the old crone did not look up, but turned a second card, revealing the queen of spades. "Mr. Lorris, Moorish lord of the Lurkmen, have you murdered my grandsons?"

"Nay madam, they are but sapped of blood," he said, noting a line of ashes strewn carefully across the threshold. "Light duty for a week, and they shall be fit as a fiddle."

"And I suppose our *moroiaca* waits outside?" the old woman guessed, her voice harsh and cracking.

"She does," he said, smearing away the ash with his boot.

"Whatever your unholy mistress wants," she said, glowering at him, "you may tell her she's come too late," and reaching out she took hold of a pair of ropes dangling from the ceiling.

A gleam like harp string caught his eye, and with a quick blade Mr. Lorris snapped a pair of silver wires stretched knee height across the doorway. Several of the lanterns shivered and dropped their watery globes, which shattered on the floor. "The lady Vaela is not my mistress, but yours," he said, pocketing the blade.

Mother Bright pursed her lips in a wrinkly frown. "Oh go to sir, disarm my traps as you like . . . much good may it do ye when the men wake. Twenty swords below will come at a snap of my fingers."

Mr. Lorris hacked down a hanging chain of garlic cloves. "You sold your school for Lord Dramen's service, and were you paid well to evict the children?"

The elderly woman pressed on the desk, rising unsteadily to her feet as she kept hold of the ropes. "What would you know of it, night worn lackey," she said sharply, taking up a gnarled walking stick to walk around the desk and creak slowly down the step. "We do what we must."

"So you place your faith in silver, and garlic, and water of baptism?" Walking along the wall Mr. Lorris knocked down another of the hanging globes with his cane, catching it as it fell. "Your gratitude is not what it was."

"Invite the devil and you shall meet his friends," she retorted, crossing the floor to a high backed chair upon which lay blankets and yarn. "My duty to Saunmoor is done, and I am broken for it. It's thirty years and more, since your mistress trod these planks."

"She is here now, Mother Bright," Mr. Lorris said, stopping to examine a network of secondary ropes tied into the ceiling from the bedstead. "She would speak with you."

Mother Bright lowered herself into the chair, taking up a wooden knitting sheath. "She wants I renew her invitation . . . and what has she to offer?"

"More than you could wish for." Mr. Lorris prodded his cane at one of the hanging billows.

"You come with riddles?" the old crone snapped, jabbing her needles to work on a long black and red scarf. "Her cursed gift to me has waned to nothing. Let her see to that! Or speak no more of her."

Outside Vaela had posted herself on the near dock, staring into ripples on the water as seven men in faceless black like their captain gathered about her. "Have you the gold?" she asked.

"Yes, mistress."

"Go, enter and prepare my way," she said, dismissing them with a gesture.

In swift order the men in black scaled the ropes, winning the decks to slip down the stairs. Vaela listened as they entered the captain's quarters, and set to dismantling the Gypsy madam's defences.

"More of you!" Mother Bright growled. "Graceless clods, there were no call to destroy my things . . ."

By the direction of their captain the Lurkmen tore down the voluminous draperies for bundling, gathered ropes in coils, collected talismans and poured the water of baptism into the river. "And swab up the rest," Mr. Lorris added. "The silver—weapons, chain, plate and cutlery—bag it all."

"You'll not steal my good silver!" Mother Bright protested. "Or have you brought with you presents enough to pay for it?"

Mr. Lorris reached into his pocket. "Your mistress offers better than silver," he said, producing the vial, "black blood from the immortal trees of Saunmoor."

Mother Bright fixated upon it, her eyes wide and searching. "Is it real? And what does she want for it?"

"That, you must ask her yourself."

Licking her lips the old woman lowered her head. "Vaela Audette de Masseine, shadow in service to the queen in the dark . . . enter freely."

Mr. Lorris stood his cane on the floor, resting his hands atop. The men arranged themselves about the perimeter, and with a rush of air the lanterns flapped as the vampiress appeared in the centre of the room.

"Hello Mother Bright," Vaela greeted, her eyes shining in the dim.

The old woman cleared her throat, twisting the knitting sheath in her hand. "*Moroiaca*—vampire, you darken my door, after so long."

Vaela lowered her hood, and crouching before the chair she placed her hands on the elderly woman's knees. "You needn't fear me," she said softly. "Despite your meagre welcome; I want no more than you are certainly prepared to give."

Mother Bright squinted with displeasure. "Since the days I danced beautiful and young, seventy years have I given you, spinning the dross of rumour to gold, dooming the worst to your judgment for the black on their souls."

"And for all the rotten apples you've rolled to my feet, I am grateful," Vaela said.

"I'll warn you, I'm blinder than I was; I'll not be glamoured by your evil eye. Why do you come to me now?"

"There is a dark mystery cast upon the queen, an affliction which slowly poisons her," Vaela said, rising to stand before her. "Drink of the sap—your gift will return to you—and I will ask you questions."

Mother Bright rubbed her nose with a sniff. "I shall require more—treasure enough to lay down with both eyes shut. And I will have the fruit of your veins, to drink, and to keep."

Vaela shook her head. "My blood will avail you nothing."

"A lie." The old crone glared up at her. "Your necessity outweighs mine! I will have your blood, and by your *willing* bestowal it shall retain its power. Or am I not the only mortal to drink the poison of the cursed trees, and live?"

Vaela leaned down, gripping the armrests as she stared into her eyes. "That is not so true as you think," she said. "In the citadel of Umbremar they are called the *children of the walls*; I will not horrify you to describe them."

"Then as the last lucid seer, my value cannot be measured." Mother Bright clicked her tongue with a dismissive noise. "You will pay for this oracle, or leave with nothing."

"Do you forget I have protected you even from the queen," Vaela said. "Were she to learn of your ability, she would have you entombed beneath the mountain, for her own particular use—even the release of death would be denied you."

"And how should she punish *you* for keeping our secret? Nay, I will not fear your queen."

"You are wiser than such boasting," Vaela said, speaking close. "Tonight you will drink of the trees, and feel your powers restored. Beside the vial you will have generous gold, which I know burns in your heart brightest of all."

A glint of metal flashed and the vampiress froze, finding a silver blade at her throat, which the old woman had pulled from the end of the knitting sheath. The Lurkmen lunged closer but Vaela raised her hand. "Wait," she commanded, tilting her head to respect the blade, "let her speak."

"And when gold is spent and vial is empty, my gift of sight worn away, I shall be left again with nothing!" Mother Bright said darkly, grabbing a fistful of Vaela's hair. "I *will* have the power in your blood, such as you've given to your precious babe of Hastelbrook."

Vaela wet her lips, digging her claws in the armrests. "Dear Ruxandra . . . to hurt me would be very foolish, and you are no fool, even if you've sold your gift to Baron Dramen and his ilk."

"I treat with whom I please!" The Gypsy madam trembled. "This curse of prophecy has afflicted me to my bones . . . Ever I age, but I do not fall sick, and I do not die. I scarcely sleep, but lay haunted by memories that are not my own."

Vaela's expression flickered with discomfort as the blade briefly touched. "I see now I have been gone too long," she said, taking the crone's hand gently, to coax the release of her hair. "Very well, you shall have what you ask."

Mother Bright relaxed with a grunt, returning the blade to its sheath. "There is a little jar upon the desk there, perfect for the occasion. When I have tasted you to my satisfaction, we shall fill it."

Mr. Lorris approached. "My lady she demeans you; you cannot consider—"

"I want her best work," Vaela said. "Help her to the table, and we shall begin."

The ship creaked as it rocked, and seated at the captain's desk the elderly fortune-teller took hold of Vaela's milky wrist as the vampiress stood beside her. By a small silver implement Mother Bright lightly cut her flesh and Vaela flinched at the pain, hissing as the old woman sucked at her wrist, drinking ravenously.

The vampiress clenched her fist, baring her teeth, until after several long swallows she pulled away. "Enough!"

Mother Bright spluttered and seethed, taken with sudden collapse, her head lolling on the desk in sleep.

Vaela found a small stout jar set by, and she punctured her arm with a sharp claw to bleed further, guiding the little stream into the glass as she glared at the sleeping crone.

With a dram or two of her own blood shed, Vaela accepted one of the Lurkmen's offer to replenish herself, and exposing only the flesh of his neck she nursed at him a few moments, before mending the hurt and taking her seat on the opposite side of the desk.

"Place the vial before her," Vaela said, wiping her mouth.

Some minutes later Mother Bright woke with a snap, stretching her arms with a wheezing cackle. "What good it does these old sinews," she said, and snatching up the black liquid in its vial she tore off the seal.

"To my curse," she said, raising a toast, "that which cannot be replaced, which no other can bear."

"How you delight in your own importance, Mother Bright," Mr. Lorris remarked.

"She is only protecting herself," Vaela said, watching her.

The Gypsy madam grinned faintly, and took a generous swallow of the viscous stuff, retching with a grimace as it went down. Making strange sounds she rattled, quivering as her bones cracked, and splaying her spidery fingers she leaned suddenly forward, staring at Vaela with eyes clouded bright white. "Your hand," she demanded, her voice low and ominous.

Vaela offered her hand across the table, and the old woman grabbed it, leaning down to lick her open palm. The vampiress tingled, watching as the same silver implement was brought to bear, and raising it high the seer stabbed it downward into Vaela's hand. The ache was liquid fire, and the vampiress gripped the chair with a shudder, her eyes wet with black.

"One name."

"Vorsadat," Vaela said. "He has betrayed his sister the queen— can you divine his future, his threat to us?"

Eyelids fluttering, Mother Bright tossed away the shard of silver, smearing the blood along the creases of Vaela's palm. "He is afflicted the same as your queen beneath the mountain," she droned. "I see revenge, hollow burning as a ring of fire in the dark. But the wandering monster is not that revenge, he is only its servant, and connected to *you*, Vaela Audette." She ran a sharp nail through the blood. "Your natural line betrays you for a murderous beast, and the line of the liver . . . for a violent death."

"My death was nigh two-hundred years ago," Vaela said. "As for *murderous beast* . . . I must disagree."

"Hush!" the Gypsy woman snapped, tracing again. "The mensal line makes vanishing angle with the vitals, portending great mischief, danger and grief."

Vaela stared at her intently. "And the wandering monster, Vorsadat, he who digs up the dead, who took my throat in his hands, do you see his fate?"

Mother Bright's nail drifted about her palm, drawing stripes of flesh which the pooling blood chased after. "I see a great black owl, round and wide as a barrow mound, with pitted eyes of fire. But the dead he has taken are never to rise again, and again, and again . . ."

"Whom does he serve? What does he want?"

"The time will soon come," Mother Bright droned. "Two ravens, old and young, will face the owl on a three-headed hill, the younger transfixed betwixt head and heart . . . but her choice is wrong, and struck from the sky the ravens will die, by ones or by two, under the mills, under the moon."

"No," Vaela snarled. "You are mistaken."

The hull yawed beneath them as wind over the water buffeted the ship, and squeezing her wounded hand tightly the Gypsy madam leaned forward, eyes wide and blind. "I see your end, clear as still water. But what is this?" she puzzled, her voice shifting strangely. "O'er an empty place, a sonorous call to preternatural grace, where twin hollows walk, without form, without face, reaching through stars, from a child's arms, to bid little raven with living branch flee, from beneath the shadow of unliving tree."

"What does it mean? What am I to learn from this?"

But with a groan the old woman collapsed, her chin dropping to her chest in sleep.

"The sight has left her?" Mr. Lorris asked.

"For now," Vaela said, rising slowly from the chair. "We must go."

"And you will gift her even so much, of your blood?"

The vampiress sighed, watching Mother Bright as she slept. "She will find it neither hastens nor heals her curse, for I bear her no affection," and turning to Mr. Lorris Vaela pulled up her hood. "Leave the vial, and the gold. Return the silver, and her things, lest the baron and his hunters anticipate our return. It behoves her to keep me secret."

Mr. Lorris nodded, signalling the others. "As you wish."

■■

To Emelyn's sleeping mind the venue was unmistakable, even seen through the monster's eyes: Charing Cross in the dead of night, where three roads converged at a tall bronze of the executed King Charles I on his steed. Atop the proud figure's head, hunched like a massive carrion bird, Vorsadat glowered over the spoils of his vexation: four bodies torn and broken, strewn about the base of the statue.

"Where is she . . . where is my little acrobat?" the great vampire growled, gnashing blood basted teeth as he scanned over sparse traffic making its way to the south road out of the city.

Wise enough to come no closer, if near enough to wonder at the grisly sight, a few men and women spoke in whispers as the monster observed them, still as stone, his hollow eyes glowing dimly in the dark.

Tentative lights began to gather, a hue and cry was raised, and Vorsadat rumbled as men of the watch found just nerve and numbers enough to approach. Irritated by their niff and noise he dug black claws into the bronze, crouching to spring, and before the torches could better discern him he launched into the night, arcing high over the gasping crowd to land on the peaked roof of the Nag's Head inn across the square.

Leaving their frighted cries behind the monstrous vampire dashed to the far edge, soaring over the back lane to catch himself by an aging steeple, where like a carven gargoyle he froze, marking every sound as he tasted the air. Mortal insects dotted the streets below, acquitting themselves of late vices, their human heat and murmurs betraying no sign of his wayward quarry . . . and heaving away again he searched on, leaping from one roof to the next.

Frustration mounted, empty windows flashed past as claws over heel Vorsadat raced along the walls, bounding high above the road between the buildings about Covent Garden park. A lonely church bell chimed from somewhere near, and conceding at last the trail was cold he dropped into the deep shadowed alley, erupting in a howl of rage.

"Where is she?" Emelyn blurted, suddenly awake. There was no sound but the sleeping breath of her companions, and rubbing her eyes she found the darkness outside standing still. "Is the wheel not repaired? Deacon?"

But her brother did not respond, and nudging Breda's shoulder Emelyn felt a twinge of alarm. "Breda? Breda wake up."

There was a face at the window, but gone before her eyes could catch it, leaving only the sure impression that it was not Vaela. Holding her breath she listened with all her might, but found neither voices nor movement outside . . . nothing but the creak of wood and wind.

The door opened, and there stood a man she had never seen. Very tall he was, long coated in black with hanging cuffs of lace, and a dishevelled twist of a cravat at his neck. Sharply handsome of features, in appearance he was perhaps twice her age, with long silver hair tied strictly back, a pair of round rimmed spectacles on his nose, gleaming in the light of the lanterns. By the unearthly aura of his presence, and the claws at his fingertips, she knew him at once for a vampire.

"Miss Emelyn Morley," he said, extending a pale hand to assist her down. "If you please."

Fear and curiosity duelled within her, but she accepted, taking hold of his fingers to descend from the coach. The night breathed cool, and watching the deep blue of his eyes she all but forgot the men, until an intruding sight of them made her gasp. Beside the open road, near piled stones anchoring a crude road sign, stood the driver, footman, and Lord Van Croft. Standing in a row they were perfectly still, their heads bowed, as though frozen in reverence for the memory of one departed . . . The horses too were very still, their heads down and tails swishing lazily.

"Your carriage has caught a wheel; the dark road is not safe," the mysterious gentleman observed.

In finding the others subdued by unnatural sleep, the fact that she was yet lucid lent her courage, and she turned to face him. "Who are you sir?"

"I am called Simeon Vietto de Rhoda, and I have waited a long time to meet you."

"Can it be that a vampire requires spectacles?" she asked before she could help it.

The vampire lord smiled. "Indeed no, Miss Morley. They are the last device I yet retain from my mortal life, crafted by my father, who was a clockmaker. I wear them to remember my origin, and keep at bay the baser instincts of immortality . . . I have assembled them anew many times, but of course their power is only imagined."

Emelyn nodded. "And you are acquainted with Vaela?"

"I am. I know her well. She will join us anon."

"And she is . . . your ally I should hope?"

"Vaela is as much family to me, as I daresay you have become, to her."

There was a chill in the air, and feeling goosepimples Emelyn embraced herself. "I am heartened to hear it," she said, stirring with envy that he would know the vampiress better than she. "I might say despite her nature, or what I know of it," she added, "Vaela has shown me more humanity than many a mortal person."

"And you have repaid her in kind," he replied, walking to the back of the leaning carriage. "I am in your debt, Miss Morley. But before we come to business, perhaps I may be of some small assistance," and rounding the corner he was out of sight.

Unsure whether to move Emelyn waited, looking over the sunken wheel, up to its hub in soft mud.

"Here we are," Lord Simeon said, and the vehicle creaked as slowly it began to rise.

Holding the neck of her cloak Emelyn came just close enough to observe him, astonished to find the vampire gentleman lifting the coach by his left hand, gripping it beneath the sturdy lower edge of the boot. As though it were no more than returning a heavy book to its shelf he set the wheels down outside the ruts.

"Thank you, my lord Vietto de Rhoda," she said, hoping she'd remembered the name.

"Lord Simeon is all the title I require," he said, and taking a kerchief from his pocket he wiped his hand. "Now, I am given to understand Vaela has shared with you her particular gift."

"She has, yes," Emelyn replied, feeling the urge to expound. "But it broke my heart to learn of her history, and I must hope she has found some measure of happiness in her life now, such as it is."

"Vaela's mortal experience casts a long shadow," he said. "Once I feared to lose her, but her vigil over Hastelbrook, and you her charge, have given her purpose."

The sense of his presence was quite different from Vaela, but there was yet something familiar in it, a sort of thoughtful stillness, as one might find in quiet moments among old and familiar books, and on a sudden Emelyn could feel Vaela's deep connection to the dark gentleman before her. "You made her," she whispered, feeling a swell of emotion at the thought. "Two-hundred years ago you found her; it was you who made her vampire."

Lord Simeon removed his spectacles, scowling as he gave them a delicate polish. "You are as perceptive as you are polite," he said. "I am her maker."

"Then you must be older still . . . older even than she."

"It was 470 years ago now, I was reborn to darkness."

Emelyn marvelled at him, imagining medieval Britain before the great monasteries were burned, when longsuffering monks hunched over their desks to copy manuscripts of the world, and strangely she wondered whether he had known or walked among them. "Are you of England?"

"I am Catalan, from Spain," he said, drawing closer, "but you needn't hear my story now. The immortal night gifts us each according to the shades of our character in life; as Vaela discerns the heart, my power allows me to peer into thought and memory."

"And you would look into mine."

"By your leave," he said, replacing his spectacles. "Vaela has spoken of the spirits you described to her, twin shadows which it might appear have protected you, even from one far older than I."

"You know of the monster . . . *Vorsadat*?"

"By occupational association. We all of us serve the queen in the dark, and he is her brother."

"As Vaela warned," Emelyn said. "I don't fully understand how it happened, but am I not made the queen's enemy by resisting him?"

"In attacking you he defied her will; she has not the heart to destroy him, but he is banished from her kingdom, and will nevermore appear to you . . . on pain of annihilation."

Finding some small comfort in the words Emelyn breathed deep, holding his gaze. "Very well, I am ready," she said.

Raising his arms he brought his hands to either side of her head, spreading his fingers. "There shall be a sense of falling into yourself," he said. "Many recollections will be brought to light, even fragments you may have repressed. Have you any questions, before we look inside?"

Emelyn trembled, unable to think as her eyes fell on his cravat. "You're wearing it Steinkirk," she said, "that is out of fashion," and reaching up she took hold of the twisted ends to pull them free and knot them smartly together, leaving the remainder to hang at his chest.

"Thank you," he said. "I have been away since the year you were born. Now, shall we begin?"

Feeling a cautious thrill she stood very still, and after a few deliberate breaths she gave him a nod.

Lord Simeon's fingertips touched her scalp; a whirl of vertigo stole her balance, and from behind she'd the warm and sudden sense of Vaela's embrace. "I'm here," the vampiress whispered.

As promised Emelyn felt a plunging bodiless sensation, losing the world around her as she fell deep into memory. A dim light shone in a dark room, and she heard the soft sweetness of Vaela's voice, singing as Emelyn lay in her infant cradle, delighting in the sound . . . The timbre of her brother's childish laughter came from outside, and the room melted away, replaced by an enormous blanket, spread all about her as she sat by her mother on the sunlit green. A branch cracked, and Deacon screamed, startling her to tears . . .

Emelyn twitched in Lord Simeon's hands, wanting desperately to help her brother—but a vision of books overtook her, a door in the shelves swung inward to darkness, and after climbing carefully down the giant stairs she nestled between caskets of stone, playing with her letter blocks as glimmers of light illumined the floor, like golden sparks breathing from the darkly hooded figure that stood bending over her . . . But when she turned to look, she was older, just high enough to tap the faceless statue on the head, pressing her cheek to the smooth carven stone as she shared of her day . . . The floor grew soft, tickling grass brushed her arms, and she was jaunting through high meadows on her way to the neighbouring estate of Candlewood under the moon, the security of a cold hand clutched in hers. Then, with angry sobs she dug into the earth to bury the heads of Isabelle's dolls in the cemetery, before drying happy tears in the light of day at the gift of Queen Bess, her beautiful Arabian mare. Her first ride was beyond the horse ring, up the hill to the old cistern in the northern woods, which was so deep one would hear what seemed an endless clatter of falling stone, before the splash . . . and then she was sitting on Vaela's cloak under the gnarled oak tree by the water, instructing her in the weaving of finger wreaths from little roots and stalks.

The grand society ball at Daulton House blazed in her eyes, and she was seventeen again, dancing her debut, where the Prince of Wales had coaxed her outside for his offer, before the vampiress interceded, and blushing bravely Emelyn shared her throat as Vaela's lips found their place for that first piercing kiss—

The party flickered away, and she sat for her portrait in Brighton Hall as elegant country ladies partnered for dancing, before she snuck away to wander the wharf, gleaning stories from old sailors as Vaela followed . . . Hastelbrook rose up again, guests mingling outdoors among merry torches, while long shadows watched from empty garret windows, and she found herself cornered alone in the maze by an elderly gentleman, who being snatched away by the scruff she was never to see again.

Colours gyred about her in a frenzy, and the bloodstone sparkled brilliant red, rising from the swaddling of its box as Emelyn lifted it out, testing the fit against her neck . . . Somewhere deep below stone ground over stone, the crimson glow winked out, and she was sitting in bed, suspended between wakefulness and sleep as a great cloaked figure crouched bird-like on the footboard, its spectral wings surrounding her, dripping with golden light—

She was twenty-one, the snow melted in the spring, and hot with news of a dashing gentleman by the name of Arkwright, Emelyn slipped her curfew to meet the vampiress again, flying down the hill only to sail into her arms as she broke a shoe. It was the only time she'd seen Vaela laugh hard enough to close her eyes.

"Wait," Emelyn said aloud, striving to hold onto the memory, but her thoughts lurched away, flitting through dreams of giant statues, and to her confident captain, courting her from the back of a white swan. Dining room candles melted into liquid smoke, and she revisited her terrible freezing fever, thrashing in bed as she fought the bloodsick—her senses waking to the power in Vaela's blood. Her ears bled, and she felt the press of Arkwright's lips, but seizing him against her she caught only air, and it was the roof of Galecliff, the captain's forbidden caress and the nightmare attack of a monster she scarcely understood.

"No," Emelyn protested, and she looked into the high dining room mirror to find a towering hooded shape looking back at her, leaning closer as the dancing guests paid it no heed. She meant this time to speak to the ghostly figure but a locking door clicked, and she was pinned against it, reliving the violent indignity of Mr. Rosch's inquisition.

"Confess!" he bellowed, the edge of his dagger gleaming, but its touch was avoided by an icy plunge into the rain battered pond, broad and black as she swam for the lady's arm, sinking far below—

And then . . . drenched with cold she stood in a dim vaulted space, centred with a great iron sarcophagus, thrice the size of a man. The weight of the bloodstone lay heavy on her chest, and as torchlike embers glowed to life upon the opposing walls, she found at either end of the long chamber towered a giant, carved in shrouded stone. From the extended fingers of each dangled a beautiful chain of twisted platinum, glinting in its own light; twin chains and twin hooded statues reaching out as though to offer them up—

The trance was broken; the vampire lord lowered his arms, and opening her eyes Emelyn gasped for breath, feeling the vampiress close behind her, clasping her shoulders.

"What's happened?" Emelyn panted. "Is it over?"

"You spoke," Vaela marvelled. "No one ever speaks."

"Don't they?" Emelyn breathed, her hand over her heart.

Lord Simeon adjusted his spectacles. "Her memories leapt and swerved like a raging current; it was all I could do to hold the path."

"Have I done something wrong?" Emelyn asked.

"Somehow you found the temerity to interrupt me," Lord Simeon said. "Perhaps I begin to apprehend how you exorcized so great an enemy from your mind, as Vorsadat. As to your shrouded phantoms, alternately indistinct as shadows and solid as cowled stone . . . undeniably I saw them."

"Please, what are they?" Emelyn asked, her head swimming from the exertion. "I cannot have imagined them."

Lord Simeon nodded thoughtfully. "More than imagination they must be, else they could not have assisted you against the monster. I must guess their presence has guarded the vault from its inception, and that perhaps it was by their will the stone door turned on the night of your birth."

"They cannot be vampires," Emelyn said. "But I dreamt of such a figure perched on the footboard of my bed, and I'd the impression of wings, surrounding me like a nest. I suppose they must be *spirits* of some sort?"

"That final memory," Lord Simeon said, "the statues, and chains hanging in the dark . . . the black sarcophagus; can it be these things lie within your family crypt?"

Emelyn furrowed her brows. "No . . . that was no memory my lord. I have never been to such a place."

Vaela stood beside her, regarding her maker. "Is it possible?"

The vampire lord folded his hands, and with a soft chuckle he looked to the sky.

"What does it mean?" Emelyn inquired, noting Vaela's chin and cheek were spattered with blood.

"I daresay it is a message, Miss Morley," Lord Simeon said, "even, perhaps, a premonition."

"Do you suppose I am haunted, or cursed?" Emelyn asked. "Long has my family been suspected of such things."

"A curse conducive to your well-being? I would not describe it so. I rather think you have been shown inside the vault itself."

"Inside! But then, to what purpose? What do they want?"

"That you find these dark figures protect you, is a riddle," he said. "One we should hope leads to the vault itself."

"Am I meant to open it on my own?"

"I cannot say . . . but I might guess the way shall be revealed only to you," Simeon said.

"As Vorsadat believed; it is why he attacked," Vaela said.

"And what of my dreams of him?" Emelyn asked. "When I dream that I am behind his eyes, feeling as though somewhere he and I are one. What is it? Is it no more than a dream?"

The vampires shared a look.

"Perhaps as you ejected him from your mind, a part of you has infected him, in turn," Simeon suggested.

The thought was overwhelming, and feeling a sudden requirement to sit down Emelyn swayed, but the vampiress caught her.

"Do not think of him," Vaela said gently. "He will come not near you now; he is forbidden."

"My family must know nothing of this," Emelyn said, her head growing light, "not of my illness, nor of Rosch, or any of it. It was only by Deacon's experiment, that Mr. Rosch was caught in the dark. And I suppose he is dead now?"

"He is not dead," Vaela said, guiding her back to the coach. "But will nevermore threaten you."

"Wait," Emelyn said, and turning to look at them both she felt as though she stood upon the uttermost boundary of one world peering into another. And yet, looking at Vaela's face, lustrous in the increscent moonlight, she beheld the melancholy visage of a woman a few years her elder, an inch or two taller, who had once lived and died, and lived again. "I know it was your blood," she said, "that saved Deacon . . . as it must have done many times before."

At this Vaela reached into her cloak. "Yes," she said simply, and taking Emelyn's hand she placed a small metal something in her palm.

"Is this . . . was this not Doctor Tarville's ring?" Emelyn asked, disconcerted to recognize the little bauble of brass. "Then he never fell on his own."

"A trophy," Vaela said. "He poisoned your brother."

Emelyn searched her eyes. "What? Why?"

"To cure the embarrassment of his inability, on pain of losing Van Croft's favour. Failing to heal he took it upon himself to satisfy the spirit of the request, by murder."

With a gasp Emelyn started to speak, but Vaela touched her lips. "I know what you would ask—I do not believe the captain was aware of the doctor's treachery."

Emelyn flung the ring away. "I do not want a trophy," she said, "though I feel nothing but hate for the man. The gift of your blood will turn me to a vengeful monster."

"You cannot charge every passion to my blood."

"But I am to be *married*," Emelyn said quietly, wishing she could speak to her in private.

Seeming to sense her reticence Lord Simeon began to whistle, the sound fading into the shadows as he slipped away from them.

"Speak freely," Vaela said, taking her hands.

Emelyn shook her head. "If this audit of my memory has taught me anything, it is that your power has sheltered my experience, all my life. You've kept me from what should have been healthy and natural fears. I do not fear the dark, nor men, nor the unknown, as I ought."

"Mortals spend the better part of their lives in fear," Vaela said, "in particular fear of the unknown. Is it not a blessing to have mastered these?"

"Is it?" Emelyn puzzled with a frown. "I will marry the captain—I will not see my family brought to ruin. But I scarcely understand what you expect of me. I don't know how to breach the vault; the crypt has been barred against me since I was a child."

"Whatever lies within the vault, the queen believes it will bring about her restoration, even her redemption. But *you* must be the one to discover it . . . If the spirits show you more, you must follow them."

Emelyn stared at her, feeling a gnawing sense that some hidden danger lay beyond Vaela's words.

The vampiress squeezed her arm. "But we needn't trouble you with shadows. You must complete your journey, return home safely, and rest. Lord Simeon will cure your brother's memory of me, forever, should you wish it."

"No, I'm well enough equipped to handle my brother," Emelyn said. "That is, he would never betray our secret. Having another to confide in wouldn't go amiss, if it does not worry you."

Vaela lifted her hand to kiss it. "It does not worry me," she said. "I am wise to trust you, even with my life, as you have proven."

"Oh, I have a gift for you," Emelyn said suddenly, digging in her pocket, whereupon she produced the little chess piece, handing it over.

"The red queen?" Vaela mused, accepting the object. "How succinctly becoming," and she handed it back.

"You don't like it?"

"Let it be our signal. Put it on the sill when you require me, and I shall come to your window."

Emelyn felt a happy flush. "Yes, very well. I will," she said, and feeling the urge to tidy her, she wet a kerchief in her mouth, applying it to wipe the blood from Vaela's face.

The vampiress smiled, lifting her chin.

Scrubbing a troublesome spot beneath her jaw Emelyn scowled. "Vaela, may I ask . . . when Lord Simeon made you vampire, did he take you against your will?"

"No. It was the first free decision I remember."

"But you took no joy in it."

"That's not true. I felt confusion, and cold, but at once such power, and possibility. There was doubt, and silence, but even when he could not reach me, I was never neglected, not as I had been in life."

Emelyn swallowed, nodding again. "Well, I'm tired of half forgetting you, the sense of you," she said. "I wish I could scold the sun to welcome you back."

"What a thing that would be."

Taking her in a parting embrace Emelyn squeezed tightly, and climbing into the carriage she found Breda and Deacon still deep in their enchanted sleep. "So I am to understand the queen is sick," she said, clearing her throat, "and that it threatens us all?"

"You needn't trouble over that now," Vaela said. "Watch and listen, but prosecute your days as you see fit. You are your own mistress."

Emelyn caught the door just before it closed. "But is her sickness unto death? Can a queen of vampires die?"

"It is not the affliction that would spell her doom, or ours," Vaela said, "but what comes after."

The door closed before Emelyn could protest, and she leaned back with a huff. With sudden grunts the men awoke outside, congratulating each other on the repair of the coach, and together they climbed aboard, as though nothing had happened.

■■

"I might have expected you sooner," Lord Simeon said.

Vaela stood very still, watching the carriage lanterns as they dwindled down the wheel rutted road.

"And how did you find Mother Bright?" Simeon asked.

"She speaks in riddles. Darkness draws near, to all of us."

"That is no vision. You might have told as much to yourself."

"Emelyn puts herself in the power of this captain, Van Croft," Vaela said, ignoring the comment, "and for the sake of her family. Their need is desperate—is it certain we can do nothing for them?"

"To intercede in their debts would only bring suspicion," he replied, watching her as she watched the road. "You do not relish sparing Mr. Rosch, but he could be in no better hands. Whatever he knows of Hastelbrook, or the vault, the old man will glean it."

"Rosch did not act alone," Vaela said, looking to the dampening sky. "He may be in league with Dramen's order of hunters—the same who captured Afaine."

"They are of little consequence," he said. "Afaine was betrayed by Vorsadat, or she'd never have been taken. Her escape renders the order no more relevant than they were a century ago."

"But they know of the vault—they speak of it in jealous whispers. In moving against them we would protect Hastelbrook; by my informer I have names."

"Nay my dear, to stir them up now could only validate their crusade. Their mortal greed is no threat to our design; only Miss Morley is chosen."

Like a host of spirits a chill wind blew across the road, murmuring over the grey meadows at either side, and Vaela crossed her arms, staring into the dark. "And these *living shadows* that attend her—have you any notion of what they are?"

"None . . . The vault's founding and purpose remain unknown to us; only the queen has any sense of its power."

"But she does not trust the prophecy; how long before she grows impatient as her brother."

"That you are bound to the Chosen Child by affection is our advantage," Lord Simeon said, squinting after the carriage, which was now but a distant spec of light in the rolling dark. "Stay close, and let us pray the vault reveals itself, before the queen thinks to attempt it by force . . ."

■ ■

Deacon and Breda had come to their senses, and once again in her stocking feet Emelyn found herself arguing with her brother.

"Have your dark curiosities," Deacon flustered, "but if there's any man who despises the supernatural, it's your dear captain."

Emelyn groaned at him. "Yes, Rosch said as much. Though I wonder why on earth it should matter to you—particularly in the company *of my lady's maid.*"

"So you will flee to *Vivere Gloria,*" Deacon carried on unabashed, "the puffed up estate of Lord Van Bloodhound of His Majesty's Navy. And what then of your *dark curiosities*; you shall keep them secret to the end of your days I suppose?"

"I'm sure I don't know what you're talking about," Emelyn said loudly. "But if I'd accepted an offer from Mr. Arkwright, rather than the captain, forgetting such a match would never answer our debts, would you deride me the same or should I be spared?"

"I'll answer your question with a question," Deacon said. "Have you still Arkwright's letter in your pocket?"

"That is none of your affair."

Deacon laughed. "Of course you have! Emelyn can you really be such a child? I know Van Croft's ilk. When by every legal measure he's made you his own, one wrong word and you shall be locked away, either for disloyalty or hysteria."

"I say," Breda protested softly.

"I am not denigrating my sister, dear Breda," Deacon said quickly. "I only mean to warn her. There was a spirited conversation you were not party to . . ."

"Nor needs she be party to this one," Emelyn said sharply. "But if I have not your blessing, I shall learn to live without it."

Bludgeoning his pillow into submission Deacon shifted his position. "Damnation Emie . . . of course you have my blessing. I only mean to say, that from where I sit Arkwright is the better man, and it's clear enough you've no idea to let him go."

"You're right, Deacon, Arkwright is a pure gentleman, with an easy spirit. I felt quite at home with him when first we met . . . but it doesn't matter now. Mama would never accept him, and he is the very last person I would inflict with my *dark curiosities* . . . He is innocent; he deserves better than to be tangled up in . . . whatever this is. I would never allow him to be put in danger."

"Danger miss?" Breda puzzled.

"And fear not, I will discard his letter the moment we arrive," Emelyn said, returning her gaze to the window.

"Good," Deacon replied, nodding with a frown as he looked out the other side.

"And I am resolved that he will forget me," Emelyn added, "and meet a beautiful young lady of warmth and," the words stuck for a moment and she cleared her throat, "and wit enough to deserve him. I do not know him so very well, after all, and I wish him every happiness."

"Not bad, but you'll have to work harder than that to convince the captain," Deacon said. "Perhaps if you pluck out your bothersome heart and stow it in the ice well . . . That should teach it a thing or two."

"Deacon, you must stop fretting for me!" Emelyn said. "It is my lot to protect Hastelbrook, and that is precisely what I mean to do. I am not the desperate romantic you imagine."

"Better," Deacon said, "I nearly believed that one."

"Did you say danger miss?" Breda interjected. "Has something happened?"

"Yes, Breda, for God's sake," Emelyn said, brandishing the ring, "I've got myself engaged, do you remember? And to a very powerful man, whom I'm sure would not tolerate a rival, so let this be an end of it."

"Yes of course miss," Breda said quietly.

The carriage jostled on. "I just want to be at home, and in bed," Emelyn sighed, finding the landscape outside relentlessly bleak.

"The sun should rise at five o'clock, just before we arrive," Deacon noted. "And I shall be sleeping all day . . . if there's any justice in the world."

Emelyn crossed her arms, checking the other window for something more interesting, and the three of them fell silent as the coach trundled along the muddied road.

■ ■

In the depths of the hidden citadel, under the false sky of a vast domed ceiling painted in the colours of a bloody sunrise, the queen in the dark, Pazoa Qiminossa, floated above the centre of the floor—gleaming marble with tines of gold that spread from her feet as the spokes of a wheel. Like a dark and evergreen angel, her slender form was sheathed in emerald silk, its tight cascades slashed to display the rich bronze of her flesh. Glitters of jewellery hung from her body like stars, while her voluminous hair was bound up high, fanning into a spined headdress of bone, ebony strands woven weblike across an intricate frame.

Pazoa's face was uncovered for her audience, blood red lips parted, high cheeks brushed, as in a wide ring surrounding the floor below her sat ancient masters before their easels, dressed each according to the royal custom of his day, many of them in rotting hats and cloaks now centuries out of fashion. By the light of hanging iron torches the portraitists painted their queen from the vantage of eighteen angles, eighteen brushes clasped in withered hands drifting methodically over canvas.

The sound of approaching footsteps tattled through the silence, breaking the spell; the masters sagged to stillness, and the queen turned to look, her dark eyes glinting in the light.

Slipping through the circle of desiccated artists, Afaine flashed close, falling to her knees before the mother of her blood. "My queen . . ."

"Our youngest shadow safely returned," the queen breathed, the welcome in her voice warming the room as she spread her arms, drifting downward.

Afaine bent low, her face near the floor. "Mother . . . I was betrayed by Vorsadat! The mortals would never have found me on their own, and I'd not have—"

But the queen stopped her voice, snatching her up in a fierce embrace. "Hush, my daughter; I have banished him, and by your escape you are redeemed."

"Why did you not come for me?" Afaine asked miserably, arms and legs wrapped about her as they rose into the air together.

Pazoa held the back of her head, cheek to cheek. "You must forgive me—I could not bear the shame of your capture, but I'd have borne your loss all the worse."

Afaine shook with little sobs, and the queen cooed her to silence.

"As the mortals dared entrap my child to torment, so shall we repay them. Morion will fetch to me this Baron Dramen's son, and together we shall feast in his flesh."

"No, not him!" Afaine protested. "Twice I escaped, and twice it was mortal men who assisted me. The baron's son broke me out by his own free will; he was imprisoned to answer for it."

"No more little words." The queen grasped her face, and with soft growls she kissed her eyes. "The lion owes no debt to the lamb."

Clinging tightly Afaine frowned. "I will return to London, when it is safe. I mean to set him free. If you would punish anyone, punish Lord Dramen; without him the hunters are lost."

The queen sighed. "I will not martyr the baron," she said, a rasp in her words as though fatigued. "He is powerless against us, and by your escape rendered impotent in the eyes of his fellows. But the others, those who put you to blade, to fire, to drowning—"

"They were disguised, masked and perfumed . . . so I would not know them. One of them was a duke—I recall his voice. But I was never drowned mother, that was Mr. Arkwright, one who knows the Chosen Child; it was only by his aid I escaped the city in a barrel."

"In a barrel?" The queen loosened her embrace to stare at her.

"Yes, the ale covered my escape, against Vorsadat's searching senses."

"Very well my daughter, then shall we spare them all?" Pazoa clucked, touching her chin with a narrow claw, "but you will venture no more beyond the boundary of my will. Hunt whom you like in the village, drink deep, and then to your room."

"But Mother, must I only—"

"Drink, and sleep, my darling creature," Pazoa said, and sinking back to the floor she released her.

The young vampiress knelt before her, the queen's slender hand wafted close, and Afaine took it, kissing her largest ring, its heavy gem carved to match the red eye of the cathedral.

"I must treat now with your elder brother," the queen said. "Go."

No sooner had Afaine reluctantly vanished than a swirl of darkness took shape in her place, and from the gathering mist the vampire lord Morion comprised himself, bowing low.

"It is nearly dawn, Mother, will you pose for portraits until you collapse with the risen sun?"

The queen trembled, coughing softly. "No peace awaits me in sleep; I take my pleasures where I will. What is your report?"

"Vorsadat cannot draw near the Chosen Child, but I will know it. As well I have ordered the Lurkmen expand their net—under the direction of Mr. Lorris they have taken thirty-nine children this night."

"So many in one? You put my best soldiers at risk . . ."

"Nay, Mother, thirteen is no longer enough. At but a single swallow from each you scarcely recover your strength. The dead hearted mortals of London are accustomed to stepping over foundlings in the street—they'll scarcely notice a few more gone missing."

The queen blinked slowly. "Have you shadowed our little raven and her maker, as I asked?"

"Yes, Mother, Vaela caught the witch hunter and surrendered him to the old man."

"Lord Tredavius is returned to our grace," Pazoa said. "I have invited he and his thrall to ensconce in the black library—there all they discover shall belong to us."

"And what of Vorsadat?" Morion asked. "Shall we expect him to lie quiet in exile? But let us not wait for his next offence—let my fury punish his betrayal."

"No, you are evenly matched. I will not risk losing you both."

Morion's eyes flashed, and vanishing from her sight he reformed outside the ring of silent masters, slashing two of them from their seats. Scarcely more than knitted bones they shattered against the floor, held vaguely to human shape by their ancient clothes. "You speak of risk," Morion growled, "while you spend your dwindling blood on vanity!"

With a snarl the queen tore away her headdress, voluminous twists of hair coming with it. The frame crashed to the floor as new tresses of black flowed from her scalp to replace them, and she drifted toward him, raven hair obscuring her face.

"Dare you waste yourself so," Morion said, stepping inside the ring, "while Vorsadat roams free to plot against us?"

"You are unhappy, my most loyal son," she muttered. "Speak your heart."

"The dead grow restless," he said, reaching out in supplication, "I see it night by night. Here and again they pause in their toil, and by the thousands they look up, as though hearing the distant call of some other voice . . ."

"The spirits of the Deadmere try me, but I will not fail their test; I will master them."

"That storm was but a ripple, and only the first," Morion rejoined, taking another step. "It came not from Saunmoor, but from the west, from whence mortal ships are lost in their dozens, from whence *his* ashes were sunk to the bottom of the sea. Let me to it, let me fly over the water and find the source of what dark will opposes you!"

Her face yet hidden Pazoa chuckled, baring her claws at him, her arm locked as though she would catch the air in her grip, and compelled by a sudden force he flew to meet her, stopping only by his throat caught in her hand.

Morion did not resist, his expression cowed in despair as lifting from the floor she took him, rising twenty yards to the peak of the dome.

"Have I aught to explain to you, my eldest," she said, speaking through the curtain of her hair, "you who should have been prince of this place, to sit at my right hand. Is my power yours to guess?"

"Mother, please," he wheezed, "I only want you should save your strength . . ."

The queen released her grasp, and Morion snapped into mist as he fell, reforming at the centre of the wheel-tiled floor. High above him her trailing gown and sleeves drifted like green tendrils in the draft. "What else have you learned, from those who are banished?" she asked, her voice resounding through stone to fill the room.

With a heavy sigh Morion dropped to his knee. "Vaela conferred with her maker; they believe the Chosen Child communes with *spirits* of the vault, and that only she will discover its ingress."

"Is that all you heard?" the queen asked, descending through the air.

Morion nodded, his eyes trained on the floor. "Yes, Mother."

"Then let us wait and see, whether it is the old man, or she, who finds our way to the treasure."

Chapter 30
The Grinning Moon

A chill shimmered over her skin, and Emelyn opened her eyes as the carriage rolled to a stop.

Breda yawned, shaking her head. "Oh, I did sleep like the angels miss . . ."

Emelyn rounded her back to stretch, and after slipping on her shoes she roused her brother. "Deacon, we're home."

Snorting awake he repaired to sitting, working his jaw. "So we are, well done."

The eminence of Hastelbrook seemed larger than she remembered, and peering up at the house her heart sank to find it still dark, with only the earliest tinge of dawn at the edge of the sky. "Like thieves in the night," she sighed.

"What do you expect at quarter to five," Deacon said, stuffing away his pocket watch. "In fact I'm surprised; we've made up the time and more."

The door opened, and with a gleaming smile Lord Van Croft offered his hand to help Emelyn down, informing her the time was quarter to five. "Yes, there's been word," she said, stepping onto the drive.

"Letters for you, Miss Morley, before I away," he said, producing the documents from his pocket to hand them over, "for each of your parents."

"Very well."

The captain pulled her close by the waist. "Darling," he said, "of course I've grown fond of your boundless curiosity, but the missive for your father is paramount; you must never see it, nor ask him after its contents."

"How mysterious," she said, scowling at the letters as he held her. "But to describe it so could only entice one's *boundless curiosity*. Why not trust it to a servant?"

"It is of a maritime matter most sensitive," he said, "and every house that keeps a servant keeps a thief."

Her answer was smothered by his kiss, and releasing her quickly he kissed her hand, before climbing the carriage again.

"Is it welcome and goodbye?" she asked, watching as coachman Graves and footman Wallace unloaded.

"I'll not invade your family's hospitality at such an hour," Van Croft said, looking down at her, "and it is imperative I return to Galecliff, with another look at that coach by the wayside. You have been wronged, Miss Morley, and Rosch is still at large. The root of his attack bears investigation."

Deacon was assisted down, Breda disembarked, and moving as close to the driver's seat as she could without climbing Emelyn addressed the captain quietly. "Can we not let the matter lie, and look to the future?" she asked, feeling some trepidation to wonder if it might not have been smarter to take Rosch's hat after all.

"Miss Morley, I'd like nothing more," Van Croft said, "but it must be understood that you are under my protection now—any slanderous word connecting my betrothed to the supernatural will not be tolerated," and with a tip of his hat he snapped the reins.

The carriage started out again, and Emelyn watched as it made good speed back to the village road. The captain's abrupt departure left a nervous weight behind, and she rather wished he'd stayed longer, if only to forget the derelict coach.

Once inside the welcoming familiar scents of pine and linseed greeted her as she stood in the grand hall, looking up to the enormous portrait of her family as she debated whether to wake them . . . There was painted Mr. Morley, standing between parted draperies, clad in smart dark colours like his son. Deacon was fifteen at the time, standing erect without crutches beside his father. Before him perched the beautiful Mrs. Morley in extravagant open collared blue, her deep red hair bundled back under a cocked hat as she held a little Isabelle in her lap. Sarah, then aged six, stood cast in white left of her mother, with Emelyn only slightly taller at nine, though like her sister painted to seem older, adjacent her sister against a backdrop of fruited shrubbery. Invariably indifferent to posing for portraits, Emelyn was presented in proud melancholy loveliness, in gilded courtly green, with lace embellishments and the bloodstone ruby gleaming at the base of her throat—

"What?" Emelyn gasped to see it. "What on earth—Deacon have they changed the portrait? Look, do you see?"

But her brother had gone up, and when she looked again, her painted throat was bare.

Emelyn rubbed her eyes. "Settle down Emie," he muttered. "You're only tired."

Soon enough her things were upstairs, Comby had taken her cloak, and the house settled to silence. Determined to be in bed before her parents and sisters arose, Emelyn was just mounting the stairs when at a sudden change of heart she turned back, making her way through double doors to the dim candle lit long gallery.

Cold and smooth, the hooded bust beckoned, its black stone seeming to hum at her touch. "You are more than a nameless statue, I'm certain of that now," she said, tracing one of the cracks with her finger, "but if there is aught your visions are meant to show me—"

"Good morning miss."

With a thrill of surprise Emelyn turned to find the creaky housekeeper, Mrs. Leicester, staring at her—gowned in retiring black as always, a candelabrum in her hand.

"I've not startled you miss."

"No, Mrs. Leicester, certainly not," Emelyn said, catching her breath, "but I should have thought you asleep."

"Not I miss."

"No, of course," Emelyn replied, summoning a smile. "You know there was a time I believed you did not sleep at all, preferring to roam the halls and catch little girls out of bed."

"Not little girls," Mrs. Leicester said, "but Miss Emelyn in particular, who fled her room at all hours, rummaging the house for secrets, or stealin' outside in the dark."

"Yes well, that was some years ago now."

"Was it?" Mrs. Leicester raised the candles close, looking her over. "It's an ill hour to be making the journey from Eastbourne miss."

"We departed late by necessity, as Galecliff hall was damaged in the storm. But I trust everyone here kept safe and indoors, and all is right with the house?"

"Broken glass in the nursery, happens some extra watering for the plants," the housekeeper answered. "Bit of weather makes no odds to the old bones of Hastelbrook," and walking past she produced a rag, with which she set about dusting the statue.

Emelyn cleared her throat, feeling a defensive twinge to see her touch it. "This sculpture, Mrs. Leicester, what do you know of it?"

"It protects the house miss."

"Does it? Then do you know anything more, of its history perhaps?"

"No miss; from the day your grandfather hired me on he made little mention of it. It protects the house, that is enough."

"Yes very well . . . then I suppose I'm for bed, if I can be trusted to my room unsupervised."

Mrs. Leicester gave her a sour expression. "Do you want I should walk you up miss?"

"No . . . never mind," Emelyn said, her smile fading. "Goodnight, or good morning, I suppose."

"Good morning miss."

Long hours on the road had taken their toll, and finding Breda dozing in a chair by the mirror Emelyn offered to manage on her own, but her lady's maid would not have it. Standing beside the bed as Breda helped her out of her layers, and into a silk night dress, Emelyn's head swam with drowse—eyelids drooping until at the slightest nudge she tipped onto the bed and swooned away.

In her dreams she enjoyed a jubilant breakfast with Margaret, catching her up on all that had passed at Galecliff, while an army of workman dug up the library floor with shovels and picks.

"What are they looking for?" Margaret asked.

"Redemption, I suppose," Emelyn said, surprised to think of it.

"But they're mortal, they don't need it," Margaret replied, sipping her coffee.

The dream shifted, and Emelyn stood once more before the mirror, the weight of the bloodstone ruby on her bare collar, pulsing red and bright in the glass. The mirror expanded, remaking itself into the wide parlour windows, and outside it was night again. Shadow steeped gardens waved under the stars, the ancient oak shivered in the wind by the water, and looking back she found the workmen had vanished, leaving a dark pit that plunged through the library floor into a lake of distant lights. With tingling toes she was just about to step off the edge, when something crashed atop her.

"Lazybug!" Isabelle cried.

Emelyn spasmed awake, hiding her eyes against the glare of daylight. "Bell no! I've only just gone to sleep—"

"You're a liar," Isabelle said, pouring over her shoulder to speak at her face. "It's nearly eleven; we've held our celebration for hours! It's time to wake up."

"What celebration?" Emelyn asked, squinting as her sister pressed close to kiss her cheek.

"For your engagement!" Isabelle chirped in her ear.

"You're wearing a ring, Emie," Sarah said, standing close by. "Are we to guess what it means? Mama has been too mysterious!"

Isabelle sat up on her knees with a happy flush. "It means she's accepted him! The captain has captured her heart, or she'd never have said yes, for all Mama's pestering."

"Do tell us, Emie," Sarah pressed. "We tried Deacon, but he won't speak of it, nor Breda! Is what happened at Galecliff some great secret?"

Emelyn groaned, curling up as she struggled to recall the dream.

"The captain proposed to you, of course he did," Isabelle said, pushing insistently on her back. "But you were not to like him at first; you must tell us how he's won you over!"

"I'll not be bullied," Emelyn said, speaking into the pillow as Isabelle jostled her. "After breakfast! I can't remember when last I ate."

"It's all in hand; your fare is being sent up," Isabelle said quickly. "Waffles and cream, with cinnamon, just as you like."

Through narrow eyes Emelyn glanced back at her. "Waffles and cream?"

"Yes, and there shall be lemon ices later. But you must wake up and tell all!"

Breakfast in bed went some way to easing her irritation: cinnamon powdered waffles doused in sweet cream, with juice of China oranges. "Very well if you must know," she sighed between chews, "yes, he has asked, and I have answered him . . . here it is."

Seizing her extended hand her sisters gawped at the stones, and their rapid questions collided. Emelyn answered as honestly as she dared, embellishing the gallantry of the captain's proposal while making no mention of the discomfiture between herself and Mrs. Akehurst, nor of saving the woman's life. Nor did she bring up her sudden illness, those missing or murdered, the tower toppled over the wall, nor the name *Rosch* in any context, which made for so lengthy a sum of omissions as to rather perplex her words.

"Shall you hesitate before every sentence?" Sarah asked. "Is it the truth Emie, or are you contriving a story?"

"Dear Sarah, it's not all for you; some things I will keep for myself," Emelyn said. "But I do care for him, I must. In a short span of time the captain and I have been through a great deal together . . . with the storm I mean, and everything. He is no less proud than ever he was, but he is honourable, and very protective."

"Honourable and protective?" Isabelle repeated, too excited to keep still. "Is that all? But he has kissed you, surely."

"I have nothing to say on that subject."

"Do you sweat when he kisses you?"

"Isabelle Marie!" Sarah scolded.

"It's all right," Emelyn said, lying back with a stretch.

"So it was upon the rooftop in the dark, overlooking the sea," Sarah said, a note of jealousy in her voice. "Of course his letter left little doubt, but we were on tenterhooks to hear your success first hand."

"What letter?" Emelyn sat up.

"Mama had one of him the day you left, then another. But she only teased it."

"Was he so sure of my answer even then? But of course he was."

"Come now there must be more," Isabelle insisted. "You've been gone two weeks!"

"Well I suppose I might tell you Deacon acquainted a particular young lady, Miss Harrington. I believe they got on very well."

"*Deacon* met a young lady?" Isabelle marvelled.

"I have invited her to call," Emelyn said, "and I hope she will. If you want more you must speak to your brother. Of course he shan't be happy I've told you. Now, what of home, how did you fair in the storm?"

"The parterres might have been shredded," Sarah said, "but we were all hands to keep them safe. One of the trees went down, but the gardeners staked tarpaulin over everything; you've never seen so much canvas, sprawling like an army in their tents. Bell and I helped; we even spread out her precious linsey woolsey."

"No we didn't," Isabelle snapped. "That's been put away since I was a child."

"Then you must be a child still, for it's under your bed."

Isabelle retorted but Emelyn shushed them, hearing a knock at the door.

There came a second knock, and Comby popped in to inform them Mrs. Morley was waiting, with Mr. Morley not expected from London until the morrow.

Emelyn stood from her bed, and after accepting final embraces of congratulations from her sisters, she showed them out.

Comby tarried a moment before leaving, giving Breda a look, and with the door closed Emelyn was reassembled—dressed and capped in elegant cream to meet her mother.

"Two letters have come for you miss," Breda said. "I've set them on the bureau. And it's not my place, but I did wonder, if it were wise to hold on to that from Mr. Arkwright? Only I'm sure we'd be in for it, were it discovered."

"Of course you're right," Emelyn said, collecting his tender note from her pocket, and crossing the room she tossed it into the fire. Or she meant to, but her fingers held fast.

"Miss?"

"Then again, really I don't see the harm in it," Emelyn said, folding the pages tightly and tucking them in her desk. "That will be all Breda, thank you."

Regally robed in white satin, Mrs. Morley was on the veranda facing out over the sun glinted lakes, her hands on the stone railing. Emelyn paused by the columns, unenthused at the prospect of repeating the half-truths of Galecliff, but steeling herself for the interview she approached, finding the railing decorated with new lanterns of globular glass along its length.

"Good morning Mama. The new lights are lovely."

Her mother breathed deeply, as though in review of a pleasant dream, and with a happy noise she welcomed her daughter for an embrace. "My dear darling girl, let me look at you," she said, releasing her with a smile. "My but you are aglow, I daresay you look more self-assured, even taller than when you left."

"I've only been gone a fortnight," Emelyn replied, handing her the letters. "These are from Mrs. Akehurst, and the captain, respectively."

"Just think of it my dearest," Mrs. Morley replied, looking them over, "you are to be mistress of a great and noble house. Lady Van Croft! Dear me how it rings. Now where is the symbol of your conquest, let me see."

Emelyn surrendered her finger for study. "There; so I've kept my promise after all . . . if only I'd wagered something."

"But I knew your charms could not be for nothing," Mrs. Morley said, examining the jewellery with delight, "I've always said it!"

"You've always said it," Emelyn echoed, and reclaiming her hand she leaned on the railing to look out over the grounds. Far below them a long mist drifted across the lakes, settling among the tarpaulin tents in the lower gardens. "But I expect, now that all is said and done . . . the tales of our destruction were exaggerated."

"On the contrary," her mother said, taking her daughter's arm to confide. "We have come to the end my dearest, and I've no doubt, had you refused the captain, the estate would be parcelled out to creditors, and your father clapped in irons for the debt."

"But is it possible," Emelyn objected. "Had Papa not high hopes for his errand to London?"

"He's gone to seek new partnership, of course he has," Mrs. Morley said, "but there will be no interest; only a fool would invest with us now."

"Had we not found some reprieve, some infusion of cash?" Emelyn asked, thinking of her ill-advised sale of the bloodstone—good for 10,000 pounds, before Vaela returned it to her.

"Well I'm sure I don't know what you mean, but more than *we* are suffering my dear. Many of our backers have lost everything, and bills are come due; it's the South Sea Company all over again! With your father in prison and the house closed to us, a miserable little cottage on your uncle's property in Leeds is the best we could hope for. My girls should be left to marry cobblers or tinkers and inherit nothing."

"Mama, really."

"But of course with your promise, gratefully these horrors are put behind us," Mrs. Morley said, cracking open the captain's letter, "so let us speak no more of debts and despair, and have a word from our dear Lord Van Croft."

"What does he say," Emelyn muttered. "Has he called our loan?"

"Don't be smart," Mrs. Morley said, holding the paper close. "Oh! Wonderful . . . *Your daughter's beauty, which pierced me from the first as the sting of Eros, now not only pierces but blinds, rendering sharply shapeless every feminine figure but hers.*"

Emelyn grimaced. "Sharply shapeless?"

"Hush now and listen: *Most precious of all is when I find her engaged to no company but her own, for she stares into the distance like an exquisite statue, looking for all the world to be lost in another, until her emerald eyes address me again, and I account myself the luckiest fellow on earth.*"

Marvelling that she could inspire so prosaic a speaker as Lord Van Croft to such words Emelyn smiled faintly, picking at the railing as she imagined a line of white wigged footman welcoming her to the high halls of her future home, the captain grasping her fingers as they mounted the steps—though even now, the idea to leave Hastelbrook snagged in her mind, as something alien, impossible.

Mrs. Morley watched her. "The point is, that my hopeless dreaming girl has grown up. Have you not? And now the very best among men is tortured with you! I am proud of you my dearest, prouder than words can say."

Emelyn stared at the intricate paths of the hedge maze. The air grew heavy, and standing there with her mother under the severely clear sky, it came to her all at once that neither Vaela, whom she cherished beyond describing, nor all the mysteries of the world after nightfall, could reach her here. In the bright hours she was on her own, surrounded by daylight people and their daylight cares, and subject to every consequence of her daylight choices, as she would be all the years of her life.

Her eyes welled at the grasp of it. "Forever is a very long time. I only worry that I will not fall in love with him . . . and I worry that I will," she added, her voice breaking.

"Emelyn, my very dearest," her mother said gently, squeezing her arm.

"I've given him my promise, Mama, but what if he changes to me, or I to him, once I've no escape?"

Mrs. Morley shook her head. "You have matched yourself to a great man who adores you completely, who has declared himself answerable to restoring our fortunes. But you are a force in your own right—else he'd never have noticed you. Some nerves over your engagement are to be expected."

Emelyn swiped her cheek with a nod.

A listless breeze tickled about them and Mrs. Morley picked at her daughter's dress. "As to him falling faster than yourself, that is only to your advantage. Many a man thinks himself too good for love, and is out of his depth when it finds him."

Emelyn sniffed, nodding again as she watched busy under-gardeners, footmen and maids struggling to drag the tarpaulins, still heavy with soak, from the flower beds. "I'm going to lend them a hand," she said.

"There is one other thing, and delicate," her mother said, catching her just as she quit the porch.

"What is it Mama?"

"Well I'm sorry to say, I've intercepted an affectionate letter from Comby to Breda. One of them will have to be dismissed."

"What? No."

"Not Adam, of course; we dare not hire a wet first footman, and none in the house are ready for the position."

"You want Breda turned out? Ten years she's been with me."

"I am sorry my girl, but one of the other maids can just as well—"

"No, Mama, absolutely not," Emelyn said. "Comby and Breda know their office. They'd never do anything untoward," and with a kiss on her mother's cheek she turned to leave.

"My dearest, we do not allow affectionate followers among the staff!" Mrs. Morley flustered, following her from the veranda.

"Then perhaps we should," Emelyn said, gliding her hand along the rail as she made her way back along the gallery over the ballroom.

"Emelyn Elizabeth, I think you forget who is mistress of this house."

Emelyn turned to face her, tapping the railing. "If you dismiss Breda, I shall rehire her, pawn my jewels, and pay her salary in advance. It's settled, Mama."

Mrs. Morley marvelled at her. "But as *Lady Van Croft* you might hire her back whenever you like!"

"And if she's found another situation? No, Mama, we shan't dismiss either one of them. Good morning."

"Good heavens." Mrs. Morley said, following her again. "You *are* changed."

"It is good to be home," Emelyn replied, just as a breathless Isabelle interrupted them—the lemon ice was ready.

Outside the air was brisk and the sun bright, occasionally shielded by young banks of cloud. The easy task of pulling wet canvas off the parterres was a welcome one, and working beside Breda allowed Emelyn to broach the subject of Adam Comberland, which delicately she did, assuring her there should be no change in staff, provided no more passionate letters were discovered.

"My mother will sniff them out better than a foxhound," Emelyn said. "You must keep everything above board."

"Yes of course. I'm ever so sorry miss," Breda said, her face and neck flushed as she helped drag a heavy tarp over the low hedge.

"Do you love him?" Emelyn asked, wrestling it free of the bushes.

Breda hesitated. "Yes miss."

"How do you know?"

A sudden gust of wind washed over the gardens, and Breda cleared her throat. "The world were a better place, miss, for him in it."

Emelyn folded the canvas smaller, squashing it in her arms. "Breda, if you and he are married, convention dictates we must turn you off and keep him on, but the way I see it, I owe you a secret . . . and I won't be parted from you."

"You owe me a secret miss?"

"My misadventures, at Galecliff, and the attack in London— you've held your tongue, and I'm grateful."

"Oh, well, I've tried to forget Mr. Rosch and all the rest."

Emelyn handed off the folded tarp to a gardener, and staring into the sky she paused for a moment of gratitude—that she and Deacon had come through the gauntlet of Galecliff and returned safely home, though she frowned to think of the four souls who had not . . . five, if Mr. Rosch ever had a soul. "Come Breda," she said, marshalling herself, "you must join me for lemon ice. We've earned it."

Thursday July 7th

Wednesday bled into Thursday, and seeking to distract herself from Van Croft's mysterious letter to her father, which when held up to the light revealed a second, smaller document folded inside, Emelyn sat down to draw in the lower gardens. She etched not a stroke, but spent the long hour staring into the lakes, finding thoughts of her *misadventures* too insistent to set aside. After nearly drawing she returned to the house for activity, where she stared into the fire beside her embroidery hoop, stared through the window as Sarah played for them on the harpsichord, and stared through a book in the small parlour while her brother smoked.

"Deacon," she said at length, "not a word on the subject has passed your lips since we arrived . . . But I suppose it's too late to convince you it was all a dream?"

"Much too late for that," he said, chewing his pipestem as he read the *Gazette.*

Evening came on with little change in the light, and seeking further diversion Emelyn played a vigorous ball-game of Wessex Fives with Isabelle against the rear wall of the house, sweating into her bodice as she waited for the over-buoyant sun to set.

"You never miss," Isabelle flustered, wiping an arm across her forehead. "Have you practiced at Galecliff?"

But Emelyn was staring up the hill into the cemetery, lost in pondering what those Morleys of generations past must have learned or guessed of the vault, if anything, and what might have driven her architectural great-grandfather to such a frenzy of expansion—

"Emie!"

The ball knocked her in the head and Emelyn startled with a laugh, catching it from the air.

"I don't want the point if you ignore the game," Isabelle huffed.

Surrendering at last the sun dissolved over the horizon, and Emelyn hurried upstairs to her room, setting the little red queen on the windowsill before tearing out of her clothes and throwing a nightdress over her head. Outside the wind rippled over the hedge maze while the flower gardens, now free of their protective coverings, doffed the bright hues of day for the blues and blacks of night.

For some while she sat in the bay window, until the door opened, and for an inane moment she thought Vaela had somehow managed to enter from the hall, but it was only her mother.

"I come in peace," Mrs. Morley said, smiling as she approached. "I shall allow you your way with Breda; there's no sense fighting over it. But in fact I have a surprise for you."

"Right now?" Emelyn asked, irritated to find no sign of the vampiress. "I've had quite my fill of surprises, Mama."

"Oh nonsense," Mrs. Morley said happily. "Look over the grounds my dearest, and make your guess. What is that one particular amusement you've always wished for?"

Emelyn looked again, her eyes moving from the gardens to the lakes, which lapped lazily at their banks, sparkling silver on black. "Not a water party?"

"Precisely!" her mother burst, rushing to share the view. "Oh you will not believe it, but when the midsummer ball is come, for which we expect a very grand company indeed, we shall have a regatta on the lakes!"

"A regatta . . . with what boats?"

"I've commissioned a half-dozen yawls for rowing," her mother said breathlessly, "which we shall watch at leisure from the deck of our very own two-sail yacht—forty-foot with the finest appointments—to be built at the shipyard in Brighton!"

Emelyn stared at her. "You've commissioned a forty-foot yacht and six yawls . . . But how on earth should we pay for them?"

With determined composure Mrs. Morley took her hand. "My dear, I do sometimes wonder whether you understand anything. Your besotted captain is won, and you cannot have missed his implications of generosity, with all the gifts he's bestowed upon you. We must act quickly to silence every rumour of our financial distress."

"So you've promised the man's money, even before I marry him," Emelyn said, her pulse rising. "But I suppose it's too much to hope Van Croft has approved of this?"

"Why should he not when it is to your benefit? You sell yourself short my dear. The worshipful captain has already commissioned, at his own expense, your portrait, to be grandly painted in duplicate, one for himself and the second to be hung downstairs in the gallery. Ten feet my dearest!"

"But the *yacht* Mama, could you not have consulted me before committing to such a project?"

"That is not how surprises work," Mrs. Morley said curtly. "The midsummer ball shall be as much to celebrate your impending marriage as anything else, and the most opulent we've ever had. And I daresay Isabelle will be celebrating with you, as word has reached us that young John Lawford himself means to attend!"

Emelyn was aghast. "John Lawford is to return? But how shall we allow it, after what he's done?"

"Oh fluff. His brawling days are long behind him, and I am satisfied he's apologized to Bell with sincerity. She might have shared the news herself, but she knows you do not approve, and fears what you think of him."

"I don't think of him at all," Emelyn said, "but it was not only his disgraceful behaviour; the man is a profligate wanderer, with nothing to his name."

"That is all changed now," Mrs. Morley said, "in fact his respectable friend, Miss Winter, writes that young Mr. Lawford finds his circumstances so changed that he wants for nothing!"

"Oh very well," Emelyn groaned, rubbing her eyes. "Perhaps he's emended himself, or perhaps not, but I wash my hands of it. I wish Isabelle every happiness."

"Excellent my dearest. So with that I shall leave you to rest, to think on your victory . . . and of our deliverance, but it is nothing less than the resurrection of Hastelbrook!"

Emelyn sat on the bed, staring vacantly, and with a happy hum her mother kissed her goodnight before swishing out of the room.

It seemed scarcely a moment later there came a light ticking sound from the window, and like a shot she rushed to see, finding Vaela clinging to the wall outside.

"Vaela!" Emelyn threw open the panes. "Come in, quickly—"

The vampiress appeared before her, and accepting Emelyn's embrace she chuckled softly. "Can you miss me already? I was only waiting for you to sleep. I've business in London; these summer nights are dreadfully short."

In Vaela's grasp the cares of day faded to softness, and closing her eyes Emelyn released her. "Have you lost my cardinal?"

"Your cloak is folded safely away, that I might keep it supple."

"I see . . . and what business have you in London, that cannot be solved in the country?"

"I have informers, who spy on my behalf," Vaela said, "but they will wait a little while. What vexes you?"

"In part it's my mother," Emelyn said, taking up the captain's letter, "so eager is she to restore Hastelbrook to glory that she will indebt us all the more. Van Croft will never find me an equal part in our union, but a vulture, a low common dependent."

Vaela sat on the bench by the window. "Your articulate fear misses the mark; you are more than a match for him, and you cannot predict the future."

"But I can; I will be mistress of Van Croft's house," Emelyn said, holding up the letter to the light of a candle, that she could examine again the folded paper within, "and returning home as often as I'd like will be difficult, particularly if I'm to find some way into the vault, if such a thing is possible. Here."

"What is this?" Vaela asked.

"Can your vampire eyes read the small page within?"

"I read hearts, not sealed letters."

"Well then I must break it open. Van Croft expressly forbid me to even ask of it . . . That man does not know me."

Rising from the bench Vaela crossed to her desk, and with a precise scratch of her claw she unsealed the wax without splitting it. Carefully she unfolded the paper, passing it to Emelyn's eager hand. "I could apply a drop and seal it again from underneath," the vampiress observed. "Have you red, blood red?"

"Blood red? Oh the wax! Yes, in the top there," and with a long breath Emelyn unfolded the letter to read:

'My Cherished, Dearest Miss Morley,'

"What?" Emelyn blinked, heat rising to her face.

'I pray you, do not harshly judge my little trick, but it would appear I know you better than you know yourself, and that I might have lost you at Galecliff to that same reckless courage is a transport of terror greater than any I've faced on the battlefield.'

"The arrogance," Emelyn said. "He could not have known I'd read it; but if my father had seen this . . ."

'You see, condemned to be master of my own inclination for too long, I suddenly wonder that my heart beats at all but for your person, and so as long as there is breath in me to defend you, you must rely on it.'

"*Condemned to be master,*" Emelyn recited, blinking slowly.

'Alas, I am obliged now to turn to a darker matter, which I include here for your father alone. T'were nothing any gentle daughter of Eve should be subject to read, so I must urge you present it to him, on your honour as my wife to be, unopened.

As for the villain Rosch, let him serve to illustrate the dangerous depravity of superstition, for he was once a man of sense, before beguiling himself with those occultic whispers that ever swirl about your home. But evil rumour seeks fertile ground, and I've an august reputation to consider. Therefore now that you are mine, it is my fervent request you shall guard yourself against all unholy thoughts and impressions, whether spoken or printed.

In closing, my fire haired Aphrodite, until next I squeeze you against me, and compel your lips to mine, I am and shall remain,

Your humble servant and captain of your heart,
Jonathan Van Croft'

"Captain of your heart?" Emelyn felt a flush, dropping the letter. "So he expects me to violate his trust in the first but not in the second," she said, examining the smaller tightly folded note of yellowing paper, and she was about to flip it open when there came a heavy sense of dread, pressing upon her as though the house itself were holding its breath. "It's only a letter," she said, looking at Vaela. "I must know what it says . . ."

The wax on this second page was but an unmarked splotch, as though sealed by the press of a thumb. With a little snap it broke free, and she unfolded the paper:

'Sir, what follows I have entrusted directly to your daughter to deliver, it being too delicate a risk in the hands of post or servants, and as I have forbid its contents from Miss Morley's eyes for her own good, should you find it unsealed upon receipt, she is to be duly reprimanded.'

"Oh am I," Emelyn said, reading on:

'Now to my purpose: As we suffer in common a tragic and unaccountable maritime loss, I've taken it in hand to share with you the last protests of one Captain Audgent, lately deceased, who stood at the helm of my ship the Old Garnet when she was sunk- turning guns hullward and scuttling to pieces in plain view of the shore. I cannot speak to how your own vessels were lost, but I know the want of their trade has put Morley Maritime to grave necessity, which perhaps this unhappy

transcription may go some way to explaining. I believe the late captain's words, as recorded by the one who found him upon the rocks, make evidence of some yet uncatalogued seafaring illness, an affliction which preys upon the mind as readily as sailor's scurvy attacks the body. Read the madman's ramblings with care, that we may consult on the matter when I return to Hastelbrook.'

Emelyn braced herself, turning to the second page:

'The following is rote transcribed from the last utterance of Eremus William Audgent, captain of the Old Garnet, which went down on Friday 13th of May 1735 in fire, near the rocks at St. Agnes, and it begins thus:'

'We were on easterly heading, in favoured winds makin' to skirt south of Cornwall for the channel. The storm would overtake us, like thick laid tar in the sky, and with no idea but to press on for the island we held fast our course, awaitin' the hurricane's befall.

The dark were upon us 'ere long, but there followed neither rain nor rough, despite a black swirlin' wind, and there came a dank fog crawlin' over the deck like fingers, the air unseasonable cold. A harrowin' din surrounds us, for all the world like the cries of men, lost and pleadin' for home, as like they were trapped by the storm, and were become a part of it.

The lanterns snuff'd away, the wretched voices a wailin' all the more, an' then rises on the deck the figure of a man, but fearsome stretched and skeletal he was, masked in white like the grinnin' moon. There came a maddenin' pain in my head, an' the sure impression we were to join them lost voices on the wind. I heard myself give the order, the crew turned all guns round, an' into the decks they set 'em off.

But in that sliver'd moment when the cannons fired me mind was me own again, and down I flee, crashing through the captain's windows and into the cold sea. All but drown'd I made the rocks, turnin' just to find the ship consumes herself in fiery collapse, the powder ignited, black smoke risin' like a gibbet, and that pale figure standin' on the prow, as like he stared right through me. The world goes dark, and hither I wakes.'

"Good Lord," Emelyn whispered, her heart pounding in her chest. "What could spur the crew to such an act, to destroy themselves to a man—but can what he describes exist? Do you know of such a *creature*?"

Slowly Vaela took the paper. "Perhaps it was only a fever of the mind, as your captain suggests . . . or perhaps not. I know only that the queen's maker is said to have worn such a mask. But he was undone, destroyed by a plot long in the making. He has been dust for some eight hundred years."

"Her own maker was her enemy?"

"I know little, but that he abused all his progeny most cruelly, a monster beyond reckoning. In the realm of Saunmoor it is forbidden to speak his name."

Emelyn trembled to think of it. "Then what does it mean?"

"I cannot tell," Vaela said quietly, "though my heart whispers this mortal captain may have witnessed the same darkness that infects our queen. But her maker it *cannot* be . . . we do not return from the second death."

Breathing through the hinges the wind shook the panes, the candles flickered, and Emelyn found herself at her wardrobe, tearing down boxes until she came upon that which hid the bloodstone ruby. Removing it quickly she clasped the stone about her neck; the weight of it seemed to settle deep within her, diffusing the phantoms of fear.

"What are you doing?" Vaela asked.

"I don't know," Emelyn replied, touching the bloodstone. "It seemed the rightful response. Often I feel the statue *wants* me to wear it, though I don't apprehend why."

Vaela stared at her. "I must copy down that letter."

"No, take it. I will not show my father such a thing . . . nor anyone. And I will bid the captain keep it to himself, whatever he thinks of me for reading it."

"I must go," Vaela said, folding the paper to tuck in her cloak.

"Wait." Emelyn came to take her hands. "I want you to stay; will you stay here with me?"

"Stay?" Vaela repeated. "Under your bed perhaps? No little one, I cannot stay."

Emelyn shivered, touching her neck. "Yes, of course you must go, to London . . . but first, will you drink?"

"No, I will not overtax you."

"I shan't be able to sleep."

"You will," Vaela said, taking her hand to kiss it. "And I shall find you in your dream, if you like."

"Yes, please."

The vampiress took her about the shoulders, holding her for a moment, and in a blink she was gone.

Emelyn came to the window, collected the little red queen, and looking out into the dark she felt a terrible chill to wonder if Captain Audgent's dreadful vision might have been the same to spell the end of her father's frigates . . . The wind rattled again, and closing the panes she locked them.

■■■

Friday July 8ᵗʰ

In the vast northern manor house of Charwell, the illustrious home of Baron Dramen, the largest space in the house was the grand dining room at the rear of the building, built with many doors of small paned glass exiting to a wide granite veranda which stepped down to the back garden walks between Spartan hedge walls and spade-manicured trees.

Tonight the dining room was bestrewn in all possible grandeur—golden drapes bedecked the walls, with a grand hardwood table split down the centre dominating the middle of the room. A churning wash of red punch flowed like a river along the table, into a marble pool before siphoning up again, coursing its way beneath an arched sculpture of sugar carved triomphe—decorated castles of snowy white walls complete with figurines along the parapets and edible heraldry. Betwixt triomphe towers, the table's grand centrepiece was in the shape of a wide-winged swan—fashioned entirely of golden skewered birds, and rooted in hollow roasted peacocks, their cooked bodies symmetrically re-planted with brilliant feathers.

Gaudily dressed men and women were gathered along the table, testing their endurance against the feast, now in its fifth course of nine. Sweet and savoury dishes crowded the surface, beckoning every eager diner: from orange roasted capons to buttered lobster, chines of veal, quail and partridge beside hearty meat pies and pasties, split salmon, puddings and tarts—every offering more ostentatious than the last. The guests were deep in their cups, with red faces and slow eyes, laughing and jeering at every distracting movement. Those whose limits were reached had pushed back their chairs in surrender, stretching their legs or drinking and talking along the windows. Colourful flautists and harpists played the courses on and off, while female performers robed in green and gold danced, and masked footmen leaned between shoulders to refresh punch glasses or serve sweets. And between the magnificent table and the high veranda doors was a wide basin of fountain tossed cider, where a small boy in a little boat rowed in circles, scooping up the drink in the ladle end of his oar to refill unsteady mugs.

Some five dozen Peers of the Realm filled out the room—lords and ladies in lavish wigs, sumptuous gowns and bulging waistcoats, all shiny fingers and wagging tongues as they partook in bottomless drinks, meats and pies. Even the young glamourous Duke Lindsor was in attendance, seated at the foot of the table in liquor stained white and cream, playing with a large leg of cooked bird as though it meant to ravish the food on his plate. The men and women about him laughed uproariously.

Ruddy with claret himself, Baron Dramen sat at the head of the table betwixt Miss Winter, gowned in black, and Lord Crennock—dressed in candied yellow and grey, his towering wig of shimmering silver.

Dramen stared at the duke, who had just opened his arms to welcome one of the more nubile dancers to sit in his lap.

"Yes, the merriest among us," Dramen sneered, "the man is an infant. Not a penny has changed hands, but he finds his pledge worthy to despoil my staff."

"Carefully," Miss Winter said, slicing a flank from the nearest roast bird—clove and onion stuffed goose. "He was promised more intimate visits to our captive. The merest thought of it inflames his deepest passions—he confides to me he has scarcely slept for the want of her."

"Nor have I scarcely slept," Dramen snapped. "But there is more at stake here than Lindsor's fantasies."

"Yes," Miss Winter conceded, snapping for more punch, "and yet I daresay those fantasies are worth even more to him than the fifty thousand he's already pledged. But we cannot put him off forever—he will begin to suspect we've lost her."

"There is no sweetening it," Lord Crennock said, rotating his goblet as he frowned at candied flags high over the lofty sugar castle.

"Walpole and all the rest shall be wondering what's become of our *vampire promise*."

As if on cue a handsome bust-proud woman stood from her chair with a sway, raising her glass. "To our generous host!" she cried.

"Lady Chilcombe," Miss Winter said. "Duke Lindsor's cousin."

"To our generous host," the besotted lady repeated, fighting ringlets of hair away from her eyes, "and, and to his captive monster! My lord, how I should dearly like to meet her." With a splash of her drink she bowed, erupting in giggles as others laughed along.

Smiling as though in pain Dramen raised his glass at her. "Look at them, fawning creatures," he grumbled. "They make show of mocking the Vampire Act, finding me for a lunatic, and here they are, happy to nurse at my hospitality . . . and *still* they demand satisfaction. Are my gifts to them not enough? Are they suddenly believers, one and all?"

"We did vow to present her at court, my lord," Miss Winter said, dabbing the corner of her mouth. "We *were* prepared, but to show the crown a living vampire were no small thing, and now she is gone."

"And the son of your name languishes in Bedlam to atone for it," Crennock put in, his low voice a growl of displeasure.

"Nay, sir," Dramen huffed. "The inconvenience of chains cannot *atone* for denying mortal science so great a lurch forward, as the discovery and proving of vampirism."

Miss Winter raised her brows, sipping her wine. "And is that where your heart is, my lord, in the discovery?"

Dramen glared at her, but he broke with a chuckle. "It is *power*, Miss Winter—there were no greater nectar for a man's soul, than dominion over his fellows," and he gave a great sigh, lifting his napkin to drop it.

Crennock's frown deepened, and Miss Winter pulled off her glove, allowing Dramen to take her hand. "More to drink, my lord," she said. "We will have that power yet, but there is another misfortune we must discuss."

"Another!"

"My man at Eastbourne, who attended Miss Morley and Lord Van Croft at Galecliff. I'd meant him to discover her fraternity with the vampire of Hastelbrook, but he's disappeared."

Lord Crennock leaned forward. "How? Where?"

"If I knew where, he'd not be disappeared," Miss Winter replied, watching as Dramen grabbed her fingers tightly to kiss them. "He was meant to arrive at Horsham days ago," she continued. "He's left word that Miss Morley's journal confesses everything—to her being in thrall, even to an unholy ritual of blood between herself and the immortal."

Lord Crennock dropped his utensils with distaste. "The House of Lords needs a distraction, Dramen," he said. "Let it be published that I am snatching up maritime debt, that these unaccountable storms in the west begin to dissipate. He who strikes first shall have the whip hand of trade to America."

Baron Dramen coughed into his drink. "You cannot mean to involve yourself in Morley's fall? Let him see debtor's prison; let the estate crumble. We shall have it for pennies on the pound soon enough."

"Hastelbrook is not likely to crumble if Miss Morley marries Van Croft," Miss Winter suggested.

"We must lay our card first," Crennock said. "Mr. Morley is in town. I shall contrive to find him at the Exchange."

A drunken Robert Abbott, wigless with his unwashed hair in a tail over storm grey frock coat and waistcoat off-centre, came suddenly to the table, leaning on his arm beside Miss Winter. "My lord, the good Lord Dramen, and his coterie," he said, waving a glass of punch. "I do regret, to permit myself, your interruption. But where is the magistrate Brule? That Justice of the Peace so deep in your pocket he cannot find the stars? I have need of him!"

"What is your business sir?" Crennock barked, as Dramen forked his kidney pie, paying no attention.

"My business, my lord, is Mr. Brule made me a promise, and I have taken every effort to see it through," he said, stopping to blink as he belched. "I've done my part, dispatched good men to see, to see your precious Miss Morley, to ascertain her hand in it . . . and it were *his*, my friend Freddy's hand—she broke it, the savage sorceress. But she knows what's become of our Lord Abbott. On my life she does, and I shall have it, sirs!"

Baron Dramen did not look up, but chewed and swallowed as the others regarded him. With a sniff he dabbed his mouth. "Winter?" he said.

Miss Winter stood quickly, and turning she took hold of Robert Abbott's chin, compelling him backward.

The young man blinked at her in surprise, finding the tip of a silver blade concealed behind her hand, just at his throat.

A few steps away she stopped. "Mr. Abbott," she said, speaking near his face. "Do not embarrass your good host. You are so much less than you imagine."

Abbott swallowed. "I will have my revenge," he said thinly. "Miss Morley knows what's become of my father; I will have my part . . . in the fall of Hastelbrook."

"Ah yes," she said, relaxing her grip. "You want your inheritance, you want satisfaction. When the vampire is in our power, when Hastelbrook is conquered, I shall send you a letter. Until that time, you shall breathe not another word of this."

"A letter," Robert repeated unhappily.

Miss Winter patted him on the cheek. "Now, this must be better than any banquet you've attended. Go enjoy yourself, and on pain of your life, trouble Lord Dramen no further."

* * *

Sunday July 10th

Emelyn awoke that morning unable to recall her dreams, though better rested than the previous day. After drifting through breakfast with hardly a word, she took her morning walk and sat for a drawing session in the gazebo with her sisters, during which she managed only a rough outline of the bridge. Over a bright afternoon dinner she stared and listened as her jubilant mother laid out plans for the week while her brother sat across, eying her in silence over his soup. After the meal was finished Emelyn set up camp on her velvet bench in the small library window, removing her shoes and tossing them somewhere. Her journal lay in her lap, unamended since her return from Eastbourne.

Deacon joined her, taking up residence in his usual wingback chair, slouching so that only his feet were visible.

Daydreams turned drowsy, and bumping her head on the glass she startled awake, finding she'd slept away the better part of an hour. Adjusting her seat she settled in to read, opening the first of her letters. That from Margaret she found cordial and informative, bearing news of her time in London, including descriptions of an intriguing masque and the revival farce of some dreadful opera . . . but Emelyn's focus wandered, and it was many tries before she reached the end of the page, where Margaret concluded warmly, talking of plans to visit relations in Cornwall with hopes of seeing Emelyn soon, and taking pains to regret how things had been left between them at Dhorings Park.

"Dear Mags," Emelyn murmured, "I've so much to tell you," and putting it aside she was amused to find the second letter was from Poppy Loganbrek—tirelessly extolling the virtues of her brother no doubt. Mr. Loganbrek, stuffed with pie and poetry, had been Emelyn's most regrettable suitor, though recalling the silly sincerity in his address seemed now almost wistful. But it was only a missive from another life, and she tossed it away without opening.

"Emelyn," Deacon said, shifting in his chair, "I should quite clarify we are never to speak of your . . . *protector* before the others."

"That's the sort of thing I should be saying to you," she replied.

"Yes, well I suppose I've yet to come to grips with it. By daylight it seems all so absurd."

"You're right, it does."

The library doors opened suddenly, and there beaming stood her father.

"Good morning my dears!" he declared, and coming to Emelyn's side he took her hand, touching it to his forehead. "Our Emelyn Elizabeth, returned in triumph! But how now, will you not give your father a smile?"

Emelyn smiled. "You have my news already, but what of yours? How fares London?"

"Well, and Deacon my good lad this is for the pair of you. I have taken, by the most astounding coincidence, a meeting with as sober a gentleman of quality as I've ever encountered, and the short of it is he has purchased the entirety of our arrears, to Lloyd's of London, to the banks and builders, to Morley Maritime and all the rest!"

"He's bought our debt Father?" Deacon asked, leaning forward to peer back at them.

"How, or why?" Emelyn asked, alarmed at the news.

"This particular gentleman is rich as Plutus, and knows an occasion for profit when he sees it," Mr. Morley said, snatching off his spectacles for a spirited polish. "It is not only Morley Maritime my dears, but a great many firms that have lost shipping, owing to dark storms in the west, which by report do not disperse but tarry, hanging over the sea like a curse . . . Therefore the country finds a plummet of mercantile capacity, and that makes for opportunity! *Buying the slow* he called it, snapping up maritime liability before the industry recovers, that he might see windfall in the coming months."

"And who is this man?" Emelyn asked.

"He is none other than the Marquess of Crennock, the very patron of Isabelle's friend, Mr. Lawford," Mr. Morley said brightly. "We met by happenstance at the exchange, and when he heard I was lord of the manor at Hastelbrook, he inquired at once of Morley Maritime, and what impediments might there be to expanding the partnership."

"Interesting," Deacon said. "An auspicious coincidence."

"Well now," Mr. Morley said, bobbing on his toes, "with Emelyn's impending match I should say we are more than secure enough, would you not agree my dear?"

"I'm not married yet, Papa."

"No, not yet," he said, and his smile faltered, a wet gleam shining in his eyes. "Not yet . . . but I shan't pretend, that it will not pain me to lose you. You are as much a fixture in this house as that old hooded statue, but of course we will manage somehow, and I will hold the captain to the very strictest of expectation. He must be answerable every moment to our good opinion."

To see her father struggle with the words panged her heart, and Emelyn stood to embrace him. "You shan't lose me, Papa, I've far too much character for Van Croft alone; he's obliged to share me with my family."

"I am glad to hear it," he breathed, holding her for a moment.

"I will visit Hastelbrook often, whatever the captain thinks of it," she said. "Anyway, I'm resolved not to leave for three months at least."

"Ah, that is good," Mr. Morley said, releasing her with a smile. "Well now, I suppose the least I might do after your journey is leave you to your leisure."

"Wait, Papa," Emelyn said, catching him as he turned. "I should like to ask you, of the crypt . . . below the library."

"Yes my dear?"

"I must have it, once and for all. Is it true the earth shook, and a piece in the floor moved, the night I was born?"

"Oh that . . . I cannot rightfully say. The panel is different now than I remember it years ago, but perhaps it only moved gradually over time, by some natural action of the earth."

Emelyn sat on the edge of the bench. "Very well, but I know why I've not been allowed into the crypt since I was a child; I had the whole truth of it from Deacon."

"Here leave me out of it if you please," Deacon remarked.

"But I'm grown now," Emelyn said quickly, recapturing her father's attention. "I should like to see it again, if only to look at our history."

"And to try the floor for a draft no doubt," Mr. Morley said wearily. "Emelyn my dear, after you are married you may wear the key round your neck if you like, but you'll not enter the crypt before then."

"But why? What's the harm?"

"There is no harm of course; there's nothing to find, but it's one more oddity of Morley folklore we need not indulge before your wedding."

"And what if I find a way to open it myself. What if there is treasure, or more likely some piece of ancient history; what if the rumours are true?"

Her father nodded with a bemused frown. "Emelyn Elizabeth, my dear daughter, if someday you open the vault, you are more than welcome to whatever lies inside, and to dispose of it how you will."

"But you've never referred to it as a vault. You *do* believe there is something there."

"We might as well believe the moon is cheese," he said. "What we *believe* is immaterial. The stone has been tested, and that crooked antiquarian found nothing."

"I suppose," Emelyn said, thinking of Mr. Gapplethorpe in London, the increasingly finger-worn coin of Saunmoor she had of him, and that sound of stone upon stone, which he claimed to have heard deep beneath the crypt . . .

"Now you've been through a great deal," her father said, "high and low as I understand, with the harrowing storm. You do well to avail yourself of these quiet moments, before your mother springs another party upon us."

"Yes, very well," she sighed, settling in her seat.

"There," Mr. Morley said. "With Deacon in his chair, and you on your bench in the window, everything is as it should be," and grasping her shoulders he kissed her forehead, before turning to take his leave.

Deacon snapped his paper, and Emelyn turned to put up her feet, embracing her knees as she stared out over the dry summer green of the hedgerows and gardens beyond. The sky was enormous, the sun high and bright, and watching a pair of collared doves that circled above the gazebo she focused on their articulate calls, pulling them closer until it were as though they fluttered and cooed just over her head.

Like a nightmare half remembered, the dead Captain Audgent's tale, and the horrors he described, returned to mind. A surge of protective conviction wet her eyes as she thought of her family, her friends, and Vaela, her kindred spirit in the dark. Distant unknowable fears clamoured for her attention, but against these there stood a sure and unbreakable sense of home—the fortress of Hastelbrook, which she knew now had a power all its own. The wind brushed over the hedge maze, the doves found a branch on which to perch together, and with a determined breath Emelyn resolved that somehow she would find her way into the vault, and whatever happened next, be it in daylight or darkness, she would be ready.

PER SANGVINEM
REGINAE
IN OCULO
VMBREMARIS

Acknowledgements

This book would not have been possible without the love and encouragement of my parents Joan and Grover, and the unwavering support of all those who have kept the candle lit, encouraging my writing over the years.

Saunmoor Book 3: Emelyn Morley and the Siege of Winter
COMING SOON